The
BELTON ESTATE

The
BELTON ESTATE

Anthony Trollope

DOVER PUBLICATIONS, INC.
NEW YORK

Published in Canada by General Publishing Company, Ltd., 30 Lesmill Road, Don Mills, Toronto, Ontario.

Published in the United Kingdom by Constable and Company, Ltd., 10 Orange Street, London WC2H 7EG.

This Dover edition, first published in 1985, is an unabridged republication of the work first published in the *Fortnightly Review* from May through December, 1865, and in book form by Chapman & Hall, London, in the same year.

Manufactured in the United States of America
Dover Publications, Inc., 31 East 2nd Street, Mineola, N.Y. 11501

Library of Congress Cataloging in Publication Data

Trollope, Anthony, 1815–1882.
    The Belton estate.

    I. Title.
PR5684.B4   1985   823′.8   84-25907
ISBN 0-486-24815-1

CONTENTS.

———◆◇◆———

viii CONTENTS.

The
BELTON ESTATE

THE BELTON ESTATE.

CHAPTER I.

THE REMNANTS OF THE AMEDROZ FAMILY.

MRS. AMEDROZ, the wife of Bernard Amedroz, Esq., of Belton Castle, and mother of Charles and Clara Amedroz, died when those children were only eight and six years old, thereby subjecting them to the greatest misfortune which children born in that sphere of life can be made to suffer. And, in the case of this boy and girl the misfortune was aggravated greatly by the peculiarities of the father's character. Mr. Amedroz was not a bad man,—as men are held to be bad in the world's esteem. He was not vicious,—was not a gambler or a drunkard, —was not self-indulgent to a degree that brought upon him any reproach; nor was he regardless of his children. But he was an idle, thriftless man, who, at the age of sixty-seven, when the reader will first make his acquaintance, had as yet done no good in the world whatever. Indeed he had done terrible evil; for his son Charles was now dead,—had perished by his own hand,—and the state of things which had brought about this woful event had been chiefly due to his father's neglect.

Belton Castle is a pretty country seat, standing in a small but beautifully-wooded park, close under the Quantock hills in Somersetshire; and the little town of Belton clusters round the park gates. Few Englishmen know the scenery of England well, and the prettinesses of Somersetshire are among those which are the least known. But the Quantock

hills are very lovely, with their rich valleys lying close
among them, and their outlying moorlands running off
towards Dulverton and the borders of Devonshire,—moorlands which are not flat, like Salisbury Plain, but are
broken into ravines and deep watercourses and rugged
dells hither and thither: where old oaks are standing, in
which life seems to have dwindled down to the last spark,
but the last spark is still there, and the old oaks give forth
their scanty leaves from year to year.

In among the hills, somewhat off the high road from
Minehead to Taunton, and about five miles from the sea,
stands the little town, or village, of Belton, and the modern
house of Mr. Amedroz, which is called Belton Castle. The
village,—for it is in truth no more, though it still main-
tains a charter for a market, and there still exists on Tues-
days some pretence of an open sale of grain and butcher's
meat in the square before the church-gate,—contains about
two thousand persons. That and the whole parish of
Belton did once,—and that not long ago,—belong to the
Amedroz family. They had inherited it from the Beltons
of old, an Amedroz having married the heiress of the family.
And as the parish is large, stretching away to Exmoor on
one side, and almost to the sea on the other, containing the
hamlet of Redicote, lying on the Taunton high road,—
Redicote, where the post-office is placed, a town almost in
itself, and one which is now much more prosperous than
Belton,—as the property when it came to the first Amedroz had limits such as these, the family had been considerable in the county. But these limits had been strait-
ened in the days of the grandfather and the father of
Bernard Amedroz; and he, when he married a Miss
Winterfield of Taunton, was thought to have done very
well, in that mortgages were paid off the property with his
wife's money to such an extent as to leave him in clear
possession of an estate that gave him two thousand a year.
As Mr. Amedroz had no grand neighbours near him, as the
place is remote and the living therefore cheap, and as with
this income there was no question of annual visits to
London, Mr. and Mrs. Amedroz might have done very well
with such of the good things of the world as had fallen to
their lot. And had the wife lived such would probably
have been the case; for the Winterfields were known to be

prudent people. But Mrs. Amedroz had died young, and things with Bernard Amedroz had gone badly.

And yet the evil had not been so much with him as with that terrible boy of his. The father had been nearly forty when he married. He had then never done any good; but as neither had he done much harm, the friends of the family had argued well of his future career. After him, unless he should leave a son behind him, there would be no Amedroz left among the Quantock hills; and by some arrangement in respect to that Winterfield money which came to him on his marriage,—the Winterfields having a long-dated connection with the Beltons of old,—the Amedroz property was, at Bernard's marriage, entailed back upon a distant Belton cousin, one Will Belton, whom no one had seen for many years, but who was by blood nearer to the squire, in default of children of his own, than any other of his relatives. And now Will Belton was the heir to Belton Castle; for Charles Amedroz, at the age of twenty-seven, had found the miseries of the world to be too many for him, and had put an end to them and to himself.

Charles had been a clever fellow,—a very clever fellow in the eyes of his father. Bernard Amedroz knew that he himself was not a clever fellow, and admired his son accordingly; and when Charles had been expelled from Harrow for some boyish freak,—in his vengeance against a neighbouring farmer, who had reported to the school authorities the doings of a few beagles upon his land, Charles had cut off the heads of all the trees in a young fir plantation,—his father was proud of the exploit. When he was rusticated a second time from Trinity, and when the father received an intimation that his son's name had better be taken from the College books, the squire was not so well pleased; but even then he found some delight in the stories which reached him of his son's vagaries; and when the young man commenced Bohemian life in London, his father did nothing to restrain him. Then there came the old story—debts, endless debts; and lies, endless lies. During the two years before his death, his father paid for him, or undertook to pay, nearly ten thousand pounds, sacrificing the life assurances which were to have made provision for his daughter; sacrificing, to a great extent, his own life income,—sacrificing everything, so that the property might

not be utterly ruined at his death. That Charles Amedroz
should be a brighter, greater man than any other Amedroz,
had still been the father's pride. At the last visit which
Charles had paid to Belton his father had called upon him
to pledge himself solemnly that his sister should not be
made to suffer by what had been done for him. Within a
month of that time he had blown his brains out in his
London lodgings, thus making over the entire property to
Will Belton at his father's death. At that last pretended
settlement with his father and his father's lawyer, he had
kept back the mention of debts as heavy nearly as those to
which he had owned ; and there were debts of honour, too,
of which he had not spoken, trusting to the next event at
Newmarket to set him right. The next event at Newmarket
had set him more wrong than ever, and so there had come
an end to everything with Charles Amedroz.

This had happened in the spring, and the afflicted father,
—afflicted with the double sorrow of his son's terrible
death and his daughter's ruin,—had declared that he would
turn his face to the wall and die. But the old squire's
health, though far from strong, was stronger than he had
deemed it, and his feelings, sharp enough, were less sharp
than he had thought them ; and when a month had passed
by, he had discovered that it would be better that he should
live, in order that his daughter might still have bread to
eat and a house of her own over her head. Though he was
now an impoverished man, there was still left to him the
means of keeping up the old home; and he told himself
that it must, if possible, be so kept that a few pounds
annually might be put by for Clara. The old carriage
horses were sold, and the park was let to a farmer, up to
the hall door of the castle. So much the squire could do ;
but as to the putting by of the few pounds, any dependence
on such exertion as that on his part would, we may say, be
very precarious.

Belton Castle was not in truth a castle. Immediately
before the front door, so near to the house as merely to
allow of a broad road running between it and the entrance
porch, there stood an old tower, which gave its name to
the residence,—an old square tower, up which the Amedroz
boys for three generations had been able to climb by means
of the ivy and broken stones in one of the inner corners,

—and this tower was a remnant of a real castle that had once protected the village of Belton. The house itself was an ugly residence, three stories high, built in the time of George II., with low rooms and long passages, and an immense number of doors. It was a large unattractive house,—unattractive, that is, as regarded its own attributes, —but made interesting by the beauty of the small park in which it stood. Belton Park did not, perhaps, contain much above a hundred acres; but the land was so broken into knolls and valleys, in so many places was the rock seen to be cropping up through the verdure, there were in it so many stunted old oaks, so many points of vantage for the lover of scenery, that no one would believe it to be other than a considerable domain. The farmer who took it, and who would not under any circumstances undertake to pay more than seventeen shillings an acre for it, could not be made to think that it was in any way considerable. But Belton Park, since first it was made a park, had never before been regarded after this fashion. Farmer Stovey, of the Grange, was the first man of that class who had ever assumed the right to pasture his sheep in Belton chase,—as the people around were still accustomed to call the woodlands of the estate.

It was full summer at Belton, and four months had now passed since the dreadful tidings had reached the castle. It was full summer, and the people of the village were again going about their ordinary business; and the shopgirls, with their lovers from Redicote, were again to be seen walking among the oaks in the park on a Sunday evening; and the world in that district of Somersetshire was getting itself back into its grooves. The fate of the young heir had disturbed the grooves greatly, and had taught many in those parts to feel that the world was coming to an end. They had not loved young Amedroz, for he had been haughty when among them, and there had been wrongs committed by the dissolute young squire, and grief had come from his misdoings upon more than one household; but to think that he should have destroyed himself with his own hand! And then, to think that Miss Clara would become a beggar when the old squire should die! All the neighbours around understood the whole history of the entail, and knew that the property was to go to Will Belton. Now Will Belton was not a gentleman! So, at least, said

the Belton folk, who had heard that the heir had been
brought up as a farmer somewhere in Norfolk. Will Bolton
had once been at the castle as a boy, now some fifteen
years ago, and then there had sprung up a great quarrel
between him and his distant cousin Charles;—and Will, who
was rough and large of stature, had thrashed the smaller
boy severely; and the thing had grown to have dimen-
sions larger than those which generally attend the quarrels
of boys; and Will had said something which had shown
how well he understood his position in reference to the
estate;—and Charles had hated him. So Will had gone,
and had been no more seen among the oaks whose name he
bore. And the people, in spite of his name, regarded him
as an interloper. To them, with their short memories and
scanty knowledge of the past, Amedroz was more honourable than Belton, and they looked upon the coming man as
an intruder. Why should not Miss Clara have the property?
Miss Clara had never done harm to any one!

Things got back into their old grooves, and at the end of
the third month the squire was once more seen in the old
family pew at church. He was a large man, who had been
very handsome, and who now, in his yellow leaf, was not
without a certain beauty of manliness. He wore his hair
and his beard long; before his son's death they were grey,
but now they were very white. And though he stooped,
there was still a dignity in his slow step,—a dignity that
came to him from nature rather than from any effort. He
was a man who, in fact, did little or nothing in the world,
—whose life had been very useless; but he had been
gifted with such a presence that he looked as though he
were one of God's nobler creatures. Though always dignified he was ever affable, and the poor liked him better
than they might have done had he passed his time in search-
ing out their wants and supplying them. They were proud
of their squire, though he had done nothing for them. It
was something to them to have a man who could so carry
himself sitting in the family pew in their parish church.
They knew that he was poor, but they all declared that he
was never mean. He was a real gentleman,—was this
last Amedroz of the family; therefore they curtseyed low,
and bowed on his reappearance among them, and made all
those signs of reverential awe which are common to the
poor when they feel reverence for the presence of a superior.

Clara was there with him, but she had shown herself in the pew for four or five weeks before this. She had not been at home when the fearful news had reached Belton, being at that time with a certain lady who lived on the further side of the county, at Perivale,—a certain Mrs. Winterfield, born a Folliott, a widow, who stood to Miss Amedroz in the place of an aunt. Mrs. Winterfield was, in truth, the sister of a gentleman who had married Clara's aunt,—there having been marriages and intermarriages between the Winterfields and the Folliotts, and the Belton-Amedroz families. With this lady in Perivale, which I maintain to be the dullest little town in England, Miss Amedroz was staying when the news reached her father, and when it was brought direct from London to herself. Instantly she hurried home, making the journey with all imaginable speed, though her heart was all but broken within her bosom. She had found her father stricken to the ground, and it was the more necessary, therefore, that she should exert herself. It would not do that she also should yield to that longing for death which terrible calamities often produce for a season.

Clara Amedroz, when she first heard the news of her brother's fate, had felt that she was for ever crushed to the ground. She had known too well what had been the nature of her brother's life, but she had not expected or feared any such termination to his career as this which had now come upon him—to the terrible affliction of all belonging to him. She felt at first, as did also her father, that she and he were annihilated as regards this world, not only by an enduring grief, but also by a disgrace which would never allow her again to hold up her head. And for many a long year much of this feeling clung to her ;— clung to her much more strongly than to her father. But strength was hers to perceive, even before she had reached her home, that it was her duty to repress both the feeling of shame and the sorrow, as far as they were capable of repression. Her brother had been weak, and in his weakness had sought a coward's escape from the ills of the world around him. She must not also be a coward! Bad as life might be to her henceforth, she must endure it with such fortitude as she could muster. So resolving she returned to her father, and was able to listen to his railings with a fortitude that was essentially serviceable both to him and to herself.

"Both of you! Both of you!" the unhappy father had said in his woe. "The wretched boy has destroyed you as much as himself!" "No, sir," she had answered, with a forbearance in her misery, which, terrible as was the effort, she forced herself to accomplish for his sake. "It is not so. No thought of that need add to your grief. My poor brother has not hurt me;—not in the way you mean." "He has ruined us all," said the father; "root and branch, man and woman, old and young, house and land. He has brought the family to an end;—ah me, to such an end!" After that the name of him who had taken himself from among them was not mentioned between the father and daughter; and Clara settled herself to the duties of her new life, striving to live as though there was no great sorrow around her—as though no cloud-storm had burst over her head.

The family lawyer, who lived at Taunton, had commu nicated the fact of Charles's death to Mr. Belton, and Belton had acknowledged the letter with the ordinary expressions of regret. The lawyer had alluded to the entail, saying that it was improbable that Mr. Amedroz would have another son. To this Belton had replied that for his cousin Clara's sake he hoped that the squire's life would be long spared. The lawyer smiled as he read the wish, thinking to himself that luckily no wish on the part of Will Belton could influence his old client either for good or evil. What man, let alone what lawyer, will ever be- lieve in the sincerity of such a wish as that expressed by the heir to a property? And yet where is the man who will not declare to himself that such, under such circum- stances, would be his own wish?

Clara Amedroz at this time was not a very young lady. She had already passed her twenty-fifth birthday, and in manners, appearance, and habits was, at any rate, as old as her age. She made no pretence to youth, speaking of her- self always as one whom circumstances required to take upon herself age in advance of her years. She did not dress young, or live much with young people, or corre- spond with other girls by means of crossed letters; nor expect that, for her, young pleasures should be provided.

Life had always been serious with her; but now, we may say, since the terrible tragedy in the family, it must be solemn as well as serious. The memory of her brother must always be upon her; and the memory also of the fact that her father was now an impoverished man, on whose behalf it was her duty to care that every shilling spent in the house did its full twelve pennies' worth of work. There was a mixture in this of deep tragedy and of little care, which seemed to destroy for her the poetry as well as the pleasure of life. The poetry and tragedy might have gone hand in hand together; and so might the cares and pleasures of life have done, had there been no black sorrow of which she must be ever mindful. But it was her lot to have to scrutinize the butcher's bill as she was thinking of her brother's fate; and to work daily among small household things while the spectre of her brother's corpse was ever before her eyes.

A word must be said to explain how it had come to pass that the life led by Miss Amedroz had been more than commonly serious before that tragedy had befallen the family. The name of the lady who stood to Clara in the place of an aunt has been already mentioned. When a girl has a mother, her aunt may be little or nothing to her. But when the mother is gone, if there be an aunt unimpeded with other family duties, then the family duties of that aunt begin—and are assumed sometimes with great vigour. Such had been the case with Mrs. Winterfield. No woman ever lived, perhaps, with more conscientious ideas of her duty as a woman than Mrs. Winterfield, of Prospect Place, Perivale. And this, as I say it, is intended to convey no scoff against that excellent lady. She was an excellent lady—unselfish, given to self-restraint, generous, pious, looking to find in her religion a safe path through life—a path as safe as the facts of Adam's fall would allow her feet to find. She was a woman fearing much for others, but fearing also much for herself, striving to maintain her house in godliness, hating sin, and struggling with the weakness of her humanity so that she might not allow herself to hate the sinners. But her hatred for the sin she found herself bound at all times to pronounce, —to show it by some act at all seasons. To fight the devil was her work,—was the appointed work of every living soul, if only living souls could be made to acknow-

ledge the necessity of the task.   Now an aunt of that kind,
when she assumes her duties towards a motherless niece,
is apt to make life serious.

But, it will be said, Clara Amedroz could have rebelled ;
and Clara's father was hardly made of such stuff that obedience to the aunt would be enforced on her by parental
anthority.   Doubtless Clara could have rebelled against
her aunt.   Indeed, I do not know that she had hitherto
been very obedient.   But there were family facts about
these Winterfield connections which would have made it
difficult for her to ignore her so-called aunt, even had she
wished to do so.   Mrs. Winterfield had twelve hundred a
year at her own disposal, and she was the only person
related to the Amedroz family from whom Mr. Amedroz
had a right to have expectations on his daughter's behalf.
Clara had, in a measure, been claimed by the lady, and the
father had made good the lady's claim, and Clara had
acknowledged that a portion of her life was due to the
demands of Perivale.   These demands had undoubtedly
made her life serious.

Life at Perivale was a very serious thing.   As regards
amusements, ordinarily so called the need of any such
institution was not acknowledged at Prospect House.
Food, drink, and raiment were acknowledged to be necessary to humanity, and, in accordance with the rules of that
house, they were supplied in plenty, and good of their
kind.   Such ladies as Mrs. Winterfield generally keep
good tables, thinking no doubt that the eatables should do
honour to the grace that is said for them.   And Mrs.
Winterfield herself always wore a thick black silk dress,—
not rusty or dowdy with age,—but with some gloss of the
silk on it ; giving away, with secret, underhand, undis-
covered charity, her old dresses to another lady of her own
sort, on whom fortune had not bestowed twelve hundred a
year.   And Mrs. Winterfield kept a low, four-wheeled, one-
horsed little phaeton, in which she made her pilgrimages
among the poor of Perivale, driven by the most solemn of
stable-boys, dressed up in a white great coat, the most prig-
gish of hats, and white cotton gloves.   At the rate of five
miles an hour was she driven about, and this driving was
to her the amusement of life.   But such an occupation to
Clara Amedroz assisted to make life serious.

In person Mrs. Winterfield was tall and thin, wearing

on her brow thin braids of false hair. She had suffered
much from acute ill health, and her jaws were sunken, and
her eyes were hollow, and there was a look of woe about
her which seemed ever to be telling of her own sorrows in
this world and of the sorrows of others in the world to come.
Ill-nature was written on her face, but in this her face
was a false face. She had the manners of a cross, peevish
woman ; but her manners also were false, and gave no
proper idea of her character. But still, such as she was,
she made life very serious to those who were called upon
to dwell with her.

I need, I hope, hardly say that a young lady such as
Miss Amedroz, even though she had reached the age of
twenty-five,—for at the time to which I am now alluding
she had nearly done so,—and was not young of her age,
had formed for herself no plan of life in which her aunt's
money figured as a motive power. She had gone to Perivale when she was very young, because she had been told
to do so, and had continued to go, partly from obedience,
partly from habit, and partly from affection. An aunt's
dominion, when once well established in early years, cannot easily be thrown altogether aside,—even though a
young lady have a will of her own. Now Clara Amedroz
had a strong will of her own, and did not at all,—at any
rate in these latter days,—belong to that school of divinity
in which her aunt shone almost as a professor. And this
circumstance, also, added to the seriousness of her life.
But in regard to her aunt's money she had entertained no
established hopes ; and when her aunt opened her mind to
her on that subject, a few days before the arrival of the
fatal news at Perivale, Clara, though she was somewhat
surprised, was by no means disappointed. Now there was
a certain Captain Aylmer in the question, of whom in this
opening chapter it will be necessary to say a few words.

Captain Frederic Folliott Aylmer was, in truth, the
nephew of Mrs. Winterfield, whereas Clara Amedroz was
not, in truth, her niece. And Captain Aylmer was also
Member of Parliament for the little borough of Perivale,
returned altogether on the Low Church interest,—for a
devotion to which, and for that alone, Perivale was noted
among boroughs. These facts together added not a little
to Mrs. Winterfield's influence and professorial power in

the place, and gave a dignity to the one-horse chaise which
it might not otherwise have possessed. But Captain
Aylmer was only the second son of his father, Sir Anthony
Aylmer, who had married a Miss Folliott, sister of our
Mrs. Winterfield. On Frederick Aylmer his mother's
estate was settled. That and Mrs. Winterfield's property
lay in the neighbourhood of Perivale ; and now, on the
occasion to which I am alluding, Mrs. Winterfield thought
it necessary to tell Clara that the property must all go
together. She had thought about it, and had doubted
about it, and had prayed about it, and now she found that
such a disposition of it was her duty.

"I am quite sure you're right, aunt," Clara had said.
She knew very well what had come of that provision which
her father had attempted to make for her, and knew also
how great were her father's expectations in regard to Mrs.
Winterfield's money.

"I hope I am; but I have thought it right to tell you.
I shall feel myself bound to tell Frederic. I have had
many doubts, but I think I am right."

"I am sure you are, aunt. What would he think of me
if, at some future time, he should have to find that I had
been in his way?"

"The future time will not be long now, my dear."

"I hope it may; but long or short, it is better so."

"I think it is, my dear; I think it is. I think it is my
duty."

It must be understood that Captain Aylmer was member
for Perivale on the Low Church interest, and that, therefore, when at Perivale he was decidedly a Low Church-
man. I am not aware that the peculiarity stuck to him
very closely at Aylmer Castle, in Yorkshire, or among his
friends in London; but there was no hypocrisy in this, as
the world goes. Women in such matters are absolutely
false if they be not sincere ; but men, with political views,
and with much of their future prospects in jeopardy also,
are allowed to dress themselves differently for different
scenes. Whatever be the peculiar interest on which a
man goes into Parliament. of course he has to live up to
that in his own borough. Whether malt, the franchise, or
teetotalism be his rallying point, of course he is full of it
when among his constituents. But it is not desirable that

he should be full of it also at his club. Had Captain
Aylmer become Prime Minister, he would no doubt have
made Low Church bishops. It was the side to which he
had taken himself in that matter, — not without good
reasons. And he could say a sharp word or two in season
about vestments ; he was strong against candles, and fought
for his side fairly well. No one had good right to complain of Captain Aylmer as being insincere ; but had his
aunt known the whole history of her nephew's life, I doubt
whether she would have made him her heir,—thinking
that in doing so she was doing the best for the good
cause.

The whole history of her niece's life she did know, and
she knew that Clara was not with her, heart and soul.
Had Clara left the old woman in doubt on this subject, she
would have been a hypocrite. Captain Aylmer did not
often spend a Sunday at Perivale, but when he did, he
went to church three times, and submitted himself to the
yoke. He was thinking of the borough votes quite as
much as of his aunt's money, and was carrying on his
business after the fashion of men. But Clara found herself
compelled to maintain some sort of a fight, though she also
went to church three times on Sunday. And there was
another reason why Mrs. Winterfield thought it right to
mention Captain Aylmer's name to her niece on this
occasion.

"I had hoped,' he said, "that it might make no difference in what way my money was left."

Clara well understood what this meant, as will, probably, the reader also. "I can't say but what it will
make a difference," she answered, smiling ; "but I shall
always think that you have done right. Why should I
stand in Captain Aylmer's way ?"

"I had hoped your ways might have been the same,"
said the old lady, fretfully.

"But they cannot be the same."

"No ; you do not see things as he sees them. Things
that are serious to him are, I fear, only light to you. Dear
Clara, would I could see you more in earnest as to the only
matter that is worth our earnestness." Miss Amedroz said
nothing as to the Captain's earnestness, though, perhaps,
her ideas as to his ideas about religion were more correct

than those held by Mrs. Winterfield. But it would not
have suited her to raise any argument on that subject. "I
pray for you, Clara," continued the old lady; "and will do
so as long as the power of prayer is left to me. I hope—I
hope you do not cease to pray for yourself?"

"I endeavour, aunt."

"It is an endeavour which, if really made, never fails."

Clara said nothing more, and her aunt also remained
silent. Soon afterwards, the four-wheeled carriage, with
the demure stable-boy, came to the door, and Clara was
driven up and down through the streets of Perivale in a
manner which was an injury to her. She knew that she
was suffering an injustice, but it was one of which she
could not make complaint. She submitted to her aunt,
enduring the penances that were required of her; and,
therefore, her aunt had opportunity enough to see her shortcomings. Mrs. Winterfield did see them, and judged her
accordingly. Captain Aylmer, being a man and a Member
of Parliament, was called upon to bear no such penances,
and, therefore, his shortcomings were not suspected.

But, after all, what title had she ever possessed to entertain expectations from Mrs. Winterfield? When she
thought of it all in her room that night, she told herself
that it was strange that her aunt should have spoken to
her in such a way on such a subject. But, then, so much
had been said to her on the matter by her father, so much,
no doubt, had reached her aunt's ears also, the hope that
her position with reference to the rich widow at Perivale
might be beneficial to her had been so often discussed at
Belton as a make-weight against the extravagance of the
heir, there had already been so much of this mistake, that
she taught herself to perceive that the communication was
needed. "In her honesty she has not chosen to leave me
with false hopes," said Clara to herself. And at that
moment she loved her aunt for her honesty.

Then, on the day but one following this conversation as
to the destiny of her aunt's property, came the terrible
tidings of her brother's death. Captain Aylmer, who had
been in London at the time, hurried down to Perivale, and
had been the first to tell Miss Amedroz what had happened.
The words spoken between them then had not been many,
but Clara knew that Captain Aylmer had been kind to

her; and when he had offered to accompany her to Belton, she had thanked him with a degree of gratitude which had almost seemed to imply more of regard between them than Clara would have acknowledged to exist. But in moments such as those, soft words may be spoken and hands may be pressed without any of that meaning which soft words and the grasping of hands generally carry with them. As far as Taunton, Captain Aylmer did go with Miss Amedroz, and there they parted, he on his journey up to town, and she for her father's desolate house at Belton.

CHAPTER II.

THE HEIR PROPOSES TO VISIT HIS COUSINS.

IT was full summer at Belton, and the sweet scent of the new hay filled the porch of the old house with fragrance, as Clara sat there, alone with her work. Immediately before the house door, between that and the old tower, there stood one of Farmer Stovey's hay-carts, now empty, with an old horse between the shafts looking as though he were asleep in the sun. Immediately beyond the tower the men were loading another cart, and the women and children were chattering as they raked the scattered remnants up to the rows. Under the shadow of the old tower, but in sight of Clara as she sat in the porch, there lay the small beer-barrels of the haymakers, and three or four rakes were standing erect against the old grey wall. It was now eleven o'clock, and Clara was waiting for her father, who was not yet out of his room. She had taken his breakfast to him in bed, as was her custom; for he had fallen into idle ways, and the luxury of his bed was, of all his remaining luxuries, the one that he liked the best. After a while he came down to her, having an open letter in his hand. Clara saw that he intended either to show it to her or to speak of it, and asked him, therefore, with some tone of interest in her voice, from whom it had come. But Mr. Amedroz was fretful at the moment, and instead of answering her began to complain of his tenant's ill-usage of him.

"What has he got his cart there for? I haven't let him

the road up to the hall door.   I suppose he will bring his
things into the parlour next."

"I rather like it, papa."

"Do you?   I can only say that you're lucky in your
tastes.   I don't like it, I can tell you."

"Mr. Stovey is out there.   Shall I ask him to have the
things moved further off?"

"No, my dear,—no.   I must bear it, as I do all the rest
of it.   What does it matter?   There'll be an end of it soon.
He pays his rent, and I suppose he is right to do as he
pleases.   But I can't say that I like it."

"Am I to see the letter, papa?" she asked, wishing to
turn his mind from the subject of the hay-cart.

"Well, yes.   I brought it for you to see; though perhaps
I should be doing better if I burned it, and said nothing
more about it.   It is a most impudent production; and
heartless,—very heartless."

Clara was accustomed to such complaints as these from
her father.   Everything that everybody did around him he
would call heartless.   The man pitied himself so much in
his own misery, that he expected to live in an atmosphere
of pity from others; and though the pity doubtless was
there, he misdoubted it.   He thought that Farmer Stovey
was cruel in that he had left the hay-cart near the house,
to wound his eyes by reminding him that he was no longer
master of the ground before his own hall door. He thought
that the women and children were cruel to chatter so near
his ears. He almost accused his daughter of cruelty, because
she had told him that she liked the contiguity of the haymaking.   Under such circumstances as those which enveloped him and her, was it not heartless in her to like
anything?   It seemed to him that the whole world of
Belton should be drowned in woe because of his misery.

"Where is it from, papa?" she asked.

"There, you may read it.   Perhaps it is better that you
should know that it has been written."   Then she read the
letter, which was as follows:—

"Plaistow Hall,—July, 186—."

Though she had never before seen the handwriting, she
knew at once from whence came the letter, for she had
often heard of Plaistow Hall.   It was the name of the farm
at which her distant cousin, Will Belton, lived, and her

father had more than once been at the trouble of explaining to her, that though the place was called a hall, the house was no more than a farmhouse. He had never seen Plaistow Hall, and had never been in Norfolk; but so much he could take upon himself to say, "They call all the farms halls down there." It was not wonderful that he should dislike his heir; and, perhaps, not unnatural that he should show his dislike after this fashion. Clara, when she read the address, looked up into her father's face. "You know who it is now," he said. And then she read the letter.

Plaistow Hall, — July, 186—.

"MY DEAR SIR,

"I have not written to you before since your bereavement, thinking it better to wait awhile; but I hope you have not taken me to be unkind in this, or have supposed me to be unmindful of your sorrow. Now I take up my pen, hoping that I may make you understand how greatly I was distressed by what has occurred. I believe, I am now the nearest male relative that you have, and as such I am very anxious to be of service to you if it may be possible. Considering the closeness of our connection, and my position in reference to the property, it seems bad that we should never meet. I can assure you that you would find me very friendly if we could manage to come together.

"I should think nothing of running across to Belton, if you would receive me at your house. I could come very well before harvest, if that would suit you, and would stay with you for a week. Pray give my kindest regards to my cousin Clara, whom I can only just remember as a very little girl. She was with her aunt at Perivale when I was at Belton as a boy. She shall find a friend in me if she wants a friend.

"Your affectionate Cousin,
"W. BELTON."

Clara read the letter very slowly, so that she might make herself sure of its tone and bearing before she was called upon by her father to express her feelings respecting it. She knew that she would be expected to abuse it violently, and to accuse the writer of vulgarity, insolence, and cruelty; but she had already learned that she must not

allow herself to accede to all her father's fantasies. For his
sake, and for his protection, it was necessary that she
should differ from him, and even contradict him. Were
she not to do so, he would fall into a state of wailing and
complaining that would exaggerate itself almost to idiotcy.
And it was imperative that she herself should exercise her
own opinion on many points, almost without reference to
him. She alone knew how utterly destitute she would be
when he should die. He, in the first days of his agony,
had sobbed forth his remorse as to her ruin; but, even
when doing so, he had comforted himself with the remembrance of Mrs. Winterfield's money, and Mrs. Winterfield's
affection for his daughter. And the aunt, when she had
declared her purpose to Clara, had told herself that the
provision made for Clara by her father was sufficient. To
neither of them had Clara told her own position. She could
not inform her aunt that her father had given up to the
poor reprobate who had destroyed himself all that had been
intended for her. Had she done so she would have been
asking her aunt for charity. Nor would she bring herself
to add to her father's misery, by destroying the hopes
which still supported him. She never spoke of her own
position in regard to money, but she knew that it had
become her duty to live a wary, watchful life, taking much
upon herself in their impoverished household, and holding
her own opinion against her father's when her doing so
became expedient. So she finished the letter in silence,
and did not speak at the moment when the movement of
her eyes declared that she had completed the task.

·" Well," said he.

" I do not think my cousin means badly."

" You don't! I do, then. I think he means very badly.
What business has he to write to me, talking of his
position?"

" I can't see anything amiss in his doing so, papa. I
think he wishes to be friendly. The property will be his
some day, and I don't see why that should not be mentioned, when there is occasion."

" Upon my word, Clara, you surprise me. But women
never understand delicacy in regard to money. They have
so little to do with it, and think so little about it, that they
have no occasion for such delicacy."

Clara could not help the thought that to her mind the subject was present with sufficient frequency to make delicacy very desirable, if only it were practicable. But of this she said nothing. "And what answer will you send to him, papa?" she asked.

"None at all. Why should I trouble myself to write to him?"

"I will take the trouble off your hands."

"And what will you say to him?"

"I will ask him to come here, as he proposes."

"Clara!"

"Why not, papa? He is the heir to the property, and why should he not be permitted to see it? There are many things in which his co-operation with you might be a comfort to you. I can't tell you whether the tenants and people are treating you well, but he can do so; and, moreover, I think he means to be kind. I do not see why we should quarrel with our cousin because he is the heir to your property. It is not through any doing of his own that he is so."

This reasoning had no effect upon Mr. Amedroz, but his daughter's resolution carried the point against him in spite of his want of reason. No letter was written that day, or on the next; but on the day following a formal note was sent off by Clara, in which Mr. Belton was told that Mr. Amedroz would be happy to receive him at Belton Castle. The letter was written by the daughter, but the father was responsible for the formality. He sat over her while she wrote it, and nearly drove her distracted by discussing every word and phrase. At last, Clara was so annoyed with her own production, that she was almost tempted to write another letter unknown to her father; but the formal note went.

"MY DEAR SIR,

"I am desired by my father to say that he will be happy to receive you at Belton Castle, at the time fixed by yourself.

"Yours truly,

"CLARA AMEDROZ."

There was no more than that, but that had the desired

effect; and by return of post there came a rejoinder, saying that Will Belton would be at the Castle on the fifteenth of August. "They can do without me for about ten days," he said in his postscript, writing in a familiar tone, which did not seem to have been at all checked by the coldness of his cousin's note,—"as our harvest will be late; but I must be back for a week's work before the partridges."

"Heartless! quite heartless!" Mr. Amedroz said as he read this. "Partridges! to talk of partridges at such a time as this!"

Clara however, would not acknowledge that she agreed with her father; but she could not altogether restrain a feeling on her own part that her cousin's good-humour towards her and Mr. Amedroz should have been repressed by the tone of her letter to him. The man was to come, however, and she would not judge of him until he was there.

In one house, in the neighbourhood, and in only one, had Miss Amedroz a friend with whom she was intimate, and as regarded even this single friend, the intimacy was the effect rather of circumstances than of real affection. She liked Mrs. Askerton, and saw her almost daily; but she could hardly tell herself that she loved her neighbour.

In the little town of Belton, close to the church, there stood a pretty, small house, called Belton Cottage. It was so near the church that strangers always supposed it to be the parsonage; but the rectory stood away out in the country, half a mile from the town, on the road to Redicote, and was a large house, three stories high, with grounds of its own, and very ugly. Here lived the old bachelor rector, seventy years of age, given much to long absences when he could achieve them, and never on good terms with his bishop His two curates lived at Redicote, where there was a second church. Belton Cottage, which was occupied by Colonel Askerton and Mrs. Askerton, was on the Amedroz property, and had been hired some two years since by the Colonel, who was then a stranger in the country and altogether unknown to the Belton people. But he had come there for shooting, and therefore his coming had been understood. Even as long ago as two years since, there had been neither use nor propriety in keeping the shooting for the squire's son, and it had been let with the cottage to

Colonel Askerton. So Colonel Askerton had come there with his wife, and no one in the neighbourhood had known anything about them. Mr. Amedroz, with his daughter, had called upon them, and gradually there had grown up an intimacy between Clara and Mrs. Askerton. There was an opening from the garden of Belton Cottage into the park, so that familiar intercourse was easy, and Mrs. Askerton was a woman who knew well how to make herself pleasant to such another woman as Miss Amedroz.

The reader may as well know at once that rumours prejudicial to the Askertons reached Belton before they had been established there for six months. At Taunton, which was twenty miles distant, these rumours were very rife, and there were people there who knew with accuracy,— though probably without a grain of truth in their accuracy, every detail in the history of Mrs. Askerton's life. And something, too, reached Clara's ears—something from old Mr. Wright, the rector, who loved scandal, and was very ill-natured. " A very nice woman," the rector had said; " but she does not seem to have any belongings in particular." " She has got a husband," Clara had replied with some little indignation, for she had never loved Mr. Wright. " Yes; I suppose she has got a husband." Then Clara had, in her own judgment, accused the rector of lying, evil-speaking, and slandering, and had increased the measure of her cordiality to Mrs. Askerton. But something more she had heard on the same subject at Perivale. " Before you throw yourself into close intimacy with the lady, I think you should know something about her," Mrs. Winterfield had said to her. " I do know something about her; I know that she has the manners and education of a lady, and that she is living affectionately with her husband, who is devoted to her. What more ought I to know?" " If you really do know all that, you know a great deal," Mrs. Winterfield had replied.

" Do you know anything against her, aunt?" Clara asked, after a pause.

There was another pause before Mrs. Winterfield answered. " No, my dear; I cannot say that I do. But I think that young ladies, before they make intimate friendships, should be very sure of their friends."

" You have already acknowledged that I know a great

deal about her," Clara replied. And then the conversation was at an end. Clara had not been quite ingenuous, as she acknowledged to herself. She was aware that her aunt would not permit herself to repeat rumours as to the truth of which she had no absolute knowledge. She understood that the weakness of her aunt's caution was due to the old lady's sense of charity and dislike of slander. But Clara had buckled on her armour for Mrs. Askerton, and was glad, therefore, to achieve her little victory. When we buckle on our armour in any cause, we are apt to go on buckling it, let the cause become as weak as it may; and Clara continued her intimacy with Mrs. Askerton, although there was something in the lady's modes of speech, and something also in her modes of thinking, which did not quite satisfy the aspirations of Miss Amedroz as to a friend.

Colonel Askerton himself was a pleasant, quiet man, who seemed to be contented with the life which he was leading. For six weeks in April and May he would go up to town, leaving Mrs. Askerton at the cottage,—as to which, probably jovial, absence in the metropolis there seemed to be no spirit of grudging on the part of the wife. On the first of September a friend would come to the cottage and remain there for six weeks' shooting ; and during the winter the Colonel and his wife always went to Paris for a fortnight. Such had been their life for the last two years ; and thus,—so said Mrs. Askerton to Clara,—did they intend to live as long as they could keep the cottage at Belton. Society at Belton they had none, and,—as they said,— desired none. Between them and Mr. Wright there was only a speaking acquaintance. The married curate at Redicote would not let his wife call on Mrs. Askerton, and the unmarried curate was a hard-worked, clerical hack,— a parochial minister at all times and seasons, who went to no houses except the houses of the poor, and who would hold communion with no man, and certainly with no woman, who would not put up with clerical admonitions for Sunday backslidings. Mr. Amedroz himself neither received guests nor went as a guest to other men's houses. He would occasionally stand for a while at the gate of the Colonel's garden, and repeat the list of his own woes as long as his neighbour would stand there to hear it. But there was no society at Belton ; and Clara, as far as she herself was aware,

was the only person with whom Mrs. Askerton held any
social intercourse, except what she might have during her
short annual holiday in Paris.

"Of course, you are right," she said, when Clara told her
of the proposed coming of Mr. Belton. "If he turned out
to be a good fellow, you will have gained a great deal.
And should he be a bad fellow, you will have lost nothing.
In either case you will know him, and considering how he
stands towards you, that itself is desirable."

"But if he should annoy papa?"

"In your papa's condition, my dear, the coming of any
one will annoy him. At least, he will say so; though I do
not in the least doubt that he will like the excitement
better even than you will."

"I can't say there will be much excitement to me."

"No excitement in a young man's coming into the house!
Without shocking your propriety, allow me to say that that
is impossible. Of course, he is coming to see whether he
can't make matters all right by marrying you."

"That's nonsense, Mrs. Askerton."

"Very well. Let it be nonsense. But why shouldn't
he? It's just what he ought to do. He hasn't got a wife;
and, as far as I know, you haven't got a lover."

"I certainly have not got a lover."

"Our religious nephew at Perivale does not seem to be
of any use."

"I wish, Mrs. Askerton, you would not speak of Captain
Aylmer in that way. I don't know any man whom I like
so much, or at any rate better, than Captain Aylmer; but
I hate the idea that no girl can become acquainted with an
unmarried man without having her name mentioned with
his, and having to hear ill-natured remarks of that kind."

"I hope you will learn to like this other man much
better. Think how nice it will be to be mistress of the old
place after all. And then to go back to the old family
name! If I were you I would make up my mind not
to let him leave the place till I had brought him to
my feet."

"If you go on like that I will not speak to you about him
again."

"Or rather not to my feet,—for gentlemen have laid
aside the humble way of making love for the last twenty

years at least; but I don't know whether the women haven't gained quite as much by the change as the men."

"As I know nothing will stop you when you once get into a vein of that kind, I shall go," said Clara. "And till this man has come and gone I shall not mention his name again in your presence."

"So be it," said Mrs. Askerton; "but as I will promise to say nothing more about him, you need not go on his account." But Clara had got up, and did leave the cottage at once.

CHAPTER III.

WILL BELTON.

MR. BELTON came to the castle, and nothing further had been said at the cottage about his coming. Clara had seen Mrs. Askerton in the mean time frequently; but that lady had kept her promise—almost to Clara's disappointment. For she,—though she had in truth disliked the proposition that her cousin could be coming with any special views with reference to herself, had nevertheless sufficient curiosity about the stranger to wish to talk about him. Her father, indeed, mentioned Belton's name very frequently, saying something with reference to him every time he found himself in his daughter's presence. A dozen times he said that the man was heartless to come to the house at such a time, and he spoke of his cousin always as though the man were guilty of a gross injustice in being heir to the property. But not the less on that account did he fidget himself about the room in which Belton was to sleep, about the food that Belton was to eat, and especially about the wine that Belton was to drink. What was he to do for wine? The stock of wine in the cellars at Belton Castle was, no doubt, very low. The squire himself drank a glass or two of port daily, and had some remnant of his old treasures by him, which might perhaps last him his time; and occasionally there came small supplies of sherry from the grocer at Taunton; but Mr. Amedroz pretended to think that Will Belton would want champagne and claret; —and he would continue to make these suggestions in spite of his own repeated complaints that the man was no better than an ordinary farmer. " I've no doubt he'll like beer," said Clara. " Beer !" said her father, and then stopped himself, as though he were lost in doubt whether it would best suit him to scorn his cousin for having so low a taste as that suggested on his behalf, or to ridicule his daughter's idea that the household difficulty admitted of so convenient a solution.

The day of the arrival at last came, and Clara certainly was in a twitter, although she had steadfastly resolved that she would be in no twitter at all. She had told her aunt by letter of the proposed visit, and Mrs. Winterfield had expressed her approbation, saying that she hoped it would lead to good results. Of what good results could her aunt be thinking? The one probable good result would surely be this—that relations so nearly connected should know each other. Why should there be any fuss made about such a visit? But, nevertheless, Clara, though she made no outward fuss, knew that inwardly she was not as calm about the man's coming as she would have wished herself to be.

He arrived about five o'clock in a gig from Taunton. Five was the ordinary dinner hour at Belton, but it had been postponed till six on this day, in the hope that the cousin might make his appearance at any rate by that hour. Mr. Amedroz had uttered various complaints as to the visitor's heartlessness in not having written to name the hour of his arrival, and was manifestly intending to make the most of the grievance should he not present himself before six ;—but this indulgence was cut short by the sound of the gig wheels. Mr. Amedroz and his daughter were sitting in a small drawing-room, which looked out to the front of the house and he, seated in his accustomed chair, near the window, could see the arrival. For a moment or two he remained quiet in his chair, as though he would not allow so insignificant a thing as his cousin's coming to ruffle him ;—but he could not maintain this dignified indifference, and before Belton was out of the gig he had shuffled out into the hall.

Clara followed her father almost unconsciously and soon found herself shaking hands with a big man, over six feet high, broad in the shoulders large limbed, with bright

quick grey eyes, a large mouth, teeth almost too perfect
and a well-formed nose, with thick short brown hair and
small whiskers which came but half way down his cheeks
—a decidedly handsome man with a florid face, but still,
perhaps, with something of the promised roughness of the
farmer. But a more good-humoured looking countenance
Clara felt at once that she had never beheld.

"And you are the little girl that I remember when I
was a boy at Mr. Folliott's?" he said. His voice was clear,
and rather loud, but it sounded very pleasantly in that sad
old house.

"Yes; I am the little girl," said Clara, smiling.

"Dear, dear! and that's twenty years ago now," said he.

"But you oughtn't to remind me of that," Mr. Belton.

"Oughtn't I? Why not?"

"Because it shows how very old I am."

"Ah, yes;—to be sure. But there's nobody here that
signifies. How well I remember this room;—and the old
tower out there. It isn't changed a bit!"

"Not to the outward eye, perhaps," said the squire.

"That's what I mean. So they're making hay still. Our
hay has been all up these three weeks. I didn't know you
ever meadowed the park." Here he trod with dreadful seve-
rity upon the corns of Mr. Amedroz, but he did not perceive
it. And when the squire muttered something about a
tenant, and the inconvenience of keeping land in his own
hands, Belton would have gone on with the subject had
not Clara changed the conversation. The squire complained
bitterly of this to Clara when they were alone, saying that
it was very heartless.

She had a little scheme of her own,—a plan arranged
for the saying of a few words to her cousin on the earliest
opportunity of their being alone together,—and she contrived that this should take place within half an hour after
his arrival, as he went through the hall up to his room.
"Mr. Belton," she said, "I am sure you will not take it
amiss if I take a cousin's privilege at once and explain to
you something of our way of living here. My dear father is
not very strong."

"He is much altered since I saw him last."

"Oh, yes. Think of all that he has had to bear! Well,
Mr. Belton, the fact is, that we are not so well off as we

used to be, and are obliged to live in a very quiet way.
You will not mind that?"

"Who? I?"

"I take it very kind of you, your coming all this way
to see us——"

"I'd have come three times the distance."

"But you must put up with us as you find us, you know.
The truth is we are very poor."

"Well, now;—that's just what I wanted to know. One
couldn't write and ask such a question; but I was sure I
should find out if I came."

"You've found it out already, you see."

"As for being poor, it's a thing I don't think very much
about,—not for young people. But it isn't comfortable
when a man gets old. Now what I want to know is this;
can't something be done?"

"The only thing to do is to be very kind to him. He
has had to let the park to Mr. Stovey, and he doesn't like
talking about it."

"But if it isn't talked about, how can it be mended?"

"It can't be mended."

"We'll see about that. But I'll be kind to him; you
see if I ain't. And I'll tell you what, I'll be kind to you
too, if you'll let me. You have got no brother now."

"No," said Clara; "I have got no brother now."
Belton was looking full into her face, and saw that her
eyes had become clouded with tears.

"I will be your brother," said he. "You see if I don't.
When I say a thing I mean it. I will be your brother."
And he took her hand, caressing it, and showing her that
he was not in the least afraid of her. He was blunt in his
bearing, saying things which her father would have called
indelicate and heartless, as though they gave him no effort,
and placing himself at once almost in a position of ascen-
dency. This Clara had not intended. She had thought
that her farmer cousin, in spite of the superiority of his
prospects as heir to the property, would have acceded to
her little hints with silent acquiescence; but instead of
this he seemed prepared to take upon himself the chief
part in the play that was to be acted between them.
"Shall it be so?" he said, still holding her hand.

"You are very kind."

" I will be more than kind; I will love you dearly if
you will let me. You don't suppose that I have looked
you up here for nothing. Blood is thicker than water,
and you have nobody now so near to you as I am. I don't
see why you should be so poor, as the debts have been
paid."

"Papa has had to borrow money on his life interest in
the place."

"That's the mischief! Never mind. We'll see if we
can't do something. And in the meantime don't make a
stranger of me. Anything does for me. Lord bless you!
if you were to see how I rough it sometimes! I can eat
beans and bacon with any one; and what's more, I can go
without 'em if I can't get 'em."

"We'd better get ready for dinner now. I always dress,
because papa likes to see it." This she said as a hint to
her cousin that he would be expected to change his coat,
for her father would have been annoyed had his guest sat
down to dinner without such ceremony. Will Belton was
not very good at taking hints; but he did understand this,
and made the necessary change in his apparel.

The evening was long and dull, and nothing occurred
worthy of remark except the surprise manifested by Mr.
Amedroz when Belton called his daughter by her Christian
name. This he did without the slightest hesitation, as
though it were the most natural thing in the world for him
to do. She was his cousin, and cousins of course addressed
each other in that way. Clara's quick eye immediately
saw her father's slight gesture of dismay, but Belton
caught nothing of this. The squire took an early opportunity of calling him Mr. Belton, with some little peculiarity of expression; but this was altogether lost upon Will,
who five times in the next five minutes addressed " Clara "
as though they were already on the most intimate terms.
She would have answed him in the same way, and would
have called him Will, had she not been afraid of offending
her father.

Mr. Amedroz had declared his purpose of coming down
to breakfast during the period of his cousin's visit, and at
nalf-past nine he was in the parlour. Clara had been there
some time but had not seen her cousin. He entered the
room immediately after her father, bringing his hat with

him in his hand, and wiping the drops of perspiration from his brow. "You have been out, Mr. Belton," said the squire.

"All round the place, sir. Six o'clock doesn't often find me in bed, summer or winter. What's the use of laying in bed when one has had enough of sleep?"

"But that's just the question," said Clara; "whether one has had enough at six o'clock."

"Women want more than men, of course. A man, if he means to do any good with land, must be out early. The grass will grow of itself at nights, but it wants looking after as soon as the daylight comes."

"I don't know that it would do much good to the grass here," said the squire, mournfully.

"As much here as anywhere. And indeed I've got something to say about that." He had now seated himselī at the breakfast-table, and was playing with his knife and fork. "I think, sir, you're hardly making the best you can out of the park."

"We won't mind talking about it, if you please," said the squire.

"Well; of course I won't, if you don't like it; but upon my word you ought to look about you; you ought indeed."

"In what way do you mean?" said Clara.

"If your father doesn't like to keep the land in his own hands, he should let it to some one who would put stock in it,—not go on cutting it year after year, and putting nothing back, as this fellow will do. I have been talking to Stovey, and that's just what he means."

"Nobody here has got money to put stock on the land," said the squire, angrily.

"Then you should look for somebody somewhere else. That's all. I'll tell you what now, Mr. Amedroz, I'll do it myself." By this time he had helped himself to two large slices of cold mutton, and was eating his breakfast and talking with an equal amount of energy for either occupation.

"That's out of the question," said the squire.

"I don't see why it should be out of the question. It would be better for you,—and better for me too, if this place is ever to be mine." On hearing this the squire winced, but said nothing. This terrible fellow was so

vehemently outspoken that the poor old man was absolutely unable to keep pace with him,—even to the repeating of his wish that the matter should be talked of no
further. "I'll tell you what I'll do, now," continued
Belton. "There's altogether, outside the palings and in,
about a hundred and fifty acres of it. I'll give you one
pound two and sixpence an acre, and I won't cut an acre of
grass inside the park;—no, nor much of it outside either;
—only just enough to give me a little fodder for the cattle
in winter."

"And give up Plaistow Hall?" asked Clara.

"Lord love you, no. I've a matter of nine hundred
acres on hand there, and most of it under the plough. I've
counted it up, and it would just cost me a thousand pounds
to stock this place. I should come and look at it twice a
year or so, and I should see my money home again, if I
didn't get any profit out of it."

Mr. Amedroz was astonished. The man had only been
in his house one night, and was proposing to take all his
troubles off his hands. He did not relish the proposition
at all. He did not like to be accused of not doing as well
for himself as others could do for him. He did not wish
to make any change,—although he remembered at the
moment his anger with Farmer Stovey respecting the hay-
carts. He did not desire that the heir should have any
immediate interest in the place. But he was not strong
enough to meet the proposition with a direct negative. "I
couldn't get rid of Stovey in that way," he said, plaintively.

"I've settled it all with Stovey already," said Belton.
"He'll be glad enough to walk off with a twenty-pound
note, which I'll give him. He can't make money out of
the place. He hasn't got means to stock it, and then see
the wages that haymaking runs away with! He'd lose
by it even at what he's paying, and he knows it. There
won't be any difficulty about Stovey."

By twelve o'clock on that day, Mr. Stovey had been
brought into the house, and had resigned the land. It had
been let to Mr. William Belton at an increased rental,—a
rental increased by nearly forty pounds per annum,—and
that gentleman had already made many of his arrangements for entering upon his tenancy. The twenty pounds

had already been paid to Stovey, and the transaction was complete. Mr. Amedroz sat in his chair bewildered, dismayed—and, as he himself declared, shocked, quite shocked, at the precipitancy of the young man. It might be for the best. He didn't know. He didn't feel at all sure. But such hurrying in such a matter was, under all the circumstances of the family, to say the least of it, very indelicate. He was angry with himself for having yielded, and angry with Clara for having allowed him to do so. "It doesn't signify much," he said, at last. "Of course he'll have it all to himself before long."

"But, papa, it really seems to be a much better arrangement for you. You'll get more money——"

"Money is not everything, my dear."

"But you'd sooner have Mr. Belton, our own cousin, about the place, than Mr. Stovey?"

"I don't know. We shall see. The thing is done now, and there is no use in complaining. I must say he hasn't shown a great deal of delicacy."

On that afternoon Belton asked Clara to go out with him, and walk round the place. He had been again about the grounds, and had made plans, and counted up capabilities, and calculated his profit and losses. "If you don't dislike scrambling about," said he, "I'll show you everything that I intend to do."

"But I can't have any changes made, Mr. Belton," said Mr. Amedroz, with some affectation of dignity in his manner. "I won't have the fences moved, or anything of that kind."

"Nothing shall be done, sir, that you don't approve. I'll just manage it all as if I was acting as your own——bailiff." Son, he was going to say, but he remembered the fate of his cousin Charles just in time to prevent the use of the painful word.

"I don't want to have anything done," said Mr. Amedroz.

"Then nothing shall be done. We'll just mend a fence or two, to keep in the cattle, and leave other things as they are. But perhaps Clara will walk out with me all the same."

Clara was quite ready to walk out, and had already tied on her hat and taken her parasol.

"Your father is a little nervous," said he, as soon as they were beyond hearing of the house.

"Can you wonder at it, when you remember all that he has suffered?"

"I don't wonder at it in the least; and I don't wonder at his disliking me either."

"I don't think he dislikes you, Mr. Belton."

"Oh, but he does. Of course he does. I'm the heir to the place instead of you. It is natural that he should dislike me. But I'll live it down. You see if I don't. I'll make him so fond of me, he'll always want to have me here. I don't mind a little dislike to begin with."

"You're a wonderful man, Mr. Belton."

"I wish you wouldn't call me Mr. Belton. But of course you must do as you please about that. If I can make him call me Will, I suppose you'll call me so too."

"Oh, yes; then I will."

"It don't much matter what a person is called; does it? Only one likes to be friendly with one's friends. I suppose you don't like my calling you Clara."

"Now you've begun you had better go on."

"I mean to. I make it a rule never to go back in the world. Your father is half sorry that he has agreed about the place; but I shan't let him off now. And I'll tell you what. In spite of what he says, I'll have it as different as possible before this time next year. Why, there's lots of timber that ought to come out of the plantation; and there's places where the roots want stubbing up horribly. These things always pay for themselves if they are properly done. Any good done in the world always pays." Clara often remembered those words afterwards when she was thinking of her cousin's character. Any good done in the world always pays!

"But you mustn't offend my father, even though it should do good," she said.

"I understand," he answered. "I won't tread on his toes. Where do you get your milk and butter?"

"We buy them."

"From Stovey, I suppose."

"Yes; from Mr. Stovey. It goes against the rent."

"And it ought to go against the grain too,—living in the country and paying for milk! I'll tell you what I'll do. I'll give you a cow. It shall be a little present from me to you. He said nothing of the more important present which this would entail upon him in the matter of the grass for the cow; but she understood the nature of the arrangement, and was anxious to prevent it.

" Oh, Mr. Belton, I think we'd better not attempt that," she said.

" But we will attempt it. I've pledged myself to do nothing to oppose your father; but I've made no such promise as to you. We'll have a cow before I'm many days older. What a pretty place this is! I do like these rocks so much, and it is such a comfort to be off the flat."

" It is pretty."

' Very pretty. You've no conception what an ugly place Plaistow is. The land isn't actual fen now, but it was once. And it's quite flat. And there is a great dike, twenty feet wide, oozing through it,—just oozing, you know; and lots of little dikes, at right angles with the big one. And the fields are all square. And there are no hedges,—and hardly a tree to be seen in the place.",

" What a picture you have drawn! I should commit suicide if I lived there."

" Not if you had so much to do as I have."

" And what is the house like ?"

" The house is good enough,—an old-fashioned manor-house, with high brick chimneys, and brick gables, tiled all over, and large square windows set in stone. The house is good enough, only it stands in the middle of a farm-yard. I said there were no trees, but there is an avenue."

" Come, that's something."

" It was an old family seat, and they used to have avenues in those days ; but it doesn't lead up to the present hall door. It comes sideways up to the farm-yard; so that the whole thing must have been different once, and there must have been a great court-yard. In Elizabeth's time Plaistow Manor was rather a swell place, and belonged to some Roman Catholics who came to grief, and then the Howards got it. There's a whole history about it, only I don't much care about those things."

" And is it yours now ?"

" It's between me and my uncle, and I pay him rent for his part. He's a clergyman, you know, and he has a living in Lincolnshire,—not far of

" And do you live all alone in that big house ?"

" There's my sister. You've heard of Mary ;—haven't you ?"

Then Clara remembered that there was a Miss Belton,— a poor sickly creature, with a twisted spine and a hump back, as to whose welfare she ought to have made inquiries.

" Oh, yes; of course," said Clara. " I hope she's better than she used to be,—when we heard of her."

" She'll never be better. But then she does not become much worse. I think she does grow a little weaker. She's older than I am, you know,—two years older; but you would think she was quite an old woman to look at her." Then, for the next half hour, they talked about Mary Belton as they visited every corner of the place. Belton still had an eye to business as he went on talking, and Clara remarked how many sticks he moved as he went, how many stones he kicked on one side, and how invariably he noted any defect in the fences. But still he talked of his sister, swearing that she was as good as gold, and at last wiping away the tears from his eyes as he described her maladies. " And yet I believe she is better off than any of us," he said, " because she is so good." Clara began to wish that she had called him Will from the beginning, because she liked him so much. He was just the man to have for a cousin,—a true loving cousin, stalwart, self-confident, with a grain or two of tyranny in his composition as becomes a man in relation to his intimate female relatives ; and one, moreover, with whom she could trust herself to be familiar without any danger of love-making ! She saw his character clearly, and told herself that she understood it perfectly. He " was a jewel of a cousin, and she must begin to call him Will as speedily as possible.

At last they came round in their walk to the gate leading into Colonel Askerton's garden ; and here in the garden, close to the gate, they found Mrs. Askerton. I fancy that she had been watching for them, or at any rate watching for Clara, so that she might know how her friend was carrying herself with her cousin. She came at once to the wicket, and there she was introduced by Clara to Mr. Belton. Mr. Belton as he made his bow muttered something awkwardly, and seemed to lose his self-posses-

sion for the moment. Mrs. Askerton was very gracious to
him, and she knew well how to be both gracious and
ungracious. She talked about the scenery, and the charms
of the old place, and the dulness of the people around
them, and the inexpediency of looking for society in
country places : till after awhile Mr. Belton was once
more at his ease.

"How is Colonel Askerton?" asked Clara.

"He's in-doors. Will you come and see him? He's
reading a French novel, as usual. It's the only thing he
ever does in summer. Do you ever read French novels,
Mr. Belton?"

"I read very little at all, and when I do I read English."

"Ah, you're a man who has a pursuit in life, no doubt."

"I should rather think so,—that is, if you mean, by a
pursuit, earning my bread. A man has not much time for
French novels with a thousand acres of land on his hands ;
even if he knew how to read French, which I don't."

"But you're not always at work on your farm?"

"It's pretty constant, Mrs. Askerton. Then I shoot,
and hunt."

"You're a sportsman?"

"All men living in the country are, more or less."

"Colonel Askerton shoots a great deal. He has the
shooting of Belton, you know. He'll be delighted, I'm
sure, to see you if you are here some time in September.
But you, coming from Norfolk, would not care for partridge-
shooting in Somersetshire."

"I don't see why it shouldn't be as good here as there."

"Colonel Askerton thinks he has got a fair head of game
upon the place."

"I dare say. Game is easily kept if people knew how
to set about it."

"Colonel Askerton has a very good keeper, and has gone
to a great deal of expense since he has been here."

"I'm my own head-keeper," said Belton ; "and so I will
be,—or rather should be, if I had this place."

Something in the lady's tone had grated against his
feelings and offended him ; or perhaps he thought that she
assumed too many of the airs of proprietorship because the
shooting of the place had been let to her husband for thirty
pounds a-year.

"I hope you don't mean to say you'll turn us out," said Mrs. Askerton, laughing.

"I have no power to turn anybody out or in," said he. "I've got nothing to do with it."

Clara, perceiving that matters were not going quite pleasantly between her old and new friend, thought it best to take her departure. Belton, as he went, lifted his hat from his head, and Clara could not keep herself from thinking that he was not only very handsome, but that he looked very much like a gentleman in spite of his occupation as a farmer.

"By-bye, Clara," said Mrs. Askerton; "come down and see me to-morrow, there's a dear. Don't forget what a dull life I have of it." Clara said that she would come. "And I shall be so happy to see Mr. Belton if he will call before he leaves you." At this Belton again raised his hat from his head, and muttered some word or two of civility. But this, his latter muttering, was different from the first, for he had altogther regained his presence of mind.

"You didn't seem to get on very well with my friend," said Clara, laughing, as soon as they had turned away from the cottage.

"Well, no;—that is to say, not particularly well or particularly badly. At first I took her for somebody else I knew slightly ever so long ago, and I was thinking of that other person at the time."

"And what was the other person's name?"

"I can't even remember that at the present moment."

"Mrs. Askerton was a Miss Oliphant."

"That wasn't the other lady's name. But, independently of that, they can't be the same. The other lady married a Mr. Berdmore."

"A Mr. Berdmore!" Clara as she repeated the name felt convinced that she had heard it before, and that she had heard it in connection with Mrs. Askerton. She certainly had heard the name of Berdmore pronounced, or had seen it written, or had in some shape come across the name in Mrs. Askerton's presence; or at any rate somewhere on the premises occupied by that lady. More than this she could not remember; but the name, as she had now heard it from her cousin, became at once distinctly connected in her memory with her friends at the cottage.

"Yes," said Belton; " a Mr. Berdmore. I knew more
of him than of her, though for the matter of that, I knew
very little of him either. She was a fast-going girl, and
his friends were very sorry. But I think they are both
dead or divorced, or that they have come to grief in
some way."

"And is Mrs. Askerton like the fast-going lady?"

" In a certain way. Not that I remember what the fast-
going lady was like; but there was something about this
woman that put me in mind of the other. Vigo was her
nam ; now I recollect it,—a Miss Vigo. It's nine or ten
years ago now, and I was little more than a boy."

" Her name was Oliphant."

" I don't suppose they have anything to do with each
other. What riled me was the way she talked of the shooting. People do when they take a little shooting. They
pay some trumpery thirty or forty pounds a-year, and then
they seem to think that it's almost the same as though they
owned the property themselves. I've known a man talk of
his manor because he had the shooting of a wood and a
small farm round it. They are generally shopkeepers out
of London, gin distillers, or brewers, or people like that."

"Why, Mr. Belton, I didn't think you could be so
furious!"

" Can't I? When my back's up, it is up! But it isn't
up yet."

" And I hope it won't be up while you remain in Somersetshire."

" I won't answer for that. There's Stovey's empty cart
standing just where it stood yesterday; and he promised
he'd have it home before three to-day. My back will be
up with him if he doesn't mind himself."

It was nearly six o'clock when they got back to the
house, and Clara was surprised to find that she had been
out three hours with her cousin. Certainly it had been
very pleasant. The usual companion of her walks, when
she had a companion, was Mrs. Askerton; but Mrs. Askerton did not like real walking. She would creep about the
grounds for an hour or so, and even such companionship as
that was better to Clara than absolute solitude; but now
she had been carried about the place, getting over stiles
and through gates, and wandering through the copses, till

she was tired and hungry, and excited and happy. "Oh, papa," she said, "we have had such a walk!"

"I thought we were to have dined at five," he replied, in a low wailing voice.

"No, papa, indeed—indeed you said six."

"That was for yesterday."

"You said we were to make it six while Mr. Belton was here."

"Very well; if it must be, I suppose it must be."

"You don't mean on my account," said Will. "I'll undertake to eat my dinner, sir, at any hour that you'll undertake to give it me. If there's a strong point about me at all, it is my appetite."

Clara, when she went to her father's room that evening, told him what Mr. Belton had said about the shooting, knowing that her father's feelings would agree with those which had been expressed by her cousin. Mr. Amedroz of course made this an occasion for further grumbling, suggesting that Belton wanted to get the shooting for himself as he had got the farm. But, nevertheless, the effect which Clara had intended was produced, and before she left him he had absolutely proposed that the shooting and the land should go together.

"I'm sure that Mr. Belton doesn't mean that at all," said Clara.

"I don't care what he means," said the squire.

"And it wouldn't do to treat Colonel Askerton in that way," said Clara.

"I shall treat him just as I like," said the squire.

CHAPTER IV.

SAFE AGAINST LOVE-MAKING.

A DEAR cousin, and safe against love-making! This was Clara's verdict respecting Will Belton, as she lay thinking of him in bed that night. Why that warranty against love-making should be a virtue in her eyes I cannot, perhaps, explain. But all young ladies are apt to talk to themselves in such phrases about gentlemen with whom they are

thrown into chance intimacy;—as though love-making
were in itself a thing injurious and antagonistic to happiness, instead of being, as it is, the very salt of life. Safe
against love-making! And yet Mrs. Askerton, her friend,
had spoken of the probability of such love-making as being
the great advantage of his coming. And there could not
be a second opinion as to the expediency of a match
between her and her cousin in a worldly point of view.
Clara, moreover, had already perceived that he was a man
fit to guide a wife, very good-humoured,—and good-tem-
pered also, anxious to give pleasure to others, a man of
energy and forethought, who would be sure to do well in the
world and hold his head always high among his fellows ;—
as good a husband as a girl could have. Nevertheless, she
congratulated herself in that she felt satisfied that he was
safe against love-making! Might it be possible that that
pressing of hands at Taunton had been so tender, and those
last words spoken with Captain Aylmer so soft, that on his
account she felt delighted to think that her cousin was
warranted not to make love ?

And what did Will Belton think about his cousin, insured as he was thus supposed to be against the dangers of
love? He, also, lay awake for awhile that night, thinking
over this new friendship. Or rather he thought of it walking about his room, and looking out at the bright harvest
moon ;—for with him to be in bed was to be asleep. He
sat himself down, and he walked about, and he leaned out
of the window into the cool night air; and he made some
comparisons in his mind, and certain calculations; and he
thought of his present home, and of his sister, and of his
future prospects as they were concerned with the old place
at which he was now staying; and he portrayed to himself,
in his mind, Clara's head and face and figure and feet ;—
and he resolved that she should be his wife. He had never
seen a girl who seemed to suit him so well. Though he
had only been with her for a day, he swore to himself that
he knew he could love her. Nay ;—he swore to himself
that he did love her. Then,—when he had quite made
up his mind, he tumbled into his bed and was asleep in five
minutes.

Miss Amedroz was a handsome young woman, tall,
well-made, active, and full of health. She carried herself

as though she thought her limbs were made for use, and
not simply for ease upon a sofa. Her head and neck stood
well upon her shoulders, and her waist showed none of
those waspish proportions of which ladies used to be more
proud than I believe them to be now, in their more advanced state of knowledge and taste. There was much
about her in which she was like her cousin, as though the
blood they had in common between them had given to
both the same proportions and the same comeliness. Her
hair was of a dark-brown colour, as was his. Her eyes
were somewhat darker than his, and perhaps not so full of
constant movement; but they were equally bright, and
possessed that quick power of expressing tenderness which
belonged to him. Her nose was more finely cut, as was
also her chin, and the oval of her face; but she had the
same large expressive mouth, and the same perfection of
ivory-white teeth. As has been said before, Clara Amedroz,
who was now nearly twenty-six years of age, was not a
young-looking young woman. To the eyes of many men
that would have been her fault; but in the eyes of Belton
it was no fault. He had not made himself fastidious as to
women by much consort with them, and he was disposed
to think that she who was to become his wife had better
be something more than a girl not long since taken out of the
nursery. He was well to do in the world, and could send
his wife out in her carriage, with all becoming bravery of
appurtenances. And he would do so, too, when he should
have a wife. But still he would look to his wife to be a
useful partner to him. She should be a woman not above
agricultural solicitude, or too proud to have a care for her
cows. Clara, he was sure, had no false pride; and yet,—
as he was sure also, she was at every point such a lady as
would do honour to the carriage and the bravery when it
should be forthcoming. And then such a marriage as this
would put an end to all the trouble which he felt in reference to the entail on the estate. He knew that he was to
be master of Belton, and of course had, in that knowledge,
the satisfaction which men do feel from the consciousness of
their future prosperity. And this with him was enhanced
by a strong sympathy with old-fashioned prejudices as to
family. He would be Belton of Belton; and there had
been Beltons of Belton in old days, for a longer time back-

wards than he was able to count. But still the prospect
had not been without its alloy, and he had felt real distress
at the idea of turning his cousin out of her father's house.
Such a marriage as that he now contemplated would put all
these things right.

When he got up in the morning he was quite as keen
about it as he had been on the previous evening;—and as
he thought about it the more, he became keener and still
more keen. On the previous evening, as he was leaning
out of the window endeavouring to settle in his own mind
what would be the proper conduct of the romance of the
thing, he had considered that he had better not make his
proposal quite at once. He was to remain eight days at
Belton, and as eight days was not a long period of acquaintance, he had reflected that it might be well for him
to lay what foundation for love it might be in his power to
construct during his present sojourn, and then return and
complete the work before Christmas. But as he was
shaving himself, the habitual impatience of his nature pre-
dominated, and he became disposed to think that delay
would be useless, and might perhaps be dangerous. It might
be possible that Clara would be unable to give him a
decisive answer so quickly as to enable him to return home
an accepted lover; but if such doubt were left, such doubt
would give him an excuse for a speedy return to Belton.
He did not omit to tell himself that very probably he
might not succeed at all. He was a man not at all apt to
feel assurance that he could carry all before him in love.
But in this matter, as in all others which required from
him any personal effort, he prepared himself to do his best,
leaving the consequences to follow as they might. When
he threw his seed-corn into the earth with all such due
appliances of agricultural skill and industry as his capital
and experience enabled him to use, he did his part towards
the production of next year's crop; and after that he must
leave it to a higher Power to give to him, or to withhold
from him, the reward of his labour. He had found that, as
a rule, the reward had been given when the labour had
been honest; and he was now prepared to follow the same
plan with the same hopes, in this matter of his love-
making.

After much consideration,—very much consideration, a

consideration which took him the whole time that he was
brushing his hair and washing his teeth,—he resolved that
he would, in the first instance, speak to Mr. Amedroz.
Not that he intended that the father should win the daughter for him. He had an idea that he would like to do that
work for himself. But he thought that the old squire
would be better pleased if his consent were asked in the
first instance. The present day was Sunday, and he would
not speak on the subject till Monday. This day he would
devote to the work of securing his future father-in-law's
good opinion; to that,—and to his prayers.

And he had gained very much upon Mr. Amedroz before
the evening of the day was over. He was a man before
whom difficulties seemed to yield, and who had his own
way simply because he had become accustomed to ask for
it,—to ask for it and to work for it. He had so softened the
squire's tone of thought towards him, that the future
stocking of the land was spoken of between them with
something like energy on both sides ; and Mr. Amedroz
had given his consent, without any difficulty, to the
building of a shed for winter stall-feeding. Clara sat by
listening, and perceived that Will Belton would soon be
allowed to do just what he pleased with the place. Her
father talked as she had not heard him talk since her poor
brother's death, and was quite animated on the subject of
woodcraft. "We don't know much about timber down
where I am," said Will, "just because we've got no
trees."

"I'll show you your way," said the old man. "I've
managed the timber on the estate myself for the last forty
years." Will Belton of course did not say a word as to
the gross mismanagement which had been apparent even
to him. What a cousin he was! Clara thought,—what a
paragon among cousins! And then he was so manifestly
safe against love-making! So safe, that he only cared to
talk about timber, and oxen, and fences, and winter-forage!
But it was all just as it ought to be; and if her father did
not call him Will before long, she herself would set the
way by doing so first. A very paragon among cousins!

"What a flatterer you are!" she said to him that night.

"A flatterer! I?"

"Yes, you. You have flattered papa out of all his

animosity already. I shall be jealous soon; for he'll think more of you than of me."

"I hope he'll come to think of us as being nearly equally near to him," said Belton, with a tone that was half serious and half tender. Now that he had made up his mind, he could not keep his hand from the work before him an instant. But Clara had also made up her mind, and would not be made to think that her cousin could mean anything that was more than cousinly.

"Upon my word," she said, laughing, "that is very cool on your part."

"I came here determined to be friends with him at any rate."

"And you did so without any thought of me. But you said you would be my brother, and I shall not forget your promise. Indeed, indeed, I cannot tell you how glad I am that you have come,—both for papa's sake and my own. You have done him so much good that I only dread to think that you are going so soon."

"I'll be back before long. I think nothing of running across here from Norfolk. You'll see enough of me before next summer."

Soon after breakfast on the next morning he got Mr. Amedroz out into the grounds, on the plea of showing him the proposed site for the cattle-shed; but not a word was said about the shed on that occasion. He went to work at his other task at once, and when that was well on hand the squire was quite unfitted for the consideration of any less important matter, however able to discuss it Belton might have been himself.

"I've got something particular that I want to say to you, sir," Belton began.

Now Mr. Amedroz was of opinion that his cousin had been saying something very particular ever since his arrival, and was rather frightened at this immediate prospect of a new subject.

"There's nothing wrong; is there?"

"No, nothing wrong;—at least, I hope it's not wrong. Would not it be a good plan, sir, if I were to marry my cousin Clara?"

What a terrible young man! Mr. Amedroz felt that his breath was so completely taken away from him that he was quite unable to speak a word of answer at the moment. Indeed, he was unable to move, and stood still, where he had been fixed by the cruel suddenness of the proposition made to him.

"Of course I know nothing of what she may think about it," continued Belton. "I thought it best to come to you before I spoke a word to her. And I know that in many ways she is above me. She is better educated, and reads more, and all that sort of thing. And it may be that she'd rather marry a London man than a fellow who passes all his time in the country. But she couldn't get one who would love her better or treat her more kindly. And then as to the property; you must own it would be a good arrangement. You'd like to know it would go to your own child and your own grandchild;—wouldn't you, sir? And I'm not badly off, without looking to this place at all, and could give her everything she wants. But then I don't know that she'd care to marry a farmer." These last words he said in a melancholy tone, as though aware that he was confessing his own disgrace.

The squire had listened to it all, and had not as yet said a word. And now, when Belton ceased, he did not know what word to speak. He was a man whose thoughts about women were chivalrous, and perhaps a little old-fashioned. Of course, when a man contemplates marriage, he could do nothing better, nothing more honourable, than consult the lady's father in the first instance. But he felt that even a father should be addressed on such a subject with great delicacy. There should be ambages in such a matter. The man who resolved to commit himself to such a task should come forward with apparent difficulty,—with great diffidence, and even with actual difficulty. He should keep himself almost hidden, as behind a mask, and should tell of his own ambition with doubtful, quivering voice. And the ambages should take time. He should approach the citadel to be taken with covered ways,—working his way slowly and painfully. But this young man, before he had been in the house three days, said all that he had to say without the slightest quaver in his voice, and evidently expected to get an answer about the squire's daughter as quickly as he had got it about the squire's land.

"You have surprised me very much," said the old man at last, drawing his breath.

"I'm quite in earnest about it. Clara seems to me to be the very girl to make a good wife to such a one as I am. She's got everything that a woman ought to have;—by George she has!"

"She is a good girl, Mr. Belton."

"She is as good as gold, every inch of her."

"But you have not known her very long, Mr. Belton."

"Quite long enough for my purposes. You see I knew all about her beforehand,—who she is, and where she comes from. There's a great deal in that you know."

Mr. Amedroz shuddered at the expressions used. It was grievous to him to hear his daughter spoken of as one respecting whom some one knew who she was and whence she came. Such knowledge respecting the daughter of such a family was, as a matter of course, common to all polite persons. "Yes," said Mr. Amedroz, stiffly; "you know as much as that about her, certainly."

"And she knows as much about me. Now the question is, whether you have any objection to make?"

"Really, Mr. Belton, you have taken me so much by surprise that I do not feel myself competent to answer you at once."

"Shall we say in an hour's time, sir?" An hour's time! Mr. Amedroz, if he could have been left to his own guidance, would have thought a month very little for such a work.

"I suppose you would wish me to see Clara first," said Mr. Amedroz.

"Oh dear, no. I would much rather ask her myself;—if only I could get your consent to my doing so."

"And you have said nothing to her?"

"Not a word."

"I am glad of that. You would have behaved badly, I think, had you done so while staying under my roof."

"I thought it best, at any rate, to come to you first. But, as I must be back at Plaistow on this day week, I haven't much time to lose. So if you could think about it this afternoon, you know——"

Mr. Amedroz, much bewildered, promised that he would do his best, and eventually did bring himself to give an answer on the next morning. "I have been thinking about this all night," said Mr. Amedroz.

"I'm sure I'm very much obliged to you," said Belton, feeling rather ashamed of his own remissness as he remembered how soundly he had himself slept.

"If you are quite sure of yourself——"

"Do you mean sure of loving her? I am as sure of that as anything."

"But men are so apt to change their fancies."

"I don't know much about my fancies; but I don't often change my purpose when I'm in earnest. In such a matter as this I couldn't change. I'll say as much as that for myself, though it may seem bold."

"Of course, in regard to money such a marriage would be advantageous to my child. I don't know whether you know it, but I shall have nothing to give her—literally nothing."

"All the better, sir, as far as I am concerned. I'm not one who wants to be saved from working by a wife's fortune."

"But most men like to get something when they marry."

"I want to get nothing;—nothing, that is, in the way of money. If Clara becomes my wife, I'll never ask you for a shilling."

"I hope her aunt will do something for her." This the old man said in a wailing voice, as though the expression of such a hope was grievous to him.

"If she becomes my wife, Mrs. Winterfield will be quite at liberty to leave her money elsewhere." There were old causes of dislike between Mr. Belton and Mrs. Winterfield, and even now Mrs. Winterfield was almost offended because Mr. Belton was staying at Belton Castle.

"But all that is quite uncertain," continued Mr. Amedroz.

"And I have your leave to speak to Clara myself?"

"Well, Mr. Belton; yes; I think so. I do not see why you should not speak to her. But I fear you are a little too precipitate. Clara has known you so very short a time, that you can hardly have a right to hope that she should learn to regard you at once as you would have her do." As he heard this, Belton's face became long and melan

choly. He had taught himself to think that he could dis-
pense with that delay till Christmas which he had at first
proposed to himself, and that he might walk into the arena
at once, and perhaps win the battle in the first round.
"Three days is such a very short time," said the squire.

"It is short, certainly," said Belton.

The father's leave was however given, and armed with
that, Belton was resolved that he would take, at any rate,
some preliminary steps in love-making before he returned
to Plaistow. What would be the nature of the preliminary
steps taken by such a one as him, the reader by this time
will probably be able to surmise.

CHAPTER V.

NOT SAFE AGAINST LOVE-MAKING.

"Why don't you call him Will?" Clara said to her father.
This question was asked on the evening of that Monday on
which Mr. Amedroz had given his consent as to the marriage proposal.

"Call him Will! Why should I?"

"You used to do so, when he was a boy."

"Of course I did; but that is years ago. He would
think it impertinent now."

"Indeed he would not; he would like it. He has told
me so. It sounds so cold to him to be called Mr. Belton
by his relations."

The father looked at his daughter as though for a
moment he almost suspected that matters had really been
arranged between her and her future lover without his
concurrence, and before his sanction had been obtained.
But if for a moment such a thought did cross his mind, it
did not dwell there. He trusted Belton; but as to his
daughter, he knew that he might be sure of her. It would
be impossible with her to keep such a secret from him,
even for half a day. And yet, how odd it was! Here was
a man who in three days had fallen in love with his
daughter; and here was his daughter apparently quite as
ready to be in love with the man. How could she, who

was ordinarily circumspect, and almost cold in her demeanour towards strangers—who was from circumstances and from her own disposition altogether hostile to flirting intimacies—how could his Clara have changed her nature so speedily? The squire did not understand it, but was prepared to believe that it was all for the best. "I'll call him Will, if you like it," said he.

"Do, papa, and then I can do so also. He is such a good fellow, and I am so fond of him."

On the next morning Mr. Amedroz did, with much awkwardness, call his guest by his Christian name. Clara caught her cousin's eye and smiled, and he also smiled. At that moment he was more in love than ever. Could anything be more charming than this? Immediately after breakfast he was going over to Redicote, to see a builder in a small way who lived there, and whom he proposed to employ in putting up the shed for the cattle; but he almost begrudged the time, so anxious was he to begin his suit. But his plan had been laid out, and he would follow it. "I think I shall be back by three o'clock," he said to Clara, "and then we'll have our walk."

"I'll be ready; and you can call for me at Mrs. Askerton's. I must go down there, and it will save you something in your walk to pick me up at the cottage." And so the arrangements for the day were made.

Clara had promised that she would soon call at the cottage, and was, indeed, rather anxious to see Mrs. Askerton on her own account. What she had heard from her cousin as to a certain Miss Vigo of old days had interested her and also what she had heard of a certain Mr. Berdmore. It had been evident to her that her cousin had thought little about it. The likeness of the lady he then saw to the lady he had before known, had at first struck him; but when he found that the two ladies were not represented by one and the same person, he was satisfied, and there was an end of the matter for him. But it was not so with Clara. Her feminine mind dwelt on the matter with more earnestness than he had cared to entertain, and her clearer intellect saw possibilities which did not occur to him. But it was not till she found herself walking across the park to the cottage that she remembered that any inquiries as to her past life might be disagreeable to Mrs. Askerton. She had thought of asking her friend plainly whether the names of Vigo and Berdmore had ever been familiar to her ; but she reminded herself that there had been rumours afloat, and that there might be a mystery. Mrs. Askerton would sometimes talk of her early life ; but she would do this with dreamy, indistinct language, speaking of the sorrows of her girlhood, but not specifying their exact nature, seldom mentioning any names, and never referring with clear personality to those who had been nearest to her when she had been a child. Clara had seen her friend's maiden name, Mary Oliphant, written in a book, and seeing it had alluded to it. On that occasion Mrs. Askerton had spoken of herself as having been an Oliphant, and thus Clara had come to know the fact. But now, as she made her way to the cottage, she remembered that she had learned nothing more than this as to Mrs. Askerton's early life. Such being the case, she hardly knew how to ask any question about the two names that had been mentioned. And yet, why should she not ask such a question? Why should she doubt Mrs. Askerton? And if she did doubt, why should not her doubts be solved?

She found Colonel Askerton and his wife together, and she certainly would ask no such question in his presence. He was a slight-built, wiry man, about fifty, with iron-grey hair and beard,—who seemed to have no trouble in life, and to desire but few pleasures. Nothing could be more regular than the course of his days, and nothing more idle. He breakfasted at eleven, smoked and read till the afternoon, when he rode for an hour or two ; then he dined, read again, smoked again, and went to bed. In September and October he shot, and twice in the year, as has been before stated, went away to seek a little excitement elsewhere. He seemed to be quite contented with his lot, and was never heard to speak an angry word to any one. Nobody cared for him much ; but then he troubled himself with no one's affairs. He never went to church, and had not eaten or drank in any house but his own since he had come to Belton.

"Oh, Clara, you naughty girl," said Mrs. Askerton, " why didn't you come yesterday? I was expecting you all day."

" I was busy. Really, we've grown to be quite industrious people since my cousin came."

"They tell me he's taking the land into his own hands," said the Colonel.

"Yes, indeed ; and he is going to build sheds, and buy cattle ; and I don't know what he doesn't mean to do; so that we shall be alive again."

"I hope he won't want my shooting."

"He has shooting of his own in Norfolk," said Clara.

"Then he'll hardly care to come here for that purpose. When I heard of his proceedings, I began to be afraid."

"I don't think he would do anything to annoy you for the world," said Clara, enthusiastically. "He's the most unselfish person I ever met."

"He'd have a perfect right to take the shooting if he liked it,—that is always supposing that he and your father agreed about it."

"They agree about everything now. He has altogether disarmed papa's prejudices, and it seems to be recognised that he is to have his own way about the place. But I don't think he'll interfere about the shooting."

"He won't my dear, if you ask him not," said Mrs. Askerton.

"I'll ask him in a moment, if Colonel Askerton wishes it."

"Oh dear no," said he. "It would be teaching the ostler to grease the horse's teeth. Perhaps he hasn't thought of it."

"He thinks of everything," said Clara.

"I wonder whether he's thinking of——" So far Mrs. Askerton spoke, and then she paused. Colonel Askerton looked up at Clara with an ill-natured smile, and Clara felt that she blushed. Was it not cruel that she could not say a word in favour of a friend and a cousin,—a cousin who had promised to be a brother to her, without being treated with such words and such looks as these ? But she was determined not to be put down. "I'm quite sure of this," she said, "that my cousin would do nothing unfair or un-gentlemanlike."

"There would be nothing unfair or ungentlemanlike in it. I shouldn't take it amiss at all ;—but I should simply take up my bed and walk. Pray tell him that I hope I shall have the pleasure of seeing him before he goes. I did call yesterday, but he was out."

"He'll be here soon. He's to come here for me." But Colonel Askerton's horse was brought to the door, and he could not therefore wait to make Mr. Belton's acquaintance on that occasion.

"What a Phœnix this cousin of yours is," said Mrs. Askerton, as soon as her husband was gone.

"He is a splendid fellow;—he is indeed. There's so much life about him! He's always doing something. He says that doing good will always pay in the long run. Isn't that a fine doctrine?"

"Quite a practical Phœnix!"

"It has done papa so much good! At this moment he's out somewhere, thinking of what is going on, instead of moping in the house. He couldn't bear the idea of Will's coming, and now he is already beginning to complain because he's going away."

"Will, indeed!"

"And why not Will? He's my cousin."

"Yes;—ten times removed. But so much the better, if he's to be anything more than a cousin."

"He is to be nothing more, Mrs. Askerton."

"You're quite sure of that?"

"I am quite sure of it. And I cannot understand why there should be such a suspicion because he and I are thrown closely together, and are fond of each other. Whether he is a sixth, eighth, or tenth cousin makes no difference. He is the nearest I have on that side; and since my poor brother's death he is papa's heir. It is so natural that he should be my friend;—and such a comfort that he should be such a friend as he is! I own it seems cruel to me that under such circumstances there should be any suspicion."

"Suspicion, my dear; suspicion of what?"

"Not that I care for it. I am prepared to love him as if he were my brother. I think him one of the finest creatures I ever knew,—perhaps the finest I ever did know. His energy and good-nature together are just the qualities to make the best kind of man. I am proud of him as my friend and my cousin, and now you may suspect what you please."

"But, my dear, why should not he fall in love with you? It would be the most proper, and also the most convenient thing in the world."

"I hate talking of falling in love;—as though a woman has nothing else to think of whenever she sees a man."

" A woman has nothing else to think of."

" I have,—a great deal else.   And so has he."

" It's quite out of the question on his part, then ?"

" Quite out of the question.   I'm sure he likes me.   I can see it in his face, and hear it in his voice, and am so happy that it is so.   But it isn't in the way that you mean. Heaven knows that I may want a friend some of these days, and I feel that I may trust to him.   His feelings to me will be always those of a brother."

" Perhaps so.   I have seen that fraternal love before under similar circumstances, and it has always ended in the same way."

" I hope it won't end in any way between us."

" But the joke is that this suspicion, as you call it,— which makes you so indignant,—is simply a suggestion that a thing should happen which, of all things in the world, would be the best for both of you."

" But the thing won't happen, and therefore let there be an end of it.   I hate the twaddle talk of love, whether it's about myself or about any one else.   It makes me feel ashamed of my sex, when I find that I cannot talk of myself to another woman without being supposed to be either in love, or thinking of love,—either looking for it or avoiding it.   When it comes, if it comes prosperously, it's a very good thing.   But I for one can do without it, and I feel myself injured when such a state of things is presumed to be impossible."

" It is worth any one's while to irritate you, because your indignation is so beautiful."

" It is not beautiful to me; for I always feel ashamed afterwards of my own energy.   And now, if you please, we won't say anything more about Mr. Will Belton."

" May I not talk about him, even as the enterprising cousin ?"

" Certainly; and in **any** other light you please.   Do you know, he seemed to think that he had known you ever so many years ago."

Clara, as she said this, did not look direct at her friend's face; but still she could perceive that Mrs. Askerton was disconcerted.   There came a shade of paleness over her face, and a look of trouble on her brow, and for a moment or two she made no reply.

"Did he?" she then said. "And when was that?"

"I suppose it was in London. But, after all, I believe it was not you, but somebody whom he remembers to have been like you. He says that the lady was a Miss Vigo." As she pronounced the name, Clara turned her face away, feeling instinctively that it would be kind to do so.

"Miss Vigo!" said Mrs. Askerton at once; and there was that in the tone of her voice which made Clara feel that all was not right with her. "I remember that there were Miss Vigos; two of them, I think. I didn't know that they were like me especially."

"And he says that the one he remembers married a Mr. Berdmore."

"Married a Mr. Berdmore!" The tone of voice was still the same, and there was an evident struggle, as though the woman was making a vehement effort to speak in her natural voice. Then Clara looked at her, feeling that if she abstained from doing so, the very fact of her so abstaining would be remarkable. There was the look of pain on Mrs. Askerton's brow, and her cheeks were still pale; but she smiled as she went on speaking. "I'm sure I'm flattered, for I remember that they were both considered beauties. Did he know anything more of her?"

"No; nothing more."

"There must have been some casual likeness I suppose." Mrs. Askerton was a clever woman, and had by this time almost recovered her self-possession. Then there came ring at the front door, and in another minute Mr. Belton was in the room. Mrs. Askerton felt that it was imperative on her to make some allusion to the conversation which had just taken place, and dashed at the subject at once. "Clara tells me that I am exactly like some old friend of yours, Mr. Belton."

Then he looked at her closely as he answered her. "I have no right to say that she was my friend, Mrs. Askerton," he said; "indeed there was hardly what might be called an acquaintance between us; but you certainly are extremely like a certain Miss Vigo that I remember."

"I often wonder that one person isn't more often found to be like another," said Mrs. Askerton.

"People often are like," said he; "but not like in such a way as to give rise to mistakes as to identity. Now, I should have stopped you in the street and called you Mrs. Berdmore."

"Didn't I once see or hear the name of Berdmore in this house?" asked Clara.

Then that look of pain returned. Mrs. Askerton had succeeded in recovering the usual tone of her countenance; but now she was once more disturbed. "I think I know the name," said she.

"I fancy that I have seen it in this house," said Clara.

"You may more likely have heard it, my dear. My memory is very poor; but if I remember rightly, Colonel Askerton did know a Captain Berdmore,—a long while ago, before he was married; and you may probably have heard him mention the name." This did not quite satisfy Clara, but she said nothing more about it then. If there was a mystery which Mrs. Askerton did not wish to have explored, why should she explore it?

Soon after this Clara got up to go, and Mrs Askerton, making another attempt to be cheerful, was almost successful. "So you're going back into Norfolk on Saturday, Clara tells me. You are making a very short visit now that you're come among us."

"It is a long time for me to be away from home. Farmers can hardly ever dare to leave their work. But in spite of my farm, I am talking of coming here again about Christmas."

"But you are going to have a farming establishment here too?"

"That will be nothing. Clara will look after that for me; will you not?" Then they went, and Belton had to consider how he would begin the work before him. He had some idea that too much precipitancy might do him an injury, but he hardly knew how to commence without coming to the point at once. When they were out together in the park, he went back at first to the subject of Mrs. Askerton.

"I would almost have sworn they were one and the same woman," he said.

"But you see that they are not."

" It's not only the likeness, but the voice. It so chanced
that I once saw that Miss Vigo in some trouble. I happened to meet her in company with a man who was,—who
was tipsy, in fact, and I had to relieve her."

" Dear me,—how disagreeable !"

" It's a long time ago, and there can't be any harm in
mentioning it now. It was the man she was going to
marry, and whom she did marry."

" What ;—the Mr. Berdmore ?"

" Yes; he was often in that way. And there was a
look about Mrs. Askerton just now so like the look of that
Miss Vigo then, that I cannot get rid of the idea."

" They can't be the same, as she was certainly a Miss
Oliphant. And you hear, too, what she says."

" Yes;—I heard what she said. You have known her
long ?"

" These two years."

" And intimately ?"

" Very intimately. She is our only neighbour ; and her
being here has certainly been a great comfort to me. It
is sad not having some woman near one that one can speak
to ;—and then, I really do like her very much."

" No doubt it's all right."

" Yes ; it's all right," said Clara. After that there was
nothing more said about Mrs. Askerton, and Belton began
his work. They had gone from the cottage, across the
park, away from the house, up to a high rock which stood
boldly out of the ground, from whence could be seen the
sea on one side, and on the other a far tract of country
almost away to the moors. And when they reached this
spot they seated themselves. " There," said Clara, " I consider this to be the prettiest spot in England."

" I haven't seen all England," said Belton.

" Don't be so matter-of-fact, Will. I say it's the prettiest
in England, and you can't contradict me."

" And I say you're the prettiest girl in England, and
you can't contradict me."

This annoyed Clara, and almost made her feel that her
paragon of a cousin was not quite so perfect as she had
represented him to be. " I see," she said, " that if I talk
nonsense I'm to be punished."

" Is it a punishment to you to know that I think you

very handsome !" he said, turning round and looking full into her face.

"It is disagreeable to me—very, to have any such subject talked about at all. What would you think if I began to pay you foolish personal compliments ?"

"What I say isn't foolish; and there's a great difference. Clara, I love you better than all the world put together."

She now looked at him; but still she did not believe it. It could not be that after all her boastings she should have made so gross a blunder. "I hope you do love me," she said; "indeed, you are bound to do so, for you promised that you would be my brother.'

"But that will not satisfy me now, Clara. Clara, I want to be your husband."

"Will !" she exclaimed.

"Now you know it all; and if I have been too sudden, I must beg your pardon."

"Oh, Will, forget that you have said this! Do not go on until everything must be over between us."

"Why should anything be over between us? Why should it be wrong in me to love you ?"

"What will papa say ?"

"Mr. Amedroz knows all about it already, and has given me his consent. I asked him directly I had made up my own mind, and he told me that I might go to you."

"You have asked papa ? Oh dear, oh dear, what am I to do ?"

"Am I so odious to you, then ?" As he said this he got up from his seat and stood before her. He was a tall, well-built, handsome man, and he could assume a look and mien that were almost noble when he was moved as he was moved now.

"Odious ! Do you not know that I have loved you as my cousin—that I have already learned to trust you as though you were really my brother ? But this breaks it all."

"You cannot love me, then, as my wife ?"

"No." She pronounced the monosyllable alone, and then he walked away from her as though that one little word settled the question for him, now and for ever. He walked away from her, perhaps a distance of two hundred yards, as though the interview was over, and he were leaving her. She, as she saw him go, wished that he would return that she might say some word of comfort to him. Not that she could have said the only word that would have comforted him. At the first blush of the thing, at the first sound of the address which he had made to her, she had been angry with him. He had disappointed her, and she was indignant. But her anger had already melted, and turned itself to ruth. She could not but love him better, in that he had loved her so well; but yet she could not love him with the love which he desired.

But he did not leave her. When he had gone from her down the hill the distance that has been named, he turned back, and came up to her slowly. He had a trick of standing and walking with his thumbs fixed into the armholes of his waistcoat, while his large hands rested on his breast. He would always assume this attitude when he was assured that he was right in his views, and was eager to carry some point at issue. Clara already understood that this attitude signified his intention to be autocratic. He now came close up to her, and again stood over her, before he spoke. "My dear," he said, "I have been rough and hasty in what I have said to you, and I have to ask you to pardon my want of manners."

"No, no, no," she exclaimed.

"But in a matter of so much interest to us both you will not let an awkward manner prejudice me."

"It is not that; indeed, it is not."

"Listen to me, dearest. It is true that I promised to be your brother, and I will not break my word unless I break it by your own sanction. I did promise to be your brother, but I did not know then how fondly I should come to love you. Your father, when I told him of this, bade me not to be hasty; but I am hasty, and I haven't .known how to wait. Tell me that I may come at Christmas for my answer, and I will not say a word to trouble you till then. I will be your brother, at any rate, till Christmas."

"Be my brother always."

A black cloud crossed his brow as this request reached his ears. She was looking anxiously into his face, watching every turn in the expression of his countenance. "Will you not let it wait till Christmas?" he asked.

She thought it would be cruel to refuse this request, and

yet she knew that no such waiting could be of service to him. He had been awkward in his love-making, and was aware of it. He should have contrived this period of waiting for himself; giving her no option but to wait and think of it. He should have made no proposal, but have left her certain that such proposal was coming. In such case she must have waited—and if good could have come to him from that, he might have received it. But, as the question was now presented to her, it was impossible that she should consent to wait. To have given such consent would have been tantamount to receiving him as her lover. She was therefore forced to be cruel.

"It will be of no avail to postpone my answer when I know what it must be. Why should there be suspense?"

"You mean that it is impossible that you should love me?"

"Not in that way, Will."

"And why not?" Then there was a pause. "But I am a fool to ask such a question as that, and I should be worse than a fool were I to press it. It must then be considered as settled?"

She got up and clung to his arm. "Oh, Will, do not look at me like that!"

"It must, then, be considered as settled?" he repeated.

"Yes, Will, yes. Pray consider it as settled." He then sat down on the rock again, and she came and sat by him, —near to him, but not close as she had been before. She turned her eyes upon him, gazing on him, but did not speak to him; and he sat also without speaking for a while, with his eyes fixed upon the ground. "I suppose we may go back to the house?" he said at last.

"Give me your hand, Will, and tell me that you still love me—as your sister."

He gave her his hand. "If you ever want a brother's care you shall have it from me," he said.

"But not a brother's love?"

"No. How can the two go together? I shan't cease to love you, because my love is vain. Instead of making me happy it will make me wretched. That will be the only difference."

"I would give my life to make you happy, if that were possible."

" You will not give me your life in the way that I would have it." After that they walked in silence back to the house, and when he had opened the front door for her, he parted from her and stood alone under the porch, thinking of his misfortune.

CHAPTER VI.

SAFE AGAINST LOVE-MAKING ONCE AGAIN.

FOR a considerable time Belton stood under the porch of the house thinking of what had happened to him, and endeavouring to steady himself under the blow which he had received. I do not know that he had been sanguine of success. Probably he had made to himself no assurances on the subject. But he was a man to whom failure, of itself, was intolerable. In any other event of life he would have told himself that he would not fail—that he would persevere and conquer. He could imagine no other position as to which he could at once have been assured of failure, in any project on which he had set his heart. But as to this project it was so. He had been told that she could not love him—that she could never love him;—and he had believed her. He had made his attempt and had failed; and as he thought of this, standing under the porch, he became convinced that life for him was altogether changed, and that he who had been so happy must now be a wretched man.

He was still standing there when Mr. Amedroz came down into the hall, dressed for dinner, and saw his figure through the open doors. "Will," he said, coming up to him, "it only wants five minutes to dinner." Belton started and shook himself, as though he were shaking off a lethargy, and declared that he was quite ready. Then he remembered that he would be expected to dress, and rushed up-stairs, three steps at a time, to his own room. When he came down, Clara and her father were already in the dining-room, and he joined them there.

Mr. Amedroz, though he was not very quick in reading facts from the manners of those with whom he lived, had

felt assured that things had gone wrong between Belton
and his daughter. He had not as yet had a minute in
which to speak to Clara, but he was certain that it was so.
Indeed, it was impossible not to read terrible disappointment and deep grief in the young man's manner. He made
no attempt to conceal it, though he did not speak of it.
Through the whole evening, though he was alone for a
while with the squire, and alone also for a time with Clara,
he never mentioned or alluded to the subject of his rejection. But he bore himself as though he knew and they
knew—as though all the world knew, that he had been rejected. And yet he did not remain silent. He talked of
his property and of his plans, and explained how things
were to be done in his absence. Once only was there
something like an allusion made to his sorrow. "But you
will be here at Christmas?" said Mr. Amedroz, in answer
to something which Belton had said as to work to be done
in his absence. "I do not know how that may be now,"
said Belton. And then they had all been silent.

It was a terrible evening to Clara. She endeavoured to
talk, but found it to be impossible. All the brightness of
the last few days had disappeared, and the world seemed
to her to be more sad and solemn than ever. She had no
idea when she was refusing him that he would have taken
it to heart as he had done. The question had come before
her for decision so suddenly, that she had not, in fact, had
time to think of this, as she was making her answer. All
she had done was to feel that she could not be to him what
he wished her to be. And even as yet she had hardly
asked herself why she must be so steadfast in her refusal.
But she had refused him steadfastly, and she did not for a
moment think of reducing the earnestness of her resolution.
It seemed to be manifest to her, from his present manner,
that he would never ask the question again; but she was
sure, let it be asked ever so often, that it could not be
answered in any other way.

Mr. Amedroz, not knowing why it was so, became cross
and querulous and scolded his daughter. To Belton, also,
he was captious, making little difficulties, and answering
him with petulance. This the rejected lover took with
most extreme patience, as though such a trifling annoyance
had no effect in adding anything to his misery. He still

held his purpose of going on the Saturday, and was still
intent on work which was to be done before he went; but
it seemed that he was satisfied to do everything now as a
duty, and that the enjoyment of the thing, which had heretofore been so conspicuous, was over.

At last they separated, and Clara, as was her wont, went
up to her father's room. "Papa," she said, "what is all
this about Mr. Belton?"

"All what, my dear? what do you mean?"

"He has asked me to be,—to be his wife; and has told
me that he came with your consent."

"And why shouldn't he have my consent? What is
there amiss with him? Why shouldn't you marry him if
he likes you? You seemed, I thought, to be very fond of
him."

This surprised Clara more than anything. She could
hardly have told herself why, but she would have thought
that such a proposition from her cousin would have made
her father angry,—unreasonably angry;—angry with him
for presuming to have such an idea; but now it seemed
that he was going to be angry with her for not accepting
her cousin out of hand.

"Yes, papa; I am fond of him; but not like that. I
did not expect that he would think of me in that way."

"But why shouldn't he think of you? It would be a
very good marriage for you as far as money is concerned."

"You would not have me marry any one for that reason;
—would you, papa?"

"But you seemed to like him. Well; of course I can't
make you like him. I meant to do for the best; and when
he came to me as he did, I thought he was behaving very
handsomely, and very much like a gentleman."

"I am sure he would do that."

"And if I could have thought that this place would be
your home when I am gone, it would have made me very
happy;—very happy."

She now came and stood close to him and took his hand.
"I hope, papa, you do not make yourself uneasy about me.
I shall do very well. I'm sure you can't want me to go
away and leave you."

"How will you do very well? I'm sure I don't know.
And if your aunt Winterfield means to provide for you, it

would only be kind in her to let me know it, so that I
might not have the anxiety always on my mind."

Clara knew well enough what was to be the disposition
of her aunt's property, but she could not tell her father of
that now. She almost felt that it was her duty to do so,
but she could not bring herself to do it. She could only
beg him not to be anxious on her behalf, making vague
assurances that she would do very well. "And you are
determined not to change your mind about Will ?" he said
at last.

" I shall not change my mind about that, papa, certainly,"
she answered. Then he turned away from her, and she
saw that he was displeased.

When alone, she was forced to ask herself why it was
that she was so certain. Alas! there could in truth be no
doubt on that subject in her own mind. When she sat
down resolved to give herself an answer, there was no
doubt. She could not love her cousin, Will Belton, because
her heart belonged to Captain Aylmer.

But she knew that she had received nothing in exchange
for her heart. He had been kind to her on that journey to
Taunton, when the agony arising from her brother's death
had almost crushed her. He had often been kind to her on
days before that,—so kind, so soft in his manners, approaching so nearly to the little tendernesses of incipient love-
making, that the idea of regarding him as her lover, had of
necessity forced itself upon her. But in nothing had he
gone beyond those tendernesses, which need not imperatively be made to mean anything, though they do often
mean so much. It was now two years since she had first
thought that Captain Aylmer was the most perfect gentleman she knew, and nearly two years since Mrs. Winterfield
had expressed to her a hope that Captain Aylmer might
become her husband. She had replied, that such a thing
was impossible,—as any girl would have replied ; and had
in consequence treated Captain Aylmer with all the coolness
which she had been able to assume whenever she was in
company with him in her aunt's presence. Nor was it
natural to her to be specially gracious to a man under such
trying circumstances, even when no Mrs. Winterfield was
there to behold. And so things' had gone on. Captain
Aylmer had now and again made himself very pleasant to

her,—at certain trying periods of joy or trouble almost
more than pleasant. But nothing had come of it, and Clara
had told herself that Captain Aylmer had no special feeling
in her favour. She had told herself this, ever since that
journey together from Perivale to Taunton ; but never till
now had she also confessed to herself what was her own
case.

She made a comparison between the two men. Her
cousin Will was, she thought, the more generous, the more
energetic,—perhaps by nature the man of the higher gifts.
In person he was undoubtedly the superior. He was full
of noble qualities,—forgetful of self, industrious, full of
resources, a very man of men, able to command, eager in
doing work for others' good and his own,—a man altogether
uncontaminated by the coldness and selfishness of the outer
world. But he was rough, awkward, but indifferently
educated, and with few of those tastes which to Clara
Amedroz were delightful. He could not read poetry to her,
he could not tell her of what the world of literature was
doing now, or of what it had done in times past. He knew
nothing of the inner world of worlds which governs the
world. She doubted whether he could have told her who
composed the existing cabinet, or have given her the name of
a single bishop beyond the see in which his own parish
was situated. But Captain Aylmer knew everybody,
and had read everything, and understood, as though by
instinct, all the movements of the world in which he
lived.

But what mattered any such comparison ? Even though
she should be able to prove to herself beyond the shadow
of a doubt that her cousin Will was of the two the fitter to
be loved,—the one more worthy of her heart,—no such
proof could alter her position. Love does not go by worth.
She did not love her cousin as she must love any man to
whom she could give her hand,—and, alas ! she did love
that other man.

On this night I doubt whether Belton did slumber with
that solidity of repose which was usual to him. At any
rate, before he came down in the morning he had found
time for sufficient thought, and had brought himself to a
resolution. He would not give up the battle as lost. To
his thinking there was something weak and almost mean

in abandoning any project which he had set before himself.
He had been awkward, and he exaggerated to himself his
own awkwardness. He had been hasty, and had gone
about his task with inconsiderate precipitancy. It might
be that he had thus destroyed all his chance of success.
But, as he said to himself, " he would never say die, as
long as there was a puff of breath left to him." He would
not mope, and hang down his head, and wear the willow.
Such a state of things would ill suit either the roughness
or the readiness of his life. No! He would bear like a
man the disappointment which had on this occasion befallen
him, and would return at Christmas, and once more try his
fortune.

At breakfast, therefore, the cloud had passed from his
brow. When he came in, he found Clara alone in the
room, and he simply shook hands with her after his ordinary fashion. He said nothing of yesterday, and almost
succeeded in looking as though yesterday had been in no-
wise memorable. She was not so much at her ease, but
she also received some comfort from his demeanour. Mr.
Amedroz came down almost immediately, and Belton soon
took an opportunity of saying that he would be back at
Christmas, if Mr. Amedroz would receive him.

" Certainly," said the squire. " I thought it had been
all settled."

" So it was ;—till I said a word yesterday which foolishly
seemed to unsettle it. But I have thought it over again,
and I find that I can manage it."

" We shall be so glad to have you!" said Clara.

" And I shall be equally glad to come. They are
already at work, sir, about the sheds."

" Yes; I saw the carts full of bricks go by," said the
squire, querulously. " I didn't know there was to be any
brickwork. You said you would have it made of deal
slabs with oak posts."

" You must have a foundation, sir. I propose to carry
the brickwork a foot and a half above the ground."

" I suppose you know best. Only that kind of thing is
so very ugly."

" If you find it to be ugly after it is done, it shall be
pulled down again."

" No ;—it can never come down again."

"It can;—and it shall, if you don't like it. I never think anything of changes like that."

"I think they'll be very pretty!" said Clara.

"I dare say," said the squire; "but at any rate it won't make much difference to me. I shan't be here long to see them."

This was rather melancholy; but Belton bore up even against this, speaking cheery words, and expressing bright hopes,—so that it seemed, both to Clara and to her father, that he had in a great measure overcome the disappointment of the preceding day. It was probable that he was a man not prone to be deeply sensitive in such matters for any long period. The period now had certainly not been long, and yet Will Belton was alive again.

Immediately after breakfast there occurred a little incident which was not without its effect upon them all. There came up on the drive, immediately before the front door, under the custody of a boy, a cow. It was an Alderney cow, and any man or woman at all understanding in cows, would at once have perceived that this cow was perfect in her kind. Her eyes were mild, and soft, and bright. Her legs were like the legs of a deer; and in her whole gait and demeanour she almost gave the lie to her own name, asserting herself to have sprung from some more noble origin among the woods, than may be supposed to be the origin of the ordinary domestic cow,—a useful animal, but heavy in its appearance, and seen with more pleasure at some little distance than at close quarters. But this cow was graceful in its movements, and almost tempted one to regard her as the far-off descendant of the elk or the antelope.

"What's that?" said Mr. Amedroz, who, having no cows of his own, was not pleased to see one brought up in that way before his hall door. "There's somebody's cow come here."

Clara understood it in a moment; but she was pained, and said nothing. Had the cow come without any such scene as that of yesterday, she would have welcomed the animal with all cordiality, and would have sworn to her cousin that the cow should be cherished for his sake. But after what had passed it was different. How was she to take any present from him now?

But Belton faced the difficulty without any bashfulness or apparent regret. "I told you I would give you a cow," said he; "and here she is."

"What can she want with a cow?" said Mr. Amedroz.

"I am sure she wants one very much. At any rate she won't refuse the present from me; will you, Clara?"

What could she say? "Not if papa will allow me to keep it."

"But we've no place to put it!" said the squire. "We haven't got grass for it!"

"'There's plenty of grass,' said Belton. "Come, Mr. Amedroz; I've made a point of getting this little creature for Clara, and you mustn't stand in the way of my gratification." Of course he was successful, and of course Clara thanked him with tears in her eyes.

The next two days passed by without anything special to mark them, and then the cousin was to go. During the period of his visit he did not see Colonel Askerton, nor did he again see Mrs. Askerton. He went to the cottage once, with the special object of returning the Colonel's call; but the master was out, and he was not specially invited in to see the mistress. He said nothing more to Clara about her friends, but he thought of the matter more than once, as he was going about the place, and became aware that he would like to ascertain whether there was a mystery, and if so, what was its nature. He knew that he did not like Mrs. Askerton, and he felt also that Mrs. Askerton did not like him. This was, as he thought, unfortunate; for might it not be the case that in the one matter which was to him of so much importance, Mrs. Askerton might have considerable influence over Clara?

During these days nothing special was said between him and Clara. The last evening passed over without anything to brighten it, or to make it memorable. Mr. Amedroz, in his passive, but gently querulous way, was sorry that Belton was going to leave him, as his cousin had been the creation of some new excitement for him; but he said nothing on the subject; and when the time for going to bed had come, he bade his guest farewell with some languid allusion to the pleasure which he would have in seeing him again at Christmas. Belton was to start very early in the morning—before six, and of course he was prepared

to take leave also of·Clara. But she told him very gently,
so gently that her father did not hear it, that she would be
up to give him a cup of coffee before he went.

"Oh no," he said.

"But I shall. I won't have you go without seeing you
out of the door."

And on the following morning she was up before him.
She hardly understood, herself, why she was doing this.
She knew that it should be her object to avoid any further
special conversation on that subject which they had discussed up among the rocks. She knew that she could give
him no comfort, and that he could give none to her. It would
seem that he was willing to let the remembrance of the
scene pass away, so that it should be as though it had never
been ; and surely it was not for her to disturb so salutary
an arrangement ! But yet she was up to bid him God-
speed as he went. She could not bear,—so she excused
the matter to herself,—she could not bear to think that he
should regard her as ungrateful. She knew all that he had
done for them. She had perceived that the taking of the
land, the building of the sheds, the life which he had
contrived in so short a time to throw into the old place, had
all come from a desire on his part to do good to those in
whose way he stood by family arrangements made almost
before his birth ; and she longed to say to him one word of
thanks. And had he not told her,—once in the heat of
his disappointment ; for then at that moment, as Clara said
to herself, she supposed that he must have been in some
measure disappointed,—had he not even then told her that
when she wanted a brother's care, a brother's care should
be given to her by him ? Was she not therefore bound to
do for him what she would do for a brother ?

She, with her own hands, brought the coffee into the little
breakfast-parlour, and handed the cup into his hands.
The gig, which had come overnight from Taunton, was
not yet at the door, and there was a minute or two during
which they must speak to each other. Who has not seen
some such girl when she has come down early, without the
full completeness of her morning toilet, and yet nicer,
fresher, prettier to the eye of him who is so favoured, than
she has ever been in more formal attire ? And what man
who has been so favoured has not loved her who has so

favoured him, even though he may not previously have
been enamoured as deeply as poor Will Belton?

"This is so good of you," he said.

"I wish I knew how to be good to you," she answered,
—not meaning to trench upon dangerous ground, but feeling, as the words came from her, that she had done so.
"You have been so good to us, so very good to papa, that
we owe you everything. I am so grateful to you for saying
that you will come back at Christmas."

He had resolved that he would refrain from further
love-making till the winter; but he found it very hard to
refrain when so addressed. To take her in his arms, and
kiss her twenty times, and swear that he would never let
her go,—to claim her at once savagely as his own, that was
the line of conduct to which temptation prompted him.
How could she look at him so sweetly, how could she stand
before him, ministering to him with all her pretty maidenly
charms brought so close to him, without intending that he
should love her? But he did refrain. "Blood is thicker
than water," said he. "That's the real reason why I first
came."

"I understand that quite, and it is that feeling that
makes you so good. But I'm afraid you are spending a
great deal of money here—and all for our sakes."

"Not at all. I shall get my money back again. And if
I didn't, what then? I've plenty of money. It is not
money that I want."

She could not ask him what it was that he did want, and
she was obliged therefore to begin again. "Papa will look
forward so to the winter now."

"And so shall I."

"But you must come for longer then;—you won't go
away at the end of a week? Say that you won't."

"I'll see about it. I can't tell quite yet. You'll write
me a line to say when the shed is finished, won't you?"

"That I will, and I'll tell you how Bessy goes on."
Bessy was the cow. "I will be so very fond of her.
She'll come to me for apples already."

Belton thought that he would go to her, wherever she
might be, even if he were to get no apples. "It's all cupboard love with them," he said. "I'll tell you what I'll
do;—when I come, I'll bring you a dog that will follow

you without thinking of apples." Then the gig was heard on the gravel before the door, and Belton was forced to go. For a moment he reflected whether, as her cousin, it was not his duty to kiss her. It was a matter as to which he had doubt,—as is the case with many male cousins : but ultimately he resolved that if he kissed her at all he would not kiss her in that light, and so he again refrained. "Good-bye," he said, putting out his great hand to her.

"Good-bye, Will, and God bless you." I almost think he might have kissed her, asking himself no questions as to the light in which it was done.

As he turned from her he saw the tears in her eyes ; and as he sat in the gig thinking of them, other tears came into his own. By heaven, he would have her yet ! He was a man who had not read much of romance. To him all the imagined mysteries of passion had not been made common by the perusal of legions of love stories ;—but still he knew enough of the game to be aware that women had been won in spite, as it were, of their own teeth. He knew that he could not now run away with her, taking her off by force ; but still he might conquer her will by his own. As he remembered the tears in her eyes, and the tone of her voice, and the pressure of her hand, and the gratitude that had become tender in its expression, he could not but think that he would be wise to love her still. Wise or foolish, he did love her still ; and it should not be owing to fault of his if she did not become his wife. As he drove along he saw little of the Quantock hills, little of the rich Somersetshire pastures, little of the early beauty of the August morning. He saw nothing but her eyes, moistened with bright tears, and before he reached Taunton he had rebuked himself with many revilings, in that he had parted from her and not kissed her.

Clara stood at the door watching the gig till it was out of sight,—watching it as well as her tears would allow. What a grand cousin he was ! Had it not been a pity,—a thousand pities,—that that grievous episode should have come to mar the brotherly love, the sisterly confidence, which might otherwise have been so perfect between them ? But perhaps it might all be well yet. Clara knew, or thought that she knew, that men and women differed in their appreciation of love. She, having once loved, could not change. Of that she was sure. Her love might be fortunate or unfortunate. It might be returned, or it might simply be her own, to destroy all hope of happiness for her on earth. But whether it were this or that, whether productive of good or evil, the love itself could not be changed. But with men she thought it might be different. Her cousin, doubtless, had been sincere in the full sincerity of his heart when he made his offer. And had she accepted it,—had she been able to accept it,—she believed that he would have loved her truly and constantly. Such was his nature. But she also believed that love with him, unrequited love, would have no enduring effect, and that he had already resolved, with equal courage and wisdom, to tread this short-lived passion out beneath his feet. One night had sufficed to him for that treading out. As she thought of this the tears ran plentifully down her cheek; and going again to her room, she remained there crying till it was time for her to wipe away the marks of her weeping, that she might go to her father.

But she was very glad that Will bore it so well;—very glad! Her cousin was safe against love-making once again.

CHAPTER VII.

MISS AMEDROZ GOES TO PERIVALE.

It had been settled for some time past that Miss Amedroz was to go to Perivale for a few days in November. Indeed it seemed to be a recognised fact in her life that she was to make the journey from Belton to Perivale and back very often, as there prevailed an idea that she owed a divided duty. This was in some degree hard upon her, as she had very little gratification in these visits to her aunt. Had there been any intention on the part of Mrs. Winterfield to provide for her, the thing would have been intelligible according to the usual arrangements which are made in the world on such matters; but Mrs. Winterfield had scarcely a right to call upon her niece for dutiful attendance, after having settled it with her own conscience that

her property was all to go to her nephew. But Clara
entertained no thought of rebelling, and had agreed to
make the accustomed journey in November, travelling
then, as she did all on such journeys, at her aunt's expense.

Two things only occurred to disturb her tranquillity
before she went, and they were not of much violence. Mr.
Wright, the clergyman, called at Belton Castle, and in the
course of conversation with Mr. Amedroz renewed some
one of those ill-natured rumours which had before been
spread about Mrs. Askerton. Clara did not see him, but
she heard an account of it all from her father.

" Does it mean, papa," she said, speaking almost with
anger, " that you want me to give up Mrs. Askerton?"

" How can you be so unkind as to ask me such a question?" he replied. " You know how I hate to be bothered.
I tell you what I hear, and then you can decide for yourself."

" But that isn't quite fair either, papa. That man comes
here——"

" That man, as you call him, is the rector of the parish,
and I've known him for forty years."

" And have never liked him, papa."

" I don't know much about liking anybody, my dear.
Nobody likes me, and so why should I trouble myself?"

" But, papa, it all amounts to this—that somebody has
said that the Askertons are not Askertons at all, but ought
to be called something else. Now we know that he served
as Captain and Major Askerton for seven years in India—
and in fact it all means nothing. If I know anything, I
know that he is Colonel Askerton."

" But do you know that she is his wife? That is what
Mr. Wright asks. I don't say anything. I think it's very
indelicate talking about such things."

" If I am asked whether I have seen her marriage certi-
ficate, certainly I have not ; nor probably did you ever do
so as to any lady that you ever knew. But I know that
she is her husband's wife, as we all of us know things of
that sort. I know she was in India with him. I've seen
things of hers marked with her name that she has had at
least for ten years."

" I don't know anything about it, my dear " said Mr.
Amedroz, angrily.

"But Mr. Wright ought to know something about it before he says such things. And then this that he's saying isn't the same that he said before."

"I don't know what he said before."

"He said they were both of them using a feigned name."

"It's nothing to me what name they use. I know I wish they hadn't come here if I'm to be troubled about them in this way—first by Wright and then by you."

"They have been very good tenants, papa."

"You needn't tell me that, Clara, and remind me about the shooting, when you know how unhappy it makes me."

After this Clara said nothing more, and simply determined that Mr. Wright and his gossip should have no effect upon her intimacy with Mrs. Askerton. But not the less did she continue to remember what her cousin had said about Miss Vigo.

And she had been ruffled a second time by certain observations which Mrs. Askerton made to her respecting her cousin—or rather by little words which were dropped on various occasions. It was very clear that Mrs. Askerton did not like Mr. Belton, and that she wished to prejudice Clara against him. "It's a pity he shouldn't be a lover of yours," the lady said, "because it would be such a fine instance of Beauty and the Beast." It will of course be understood that Mrs. Askerton had never been told of the offer that had been made.

"You don't mean to say that he's not a handsome man," said Clara.

"I never observe whether a man is handsome or not; but I can see very well whether he knows what to do with his arms and legs, or whether he has the proper use of his voice before ladies." Clara remembered a word or two spoken by her cousin to herself, in speaking which he had seemed to have a very proper use of his voice. "I know when a man is at ease like a gentleman, and when he is awkward like a——"

"Like a what?" said Clara. "Finish what you've got to say."

"Like a ploughboy, I was going to say," said Mrs. Askerton.

"I declare I think you have a spite against him, because

he said you were like some Miss Vigo," replied Clara,
sharply.   Mrs. Askerton was on that occasion silenced, and
she said nothing more about Mr. Belton till after Clara had
returned from Perivale.

The journey itself from Belton to Perivale was always a
nuisance, and was more so now than usual, as it was made
in the disagreeable month of November.   There was kept
at the little inn at Redicote an old fly—so called—which
habitually made the journey to the Taunton railway-station,
under the conduct of an old grey horse and an older and
greyer driver, whenever any of the old ladies of the neighbourhood were minded to leave their homes.   This vehicle
usually travelled at the rate of five miles an hour; but the
old grey driver was never content to have time allowed to
him for the transit calculated upon such a rate of speed.
Accidents might happen, and why should he be made, as
he would plaintively ask, to drive the poor beast out of its
skin ?   He was consequently always at Belton a full hour
before the time, and though Clara was well aware of all
this, she could not help herself.   Her father was fussy and
impatient, the man was fussy and impatient; and there
was nothing for her but to go.   On the present occasion
she was taken off in this way the full sixty minutes too
soon, and after four dreary hours spent upon the road,
found herself landed at the Taunton station, with a terrible
gulf of time to be passed before she could again proceed on
her journey.

One little accident had occurred to her.   The old horse,
while trotting leisurely along the level high road, had contrived to tumble down.   Clara did not think very much of
this, as the same thing had happened with her before; but,
even with an hour or more to spare, there arises a question
whether under such circumstances the train can be saved.
But the grey old man reassured her.   " Now, miss," said
he, coming to the window, while he left his horse recum-
bent and apparently comfortable on the road, " where'd
you have been now, zure, if I hadn't a few minutes in hand
for you ?"   Then he walked off to some neighbouring cottage, and having obtained assistance, succeeded in putting
his beast again upon his legs.   After that he looked once
more in at the window.   " Who's right now, I wonder?"
he said, with an air of triumph.   And when he came to

her for his guerdon at Taunton, he was evidently cross in not having it increased because of the accident.

That hour at the Taunton station was terrible to her. I know of no hours more terrible than those so passed. The minutes will not go away, and utterly fail in making good their claim to be called winged. A man walks up and down the platform, and in that way obtains something of the advantage of exercise, but a woman finds herself bound to sit still within the dreary dulness of the waiting-room. There are, perhaps, people who under such circumstances can read, but they are few in number. The mind altoge- ther declines to be active, whereas the body is seized by a spirit of restlessness to which delay and tranquillity are loathsome. The advertisements on the walls are examined, the map of some new Eden is studied—some Eden in which an irregular pond and a church are surrounded by a mul- tiplicity of regular villas and shrubs—till the student feels that no considerations even of health or economy would induce him to live there. Then the porters come in and out, till each porter has made himself odious to the sight. Everything is hideous, dirty, and disagreeable; and the mind wanders away, to consider why station-masters do not more frequently commit suicide. Clara Amedroz had al- ready got beyond this stage, and was beginning to think of herself rather than of the station-master, when at last there sounded close to her ears, the bell of promise, and she knew that the train was at hand.

At Taunton there branched away from the main line that line which was to take her to Perivale, and therefore she was able to take her own place quietly in the carriage, when she found that the down-train from London was at hand. This she did, and could then watch with equani- mity, while the travellers from the other train went through the penance of changing their seats. But she had not been so watching for many seconds when she saw Captain Frederick Aylmer appear upon the platform. Immediately she sank back into her corner, and watched no more. Of course he was going to Perivale; but why had not her aunt told her that she was to meet him? Of course she would be staying in the same house with him, and her present small attempt to avoid him would thus be futile. The attempt was made; but nevertheless she was probably

pleased when she found that it was made in vain. He
came at once to the carriage in which she was sitting, and
had packed his coats, and dressing-bag, and desk, about
the carriage before he had discovered who was his fellow-
traveller. " How do you do, Captain Aylmer ?" she said,
as he was about to take his seat.

" Miss Amedroz! Dear me, how very odd! I had not
the slightest expectation of meeting you here. The pleasure is, of course, the greater."

" Nor I of seeing you. Mrs. Winterfield has not mentioned to me that you were coming to Perivale."

" I didn't know it myself till the day before yesterday.
I'm going to give an account of my stewardship to the
good-natured Perivalians who send me to Parliament. I'm
to dine with the mayor to-morrow, and as some big-wig
has come in his way who is going to dine with him also,
the thing has been got up in a hurry. But I'm delighted
to find that you are to be with us."

" I generally go to my aunt about this time of the year."

" It is very good-natured of you." Then he asked after
her father, and she told him of Mr. Belton's visit, telling
him nothing— as the reader will hardly require to be told
—of Mr. Belton's offer. And so, by degrees, they fell into
close and intimate conversation.

" I am so glad, for your father's sake !" said the captain,
with sympathetic voice, speaking still of Mr. Belton's visit.

" That's what I feel, of course."

" It is just as it should be, as he stands in that position
to the property. And so he is a nice sort of fellow, is
he ?"

" Nice is no word for him. He is perfect!"

" Dear me! This is terrible! You remember that they
hated some old Greek patriot when they could find no
fault in him ?"

" I'll defy you to hate my cousin Will."

" What sort of looking man is he ?"

" Extremely handsome ;—at least I should say so."

" Then I certainly must hate him. And clever?"

" Well ;—not what you would call clever. He is very
clever about fields and cattle."

" Come ; there is some relief in that."

" But you must not mistake me. He is clever; and then

there's a way about him of doing everything just as he likes it, which is wonderful. You feel quite sure that he'll become master of everything."

"But I do not feel at all sure that I should like him the better for that."

"But he doesn't meddle in things that he doesn't understand. And then he is so generous! His spending all that money down there is only done because he thinks it will make the place pleasanter to papa."

"Has he got plenty of money?"

"Oh, plenty! At least, I think so. He says that he has."

"The idea of any man owning that he had got plenty of money! What a happy mortal! And then to be handsome, and omnipotent, and to understand cattle and fields! One would strive to emulate him rather than envy him, had not one learned to acknowledge that it is not given to every one to get to Corinth."

"You may laugh at him, but you'd like him if you knew him."

"One never can be sure of that from a lady's account of a man. When a man talks to me about another man, I can generally tell whether I should like him or not—particularly if I know the man well who is giving the description; but it is quite different when a woman is the describer."

"You mean that you won't take my word?"

"We see with different eyes in such matters. I have no doubt your cousin is a worthy man—and as prosperous a gentleman as the Thane of Cawdor in his prosperous days; but probably if he and I came together we shouldn't have a word to say to each other."

Clara almost hated Captain Aylmer for speaking as he did, and yet she knew that it was true. Will Belton was not an educated man, and were they two to meet in her presence,—the captain and the farmer,—she felt that she might have to blush for her cousin. But yet he was the better man of the two. She knew that he was the better man of the two, though she knew also that she could not love him as she loved the other."

Then they changed the subject of their conversation, and discussed Mrs. Winterfield, as they had often done before. Captain Aylmer had said that he should return to London

on the Saturday, the present day being Tuesday, and Clara
accused him of escaping always from the real hard work of
his position. "I observe that you never stay a Sunday at
Perivale," she said.

"Well;—not often. Why should I? Sunday is just the
day that people like to be at home."

"I should have thought it would not have made much
difference to a bachelor in that way."

"But Sunday is a day that one specially likes to pass
after one's own fashion."

"Exactly;—and therefore you don't stay with my aunt.
I understand it all completely."

"Now you mean to be ill-natured."

"I mean to say that I don't like Sundays at Perivale at
all, and that I should do just as you do, if I had the power.
But women,—women, that is, of my age,—are such slaves!
We are forced to give an obedience for which we can see
no cause, and for which we can understand no necessity.
I couldn't tell my aunt that I meant to go away on
Saturday."

"You have no business which makes imperative calls
upon your time."

"That means that I can't plead pretended excuses. But
the true reason is that we are dependent."

"There is something in that, I suppose."

"Not that I am dependent on her. But my position
generally is dependent, and I cannot assist myself."

Captain Aylmer found it difficult to make any answer to
this, feeling the subject to be one which could hardly be
discussed between him and Miss Amedroz. He not un-
naturally looked to be the heir of his aunt's property, and
any provision made out of that property for Clara, would
so far lessen that which would come to him. For anything
that he knew, Mrs. Winterfield might leave everything she
possessed to her niece. The old lady had not been open
and candid to him, whom she meant to favour in her will,
as she had been to her to whom no such favour was to be
shown. But Captain Aylmer did know, with tolerable
accuracy, what was the state of affairs at Belton, and was
aware that Miss Amedroz had no prospect of maintenance
on which to depend, unless she could depend on her aunt.
She was now pleading that she was not dependent on that

lady, and Captain Aylmer felt that she was wrong. He was a man of the world, and was by no means inclined to abandon any right that was his own ; but it seemed to him that he was almost bound to say some word to show that in his opinion Clara should hold herself bound to comply with her aunt's requirements.

"Dependence is a disagreeable word," he said ; "and one never quite knows what it means."

"If you were a woman you'd know. It means that I must stay at Perivale on Sundays, while you can go up to London, or down to Yorkshire. That's what it means."

"What you do mean, I think, is this ;—that you owe a duty to your aunt, the performance of which is not alto-gether agreeable. Nevertheless it would be foolish in you to omit it."

"It isn't that ;—not that at all. It would not be foolish, not in your sense of the word ; but it would be wrong. My aunt has been kind to me, and therefore I am bound to her for this service. But she is kind to you also, and yet you are not bound. That's why I complain. You sail away under false pretences, and yet you think you do your duty. You have to see your lawyer,—which means going to your club ; or to attend to your tenants,—which means hunting and shooting."

"I haven't got any tenants."

"You know very well that you could remain over Sun-day without doing any harm to anybody ;—only you don't like going to church three times, and you don't like hear-ing my aunt read a sermon afterwards. Why shouldn't you stay, and I go to the club ?"

"With all my heart, if you can manage it."

"But I can't ; we ain't allowed to have clubs, or shoot-ing, or to have our own way in anything, putting forward little pretences about lawyers."

"Come, I'll stay if you'll ask me."

"I'm sure I won't do that. In the first place you'd go to sleep, and then she would be offended ; and I don't know that your sufferings would make mine any lighter. I'm not prepared to alter the ways of the world ; but I feel myself entitled to grumble at them sometimes."

Mrs. Winterfield inhabited a large brick house in the centre of the town. It had a long frontage to the street ;

for there was not only the house itself, with its three
square windows on each side of the door, and its seven
windows over that, and again its seven windows in the
upper story,—but the end of the coach-house also abutted
on the street, on which was the family clock, quite as
much respected in Perivale as was the town-clock; and
between the coach-house and the mansion there was the
broad entrance into the yard, and the entrance also to the
back door. No Perivalian ever presumed to doubt that
Mrs. Winterfield's house was the most important house in
the town. Nor did any stranger doubt it on looking at the
frontage. But then it was in all respects a town house to
the eye,—that is, an English town house, being as ugly
and as respectable as unlimited bricks and mortar could
make it. Immediately opposite to Mrs. Winterfield lived
the leading doctor and a retired builder, so that the lady's
eye was not hurt by any sign of a shop. The shops,
indeed, came within a few yards of her on either side; but
as the neighbouring shops on each side were her own property, this was not unbearable. To me, had I lived there,
the incipient growth of grass through some of the stones
which formed the margin of the road, would have been
altogether unendurable. There is no sign of coming decay
which is so melancholy to the eye as any which tells of a
decrease in the throng of men. Of men or horses there
was never any throng now in that end of Perivale. That
street had formed part of the main line of road from Salisbury to Taunton, and coaches, waggons, and posting-
carriages had been frequent on it; but now, alas! it was
deserted. Even the omnibuses from the railway-station
never came there unless they were ordered to call at Mrs.
Winterfield's door. For Mrs. Winterfield herself, this
desolation had, I think, a certain melancholy attraction.
It suited her tone of mind and her religious views, that
she should be thus daily reminded that things of this world
were passing away and going to destruction. She liked to
have ocular proof that grass was growing in the highways
under mortal feet, and that it was no longer worth man's
while to renew human flags in human streets. She was
drawing near to the pavements which would ever be
trodden by myriads of bright sandals, and which yet would
never be worn, and would be carried to those jewelled

causeways on which no weed could find a spot for its useless growth.

Behind the house there was a square prim garden, arranged in parallelograms, tree answering to tree at every corner, round which it was still her delight to creep when the weather permitted. Poor Clara! how much advice she had received during these creepings, and how often had she listened to inquiries as to the schooling of the gardener's children. Mrs. Winterfield was always unhappy about her gardener. Serious footmen are very plentiful, and even coachmen are to be found who, at a certain rate of extra payment, will be punctual at prayer-time, and will promise to read good little books; but gardeners, as a class, are a profane people, who think themselves entitled to claim liberty of conscience, and who will not submit to the domestic despotism of a serious Sunday. They live in cottages by themselves, and choose to have an opinion of their own on church matters. Mrs. Winterfield was aware that she ought to bid high for such a gardener as she wanted. A man must be paid well who will submit to daily inquiries as to the spiritual welfare of himself, his wife, and family. But even though she did bid high, and though she paid generously, no gardener would stop with her. One conscientious man attempted to bargain for freedom from religion during the six unimportant days of the week, being strong, and willing therefore to give up his day of rest; but such liberty could not be allowed to him, and he also went. "He couldn't stop," he said, "in justice to the greenhouses, when missus was so constant down upon him about his sprittual backslidings. And, after all, where did he backslide? It was only a pipe of tobacco with the babby in his arms, instead of that darned evening lecture."

Poor Mrs. Winterfield! She had been strong in her youth, and had herself sat through evening lectures with a fortitude which other people cannot attain. And she was strong too in her age, with the strength of a martyr, submitting herself with patience to wearinesses which are insupportable to those who have none of the martyr spirit. The sermons of Perivale were neither bright, nor eloquent, nor encouraging. All the old vicar or the young curate could tell she had heard hundreds of times. She knew it all by heart, and could have preached their sermons to them better than they could preach them to her. It was impossible that she could learn anything from them; and yet she would sit there thrice a day, suffering from cold in winter, from cough in spring, from heat in summer, and from rheumatism in autumn; and now that her doctor had forbidden her to go more than twice, recommending her to go only once, she really thought that she regarded the prohibition as a grievance. Indeed, to such as her, that expectation of the jewelled causeway, and of the perfect pavement that shall never be worn, must be everything. But if she was right—right as to herself and others,—then why has the world been made so pleasant? Why is the fruit of the earth so sweet; and the trees,—why are they so green; and the mountains so full of glory? Why are women so lovely; and why is it that the activity of man's mind is the only sure forerunner of man's progress? In listening thrice a day to outpourings from the clergymen at Perivale, there certainly was no activity of mind.

Now, in these days, Mrs. Winterfield was near to her reward. That she had insured that I cannot doubt. She had fed the poor, and filled the young full with religious teachings,—perhaps not wisely, and in her own way only too well, but yet as her judgment had directed her. She had cared little for herself,—forgiving injuries done to her, and not forgiving those only which she thought were done to the Lord. She had lived her life somewhat as the martyr lived, who stood for years on his pillar unmoved, while his nails grew through his flesh. So had she stood, doing, I fear, but little positive good with her large means, —but thinking nothing of her own comfort here, in comparison with the comfort of herself and others in the world to which she was going.

On this occasion her nephew and niece reached her together; the prim boy, with the white cotton gloves and the low four-wheeled carriage, having been sent down to meet Clara; for Mrs. Winterfield was a lady who thought it unbecoming that her niece,—though only an adopted niece,—should come to her door in an omnibus. Captain Aylmer had driven the four-wheeled carriage from the station, dispossessing the boy, and the luggage had been confided to the public conveyance.

"It is very fortunate that you should come together," said Mrs. Winterfield. "I didn't know when to expect you, Fred. Indeed, you never say at what hour you'll come."

"I think it safer to allow myself a little margin, aunt, because one has so many things to do."

"I suppose it is so with a gentleman," said Mrs. Winterfield. After which Clara looked at Captain Aylmer, but did not betray any of her suspicions. "But I knew Clara would come by this train," continued the old lady; "so I sent Tom to meet her. Ladies always can be punctual; they can do that at any rate." Mrs. Winterfield was one of those women who have always believed that their own sex is in every respect inferior to the other.

CHAPTER VIII.

CAPTAIN AYLMER MEETS HIS CONSTITUENTS.

On the first evening of their visit Captain Aylmer was very attentive to his aunt. He was quite alive to the propriety of such attentions, and to their expediency; and Clara was amused as she watched him while he sat by her side, by the hour together, answering little questions and making little remarks suited to the temperament of the old lady's mind. She, herself, was hardly called upon to join in the conversation on that evening, and as she sat and listened, she could not but think that Will Belton would have been less adroit, but that he would also have been more straightforward. And yet why should not Captain Aylmer talk to his aunt? Will Belton would also have talked to his aunt if he had one, but then he would have talked his own talk, and not his aunt's talk. Clara could hardly make up her mind whether Captain Aylmer was or was not a sincere man. On the following day Aylmer was out all the morning, paying visits among his constituents, and at three o'clock he was to make his speech in the Town-hall. Special places in the gallery were to be kept for Mrs. Winterfield and her niece, and the old woman was quite resolved that she would be there. As the day advanced

she became very fidgety, and at length she was quite alive
to the perils of having to climb up the Town-hall stairs ;
but she persevered, and at ten minutes before three she
was seated in her place.

"I suppose they will begin with prayer," she said to
Clara.   Clara, who knew nothing of the manner in which
things were done at such meetings, said that she supposed
so.   A town councillor's wife who sat on the other side of
Mrs. Winterfield, here took the liberty of explaining that
as the Captain was going to talk politics there would be
no prayers.   "But they have prayers in the Houses of
Parliament," said Mrs. Winterfield, with much anger.   To
this the town councillor's wife, who was almost silenced
by the great lady's wrath, said that indeed she did not
know.   After this Mrs. Winterfield continued to hope for
the best, till the platform was filled and the proceedings
had commenced.   Then she declared the present men of
Perivale to be a godless set, and expressed herself very
sorry that her nephew had ever had anything to do with
them.   "No good can come of it, my dear," she said.
Clara from the beginning had feared that no good would
come of her aunt's visit to the Town-hall.

The business was put on foot at once, and with some
little flourishing at the commencement, Captain Aylmer
made his speech;—the same speech which we have all
heard and read so often, specially adapted to the meridian
of Perivale.   He was a Conservative, and of course he
told his hearers that a good time was coming ; that he and
his family were really about to buckle themselves to the
work, and that Perivale would hear things that would surprise it.   The malt tax was to go, and the farmers were
to have free trade in beer;—the arguments from the other
side having come beautifully round in their appointed
circle,—and old England was to be old England once
again.   He did the thing tolerably well, as such gentlemen usually do, and Perivale was contented with its
member, with the exception of one Perivalian.   To Mrs.
Winterfield, sitting up there and listening with all her
ears, it seemed that he had hitherto omitted all allusion
to any subject that was worthy of mention.   At last he
said some word about the marriage and divorce court,
condemning the iniquity of the present law to which

Perivale had opposed itself violently by petition and general meetings; and upon hearing this, Mrs. Winterfield had thumped with her umbrella, and faintly cheered him with her weak old voice. But the surrounding Perivalians had heard the cheer, and it was repeated backwards and forwards through the room, till the member's aunt thought that it might be her nephew's mission to annul that godless Act of Parliament, and restore the matrimonial bonds of England to their old rigidity. When Captain Aylmer came out to hand her up to her little carriage, she patted him, and thanked him, and encouraged him; and on her way home she congratulated herself to Clara that she should have such a nephew to leave behind her in her place.

Captain Aylmer was dining with the mayor on that evening, and Mrs. Winterfield was therefore able to indulge herself in talking about him. "I don't see much of young men, of course," she said; "but I do not even hear of any that are like him." Again Clara thought of her cousin Will. Will was not at all like Frederic Aylmer; but was he not better? And yet, as she thought thus, she remembered that she had refused her cousin Will because she loved that very Frederic Aylmer whom her mind was thus condemning.

"I'm sure he does his duty as a member of Parliament very well," said Clara.

"That alone would not be much; but when that is joined to so much that is better, it is a great deal. I am told that very few of the men in the House now are believers at all."

"Oh, aunt!"

"It is terrible to think of, my dear."

"But, aunt, they have to take some oath, or something of that sort, to show that they are Christians."

"Not now, my dear. They've done away with all that, since we had Jew members. An atheist can go into Parliament now; and I'm told that most of them are that, or nearly as bad. I can remember when no Papist could sit in parliament. But they seem to me to be doing away with everything. It's a great comfort to me that Frederic is what he is."

"I'm sure it must be, aunt."

Then there was a pause, during which, however, Mrs. Winterfield gave no sign that the conversation was to be considered as being over.   Clara knew her aunt's ways so well, that she was sure something more was coming, and therefore waited patiently, without any thought of taking up her book.   "I was speaking to him about you yesterday," Mrs. Winterfield said at last.

"That would not interest him very much."

"Why not?   Do you suppose he is not interested in those I love?   Indeed, it did interest him; and he told me what I did not know before, and what you ought to have told me."

Clara now blushed, she knew not why, and became agitated.   "I don't know that I have kept anything from you that I ought to have told," she said.

"He says that the provision made for you by your father has all been squandered."

"If he used that word he has been very unkind," said Clara, angrily.

"I don't know what word he used, but he was not unkind at all; he never is.   I think he was very generous."

"I do not want his generosity, aunt."

"That is nonsense, my dear.   If he has told me the truth, what have you to depend on?"

"I don't want to depend on anything.   I hate hearing about it."

"Clara, I wonder you can talk in that way.   If you were only seventeen it would be very foolish; but at your age it is inexcusable.   When I am gone, and your father is gone, who is to provide for you?   Will your cousin do it—Mr. Belton, who is to have the property?"

"Yes, he would—if I would let him;—of course I would not let him.   But, aunt, pray do not go on.   I would sooner have to starve than talk about it at all."

There was another pause; but Clara again knew that the conversation was not over; and she knew also that it would be vain for her to endeavour to begin another subject.   Nor could she think of anything else to say, so much was she agitated.

"What makes you suppose that Mr. Belton would be so liberal?" asked Mrs. Winterfield.

"I don't know.   I can't say.   He is the nearest relation

I shall have; and of all the people I ever knew he is the best, and the most generous, and the least selfish. When he came to us papa was quite hostile to him—disliking his very name; but when the time came, papa could not bear to think of his going, because he had been so good."

"Clara!"

"Well, aunt."

"I hope you know my affection for you."

"Of course I do, aunt; and I hope you trust mine for you also."

"Is there anything between you and Mr. Belton besides cousinship?"

"Nothing."

"Because if I thought that, my trouble would of course be at an end."

"There is nothing;—but pray do not let me be a trouble to you." Clara, for a moment, almost resolved to tell her aunt the whole truth; but she remembered that she would be treating her cousin badly if she told the story of his rejection.

There was another short period of silence, and then Mrs. Winterfield went on. "Frederic thinks that I should make some provision for you by will. That, of course, is the same as though he offered to do it himself. I told him that it would be so, and I read him my will last night. He said that that made no difference, and recommended me to add a codicil. I asked him how much I ought to give you, and he said fifteen hundred pounds. There will be as much as that after burying me without burden to the estate. You must acknowledge that he has been very generous."

But Clara, in her heart, did not at all thank Captain Aylmer for his generosity. She would have had everything from him, or nothing. It was grievous to her to think that she should owe to him a bare pittance to keep her out of the workhouse,—to him who had twice seemed to be on the point of asking her to share everything with him. She did did not love her cousin Will as she loved him; but her cousin Will's assurance to her that he would treat her with a brother's care was sweeter to her by far than Frederic Aylmer's well-balanced counsel to his aunt on her behalf. In her present mood, too, she wanted no one to have fore-

thought for her; she desired no provision; for her, in the
discomfiture of heart there was consolation in the feeling
that when she should find herself alone in the world, she
would have been ill-treated by her friends all round her.
There was a charm in the prospect of her desolation of
which she did not wish to be robbed by the assurance of
some seventy pounds a year, to be given to her by Captain
Frederic Aylmer. To be robbed of one's grievance is the
last and foulest wrong,—a wrong under which the most
enduring temper will at last yield and become soured,—by
which the strongest back will be broken. "Well, my
dear," continued Mrs. Winterfield, when Clara made no
response to this appeal for praise.

"It is so hard for me to say anything about it, aunt.
What can I say but that I don't want to be a burden to any
one?"

"That is a position which very few women can attain,
—that is, very few single women."

"I think it would be well if all single women were
strangled by the time they are thirty," said Clara, with a
fierce energy which absolutely frightened her aunt.

"Clara! how can you say anything so wicked,—so abo-
minably wicked."

"Anything would be better than being twitted in this
way. How can I help it that I am not a man and able to
work for my bread? But I am not above being a housemaid, and so Captain Aylmer shall find. I'd sooner be a
housemaid, with nothing but my wages, than take the
money which you say he is to give me. It will be of no
use, aunt, for I shall not take it."

"It is I that am to leave it to you. It is not to be a
present from Frederic."

"It is the same thing, aunt. He says you are to do it;
and you told me just now that it was to come out of his
pocket."

"I should have done it myself long ago, had you told me
all the truth about your father's affairs."

"How was I to tell you? I would sooner have bitten
my tongue out. But I will tell you the truth now. If I
had known that all this was to be said to-me about money,
and that our poverty was to be talked over between you
and Captain Aylmer, I would not have come to Perivale.

I would rather that you should be angry with me, and think that I had forgotten you."

" You would not say that, Clara, if you remembered that this will probably be your last visit to me."

" No, no; it will not be the last. But do not talk about these things. And it will be so much better that I should be here when he is not here."

" I had hoped that when I died you might both be with me together,—as husband and wife."

" Such hopes never come to anything."

" I still think that he would wish it."

" That is nonsense, aunt. It is indeed, for neither of us wish it." A lie on such a subject from a woman under such circumstances is hardly to be considered a lie at all. It is spoken with no mean object, and is the only bulwark which the woman has ready at her need to cover her own weakness.

" From what he said yesterday," continued Mrs. Winterfield, " I think it is your own fault."

" Pray--pray do not talk in that way. It cannot be matter of any fault that two people do not want to marry each other."

" Of course I asked him no positive question. It would be indelicate even in me to have done that. But he spoke as though he thought very highly of you."

" No doubt he does. And so do I of Mr. Possitt."

" Mr. Possitt is a very excellent young man," said Mrs. Winterfield, gravely. Mr. Possitt was, indeed, her favourite curate at Perivale, and always dined at the house on Sundays between services, when Mrs. Winterfield was very particular in seeing that he took two glasses of her best port wine to support him. " But Mr. Possitt has nothing but his curacy."

" There is no danger, aunt, I can assure you."

" I don't know what you call danger; but Frederic seemed to think that you are always sharp with him. You don't want to quarrel with him, I hope, because I love him better than any one in the world?"

" Oh, aunt, what cruel things you say to me without thinking of them!"

" I do not mean to be cruel; but I will say nothing more about him. As I told you before, that I had not thought it expedient to leave away any portion of my little property from Frederic,—believing, as I did then, that the money intended for you by your father was still remaining,—it is best that you should now know that I have at last learnt the truth, and that I will at once see my lawyer about making this change."

"Dear aunt, of course I thank you."

"I want no thanks, Clara. I humbly strive to do what I believe to be my duty. I have never felt myself to be more than a steward of my money. That I have often failed in my stewardship I know well ;—for in what duties do we not all fail ?" Then she gently laid herself back in her arm-chair, closing her eyes, while she kept fast clasped in her hands the little book of daily devotion which she had been striving to read when the conversation had been commenced. Clara knew then that nothing more was to be said, and that she was not at present to interrupt her aunt. From her posture, and the closing of her eyelids, Mrs. Winterfield might have been judged to be asleep; but Clara could see the gentle motion of her lips, and was aware that her aunt was solacing herself with prayer.

Clara was angry with herself, and angry with all the world. She knew that the old lady who was sitting then before her was very good ; and that all this that had now been said had come from pure goodness, and a desire that strict duty might be done, and Clara was angry with her self in that she had not been more ready with her thanks, and more demonstrative with her love and gratitude. Mrs. Winterfield was affectionate as well as good, and her niece's coldness, as the niece well knew, had hurt her sorely. But still what could Clara have done or said ? She told herself that it was beyond her power to burst out into loud praises of Captain Aylmer ; and of such nature was the gratitude which Mrs. Winterfield had desired. She was not grateful to Captain Aylmer, and wanted nothing that was to come from his generosity. And then her mind went away to that other portion of her aunt's discourse. Could it be possible that this man was in truth attached to her, and was repelled simply by her own manner ? She was aware that she had fallen into a habit of fighting with him, of sparring against him with words about indifferent things, and calling his conduct in question in a manner

half playful and half serious. Could it be the truth that
she was thus robbing herself of that which would be to her,
—as to herself she had frankly declared,—the one treasure
which she would desire ? Twice, as has been said before,
words had seemed to tremble on his lips which might have
settled the question for her for ever; and on both occasions,
as she knew, she herself had helped to laugh off the pre-
cious word that had been coming. But had he been thoroughly in earnest,—in earnest as she would have him to
be,—no laugh would have deterred him from his purpose.
Could she have laughed Will Belton out of his declaration ?

At last the lips ceased to move, and she knew that her
aunt was in truth asleep. The poor old lady hardly ever
slept at night; but nature, claiming something of its due,
would give her rest such as this in her arm-chair by the
fireside. They were sitting in a large double drawing-
room upstairs, in which there were, as was customary with
Mrs. Winterfield in winter, two fires ; and the candles were
in the back room, while the two ladies sat in that looking
out into the street. This Mrs. Winterfield did to save her
eyes from the candles, and yet to be within reach of light
if it were wanted. And Clara also sat motionless in the
dark, careful not to disturb her aunt, and desirous of being
with her when she should awake. Captain Aylmer had
declared his purpose of being home early from the mayor's
dinner, and the ladies were to wait for his arrival before
tea was brought to them. Clara was herself almost asleep
when the door was opened, and Captain Aylmer entered
the room.

"H—sh !" she said, rising gently from her chair, and
putting up her finger. He saw her by the dull light of the
fire, and closed the door without a sound. Clara then crept
into the back room, and he followed her with noiseless
step. "She did not sleep at all last night," said Clara ;
" and now the unusual excitement of the day has fatigued
ner, and I think it is better not to wake her." The rooms
were large, and they were able to place themselves at such
a distance from the sleeper, that their low words could
hardly disturb her.

" Was she very tired when she got home ?" he asked.
"Not very. She has been talking much since that."

"Has she spoken about her will to you?"

"Yes;—she has."

"I thought she would." Then he was silent, as though he expected that she would speak again on that matter. But she had no wish to discuss her aunt's will with him, and therefore, to break the silence, asked him some trifling question. "Are you not home earlier than you expected?"

"It was very dull, and there was nothing more to be said. I did come away early, and perhaps have given affront. I hope you will accept the compliment implied."

"Your aunt will, when she wakes. She will be delighted to find you here."

"I am awake," said Mrs. Winterfield. "I heard Frederic come in. It is very good of him to come so soon. Clara, my dear, we will have tea."

During tea, Captain Aylmer was called upon to give an account of the mayor's feast,—how the rector had said grace before dinner, and Mr. Possitt had done so after dinner, and how the soup had been uneatable. "Dear me!" said Mrs. Winterfield. "And yet his wife was housekeeper formerly in a family that lived very well!" The Mrs. Winterfields of this world allow themselves little spiteful pleasures of this kind, repenting of them, no doubt, in those frequent moments in which they talk to their friends of their own terrible vilenesses. Captain Aylmer then explained that his own health had been drunk, and his aunt desired to know whether, in returning thanks, he had been able to say anything further against that wicked Divorce Act of Parliament. This her nephew was constrained to answer with a negative, and so the conversation was carried on till tea was over. She was very anxious to hear every word that he could be made to utter as to his own doings in Parliament, and as to his doings in Perivale, and hung upon him with that wondrous affection which old people with warm hearts feel for those whom they have selected as their favourites. Clara saw it all, and knew that her aunt was almost doting.

"I think I'll go up to bed now, my dears," said Mrs. Winterfield, when she had taken her cup of tea. "I am tired with those weary stairs in the Town-hall, and I shall be better in my own room." Clara offered to go with her but this attendance her aunt declined,—as she did always.

So the bell was rung, and the old maid-servant walked off
with her mistress, and Miss Amedroz and Captain Aylmer
were left together.

"I don't think she will last long," said Captain Aylmer,
soon after the door was closed.

"I should be sorry to believe that; but she is certainly
much altered."

"She has great courage to keep her up,—and a feeling
that she should not give way, but do her duty to the last.
In spite of all that, however, I can see how changed she is
since the summer. Have you ever thought how sad it will
be if she should be alone when the day comes?"

"She has Martha, who is more to her now than any one
else,—unless it is you."

"You could not remain with her over Christmas, I
suppose?"

"Who, I? What would my father do? Papa is as old,
or nearly as old, as my aunt."

"But he is strong."

"He is very lonely. He would be more lonely than she
is, for he has no such servant as Martha to be with him.
Women can do better than men, I think, when they come
to my aunt's age."

From this they got into a conversation as to the
character of the lady with whom they were both so nearly
connected, and, in spite of all that Clara could do to prevent it, continual references were made by Captain Aylmer
to her money, and her will, and the need of an addition to
that will on Clara's behalf. At last she was driven to
speak out. "Captain Aylmer," she said, "the subject is
so distasteful to me, that I must ask you not to speak about
it."

"In my position I am driven to think about it."

"I cannot, of course, help your thoughts; but I can
assure you that they are unnecessary."

"It seems to me so hard that there should be such a gulf
between you and me." This he said after he had been
silent for a while; and as he spoke he looked away from
her at the fire.

"I don't know that there is any particular gulf," she
replied.

"Yes, there is. And it is you that makes it. Whenever

I attempt to speak to you as a friend you draw yourself off from me, and shut yourself up. I know that it is not jealousy."

"Jealousy, Captain Aylmer !"

"Jealousy with my aunt, I mean."

"No, indeed."

"You are infinitely too proud for that; but I am sure that a stranger seeing it all would think that it was so."

"I don't know what it is that I do or that I ought not to do. But all my life everything that I have done at Perivale has always been wrong."

"It would have been so natural that you and I should be friends."

"If we are enemies, Captain Aylmer, I don't know it."

"But if ever I venture to speak of your future life, you always repel me ;—as though you were determined to let me know that it should not be a matter of care to me."

"That is exactly what I am determined to let you know. You are, or will be, a rich man, and you have everything the world can give you. I am, or shall be, a very poor woman."

"Is that a reason why I should not be interested in your welfare ?"

"Yes ;—the best reason in the world. We are not related to each other, though we have a common connection in dear Mrs. Winterfield. And nothing, to my idea, can be more objectionable than any sort of dependence from a woman of my age on a man of yours,—there being no real tie of blood between them. I have spoken very plainly, Captain Aylmer, for you have made me do it."

"Very plainly," he said.

"If I have said anything to offend you, I beg your pardon ; but I was driven to explain myself." Then she got up and took her bed-candle in her hand.

"You have not offended me," he said, as he also rose.

"Good-night, Captain Aylmer."

He took her hand and kept it. "Say that we are friends."

"Why should we not be friends ?"

"There is no reason on my part why we should not be the dearest friends," he said. "Were it not that I am so utterly without encouragement, I should say the very dearest." He still held her hand, and was looking into her face as he spoke. For a moment she stood there, bearing his gaze, as though she expected some further words to be spoken. Then she withdrew her hand, and again saying, in a clear voice, " Good-night, Captain Aylmer," she left the room.

CHAPTER IX.

CAPTAIN AYLMER'S PROMISE TO HIS AUNT.

WHAT had Captain Aylmer meant by telling her that they might be the dearest friends—by saying so much as that, and then saying no more ? Of course, Clara asked herself that question as soon as she was alone in her bedroom, after leaving Captain Aylmer below. And she made two answers to herself—two answers which were altogether distinct, and contradictory one of the other. At first she decided that he had said so much and no more because he was deceitful—because it suited his vanity to raise hopes which he had no intention of fulfilling—because he was fond of saying soft things which were intended to have no meaning. This was her first answer to herself. But in her second she accused herself as much as she had before accused him. She had been cold to him, unfriendly, and harsh. As her aunt had told her, she spoke sharp words to him, and repulsed the kindness which he offered her. What right had she to expect from him a declaration of love when she was studious to stop him at every avenue by which he might approach it ? A little management on her side would, she almost knew, make things right. But then the idea of any such management distressed her ;—nay, more, disgusted her. The management, if any were necessary, must come from him. And it was manifest enough that if he had any strong wishes in this matter, he was not a good manager. Her cousin, Will Belton, knew how to manage much better.

On the next morning, however, all her thoughts respecting Captain Aylmer were dissipated by tidings which Martha brought to her bedside. Her aunt was ill. Martha was afraid that her mistress was very ill. She did not

dare to send specially for the doctor on her own responsi-
bility, as Mrs. Winterfield had strong and peculiar feelings
about doctors' visits, and had on this very morning declined to be so visited. On the next day the doctor would
come in the usual course of things, for she had, submitted
for some years back to such periodical visitings; but she
had desired that nothing might be done out of the common
way. Martha, however, declared that if she were alone
with her mistress the doctor would be sent for; and she
now petitioned for aid from Clara. Clara was, of course, by
her aunt's bedside in a few minutes, and in a few minutes
more the doctor from the other side of the way was there
also.

It was ten o'clock before Captain Aylmer and Miss
Amedroz met at breakfast, and they had before that been
together in Mrs. Winterfield's room. The doctor had
told Captain Aylmer that his aunt was ill—very ill,
dangerously ill. She had been wrong to go into such a
place as the cold, unaired Court House, and that, too, in
the month of November; and the fatigue had also been too
much for her. Mrs. Winterfield, too, had admitted to
Clara that she knew herself to be very ill. "I felt it
coming on me last night," she said, "when I was talking
to you; and I felt it still more strongly when I left you
after tea. I have lived long enough. God's will be done."
At that moment, when she said she had lived long enough,
she forgot her intention with reference to her will. But
she remembered it before Clara had left the room. "Tell
Frederic," she said, "to send at once for Mr. Palmer."
Now Clara knew that Mr. Palmer was the attorney, and
resolved that she would give no such message to Captain
Aylmer. But Mrs. Winterfield sent for her nephew, who
had just left her, and herself gave her orders to him. In
the course of the morning there came tidings from the
attorney's office that Mr. Palmer was away from Perivale,
that he would be back on the morrow, and that he would
of course wait on Mrs. Winterfield immediately on his
return.

Captain Aylmer and Miss Amedroz discussed nothing
but their aunt's state of health that morning over the
breakfast-table. Of course, under such circumstances in
the house, there was no further immediate reference made

to that offer of dearest friendship. It was clear to them
both that the doctor did not expect that Mrs. Winterfield
would again leave her bed ; and it was clear to Clara also
that her aunt was of the same opinion.

" I shall hardly be able to go home now," she said.

" It will be kind of you if you can remain."

" And you ?"

" I shall remain over the Sunday. If by that time she
is at all better, I will run up to town and come down again
before the end of the week. I know you don't believe it,
but a man really has some things which he must do."

" I don't disbelieve you, Captain Aylmer."

" But you must write to me daily if I do go." ·

To this Clara made no objection ;—and she must write
also to some one else. She must let her cousin know how
little chance there was that she would be at home at Christmas, explaining to him at the same time that his visit to
her father would on that account be all the more welcome.

" Are you going to her now ?" he asked, as Clara got up
immediately after breakfast. " I shall be in the house all
the morning, and if you want me you will of course send
for me."

" She may perhaps like to see you."

" I will come up every now and again. I would remain
there altogether, only I should be in the way." Then
ne got a newspaper, and made himself comfortable over
the fire, while she went up to her weary task in her
aunt's room.

Neither on that day nor on the next did the lawyer come,
and on the following morning all earthly troubles were
over with Mrs. Winterfield. It was early on the Sunday
morning that she died, and late on the Saturday evening
Mr. Palmer had sent up to say that he had been detained
at Taunton, but that he would wait on Mrs. Winterfield
early on the Monday morning. On the Friday the poor
lady had said much on the subject, but had been comforted by an assurance from her nephew that the arrangement should be carried out exactly as she wished it, whether
the codicil was or was not added to the will. To Clara
she said nothing more on the subject, nor at such a time
did Captain Aylmer feel that he could offer her any assurance on the matter. But Clara knew that the will **was**

not altered ; and though at that time she was not thinking much about money, she had, nevertheless, very clearly made up her own mind as to her own conduct. Nothing should induce her to take a present of fifteen hundred pounds,— or, indeed, of as many pence from Captain Aylmer. During those hours of sickness in the house they had been much thrown together, and no one could have been kinder or more gentle to her than he had been. He had come to call her Clara, as people will do when joined together in such duties, and had been very pleasant as well as affectionate in his manner with her. It had seemed to her that he also wished to take upon himself the cares and love of an adopted brother. But as an adopted brother she would have nothing to do with him. The two men whom she liked best in the world would assume each the wrong place ; and between them both she felt that she would be left friendless.

On the Saturday afternoon they had both surmised how it was going to be with Mrs. Winterfield, and Captain Aylmer had told Mr. Palmer that he feared his coming on the Monday would be useless. He explained also what was required, and declared that he would be at once ready to make good the deficiency in the will. Mr. Palmer seemed to think that this would be better even than the making of a codicil in the last moments of the lady's life ; and, therefore, he and Captain Aylmer were at rest on that subject.

During the greater part of the Saturday night both Clara and Captain Aylmer remained with their aunt ; and once, when the morning was almost there, and the last hour was near at hand, she had said a word or two which both of them had understood, in which she implored her darling Frederic to take a brother's care of Clara Amedroz. Even in that moment Clara had repudiated the legacy, feeling sure in her heart that Frederic Aylmer was aware what was the nature of the care which he ought to owe, if he would consent to owe any care to her. He promised his aunt that he would do as she desired him, and it was impossible that Clara should then, aloud, repudiate the compact. But she said nothing, merely allowing her hand to rest with his beneath the thin, dry hand of the dying woman. To her aunt, however, when for a moment they

were alone together, she showed all possible affection, with
thanks and tears, and warm kisses, and prayers for forgiveness, as to all those matters in which she had offended.
"My pretty one;—my dear," said the old woman,
raising her hand on to the head of the crouching girl,
who was hiding her moist eyes on the bed. Never
during her life had her aunt appeared to her in so loving
a mood as now, when she was leaving it. Then, with
some eager impassioned words, in which she pronounced
her ideas of what should be the religious duties of a
woman, Mrs. Winterfield bade farewell to her niece.
After that, she had a longer interview with her nephew,
and then it seemed that all worldly cares were over with
her.

The Sunday was passed in all that blankness of funereal
grief which is absolutely necessary on such occasions. It
cannot be said that either Clara or Captain Aylmer were
stricken with any of that agony of woe which is produced
on us by the death of those whom we have loved so well
that we cannot bring ourselves to submit to part with
them. They were both truly sorry for their aunt, in the
common parlance of the world; but their sorrow was of
that modified sort which does not numb the heart, and
make the surviving sufferer feel that there never can be a
remedy. Nevertheless, it demanded sad countenances, few
words, and those spoken hardly above a whisper, an absence
of all amusement and almost of all employment and a full
surrender to the trappings of woe. They two were living
together without other companion in the big house,—sitting
down together to dinner and to tea; but on this day hardly
a dozen words were spoken between them, and those dozen
were spoken with no purport. On the Monday Captain
Aylmer gave orders for the funeral, and then went away
to London, undertaking to be back on the day before the
last ceremony. Clara was rather glad that he should be
gone, though she feared the solitude of the big house. She
was glad that he should be gone, as she found it impossible
to talk to him with ease to herself. She knew that he was
about to assume some position as protector or quasi guardian over her, in conformity with her aunt's express wish,
and she was quite resolved that she would submit to no such
guardianship from his hands. That being so, the shorter

period there might be for any such discussion the
better.

The funeral was to take place on the Saturday, and
during the four days that intervened she received two
visits from Mr. Possitt. Mr. Possitt was very discreet in
what he said, and Clara was angry with herself for not
allowing his words to have any avail with her. She told
herself that they were commonplace; but she told herself,
also, after his first visit, that she had no right to expect
anything else but commonplace words. How often are
men found who can speak words on such occasions that are
not commonplaces,—that really stir the soul, and bring true
comfort to the listener? The humble listener may receive
comfort from commonplace words; but Clara was not
humble, and rebuked herself for her own pride. On the
second occasion of his coming she did endeavour to receive
him with a meek heart, and to accept what he said with an
obedient spirit. But the struggle within her bosom was
hard, and when he bade her to kneel and pray with him,
she doubted for a moment between rebellion and hypocrisy.
But she had determined to be meek, and so hypocrisy
carried the hour.

What would a clergyman say on such an occasion if the
object of his solicitude were to decline the offer, remarking
that prayer at that moment did not seem to be opportune;
and that, moreover, he, the person thus invited, would like,
first of all, to know what was to be the special object of the
proposed prayer, if he found that he could, at the spur of
the moment, bring himself at all into a fitting mood for the
task? Of him who would decline, without argument,
the clergyman would opine that he was simply a reprobate. Of him who would propose to accompany an
hypothetical acceptance with certain stipulations, he
would say to himself that he was a stiff-necked wrestler
against grace, whose condition was worse than that of the
reprobate. Men and women, conscious that they will be
thus judged, submit to the hypocrisy, and go down upon
their knees unprepared, making no effort, doing nothing
while they are there, allowing their consciences to be eased
if they can only feel themselves numbed into some ceremo-
nial awe by the occasion. So it was with Clara, when
Mr. Possitt, with easy piety, went through the formula of

his devotion, hardly ever having realised to himself the fact that, of all works in which man can engage himself, that of prayer is the most difficult.

"It is a sad loss to me," said Mr. Possitt, as he sat for half an hour with Clara, after she had thus submitted herself. Mr. Possitt was a weakly, pale-faced little man, who worked so hard in the parish that on every day, Sundays included, he went to bed as tired in all his bones as a day labourer from the fields ;—"a very great loss. There are not many now who understand what a clergyman has to go through, as our dear friend did." If he was mindful of his two glasses of port wine on Sundays, who could blame him ?

"She was a very kind woman, Mr. Possitt."

"Yes, indeed ;—and so thoughtful! That she will have an exceeding great reward, who can doubt? Since I knew her she always lived as a saint upon earth. I suppose there's nothing known as to who will live in this house, Miss Amedroz ?"

"Nothing ;—I should think."

"Captain Aylmer won't keep it in his own hands."

"I cannot tell in the least ; but as he is obliged to live in London because of Parliament, and goes to Yorkshire always in the autumn, he can hardly want it."

"I suppose not. But it will be a sad loss,—a sad loss to have this house empty. Ah!—I shall never forget her kindness to me. Do you know, Miss Amedroz,"— and as he told his little secret he became beautifully confidential ;—"do you know, she always used to send me ten guineas at Christmas to help me along. She understood, as well as any one, how hard it is for a gentleman to live on seventy pounds a year. You will not wonder that I should feel that I've had a loss." It is hard for a gentleman to live upon seventy pounds a year ; and it is very hard, too, for a lady to live upon nothing a year, which lot in life fate seemed to have in store for Miss Amedroz.

On the Friday evening Captain Aylmer came back, and Clara was in truth glad to see him. Her aunt's death had been now far enough back to admit of her telling Martha that she would not dine till Captain Aylmer had come, and to allow her to think somew of his comfort. People must eat and drink even when the grim monarch is in the house; and it is a relief when they first dare to do so with some attention to the comforts which are ordinarily so important to them. For themselves alone women seldom care to exercise much trouble in this direction; but the presence of a man at once excuses and renders necessary the ceremony of a dinner. So Clara prepared for the arrival, and greeted the comer with some returning pleasantness of manner. And he, too, was pleasant with her, telling her of his plans, and speaking to her as though she were one of those whom it was natural that he should endeavour to interest in his future welfare.

"When I come back to-morrow," he said, "the will must be opened and read. It had better be done here." They were sitting over the fire in the dining-room, after dinner, and Clara knew that the coming back to which he alluded was his return from the funeral. But she made no answer to this, as she wished to say nothing about her aunt's will. "And after that," he continued, "you had better let me take you out."

"I am very well," she said; "I do not want any special taking out."

"But you have been confined to the house the whole week."

"Women are accustomed to that, and do not feel it as you would. However, I will walk with you if you'll take me."

"Of course I'll take you. And then we must settle our future plans. Have you fixed upon any day yet for returning? Of course, the longer you stay, the kinder you will be."

"I can do no good to any one by staying."

"You do good to me;—but I suppose I'm nobody. I wish I could tell what to do about this house. Dear, good old woman! I know she would have wished that I should keep it in my own hands, with some idea of living here at some future time;—but of course I never shall live here."

"Why not?"

"Would you like it yourself?"

"I am not Member of Parliament for Perivale, and

should not be the leading person in the town. You would be a sort of king here; and then, some day, you will have your mother's property as well as your aunt's; and you would be near to your own tenants."

"But that does not answer my question. Could you bring yourself to live here,—even if it were your own?"

"Why not?"

"Because it is so deadly dull;—because it has no attraction whatever;—because of all lives it is the one you would like the least. No one should live in a provincial town but they who make their money by doing so."

"And what are the wives and daughters of such people to do,—and especially their widows? I have no doubt I could live here very happily if I had anybody near me that I liked. I should not wish to have to depend altogether on Mr. Possitt for society."

"And you would find him about the best."

"Mr. Possitt has been with me twice whilst you were away, and he, too, asked what you meant to do about the house."

"And what did you say?"

"What could I say? Of course I said I did not know. I suppose he was meditating whether you would live here and ask him to dinner on Sundays!"

"Mr. Possitt is a very good sort of man," said the Captain, gravely;—for Captain Aylmer, in the carrying out of his principles, always spoke seriously of everything connected with the Church in Perivale.

"And quite worthy to be asked to dinner on Sundays," said Clara. "But I did not give him any hope. How could I? Of course I knew that you would not live here, though I did not tell him so."

"No; I don't suppose I shall. But I see very plainly that you think I ought to do so."

"I've the old-fashioned idea as to a man's living near to his own property; that is all. No doubt it was good for other people in Perivale, besides Mr. Possitt, that my dear aunt lived here; and if the house is shut up, or let to some stranger, they will feel her loss the more. But I don't know that you are bound to sacrifice yourself to them."

"If I were to marry," said Captain Aylmer, very slowly

and in a low voice, " of course I should have to think of my wife's wishes."

" But if your wife, when she accepted you, knew that you were living here, she would hardly take upon herself to demand that you should give up your residence."

" She might find it very dull."

" She would make her own calculations as to that before she accepted you."

" No doubt;—but I can't fancy any woman taking a man who was tied by his leg to Perivale. What do the people do who live in Perivale?"

" Earn their bread."

" Yes;—that's just what I said. But I shouldn't earn mine here."

" I have the feeling I spoke of very strongly about papa's place," said Clara, changing the conversation suddenly. " I very often think of the future fate of Belton Castle when papa shall have gone. My cousin has got his house at Plaistow, and I don't suppose he'd live there."

" And where will you go?" he asked.

As soon as she had spoken, Clara regretted her own imprudence in having ventured to speak upon her own affairs. She had been well pleased to hear him talk of his plans, and had been quite resolved not to talk of her own. But now, by her own speech, she had set him to make inquiries as to her future life. She did not at first answer the question; but he repeated it. " And where will you live yourself?"

" I hope I may not have to think of that for some time to come yet."

" It is impossible to help thinking of such things."

" I can assure you that I haven't thought about it; but I suppose I shall endeavour to—to—; I don't know what I shall endeavour to do."

" Will you come and live at Perivale?"

" Why here more than anywhere else?"

" In this house I mean."

" That would suit me admirably;—would it not? I'm afraid Mr. Possitt would not find me a good neighbour. To tell the truth, I think that any lady who lives here alone ought to be older than I am. The Perivalians would not show to a young woman that sort of respect which they have always felt for this house."

"I didn't mean alone," said Captain Aylmer.

Then Clara got up and made some excuse for leaving him, and there was nothing more said between them,—nothing, at least, of moment. on that evening. She had become uneasy when he asked her whether she would like to live in his house at Perivale. But afterwards, when he suggested that she was to have some companion with her there, she felt herself compelled to put an end to the conversation. And yet she knew that this was always the way, both with him and with herself. He would say things which would seem to promise that in another minute he would be at her feet, and then he would go no further. And she, when she heard those words,—though in truth she would have had him at her feet if she could,—would draw away, and recede, and forbid him as it were to go on. But Clara continued to make her comparisons, and knew well that her cousin Will would have gone on in spite of any such forbiddings.

On that night, however, when she was alone, she could console herself with thinking how right she had been. In that front bedroom, the door of which was opposite to her own, with closed shutters, in the terrible solemnity of life-less humanity, was still lying the body of her aunt! What would she have thought of herself if at such a moment she could have listened to words of love, and promised herself as a wife, while such an inmate was in the house? She little knew that he, within that same room, had pledged himself, to her who was now lying there waiting for her last removal—had pledged himself, just seven days since, to make the offer which, when he was talking to her, she was always half hoping and half fearing!

He could have meant nothing else when he told her that he had not intended to suggest that she should live there alone in that great house at Perivale. She could not hinder herself from thinking of this, unfit as was the present moment for any such thoughts. How was it possible that she should not speculate on the subject, let her resolutions against any such speculation be ever so strong? She had confessed to herself that she loved the man, and what else could she wish but that he also should love her?

But there came upon her some faint suspicion—some glimpse of what was almost a dream—that he might possibly in this matter be guided rather by duty than by love. It might be that he would feel himself constrained to offer his hand to her—constrained by the peculiarity of his position towards her. If so—should she discover that such were his motives—there would be no doubt as to the nature of her answer.

CHAPTER X.

SHOWING HOW CAPTAIN AYLMER KEPT HIS PROMISE.

THE next day was necessarily very sad. Clara had declared her determination to follow her aunt to the churchyard, and did so, together with Martha, the old servant. There were three or four mourning coaches, as family friends came over from Taunton, one or two of whom were to be present at the reading of the will. How melancholy was the occasion, and how well the work was done : how substantial and yet how solemn was the luncheon, spread after the funeral for the gentlemen ; and how the will was read, without a word of remark, by Mr. Palmer, need hardly be told here. The will contained certain substantial legacies to servants—the amount to that old handmaid Martha being so great as to produce a fit of fainting, after which the old handmaid declared that if ever there was, by any chance, an angel of light upon the earth, it was her late mistress; and yet Martha had had her troubles with her mistress; and there was a legacy of two hundred pounds to the gentleman who was called upon to act as co-executor with Captain Aylmer. Other clause in the will there was none, except that one substantial clause which bequeathed to her well-beloved nephew, Frederic Folliott Aylmer, everything of which the testatrix died possessed. The will had been made at some moment in which Clara's spirit of independence had offended her aunt, and her name was not mentioned. That nothing should have been left to Clara was the one thing that surprised the relatives from Taunton who were present. The relatives from

Taunton, to give them their due, expected nothing for themselves; but as there had been great doubt as to the proportions in which the property would be divided, between the nephew and adopted niece, there was aroused a considerable excitement as to the omission of the name of Miss Amedroz—an excitement which was not altogether unpleasant. When people complain of some cruel shame, which does not affect themselves personally, the complaint is generally accompanied by an unexpressed and unconscious feeling of satisfaction.

On the present occasion, when the will had been read and refolded, Captain Aylmer, who was standing on the rug near the fire, spoke a few words. His aunt, he said, had desired to add a codicil to the will, of the nature of which Mr. Palmer was well aware. She had expressed her intention to leave fifteen hundred pounds to her niece, Miss Amedroz; but death had come upon her too quickly to enable her to perform her purpose. Of this intention on the part of Mrs. Winterfield, Mr. Palmer was as well aware as himself; and he mentioned the subject now, merely with the object of saying that as a matter of course the legacy to Miss Amedroz was as good as though the codicil had been completed. On such a question as that there could arise no question as to legal right; but he understood that the legal claim of Miss Amedroz, under such circumstances, was as valid as his own. It was therefore no affair of generosity on his part. Then there was a little buzz of satisfaction on the part of those present, and the meeting was broken up.

A certain old Mrs. Folliott, who was cousin to everybody concerned, had come over from Taunton to see how things were going. She had always been at variance with Mrs. Winterfield, being a woman who loved cards and supper parties, and who had throughout her life stabled her horses in stalls very different to those used by the lady of Perivale. Now this Mrs. Folliott was the first to tell Clara of the will. Clara, of course, was altogether indifferent. She had known for months past that her aunt had intended to leave nothing to her, and her only hope had been that she might be left free from any commiseration or remark on the subject. But Mrs. Folliott, with sundry shakings of the head, told her how her aunt had omitted to name her—and then told her also of Captain Aylmer's generosity. "We all did think, my dear," said Mrs. Folliott, "that she would have done better than that for you, or at any rate that she would not have left you dependent on him." Captain Aylmer's horses were also supposed to be stabled in strictly Low Church stalls, and were therefore regarded by Mrs. Folliott with much dislike.

"I and my aunt understood each other perfectly," said Clara.

"I dare say. But if so, you really were the only person that did understand her. No doubt what she did was quite right, seeing that she was a saint; but we sinners would have thought it very wicked to have made such a will, and then to have trusted to the generosity of another person after we were dead."

"But there is no question of trusting to any one's generosity, Mrs. Folliott."

"He need not pay you a shilling, you know, unless he likes it."

"And he will not be asked to pay me a shilling."

"I don't suppose he will go back after what he has said publicly."

"My dear Mrs. Folliott," said Clara earnestly, "pray do not let us talk about it. It is quite unnecessary. I never expected any of my aunt's property, and knew all along that it was to go to Captain Aylmer,—who, indeed, was Mrs. Winterfield's heir naturally. Mrs. Winterfield was not really my aunt, and I had no claim on her."

"But everybody understood that she was to provide for you."

"As I was not one of the everybodies myself, it will not signify." Then Mrs. Folliott retreated, having, as she thought, performed her duty to Clara, and contented herself henceforth with abusing Mrs. Winterfield's will in her own social circles at Taunton.

On the evening of that day, when all the visitors were gone and the house was again quiet, Captain Aylmer thought it expedient to explain to Clara the nature of his aunt's will, and the manner in which she would be allowed to inherit under it the amount of money which her aunt had intended to bequeath to her. When she became im

patient ana onjected to listen to him, he argued with her,
pointing out to her that this was a matter of business to
which it was now absolutely necessary that she should attend.
" It may be the case," he said, " and, indeed, I hope it will,
that no essential difference will be made by it;—except
that it will gratify you to know how careful she was of
your interest in her last moments. But you are bound in
duty to learn your own position; and I, as her executor,
am bound to explain it to you. But perhaps you would
rather discuss it with Mr. Palmer."

" Oh no ;—save me from that."

" You must understand, then, that I shall pay over to
you the sum of fifteen hundred pounds as soon as the will
has been proved."

" I understand nothing of the kind. I know very well
that if I were to take it, I should be accepting a present
from you, and to that I cannot consent."

" But, Clara——"

" It is no good, Captain Aylmer. Though I don't pretend to understand much about law, I do know that I can
have no claim to anything that is not put into the will;
and I won't have what I could not claim. My mind is
quite made up, and I hope I may'nt be annoyed about it.
Nothing is more disagreeable than having to discuss
money matters."

Perhaps Captain Aylmer thought that the having no
money matters to discuss might be even more disagreeable.

" Well," he said, " I can only ask you to consult any
friend whom you can trust upon the matter. Ask your
father, or Mr. Belton, and I have no doubt that either of
them will tell you that you are as much entitled to the
legacy as though it had been written in the will."

" On such a matter, Captain Aylmer, I don't want to ask
anybody. You can't pay me the money unless I choose to
take it, and I certainly shall not do that." Upon hearing
this he smiled, assuming, as Clara fancied that he was
sometimes wont to do, a look of quiet superiority; and
then, for that time, he allowed the subject to be dropped
between them.

But Clara knew that she must discuss it at length with
her father, and the fear of that discussion made her un-
happy. She had already written to say that she would

return home on the day but one after the funeral, and had told Captain Aylmer of her purpose. So very prudent a man as he, of course, could not think it right that a young lady should remain with him, in his house, as his visitor; and to her decision on this point he had made no objection. She now heartily wished that she had named the day after the funeral, and that she had not been deterred by her dislike of making a Sunday journey. She dreaded this day, and would have been very thankful if he would have left her and gone back to London. But he intended, he said, to remain at Perivale throughout the next week, and she must endure the day as best she might be able. She wished that it were possible to ask Mr. Possitt to his accustomed dinner; but she did not dare to make the proposition to the master of the house. Though Captain Aylmer had declared Mr. Possitt to be a very worthy man, Clara surmised that he would not be anxious to commence that practice of a Sabbatical dinner so soon after his aunt's decease. The day, after all, would be but one day, and Clara schooled herself into a resolution to bear it with good humour.

Captain Aylmer had made a positive promise to his aunt on her deathbed that he would ask Clara Amedroz to be his wife, and he had no more idea of breaking his word than he had of resigning the whole property which had been left to him. Whether Clara would accept him he had much doubt. He was a man by no means brilliant, not naturally self-confident, nor was he, perhaps, to be credited with the possession of high principles of the finest sort; but he was clever, in the ordinary sense of the word, knowing his own interest, knowing, too, that that interest depended on other things besides money; and he was a just man, according to the ordinary rules of justice in the world. Not for the first time when he was sitting by the bedside of his dying aunt had he thought of asking Clara to marry him. Though he had never hitherto resolved that he would do so—though he had never till then brought himself absolutely to determine that he would take so important a step—he had pondered over it often, and was aware that he was very fond of Clara. He was, in truth, as much in love with her as it was in his nature to be in love. He was not a man to break his heart for a

girl;—nor even to make a strong fight for a wife, as
Belton was prepared to do. If refused once, he might
probably ask again,—having some idea that a first refusal
was not always intended to mean much,—and he might
possibly make a third attempt, prompted by some further
calculation of the same nature. But it might be doubted
whether, on the first, second, or third occasion, he would
throw much passion into his words; and those who knew
him well would hardly expect to see him die of a broken
heart, should he ultimately be unsuccessful.

When he had first thought of marrying Miss Amedroz
he had imagined that she would have shared with him his
aunt's property, and indeed such had been his belief up to
the days of the last illness of Mrs. Winterfield. The
match therefore had recommended itself to him as being
prudent as well as pleasant; and though his aunt had
never hitherto pressed the matter upon him, he had understood what her wishes were. When she first told him,
three or four days before her death, that her property was
left altogether to him, and then, on hearing how totally
her niece was without hope of provision from her father,
had expressed her desire to give a sum of money to Clara,
she had spoken plainly of her desire;—but she had not on
that occasion asked him for any promise. But afterwards,
when she knew that she was dying, she had questioned
him as to his own feelings, and he in his anxiety to gratify
her in her last wishes, had given her the promise which
she was so anxious to hear. He made no difficulty in doing
so. It was his own wish as well as hers. In a money
point of view he might no doubt now do better; but then
money was not everything. He was very fond of Clara,
and felt that if she would accept him he would be proud
of his wife. She was well born and well educated, and it
was the proper sort of thing for him to do. No doubt he
had some idea, seeing how things had now arranged themselves, that he would be giving much more than he would
get; and perhaps the manner of his offer might be affected
by that consideration; but not on that account did he feel
at all sure that he would be accepted. Clara Amedroz was
a proud girl,—perhaps too proud. Indeed, it was her fault.
If her pride now interfered with her future fortune in life,
it should be her own fault, not his. He would do his duty

to her and to his aunt; he would do it perseveringly and kindly; and then, if she refused him, the fault would not be his.

Such, I think, was the state of Captain Aylmer's mind when he got up on the Sunday morning, resolving that he would on that day make good his promise. And it must be remembered, on his behalf, that he would have prepared himself for his task with more animation if he had hitherto received warmer encouragement. He had felt himself to be repulsed in the little efforts which he had already made to please the lady, and had no idea whatever as to the true state of her feelings. Had he known what she knew, he would, I think, have been animated enough, and gone to his task as happy and thriving a lover as any. But he was a man somewhat diffident of himself, though sufficiently conscious of the value of the worldly advantages which he possessed;—and he was, perhaps, a little afraid of Clara, giving her credit for an intellect superior to his own.

He had promised to walk with her on the Saturday after the reading of the will, intending to take her out through the gardens down to a farm, now belonging to himself, which lay at the back of the town, and which was held by an old widow who had been senior in life to her late landlady; but no such walk had been possible, as it was dark before the last of the visitors from Taunton had gone. At breakfast on Sunday he again proposed the walk, offering to take her immediately after luncheon. "I suppose you will not go to church?" he said.

"Not to-day. I could hardly bring myself to do it to-day."

"I think you are right. I shall go. A man can always do these things sooner than a lady can. But you will come out afterwards?" To this she assented, and then she was left alone throughout the morning. The walk she did not mind. That she and Captain Aylmer should walk together was all very well. They might probably have done so had Mrs. Winterfield been still alive. It was the long evening afterwards that she dreaded—the long winter evening, in which she would have to sit with him as his guest, and with him only. She could not pass these hours without talking to him, and she felt that she could not talk to him naturally and easily. It would, however, be but for once, and she would bear it.

They went together down to the house of Mrs. Partridge, the tenant, and made their kindly speeches to the old woman. Mrs. Partridge already knew that Captain Aylmer was to be her landlord, but having hitherto seen more of Miss Amedroz than of the Captain, and having always regarded her landlady's niece as being connected irrevocably with the property, she addressed them as though the estate were a joint affair.

"I shan't be here to trouble you long;—that I shan't, Miss Clara," said the old woman.

"I am sure Captain Aylmer would be very sorry to lose you," replied Clara, speaking loud, and close to the poor woman's ear, for she was deaf.

"I never looked to live after she was gone, Miss Clara; —never. No more I didn't. Deary;—deary! And I suppose you'll be living at the big house now; won't ye?"

"The big house belongs to Captain Aylmer, Mrs. Partridge." She was driven to bawl out her words, and by no means liked the task. Then Captain Aylmer said something, but his speech was altogether lost.

"Oh;—it belongs to the Captain, do it? They told me that was the way of the will; but I suppose it's all one."

"Yes; it's all one," said Captain Aylmer, gaily.

"It's not exactly all one, as you call it," said Clara, attempting to laugh, but still shouting at the top of her voice.

"Ah;—I don't understand; but I hope you'll both live there together,—and I hope you'll be as good to the poor as she that is gone. Well, well; I didn't ever think that I should be still here, while she is lying under the stones up in the old church!"

Captain Aylmer had determined that he would ask his question on the way back from the farm, and now resolved that he might as well begin with some allusion to Mrs. Partridge's words about the house. The afternoon was bright and cold, and the lane down to the farm-house had been dried by the wind, so that the day was pleasant for walking. "We might as well go on to the bridge," he said, as they left the farm-yard. "I always think that Perivale church looks better from Creevy bridge than any other point." Perivale church stood high in the centre of

the town, on an eminence, and was graced with a spire
which was declared by the Perivalians to be preferable to
that of Salisbury in proportion, though it was acknowledged to be somewhat inferior to it in height. The little
river Creevy, which ran through a portion of the suburbs
of the town, and which, as there seen, was hardly more
than a ditch, then sloped away behind Creevy Grange, as
the farm of Mrs. Partridge was called, and was crossed by
a small wooden bridge, from which there was a view not
only of the church, but of all that side of the hill on which
Mrs. Winterfield's large brick house stood conspicuously.
So they walked down to Creevy bridge, and, when there,
stood leaning on the parapet and looking back upon the
town.

"How well I know every house and spot in the place as
I see them from here," he said.

"A good many of the houses are your own,—or will be
some day ; and therefore you should know them."

"I remember, when I used to be here as a boy fishing,
I always thought Aunt Winterfield's house was the biggest
house in the county."

"It can't be nearly so large as your father's house in
Yorkshire."

"No ; certainly it is not. Aylmer Park is a large place ;
but the house does not stretch itself out so wide as that ;
nor does it stand on the side of a hill so as to show out its
proportions with so much ostentation. The coach-house
and the stables, and the old brewhouse, seem to come half
way down the hill. And when I was a boy I had much
more respect for my aunt's red-brick house in Perivale
than I had for Aylmer Park."

"And now it's your own."

"Yes ; now it's my own,—and all my respect for it is
gone. I used to think the Creevy the best river in England for fish ; but I wouldn't give a sixpence now for all
the perch I ever caught in it."

"Perhaps your taste for perch is gone also."

"Yes ; and my taste for jam. I never believed in the
store-room at Aylmer Park as I did in my aunt's store-
room here."

"I don't doubt but what it is full now."

"I dare say ; but I shall never have the curiosity even

to inquire. Ah, dear,—I wish I knew what to do about the house."

" You won't sell it, I suppose ?"

"Not if I could either live in it, or let it. It would be wrong to let it stand idle."

" But you need not decide quite at once."

" That's just what I want to do. I want to decide at once."

" Then I'm sure I cannot advise you. It seems to me very unlikely that you should come and live here by yourself. It isn't like a country-house exactly."

" I shan't live here by myself certainly. You heard what Mrs. Partridge said just now."

" What did Mrs. Partridge say ?"

" She wanted to know whether it belonged to both of us, and whether it was not all one. Shall it be all one, Clara ?"

She was leaning over the rail of the bridge as he spoke, with her eyes fixed on the slowly-moving water. When she heard his words, she raised her face and looked full upon him. She was in some sort prepared for the moment, though it would be untrue to say that she had now expected it. Unconsciously she had made some resolve that if ever the question were put to her by him, she would not be taken altogether off her guard ; and now that the question was put to her, she was able to maintain her composure. Her first feeling was one of triumph,—as it must be in such a position to any woman who has already acknowledged to herself that she loves the man who then asks her to be his wife. She looked up into Captain Aylmer's face, and his eyes almost quailed beneath hers. Even should he be triumphant, he was not perfectly assured that his triumph would be a success.

"Shall what be all one ?" she asked.

" Shall it be your house and my house ? Can you tell me that you will love me and be my wife ?" Again she looked at him, and he repeated his question. " Clara, can you love me well enough to take me for your husband ?"

" I can," she said. Why should she hesitate, and play the coy girl, and pretend to any doubts in her mind which did not exist there ? She did love him, and had so told herself with much earnestness. To him, while his words had been doubtful,—while he had simply played at making love to her, she had given no hint of the state of her affections. She had so carried herself before him as to make him doubt whether success could be possible for him. But now,—why should she hesitate now? It was as she had hoped,—or as she had hardly dared to hope. He did love her. "I can," she said; and then, before he could speak again, she repeated her words with more emphasis. "Indeed I can; with all my heart."

As regarded herself, she was quite equal to the occasion; but had she known more of the inner feelings of men and women in general, she would have been slower to show her own. What is there that any man desires,—any man or any woman,—that does not lose half its value when it is found to be easy of access, and easy of possession? Wine is valued by its price, not its flavour. Open your doors freely to Jones and Smith, and Jones and Smith will not care to enter them. Shut your doors obdurately against the same gentlemen, and they will use all their little diplomacy to effect an entrance. Captain Aylmer, when he heard the hearty tone of the girl's answer, already began almost to doubt whether it was wise on his part to devote the innermost bin of his cellar to wine that was so cheap.

Not that he had any idea of receding. Principle, if not love, prevented that. "Then the question about the house is decided," he said, giving his hand to Clara as he spoke.

"I don't care a bit about the house now," she answered.

"That's unkind."

"I am thinking so much more of you,—of you and of myself. What does an old house matter?"

"It's in very good repair," said Captain Aylmer.

"You must not laugh at me," she said; and in truth he was not laughing at her. "What I mean is that anything about a house is indifferent to me now. It is as though I had got all that I want in the world. Is it wrong of me to say so?"

"Oh, dear, no;—not wrong at all. How can it be wrong?" He did not tell her that he also had got all he wanted; but his lack of enthusiasm in this respect did not surprise her, or at first even vex her. She had always known him to be a man careful of his words,—knowing their value,—not speaking with hurried rashness as would her dear cousin Will. And she doubted whether, after all, such hurried words mean as much as words which are slower and calmer. After all his heat in love and consequent disappointment, Will Belton had left her apparently well contented. His fervour had been short-lived. She loved her cousin dearly, and was so very glad that his fervour had been short-lived!

"When you asked me, I could but tell you the truth," she said, smiling at him.

The truth is very well, but he would have liked it better had the truth come to him by slower degrees. When his aunt had told him to marry Clara Amedroz, he had been at once reconciled to the order by a feeling on his own part that the conquest of Clara would not be too facile. She was a woman of value, not to be snapped up easily,—or by any one. So he had thought then; but he began to fancy now that he had been wrong in that opinion.

The walk back to the house was not of itself very exciting, though to Clara it was a short period of unalloyed bliss. No doubt had then come upon her to cloud her happiness, and she was "wrapped up in measureless content." It was well that they should both be silent at such a moment. Only yesterday had been buried their dear old friend,—the friend who had brought them together, and been so anxious for their future happiness! And Clara Amedroz was not a young girl, prone to jump out of her shoes with elation because she had got a lover. She could be steadily happy without many immediate words about her happiness. When they had reached the house, ·and were once more together in the drawing-room, she again gave him her hand, and was the first to speak. "And you; are you contented?" she asked. Who does not know the smile of triumph with which a girl asks such a question at such a moment as that?

"Contented?—well,—yes; I think I am," he said.

But even those words did not move her to doubt. "If you are," she said, "I am. And now I will leave you till dinner, that you may think over what you have done."

"I had thought about it before, you know," he replied.

Then he stooped over her and kissed her.   It was the first time he had done so; but his kiss was as cold and proper as though they had been man and wife for years!   But it sufficed for her, and she went to her room as happy as a queen.

CHAPTER XI.

MISS AMEDROZ IS TOO CANDID BY HALF.

CLARA, when she left her accepted lover in the drawing-room and went up to her chamber, had two hours for consideration before she would see him again; and she had two hours for enjoyment.   She was very happy.   She thoroughly believed in the man who was to be her husband, feeling confident that he possessed those qualities which she thought to be most necessary for her married happiness.   She had quizzed him at times, pretending to make it matter of accusation against him that his life was not in truth all that his aunt believed it to be;—but had it been more what Mrs. Winterfield would have wished, it would have been less to Clara's taste.   She liked his position in the world; she liked the feeling that he was a man of influence; perhaps she liked to think that to some extent he was a man of fashion.   He was not handsome, but he looked always like a gentleman.   He was well educated, given to reading, prudent, steady in his habits, a man likely to rise in the world; and she loved him.   I fear the reader by this time may have begun to think that her love should never have been given to such a man.   To this accusation I will make no plea at present, but I will ask the complainant whether such men are not always loved.   Much is said of the rashness of women in giving away their hearts wildly; but the charge when made generally is, I think, an unjust one.   I am more often astonished by the prudence of girls than by their recklessness.   A woman of thirty will often love well and not wisely; but the girls of wenty seem to me to like propriety of demeanour, decency of outward life, and a competence.   It is, of course, good that it should be so; but if it is so, they should not also claim a general character for generous and passionate in-

discretion, asserting as their motto that Love shall still be
Lord of All. Clara was more than twenty; but she was
not yet so far advanced in age as to have lost her taste for
decency of demeanour and propriety of life. A Member of
Parliament, with a small house near Eaton Square, with a
moderate income, and a liking for committees, who would
write a pamphlet once every two years, and read Dante
critically during the recess, was, to her, the model for a
husband. For such a one she would read his blue books,
copy his pamphlets, and learn his translations by heart.
She would be safe in the hands of such a man, and would
know nothing of the miseries which her brother had encountered. Her model may not appear, when thus described, to be a very noble one ; but I think it is the model
most approved among ladies of her class in England.

She made up her mind on various points during those
two hours of solitude. In the first place, she would of
course keep her purpose of returning home on the following day. It was not probable that Captain Aylmer would
ask her to change it; but let him ask ever so much it
must not be changed. She must at once have the pleasure
of telling her father that all his trouble about her would
now be over ; and then, there was the consideration that
her further sojourn in the house, with Captain Aylmer as
her lover, would hardly be more proper than it would have
been had he not occupied that position. And what was
she to say if he pressed her as to the time of their marriage? Her aunt's death would of course be a sufficient
reason why it should be delayed for some few months;
and upon the whole, she thought it would be best to postpone it till the next session of Parliament should have
nearly expired. But she would be prepared to yield to
Captain Aylmer, should he name any time after Easter.
It was clearly his intention to keep up the house in Perivale
as his country residence. She did not like Perivale or the
house, but she would say nothing against such an arrangement. Indeed with what face could she do so? She was
going to bring nothing to the common account, —absolutely
nothing but herself! As she thought of this her love grew
warmer, and she hardly knew how sufficiently to testify
to herself her own gratitude and affection.

She became conscious, as she was preparing herself for

dinner, of some special attention to her toilet. She was
more than ordinarily careful with her hair, and felt herself
to be aware of an anxiety to look her best. She had now
been for some time so accustomed to dress herself in black,
that in that respect her aunt's death had made no difference
to her. Deep mourning had ceased from habit to impress
her with any special feeling of funereal solemnity. But
something about herself, or in the room, at last struck her
with awe, bidding her remember how death had of late
been busy among those who had been her dearest and
nearest friends; and she sat down, almost frightened at her
own heartlessness, in that she was allowing herself to be
happy at such a time. Her aunt had been carried away to
her grave only yesterday, and her brother's death had
occurred under circumstances of peculiar distress within
the year;—and yet she was happy, triumphant,—almost
lost in the joy of her own position! She remained for a
while in her chair, with her black dress hanging across
her lap, as she argued with herself as to her own state of
mind. Was it a sign of a hard heart within her, that she
could be happy at such a time? Ought the memory of her
poor brother to have such an effect upon her as to make any
joy of spirits impossible to her? Should she at the present
moment be so crushed by her aunt's demise, as to be incapable of congratulating herself upon her own success?
Should she have told him, when he asked her that question upon the bridge, that there could be no marrying or
giving in marriage between them, no talking on such a
subject in days so full of sorrow as these? I do not know
that she quite succeeded in recognising it as a truth that
sorrow should be allowed to bar out no joy that it does not
bar out of absolute necessity,—by its own weight, without
reference to conventional ideas; that sorrow should never,
under any circumstances, be nursed into activity, as though
it were a thing in itself divine or praiseworthy. I do not
know that she followed out her arguments till she had taught
herself that it is the Love that is divine,—the Love which,
when outraged by death or other severance, produces that
sorrow which man would control if he were strong enough,
but which he cannot control by reason of the weakness of
his humanity. I doubt whether so much as this made
itself plain to her as she sat there before her toilet table,

with her sombre dress hanging from her hands on to
the ground. But something of the strength of such reasoning was hers. Knowing herself to be full of joy, she
would not struggle to make herself believe that it behoved her to be unhappy. She told herself that she
was doing what was good for others as well as for herself;—what would be very good for her father, and what
should be good, if it might be within her power to make
it so, for him who was to be her husband. The black-
ness of the cloud of her brother's death would never altogether pass away from her. It had tended, as she knew
well, to make her serious, grave, and old, in spite of her
own efforts to the contrary. The cloud had been so black
with her that it had nearly lost for her the prize which
was now her own. But she told herself that that black-
ness was an injury to her, and not a benefit, and that
it had now become a duty to her,—for his sake, if not
for her own,—to dispel its shadows rather than encourage
them. She would go down to him full of joy, though
not full of mirth, and would confess to him frankly, that
in receiving the assurance of his love, she had received
everything that had seemed to have any value for her
in the world. Hitherto she had been independent;—she
had specially been careful to show to him her resolve to
be independent of him. Now she would put aside all
that, and let him know that she recognised in him her
lord and master as well as husband. To her father had
been left no strength on which she could lean, and she
had been forced therefore to trust to her own strength.
Now she would be dependent on him, who was to be her
husband. As heretofore she had rejected his offers of
assistance almost with disdain, so now would she accept
them without scruple, looking to him to be her guide in
all things, putting from her that carping spirit in which
she had been wont to judge of his actions, and believing
in him,—as a wife should believe in her husband.

Such were the resolutions which Clara made in the first
hour of solitude which came to her after her engagement;
and they would have been wise resolutions but for this flaw
—that the stronger was submitting itself to the weaker,
the greater to the less, the more honest to the less honest,
that which was nearly true to that which was in great

part false. The theory of man and wife — that special
theory in accordance with which the wife is to bend herself in loving submission before her husband, is very
beautiful ; and would be good altogether if it could only be
arranged that the husband should be the stronger and the
greater of the two.   The theory is based upon that hypothesis ;—and the hypothesis sometimes fails of confirma-
tion.   In ordinary marriages the vessel rights itself, and
the stronger and the greater takes the lead, whether
clothed in petticoats, or in coat, waistcoat, and trousers ;
but there sometimes comes a terrible shipwreck, when the
woman before marriage has filled herself full with ideas
of submission, and then finds that her golden-headed god
has got an iron body and feet of clay.

Captain Aylmer when he was left alone had also something to think about ; and as there were two hours left for
such thought before he would again meet Clara, and as he
had nothing else with which to occupy himself during
those two hours, he again strolled down to the bridge
on which he made his offer. He strolled down there,
thinking that he was thinking, but hardly giving much
mind to his thoughts, which he allowed to run away with
themselves as they listed.   Of course, he was going to be
married.   That was a thing settled.   And he was perfectly
satisfied with himself in that he had done nothing in a
hurry, and could accuse himself of no folly even if he had
no great cause for triumph. He had been long thinking
that he should like to have Clara Amedroz for his wife ;—
long thinking that he would ask her to marry him ; and
having for months indulged such thoughts he could not
take blame to himself for having made to his aunt that
deathbed promise which she had exacted.   At the moment
in which she asked him the question, he was himself
anxious to do the thing she desired of him.   How then
could he have refused her ?   And, having given the promise, it was a matter of course with him to fulfil it.   He
was a man who would have never respected himself again—
would have hated himself for ever, had he failed to keep a promise from which no living being could absolve him.   He had
been right therefore to make the promise, and having made
it, had been right to keep it, and to do the thing at once.
And Clara was very good and very wise, and. sometimes

looked very well, and would never disgrace him; and as
she was in worldly matters to receive much and give
nothing, she would probably be willing to make herself
amenable to any arrangements as to their future mode of
life which he might propose. In respect of this matter he
was probably thinking of lodgings for himself in London
during the parliamentary session, while she remained
alone in the big red house upon which his eyes were fixed
at the time. There was much of convenience in all this
which might perhaps atone to him for the sacrifice which
he was undoubtedly making of himself. Had marriage
simply been of itself a thing desirable he could doubtless
have disposed of himself to better advantage. His prospects, present fortune, and general position were so favourable, that he might have dared to lift his expectations, in
regard both to wealth and rank, very high. The Aylmers
were a considerable people, and he, though a younger
brother, had much more than a younger brother's portion.
His seat in Parliament was safe; his position in society
was excellent and secure; he was exactly so placed that
marriage with a fortune was the only thing wanting to put
the finishing coping-stone to his edifice;—that, and perhaps also the useful glory of having some Lady Mary or
Lady Emily at the top of his table. Lady Emily Aylmer?
Yes;—it would have sounded better, and there was a certain Lady Emily who might have suited. Now, as some
slight regrets stole upon him gently, he failed to remember that this Lady Emily had not a shilling in the
world.

Yes; some faint regrets did steal upon him, though he
went on telling himself that he had acted rightly. His
stars, which were generally very good to him, had not
perhaps on this occasion been as good as usual. No doubt
he had to a certain degree become encumbered with Clara
Amedroz. Had not the direct and immediate leap with
which she had come into his arms shown him somewhat
too plainly that one word of his mouth tending towards
matrimony had been regarded by her as being too valuable
to be lost? The fruit that falls easily from the tree,
though it is ever the best, is never valued by the gardener.
Let him have well-nigh broken his neck in gathering it,
unripe and crude, from the small topmost boughs of the

branching tree, and the pippin will be esteemed by him as invaluable. On that morning, as Captain Aylmer had walked home from church, he had doubted much what would be Clara's answer to him. Then the pippin was at the end of the dangerous bough. Now it had fallen to his feet, and he did not scruple to tell himself that it was his and always might have been his as a matter of course. Well, the apple had come of a good kind, and, though there might be specks upon it, though it might not be fit for any special glory of show or pride of place among the dessert service, still it should be garnered and used, and no doubt would be a very good apple for eating. Having so concluded, Captain Aylmer returned to the house, washed his hands, changed his boots, and went down to the drawing-room just as dinner was ready.

She came up to him almost radiant with joy, and put her hand upon his arm. " Martha did not know but what you were here," she said, " and told them to put dinner on the table."

" I hope I have not kept you waiting."

" Oh, dear, no. And what if you did ? Ladies never care about things getting cold. It is gentlemen only who have feelings in such matters as that."

" I don't know that there is much difference; but, however——" Then they were in the dining-room, and as the servant remained there during dinner, there was nothing in their conversation worth repeating. After dinner they still remained down stairs, seating themselves on the two sides of the fire, Clara having fully resolved that she would not on such an evening as this leave Captain Aylmer to drink his glass of port wine by himself.

" I suppose I may stay with you, mayn't I ?" she said.

" Oh, dear, yes ; I'm sure I'm very much obliged. I'm not at all wedded to solitude." Then there was a slight pause.

" That's lucky," she said, "as you have made up your mind to be wedded in another sort of way." Her voice as she spoke was very low, but there was a gentle ring of restrained joyousness in it which ought to have gone at once to his heart and made him supremely blessed for the time.

" Well,—yes," he answered. " We are in for it now, both of us ;—are we not ? I hope you have no misgivings about it, Clara !"

" Who; I? I have misgivings? No, indeed. I have
no misgivings, Frederic; no doubts, no scruples, no alloy
in my happiness. With me it is all as I would have it be.
Ah; you haven't understood why it has been that I have
seemed to be harsh to you when we have met."

" No, I have not," said he. This was true; but it is
true also that it would have been well that he should be
kept in his ignorance. She was minded, however, to tell
him everything, and therefore she went on.

" I don't know how to tell you; and yet, circumstanced
as we are now, it seems that I ought to tell you everything."

" Yes, certainly; I think that," said Aylmer. He was
one of those men who consider themselves entitled to see,
hear, and know every little detail of a woman's conduct, as
a consequence of the circumstances of his engagement, and
who consider themselves shorn of their privilege if anything be kept back. If any gentleman had said a soft word
to Clara eight years ago, that soft word ought to be repeated
to him now. I am afraid that these particular gentlemen
sometimes hear some fibs; and I often wonder that their
own early passages in the tournays of love do not warn
them that it must be so. When James has sat deliciously
through all the moonlit night with his arm round Mary's
waist, and afterwards sees Mary led to the altar by John,
does it not occur to him that some John may have also sat
with his arm round Anna's waist—that Anna whom he is
leading to the altar? These things should not be inquired
into too curiously; but the curiosity of some men on such
matters has no end. For the most part, women like telling,
—only they do not choose to be pressed beyond their own
modes of utterance. " I should like to know that I have
your full confidence," said he.

" You have got my full confidence," she replied.

" I mean that you should tell me anything that there is
to be told."

" It was only this; that I had learned to love you before
I thought that my love would be returned."

" Oh;—was that it?" said Captain Aylmer, in a tone
which seemed to imply something like disappointment.

" Yes, Fred; that was it. And how could I, under such
circumstances, trust myself to be gentle with you, or to

look to you for assistance ?   How could I guess then all
that I know now ?"

" Of course you couldn't."

" And therefore I was driven to be harsh. My aunt
used to speak to me about it."

" I don't wonder at that, for she was very anxious that
we should be married."

Clara for a moment felt herself to be uncomfortable as
she heard these words, half perceiving that they implied
some instigation on the part of Mrs. Winterfield. Could
it be that Captain Aylmer's offer had been made in obedience to a promise ? " Did you know of her anxiety ?"
she asked.

" Well ;—yes ; that is to say, I guessed it. It was
natural enough that the same idea should come to her and
to me too. Of course, seeing us so much thrown together,
she could not but think of our being married as a chance
upon the cards."

" She used to tell me that I was harsh to you ;—abrupt,
she called it. But what could I do ? I'll tell you, Fred,
how I first found out that I really cared for you. What I
tell you now is of course a secret ; and I should speak of
it to no one under any circumstances but those which unite
us two together. My cousin Will, when he was at Belton,
made me an offer."

" He did, did he ? You did not tell me that when you
were saying all those fine things in his praise in the railway
carriage."

" Of course I did not. Why should I ? I wasn't bound
to tell you my secrets then, sir."

" But he did absolutely offer to you ?"

" Is there anything so wonderful in that ? But, wonderful
or not, he did."

" And you refused him ?"

" I refused him, certainly."

" It wouldn't have been a bad match, if all that you say
about his property is true."

" If you come to that, it would have been a very good
match ; and perhaps you think I was silly to decline it ?"

" I don't say that."

" Papa thought so ;—but, then, I couldn't tell papa the
whole truth, as I can tell it to you now, Captain Aylmer. I

couldn't tell dear papa that my heart was not my own to
give to my cousin Will; nor could I give Will any such
reason. Poor Will! I could only say to him bluntly
that I wouldn't have him."

"And you would, if it hadn't been,—hadn't been—for
me."

"Nay, Fred; there you tax me too far. What might
have come of my heart if you hadn't fallen in my way, who
can say? I love Will Belton dearly, and hope that you
may do so——"

"I must see him first."

"Of course;—but, as I was saying, I doubt whether,
under any circumstances, he would have been the man I
should have chosen for a husband. But as it was,—it was
impossible. Now you know it all, and I think that I have
been very frank with you."

"Oh! very frank." He would not take her little jokes,
nor understand her little prettinesses. That he was a man
not prone to joking she knew well, but still it went against
the grain with her to find that he was so very hard in his
replies to her attempts.

It was not easy for Clara to carry on the conversation
after this, so she proposed that they should go upstairs into
the drawing-room. Such a change even as that would
throw them into a different way of talking, and prevent
the necessity of any further immediate allusion to Will
Belton. For Clara was aware, though she hardly knew
why, that her frankness to her future husband had hardly
been successful, and she regretted that she had on this
occasion mentioned her cousin's name. They went upstairs
and again sat themselves in chairs over the fire; but for a
while conversation did not seem to come to them freely.
Clara felt that it was now Captain Aylmer's turn to begin,
and Captain Aylmer felt—that he wished he could read the
newspaper. He had nothing in particular that he desired
to say to his lady-love. That morning, as he was shaving
himself, he had something to say that was very particular,
—as to which he was at that moment so nervous that he
had cut himself slightly through the trembling of his hand.
But that had now been said, and he was nervous no longer.
That had now been said, and the thing settled so easily,
that he wondered at his own nervousness. He did not

know that there was anything that required much further immediate speech. Clara had thought somewhat of the time which might be proposed for their marriage, making some little resolves, with which the reader is already acquainted ; but no ideas of this kind presented themselves to Captain Aylmer. He had asked his cousin to be his wife, thereby making good his promise to his aunt. There could be no further necessity for pressing haste. Sufficient for the day is the evil thereof.

It is not to be supposed that the thriving lover actually spoke to himself in such language as that,—or that he confessed to himself that Clara Amedroz was an evil to him rather than a blessing. But his feelings were already so far tending in that direction, that he was by no means disposed to make any further promise, or to engage himself in closer connection with matrimony by the mention of any special day. Clara, finding that her companion would not talk without encouragement from her, had to begin again, and asked all those natural questions about his family, his brother, his sister, his home habits, and the old house in Yorkshire, the answers to which must be so full of interest to her. But even on these subjects he was dry, and indisposed to answer with the full copiousness of free communication which she desired. And at last there came a question and an answer,—a word or two on one side, and then a word or two on the other, from which Clara got a wound which was very sore to her.

"I have always pictured to myself," she said, "your mother as a woman who has been very handsome."

"She is still a handsome woman, though she is over sixty."

"Tall, I suppose ?"

"Yes, tall, and with something of—of—what shall I say —dignity, about her."

"She is not grand, I hope."

"I don't know what you call grand."

"Not grand in a bad sense ;—I'm sure she's not that. But there are some ladies who seem to stand so high above the level of ordinary females as to make us who are ordinary quite afraid of them."

"My mother is certainly not ordinary," said Captain Aylmer.

"And I am," said Clara, laughing. "I wonder what she'll say to me,—or, rather, what she will think of me." Then there was a moment's silence, after which Clara, still laughing, went on. "I see, Fred, that you have not a word of encouragement to give me about your mother."

"She is rather particular," said Captain Aylmer.

Then Clara drew herself up, and ceased to laugh. She had called herself ordinary with that half-insincere depreciation of self which is common to all of us when we speak of our own attributes, but which we by no means intend that they who hear us shall accept as strictly true, or shall re-echo as their own approved opinions. But in this instance Captain Aylmer, though he had not quite done that, had done almost as bad.

"Then I suppose I had better keep out of her way," said Clara, by no means laughing as she spoke.

"Of course when we are married you must go and see her."

You do not, at any rate, promise me a very agreeable visit, Fred. But I dare say I shall survive it. After all, it is you that I am to marry, and not your mother; and as long as you are not majestic to me, I need not care for her majesty."

"I don't know what you mean by majesty."

"You must confess that you speak of her as of something very terrible."

"I say that she is particular;—and so she is. And as my respect for her opinion is equal to my affection for her person, I hope that you will make a great effort to gain her esteem."

"I never make any efforts of that kind. If esteem doesn't come without efforts it isn't worth having."

"There I disagree with you altogether:—but I especially disagree with you as you are speaking about my mother, and about a lady who is to become your own mother-in-law. I trust that you will make such efforts, and that you will make them successfully. Lady Aylmer is not a woman who will give you her heart at once, simply because you have become her son's wife. She will judge you by your own qualities, and will not scruple to condemn you should she see cause."

Then there was a longer silence, and Clara's heart was

almost in rebellion even on this, the first day of her engagement. But she quelled her high spirit, and said no further word about Lady Aylmer. Nor did she speak again till she had enabled herself to smile as she spoke.

"Well, Fred," she said, putting her hand upon his arm, "I'll do my best, and woman can do no more. And now I'll say good night, for I must pack for to-morrow's journey before I go to bed." Then he kissed her,—with a cold, chilling kiss,—and she left him for the night.

CHAPTER XII.

MISS AMEDROZ RETURNS HOME.

CLARA was to start by a train leaving Perivale at eight on the following morning, and therefore there was not much time for conversation before she went. During the night she had endeavoured so to school herself as to banish from her breast all feeling of anger against her lover, and of regret as regarded herself. Probably, as she told herself, she had made more of what he had said than he had intended that she should do; and then, was it not natural that he should think much of his mother, and feel anxious as to the way in which she might receive his wife? As to that feeling of anger on her own part, she did get quit of it;—but the regret was not to be so easily removed. It was not only what Captain Aylmer had said about his mother that clung to her, doing much to quench her joy; but there had been a coldness in his tone to her throughout the evening which she recognised almost unconsciously, and which made her heart heavy in spite of the joy which she repeatedly told herself ought to be her own. And she also felt,—though she was not clearly aware that she did so,—that his manner towards her had become less affectionate, less like that of a lover, since the honest tale she had told him of her own early love for him. She should have been less honest, and more discreet; less bold, and more like in her words to the ordinary run of women. She had known this as she was packing last night, and she told herself that it was so as she was dressing on this her last morning at Perivale. That frankness of hers had not been successful, and she regretted that she had not imposed on herself some little reticence,— or even a little of that coy pretence of indifference which is so often used by ladies when they are wooed. She had been boldly honest, and had found her honesty to be bad policy. She thought, at least, that she had found its policy to be bad. Whether in truth it may not have been very good,—have been the best policy in the world,—tending to give her the first true intimation which she had ever yet received of the real character of the man who was now so much to her,—that is altogether another question.

But it was clearly her duty to make the best of her present circumstances, and she went down-stairs with a smiling face and with pleasant words on her tongue. When she entered the breakfast-room, Captain Aylmer was there; but Martha was there also, and her pleasant words were received indifferently in the presence of the servant. When the old woman was gone, Captain Aylmer assumed a grave face, and began a serious little speech which he had prepared. But he broke down in the utterance of it, and was saying things very different from what he had intended before he had completed it.

"Clara," he began, "what occurred between us yesterday is a source of great satisfaction to me."

"I am glad of that, Frederick," said she, trying to be a little less serious than her lover.

"Of very great satisfaction," he continued; "and I cannot but think that we were justified by the circumstances of our position in forgetting for a time the sad solemnity of the occasion. When I remember that it was but the day before yesterday that I followed my dear old aunt to the grave, I am astonished to think that yesterday I should have made an offer of marriage."

What could be the good of his talking in this strain? Clara, too, had had her own misgivings on the same subject, —little qualms of conscience that had come to her as she remembered her old friend in the silent watches of the night; but such thoughts were for the silent watches, and not for open expression in the broad daylight. But he had paused, and she must say something.

"One's excuse to oneself is this,—that she would have wished it so."

"Exactly. She would have wished it. Indeed she did wish it, and therefore——" He paused in what he was saying, and felt himself to be on difficult ground. Her eye was full upon him, and she waited for a moment or two as though expecting that he would finish his words. But as he did not go on, she finished them for him.

"And therefore you sacrificed your own feelings." Her heart was becoming sore, and she was unable to restrain the utterance of her sarcasm.

"Just so," said he; "or, rather, not exactly that. I don't mean that I am sacrificed; for, of course, as I have just now said, nothing as regards myself can be more satisfactory. But yesterday should have been a solemn day to us; and as it was not——"

"I thought it very solemn."

"What I mean is that I find an excuse in remembering that I was doing what she asked me to do."

"What she asked you to do, Fred?"

"What I had promised, I mean."

"What you had promised? I did not hear that before." These last words were spoken in a very low voice, but they went direct to Captain Aylmer's ears.

"But you have heard me declare," he said, "that as regards myself nothing could be more satisfactory."

"Fred," she said, "listen to me for a moment. You and engaged ourselves to each other yesterday as man and wife."

"Of course we did."

"Listen to me, dear Fred. In doing that there was nothing in my mind unbefitting the sadness of the day. Even in death we must think of life, and if it were well for you and me that we should be together, it would surely have been but a foolish ceremony between us to have abstained from telling each other that it would be so, because my aunt had died last week. But it may be, and I think it is the case, that the feelings arising from her death have made us both too precipitate."

"I don't understand how that can be."

"You have been anxious to keep a promise made to her, without considering sufficiently whether in doing so you would secure your own happiness; and I——"

" I don't know about you, but as regards myself I must
be considered to be the best judge."

" And I have been too much in a hurry in believing
that which I wished to believe."

" What do you mean by all this, Clara ?"

" I mean that our engagement shall be at an end ;—not
necessarily so for always. But that as an engagement
binding us both, it shall for the present cease to exist.
You shall be again free——"

" But I don't choose to be free."

" When you think of it you will find it best that it
should be so. You have performed your promise honestly,
even though at a sacrifice to yourself. Luckily for you,—
for both of us, I should say,—the full truth has come out ;
and we can consider quietly what will be best for us to do,
independently of that promise. We will part, therefore,
as dear friends, but not as engaged to each other as man
and wife."

" But we are engaged, and I will not hear of its being
broken."

" A lady's word, Fred, is always the most potential
before marriage ;—and you must therefore yield to me in
this matter. I am sure your judgment will approve of my
decision when you think of it. There shall be no engagement between us. I shall consider myself quite free,—
free to do as I please altogether ; and you, of course, will
be free also."

" If you please, of course it must be so."

" I do please, Fred."

" And yesterday, then, is to go for nothing."

" Not exactly. It cannot go for nothing with me. I told
you too many of my secrets for that. But nothing that
was done or said yesterday is to be held as binding upon
either of us."

" And you made up your mind to that last night ?"

" It is at any rate made up to that now. Come,—I shall
have to go without my breakfast if I do not eat it at once.
Will you have your tea now, or wait and take it comfortably when I am gone ?"

Captain Aylmer breakfasted with her, and took her to
the station, and saw her off with all possible courtesy and
attention, and then he walked back by himself to his own

great house in Perivale. Not a word more had been said
between him and Clara as to their engagement, and he
recognised it as a fact that he was no longer bound to her
as her future husband. Indeed, he had no power of not
recognising the fact, so decided had been her language, and
so imperious her manner. It had been of no avail that he
had said that the engagement should stand. She had told
him that her voice was to be the more potential, and he
had felt that it was so. Well;—might it not be best for
him that it should be so? He had kept his promise to his
aunt, and had done all that lay in his power to make Clara
Amedroz his wife. If she chose to rebel against her own
good fortune simply because he spoke to her a few words
which seemed to him to be fitting, might it not be well for
him to take her at her word?

Such were his first thoughts; but as the day wore on
with him, something more generous in his nature came to
his aid, and something also that was akin to real love.
Now that she was no longer his own, he again felt a desire
to have her. Now that there would be again something to
be done in winning her, he was again stirred by a man's
desire to do that something. He ought not to have told
her of the promise. He was aware that what he had said
on that point had been dropped by him accidentally,
and that Clara's resolution after that had not been unnatural. He would, therefore, give her another chance,
and resolved before he went to bed that night that he
would allow a fortnight to pass away, and would then
write to her, renewing his offer with all the strongest
declarations of affection which he would be enabled to
make.

Clara on her way home was not well satisfied with herself or with her position. She had had great joy, during
the few hours of joy which had been hers, in thinking of
the comfort which her news would give to her father. He
would be released from all further trouble on her account
by the tidings which she would convey to him,—by the
tidings which she had intended to convey to him. But
now the story which she would have to tell would by no
means be comfortable. She would have to explain to him
that her aunt had left no provision for her, and that would
be the beginning and the end of her story. As for those

conversations about the fifteen hundred pounds,—of them she would say nothing. When she reflected on what had taken place between herself and Captain Aylmer she was more resolved than ever that she would not touch any portion of that money,—or of any money that should come from him. Nor would she tell her father anything of the marriage engagement which had been made on one day and unmade on the next. Why should she add to his distress by showing him what good things might have been hers had she only had the wit to keep them? No; she would tell her father simply of the will, and then comfort him in his affliction as best she might.

As regarded her position with Captain Aylmer, the more she though of it the more sure she became that everything was over in that quarter. She had, indeed, told him that such need not necessarily be the case,—but this she had done in her desire at the moment to mitigate the apparent authoritativeness of her own decision, rather than with any idea of leaving the matter open for further consideration. She was sure that Captain Aylmer would be glad of a means of escape, and that he would not again place himself in the jeopardy which the promise exacted from him by his aunt had made so nearly fatal to him. And for herself, though she still loved the man,—so loved him that she lay back in the corner of her carriage weeping behind her veil as she thought of what she had lost,—still she would not take him, though he should again press his suit upon her with all the ardour at his command. No, indeed. No man should ever be made to regard her as a burden imposed upon him by an extorted promise! What;—let a man sacrifice himself to a sense of duty on her behalf! And then she repeated the odious words to herself, till she came to think that it had fallen from his lips and not from her own.

In writing to her father from Perivale, she had merely told him of Mrs. Winterfield's death, and of her own intended return. At the Taunton station she met the well-known old fly and the well-known old driver, and was taken home in the accustomed manner. As she drew nearer to Belton the sense of her distress became stronger and stronger, till at last she almost feared to meet her father. What could she say to him when he should repeat to her, as he would be sure to do, his lamentation as to her future poverty?

On arriving at the house she learned that he was up-stairs in his bedroom. He had been ill, the servant said, and though he was not now in bed, he had not come down stairs. So she ran up to his room, and finding him seated in an old arm-chair by the fire-side, knelt down at his feet, as she took his hand and asked him as to his health.

"What has Mrs. Winterfield done for you in her will?" These were the first words he spoke to her.

"Never mind about wills now, papa. I want you to tell me of yourself."

"Nonsense, Clara. Answer my question."

"Oh, papa, I wish you would not think so much about money for me."

"Not think about it? Why am I not to think about it? What else have I got to think of? Tell me at once, Clara, what she has done. You ought to have written to me directly the will was made known."

There was no help for her, and the terrible word must be spoken. "She has left her property to Captain Aylmer, papa; and I must say that I think she is right."

"You do not mean everything."

"She has provided for her servants."

"And has made no provision for you?"

"No, papa."

"Do you mean to tell me that she has left you nothing, absolutely nothing?" The old man's manner was alto-gether altered as he asked this question; and there came over his face so unusual a look of energy,—of the energy of anger,—that Clara was frightened, and knew not how to answer him with that tone of authority which she was accustomed to use when she found it necessary to exercise control over him. "Do you mean to say that there is nothing,—nothing?" And as he repeated the question he pushed her away from his knees and stood up with an effort, leaning against the back of his chair.

"Dear papa, do not let this distress you."

"But is it so? Is there in truth nothing?"

"Nothing, papa. Remember that she was not really my aunt."

"Nonsense, child;—nonsense! How can you talk such

trash to me as that? And then you tell me not to distress myself! I am to know that you will be a beggar in a year or two,—probably in a few months,—and that is not to distress me! She has been a wicked woman!"

"Oh, papa, do not say that."

"A wicked woman. A very wicked woman. It is always so with those who pretend to be more religious than their neighbours. She has been a very wicked woman, alluring you into her house with false hopes."

"No, papa;—no; I must contradict you. She had given me no ground for such hope."

"I say she had,—even though she may not have made a promise. I say she had. Did not everybody think that you were to have her money?"

"I don't know what people may have thought. Nobody has had any right to think about it at all."

"That is nonsense, Clara. You know that I expected it; —that you expected it yourself."

"No;—no, no!"

"Clara,—how can you tell me that?"

"Papa, I knew that she intended to leave me nothing. She told me so when I was there in the spring."

"She told you so?"

"Yes, papa. She told me that Frederic Aylmer was to have all her property. She explained to me everything that she meant to do, and I thought that she was right."

"And why was not I told when you came home?"

"Dear papa!"

"Dear papa, indeed. What is the meaning of dear papa? Why have I been deceived?"

"What good could I do by telling you? You could not change it."

"You have been very undutiful; and as for her, her wickedness and cruelty shock me,—shock me. They do, indeed. That she should have known your position, and had you with her always,—and then have made such a will as that! Quite heartless! She must have been quite heartless."

Clara now began to find that she must in justice to her aunt's memory tell her father something more. And yet it would be very difficult to tell him anything that would not bring greater affliction upon him, and would not also lead her into deeper trouble. Should it come to pass that her aunt's intention with reference to the fifteen hundred pounds was mentioned, she would be subjected to an endless persecution as to the duty of accepting that money from Captain Aylmer. But her present feelings would have made her much prefer to beg her bread upon the roads than accept her late lover's generosity. And then again, how could she explain to her father Mrs. Winterfield's mistake about her own position without seeming to accuse her father of having robbed her? But nevertheless she must say something, as Mr. Amedroz continued to apply that epithet of heartless to Mrs. Winterfield, going on with it in a low droning tone, that was more injurious to Clara's ears than the first full energy of his anger. " Heartless, — quite heartless; — shockingly heartless,— shockingly heartless!"

" The truth is, papa," Clara said at last, " that when my aunt told me about her will, she did not know but what I had some adequate provision from my own family."

" Oh, Clara!"

" That is the truth, papa ;—for she explained the whole thing to me. I could not tell her that she was mistaken, and thus ask for her money."

" But she knew everything about that poor wretched boy." And now the father dropped back into his chair, and buried his face in his hands.

When he did this Clara again knelt at his feet. She felt that she had been cruel, and that she had defended her aunt at the cost of her own father. She had, as it were, thrown in his teeth his own imprudence, and twitted him with the injuries which he had done to her. " Papa," she said, " dear papa, do not think about it at all. What is the use ? After all, money is not everything. I care nothing for money. If you will only agree to banish the subject altogether, we shall be so comfortable."

" How is it to be banished ?"

" At any rate we need not speak of it. Why should we talk on a subject which is simply uncomfortable, and which we cannot mend ?"

" Oh dear, oh dear, oh dear !" and now he swayed himself backwards and forwards in his chair, bewailing his own condition and hers, and his past imprudence, while the

tears ran down his cheeks. She still knelt there at his
feet, looking up into his face with loving, beseeching eyes,
praying him to be comforted, and declaring that all would
still be well if he would only forget the subject, or, at any
rate, cease to speak of it. But still he went on wailing,
complaining of his lot as a child complains, and refusing
all consolation. "Yes; I know," said he, "it has all been
my fault. But how could I help it? What was I to do?"

"Papa, nobody has said that anything was your fault;
nobody has thought so."

"I never spent anything on myself—never, never; and
yet,—and yet,—and yet——!"

"Look at it with more courage, papa. After all, what
harm will it be if I should have to go out and earn my own
bread like any other young woman? I am not afraid."

At last he wept himself into an apathetic tranquillity, as though he had at present no further power for
any of the energy of grief; and she left him while she
went about the house and learned how things had gone
on during her absence. It seemed, from the tidings
which the servant gave her, that he had been ill almost
since she had been gone. He had, at any rate, chosen to
take his meals in his own room, and, as far as was remembered, had not once left the house since she had been
away. He had on two or three occasions spoken of Mr.
Belton, appearing to be anxious for his coming, and asking
questions as to the cattle and the work that was still going
on about the place; and Clara, when she returned to his
room, tried to interest him again about her cousin. But
he had in truth been too much distressed by the ill news
as to Mrs. Winterfield's will to be able to rally himself, and
the evening that was spent up in his room was very comfortless to both of them. Clara had her own sorrows to
bear as well as her father's, and could take no pleasant look
out into the world of her own circumstances. She had
gained her lover merely to lose him,—and had lost him
under circumstances that were very painful to her woman's
feeling. Though he had been for one night betrothed to
her as her husband, he had never loved her. He had asked
her to be his wife simply in fulfilment of a deathbed promise! The more she thought of it the more bitter did the
idea of it become to her. And she could not also but

think of her cousin. Poor Will! He, at any rate, had
loved her, though his eagerness in love had been, as she
told herself, but short-lived. As she thought of him, it
seemed but the other day that he had been with her up on
the rock in the park;—but as she thought of Captain
Aylmer, to whom she had become engaged only yesterday,
and from whom she had separated herself only that morning, she felt that an eternity of time had passed since she
had departed from him.

On the following day, a dull, dark, melancholy day, towards the end of November, she went out to saunter about
the park, leaving her father still in his bedroom, and after
a while made her way down to the cottage. She found
Mrs. Askerton as usual alone in the little drawing-room,
sitting near the window with a book in her hand; but
Clara knew at once that her friend had not been reading,—
that she had been sitting there looking out upon the clouds,
with her mind fixed upon things far away. The general
cheerfulness of this woman had often been cause of wonder
to Clara, who knew how many of her hours were passed in
solitude; but there did occasionally come upon her periods
of melancholy in which she was unable to act up to the
settled rule of her life, and in which she would confess that
the days and weeks and months were too long for her.

"So you are back," said Mrs. Askerton, as soon as the
first greeting was over.

"Yes; I am back."

"I supposed you would not stay there long after the
funeral."

"No; what good could I do?"

"And Captain Aylmer is still there, I suppose?"

"I left him at Perivale."

There was a slight pause, as Mrs. Askerton hesitated
before she asked her next question. "May I be told anything about the will?" she said.

"The weary will! If you knew how I hated the
subject you would not ask me. But you must not think I
hate it because it has given me nothing."

"Given you nothing?"

"Nothing! But that does not make me hate it. It is
the nature of the subject that is so odious. I have now
told you all,—everything that there is to be told, though

we were to talk for a week. If you are generous you will
not say another word about it."

"But I am so sorry."

"There,—that's it. You won't perceive that the expression of such sorrow is a personal injury to me. I don't
want you to be sorry." ·

"How am I to help it?"

"You need not express it. I don't come pitying you for
supposed troubles. You have plenty of money; but if
you were so poor that you could eat nothing but cold
mutton, I shouldn't condole with you as to the state of
your larder. I should pretend to think that poultry and
piecrust were plentiful with you."

"No, you wouldn't, dear;—not if I were as dear to you
as you are to me."

"Well, then, be sorry; and let there be an end of it.
Remember how much of all this I must of necessity have
to go through with poor papa."

"Ah, yes; I can believe that."

"And he is so far from well. Of course you have not
seen him since I have been gone."

"No; we never see him unless he comes up to the gate
there." Then there was another pause for a moment.
"And what about Captain Aylmer?" asked Mrs. Askerton.

"Well;—what about him?"

"He is the heir now?"

"Yes;—he is the heir."

"And that is all?"

"Yes; that is all. What more should there be? The
poor old house at Perivale will be shut up, I suppose."

"I don't care about the old house much, as it is not to
be your house."

"No; it is not to be my house certainly."

"There were two ways in which it might have become
yours."

"Though there were ten ways, none of those ways have
come my way," said Clara.

"Of course I know that you are so close that though
there were anything to tell you would not tell it."

"I think I would tell you anything that was proper to
be told; but now there is nothing proper,—or improper."

"Was it proper or improper when Mr. Belton made an

offer to you,—as I knew he would do, of course; as I told you that he would? Was that so improper that it could not be told?"

Clara was aware that the tell-tale colour in her face at once took from her the possibility of even pretending that the allegation was untrue, and that in any answer she might give she must acknowledge the fact. "I do not think," she said, "that it is considered fair to gentlemen to tell such stories as that."

"Then I can only say that the young ladies I have known are generally very unfair."

"But who told you?"

"Who told me? My maid. Of course she got it from yours. Those things are always known."

"Poor Will!"

"Poor Will indeed. He is coming here again, I hear, almost immediately, and it needn't be 'Poor Will' unless you like it. But as for me, I am not going to be an advocate in his favour. I tell you fairly that I did not like what little I saw of poor Will."

"I like him of all things."

"You should teach him to be a little more courteous in his demeanour to ladies : that is all. I will tell you something else, too, about poor Will—but not now. Some other day I will tell you something of your cousin Will."

Clara did not care to ask any questions as to this something that was to be told, and therefore took her leave and went away.

CHAPTER XIII.

MR. WILLIAM BELTON TAKES A WALK IN THE COUNTRY.

CLARA AMEDROZ had made one great mistake about her cousin, Will Belton, when she came to the conclusion that she might accept his proffered friendship without any apprehension that the friend would become a lover ; and she made another, equally great, when she convinced herself that his love had been as short-lived as it had been eager. Throughout his journey back to Plaistow he had

thought of nothing else but his love, and had resolved to
persevere, telling himself sometimes that he might perhaps
be successful, and feeling sure at other times that he would
encounter renewed sorrow and permanent disappointment,
—but equally resolved in either mood that he would persevere. Not to persevere in pursuit of any desired object,—
let the object be what it might,—was, to his thinking,
unmanly, weak, and destructive of self-respect. He would
sometimes say of himself, joking with other men, that if
he did not succeed in this or that thing, he could never
speak to himself again. To no man did he talk of
his love in such a strain as this; but there was a woman
to whom he spoke of it; and though he could not joke on
such a matter, the purport of what he said showed the
same feeling. To be finally rejected, and to put up with
such rejection, would make him almost contemptible in his
own eyes.

This woman was his sister, Mary Belton. Something
has been already said of this lady, which the reader may
perhaps remember. She was a year or two older than her
brother, with whom she always lived; but she had none of
those properties of youth which belonged to him in such
abundance. She was, indeed, a poor cripple, unable to
walk beyond the limits of her own garden, feeble in health,
dwarfed in stature, robbed of all the ordinary enjoyments
of life by physical deficiencies, which made even the task
of living a burden to her. To eat was a pain, or at best a
trouble. Sleep would not comfort her in bed, and weari-
ness during the day made it necessary that the hours
passed in bed should be very long. She was one of those
whose lot in life drives us to marvel at the inequalities of
human destiny, and to inquire curiously within ourselves
whether future compensation is to be given.

It is said of those who are small and crooked-backed in
their bodies, that their minds are equally cross-grained, and
their tempers as ungainly as their stature. But no one
had ever said this of Mary Belton. Her friends, indeed,
were very few in number; but those who knew her well,
loved her as they knew her, and there were three or four
persons in the world who were ready at all times to swear
that she was faultless. It was the great happiness of her
life that among those three or four her own brother was the

foremost. Will Belton's love for his sister amounted almost to veneration; and his devotion to her was so great, that in all the affairs of his life he was prepared to make her comfort one of his first considerations. And she, knowing this, had come to fear that she might be an embargo on his prosperity, and a stumbling-block in the way of his success. It had occurred to her that he would have married earlier in life if she had not been, as it were, in his way; and she had threatened him playfully,—for she could be playful,—that she would leave him if he did not soon bring a mistress home to Plaistow Hall. " I will go to uncle Robert," she had said. Now, uncle Robert was the clergyman in Lincolnshire of whom mention has been made, and he was among those two or three who believed in Mary Belton with an implicit faith,—as was also his wife. " I will go to uncle Robert, Will, and then you will be driven to get a wife."

" If my sister ever leaves my house, whether there be a wife in it or not," Will had answered, " I will never put trust in any woman again."

Plaistow Manorhouse or Hall was a fine brick mansion, built in the latter days of Tudor house architecture, with many gables and countless high chimneys,—very picturesque to the eye, but not in all respects comfortable as are the modern houses of the well-to-do squirearchy of England. And, indeed, it was subject to certain objectionable characteristics which in some degree justified the scorn which Mr. Amedroz intended to throw upon it when he declared it to be a farmhouse. The gardens belonging to it were large and excellent; but they did not surround it, and allowed the farm appurtenances to come close up to it on two sides. The door which should have been the front door, opening from the largest room in the house, which had been the hall and which was now the kitchen, led directly into the farmyard. From the further end of this farmyard a magnificent avenue of elms stretched across the home pasture down to a hedge which crossed it at the bottom. That there had been a road through the rows of trees—or, in other words, that there had in truth been an avenue to the house on that side,—was, of course, certain. But now there was no vestige of such road, and the front entrance to Plaistow Hall was by a little path across the garden from a modern road which had been made to run cruelly near to the house. Such was Plaistow Hall, and such was its mistress. Of the master, the reader, I hope, already knows so much as to need no further description.

As Belton drove himself home from the railway-station late on that August night, he made up his mind that he would tell his sister all his story about Clara Amedroz. She had ever wished that he should marry, and now he had made his attempt. Little as had been her opportunity of learning the ways of men and women from experience in society, she had always seemed to him to know exactly what every one should do in every position of life. And she would be tender with him, giving him comfort even if she could not give him hope. Moreover, Mary might be trusted with his secret; for Belton felt, as men always do feel, a great repugnance to have it supposed that his suit to a woman had been rejected. Women, when they have loved in vain, often almost wish that their misfortune should be known. They love to talk about their wounds mystically,—telling their own tales under feigned names, and extracting something of a bitter sweetness out of the sadness of their own romance. But a man when he has been rejected,—rejected with a finality that is acknowledged by himself,—is unwilling to speak or hear a word upon the subject, and would willingly wash the episode out from his heart if it were possible.

But not on that his first night would he begin to speak of Clara Amedroz. He would not let his sister believe that his heart was too full of the subject to allow of his thinking of other matters. Mary was still up, waiting for him when he arrived, with tea, and cream, and fruit ready for him. "Oh, Mary!" he said, "why are you not in bed? You know that I would have come to you upstairs. She excused herself smiling, declaring that she could not deny herself the pleasure of being with him for half an hour on his first return from his travels. "Of course I want to know what they are like," she said.

"He is a nice-looking old man," said Will, "and she is a nice-looking young woman."

"That is graphic and short, at any rate."

" And he is weak and silly, but she is strong and—and .— and——"

" Not silly also, l hope ?"

" Anything but that. I should say she is very clever."

" I'm afraid you don t like her, Will."

' Yes, I do."

" Really ?"

" Yes ; really."

" And did she take your coming well ?"

" Very well. I think she is much obliged to me for going."

" And Mr. Amedroz ?"

" He liked my coming too,—very much."

" What—after that cold letter ?"

" Yes, indeed. I shall explain it all by degrees. I have taken a lease of all the land, and I'm to go back at Christmas ; and as to the old gentleman,—he'd have me live there altogether if I would."

" Why, Will ?"

" Is it not odd ? I'm so glad I didn't make up my mind not to go when I got that letter. And yet I don't know." These last words he added slowly, and in a low voice, and Mary at once knew that everything was not quite as it ought to be.

" Is there anything wrong, Will ?"

" No, nothing wrong ; that is to say, there is nothing to make me regret that I went. I think I did some good to them."

" It was to do good to them that you went there."

" They wanted to have some one near them who could be to them as one of their own family. He is too old,—too much worn out to be capable of managing things ; and the people there were, of course, robbing him. I think I have put a stop to that."

" And you are to go again at Christmas ?"

" Yes ;—they can do without me at my uncle's, and you will be there. I have taken the land, and already bought some of the stock for it, and am going to buy more."

" I hope you won't lose money, Will."

" No ;—not ultimately, that is. I shall get the place in good condition, and I shall have paid myself when he goes, in that way, if in no other. Besides, what's a little

money? I owe it to them for robbing her of her inheritance."

"You do not rob her, Will."

"It is hard upon her, though."

"Does she feel it hard?"

"Whatever may be her feelings on such a matter, she is
a woman much too proud to show them."

"I wish I knew whether you liked her or not."

"I do like her,—I love her better than any one in the
world; better even than you, Mary; for I have asked her
to be my wife."

"Oh, Will!"

"And she has refused me. Now you know the whole of
it,—the whole history of what I have done while I have
been away." And he stood up before her, with his thumbs
thrust into the arm-holes of his waistcoat, with something
serious and almost solemn in his gait, in spite of a smile
which played about his mouth."

"Oh, Will!"

"I meant to have told you, of course, Mary,—to have
told you everything; but I did not mean to tell it to-
night;—only it has somehow fallen from me. Out of the
full heart the mouth speaks, they say."

"I never can like her if she refuses your love."

"Why not? That is unlike you, Mary. Why should
she be bound to love me because I love her?"

"Is there any one else, Will?"

"How can I tell? I did not ask her. I would not have
asked her for the world, though I would have given the
world to know."

"And is she so very beautiful?"

"Beautiful! It isn't that so much;—though she is
beautiful. But,—but,—I can't tell you why,—but she is
the only girl that I ever saw who would suit me for a wife.
Oh, dear!"

"My own Will!"

"But I'm not going to keep you up all night, Mary.
And I'll tell you something else; I'm not going to break
my heart for love. And I'll tell you something else again;
I'm not going to give it up yet. I believe I've been a fool.
Indeed, I know I've been a fool. I went about it just as if
I were buying a horse, and had told the seller that that

was my price,—he might take it or leave it. What right
had I to suppose that any girl was to be had in that way;
much less such a girl as Clara Amedroz?"

" It would have been a great match for her."

" I'm not so sure of that, Mary. Her education has been
different from mine, and it may well be that she should
marry above me. But I swear I will not speak another
word to you to-night. To-morrow, if you're well enough,
I'll talk to you all day." Soon after that he did get her to
go up to her room, though, of course, he broke that oath of
his as to not speaking another word. After that he walked
out by moonlight round the house, wandering about the
garden and farmyard, and down through the avenue, having in his own mind some pretence of the watchfulness of
ownership, but thinking little of his property and much of
his love. Here was a thing that he desired with all his
heart, but it seemed to be out of his reach,—absolutely out
of his reach. He was sick and weary with a feeling of
longing,—sick with that covetousness wherewith Ahab
coveted the vineyard of Naboth. What was the world to
him if he could not have this thing on which he had set
his heart? He had told his sister that he would not break
his heart; and so much, he did not doubt, would be true.
A man or woman with a broken heart was in his estimation a man or woman who should die of love; and he did
not look for such a fate as that. But he experienced the
palpable misery of a craving emptiness within his breast,
and did believe of himself that he never could again be in
comfort unless he could succeed with Clara Amedroz. He
stood leaning against one of the trees, striking his hands
together, and angry with himself at the weakness which
had reduced him to such a state. What could any man be
worth who was so little master of himself as he had now
become?

After awhile he made his way back through the farm-
yard, and in at the kitchen door, which he locked and
bolted; and then, throwing himself down into a wooden
arm-chair which always stood there, in the corner of the
huge hearth, he took a short pipe from the mantelpiece,
filled it with tobacco, and lighting it almost unconsciously,
began to smoke with vehemence. Plaistow Hall was already odious to him, and he longed to be back at Belton,

which he had left only that morning. Yes, on that very morning she had brought to him his coffee, looking sweetly into his face,—so sweetly as she ministered to him. And he might then well have said one word more in pleading his suit, if he had not been too awkward to know what that word should be. And was it not his own awkwardness that had brought him into this state of misery? What right had he to suppose that any girl should fall in love with such a one as he at first sight,—without a moment's notice to her own heart? And then, when he had her there, almost in his arms, why had he let her go without kissing her? It seemed to him now that if he might have once kissed her, even that would have been a comfort to him in his present affliction. "D——tion!" he said at last, as he jumped to his feet and kicked the chair on one side, and threw the pipe among the ashes. I trust it will be understood that he addressed himself, and not his lady-love in this uncivil way,—"D——tion!" Then when the chair had been well kicked out of his way, he took himself to bed. I wonder whether Clara's heart would have been hardened or softened towards him had she heard the oath, and understood all the thoughts and motives which had produced it.

On the next morning poor Mary Belton was too ill to come down stairs; and as her brother spent his whole day out upon the farm, remaining among reapers and wheat stacks till nine o'clock in the evening, nothing was said about Clara on that day. Then there came a Sunday, and it was a matter of course that the subject of which they both were thinking should be discussed. Will went to church, and, as was their custom on Sundays, they dined immediately on his return. Then, as the afternoon was very warm, he took her out to a favourite seat she had in the garden, and it became impossible that they could longer abstain.

"And you really mean to go again at Christmas?" she asked.

"Certainly I shall;—I promised."

"Then I'm sure you will."

"And I must go from time to time because of the land I have taken. Indeed there seems to be an understanding that I am to manage the property for Mr. Amedroz."

"And does she wish you to go?"

"Yes,—she says so."

"Girls, I believe, think sometimes that men are indif ferent in their love. They suppose that a man can forget it at once when he is not accepted, and that things can go on just as before."

"I suppose she thinks so of me," said Belton wofully.

"She must either think that, or else be willing to give herself the chance of learning to like you better."

"There's nothing of that, I'm sure. She's as true as steel."

"But she would hardly want you to go there unless she thought you might overcome either your love or her indif-ference. She would not wish you to be there that you might be miserable."

"Before I had asked her to be my wife I had promised to be her brother. And so I will, if she should ever want a brother. I am not going to desert her because she will not do what I want her to do, or be what I want her to be. She understands that. There is to be no quarrel between us."

"But she would be heartless if she were to encourage you to be with her simply for the assistance you may give her, knowing at the same time that you could not be happy in her presence."

"She is not heartless."

"Then she must suppose that you are."

"I dare say she doesn't think that I care much about it. When I told her, I did it all of a heap, you see; and I fancy she thought I was just mad at the time."

"And did you speak about it again?"

"No; not a word. I shouldn't wonder if she hadn't forgotten it before I went away."

"That would be impossible."

"You wouldn't say so if you knew how it was done. It was all over in half an hour; and she had given me such an answer that I thought I had no right to say anything more about it. The morning when I left her she did seem to be kinder."

"I wish I knew whether she cares for any one else."

"Ah! I so often think of that. But I couldn't ask her, you know. I had no right to pry into her secrets. When

I came away, she got up to see me off; and I felt almost tempted to carry her into the gig and drive her off."

"I don't think that would have done, Will."

"I don't suppose anything will do. We all know what happens to the child who cries for the top brick of the chimney. The child has to do without it. The child goes to bed and forgets it; but I go to bed,—and can't forget it."

"My poor Will!"

Then he got up and shook himself, and stalked about the garden,—always keeping within a few yards of his sister's chair,—and carried on a strong battle within his breast, struggling to get the better of the weakness which his love produced, though resolved that the love itself should be maintained.

"I wish it wasn't Sunday," he said at last, "because then I could go and do something. If I thought that no one would see me, I'd fill a dung-cart or two, even though it is Sunday. I'll tell you what;—I'll go and take a walk as far as Denvir Sluice; and I'll be back to tea. You won't mind?"

"Denvir Sluice is eight miles off."

"Exactly,—I'll be there and back in something over three hours."

"But, Will,—there's a broiling sun."

"It will do me good. Anything that will take something out of me is what I want. I know I ought to stay and read to you; but I couldn't do it. I've got the fidgets inside, if you know what that means. To have the big hay-rick on fire or something of that sort is what would do me most good."

Then he started, and did walk to Denvir Sluice and back in three hours. The road from Plaistow Hall to Denvir Sluice was not in itself interesting. It ran through a perfectly flat country, without a tree. For the greater part of the way it was constructed on the top of a great bank, by the side of a broad dike; and for five miles its course was straight as a line. A country walk less picturesque could hardly be found in England. The road, too, was very dusty, and the sun was hot above Belton's head as he walked. But, nevertheless, he persevered, going on till he struck his stick against the waterfall which was called Denvir

Sluice, and then returned,—not once slackening his pace, and doing the whole distance at a rate somewhat above five miles an hour. They used to say in the nursery that cold pudding is good to settle a man's love; but the receipt which Belton tried was a walk of sixteen miles, along a dusty road, after dinner, in the middle of an August day.

I think it did him some good. When he got back he took a long draught of home-brewed beer, and then went up stairs to dress himself.

"What a state you are in," Mary said to him when he showed himself for a moment in the sitting-room.

"I did it from milestone to milestone in eleven minutes, backwards and forwards, all along the five-mile reach."

Then Mary knew from his answer that the exercise had been of service to him, perceiving that he had been able to take an interest in his own prowess as a walker.

"I only hope you won't have fever," she said.

"The people who stand still are they who get fevers," he answered. "Hard work never does harm to any one. If John Bowden would walk his five miles an hour on a Sunday afternoon he wouldn't have the gout so often."

John Bowden was a neighbour in the next parish; and Mary was delighted to find that her brother could take a pride in his performance.

By degrees Miss Belton began to know with some accuracy the way in which Will had managed his affairs at Belton Castle, and was enabled to give him salutary advice.

"You see, Will," she said, "ladies are different from men in this, that they cannot allow themselves to be in love so suddenly."

"I don't see how a person is to help it. It isn't like jumping into a river, which a person can do or not, just as he pleases."

"But I fancy it is something like jumping into a river, and that a person can help it. What the person can't help is being in when the plunge has once been made."

"No, by George. There's no getting out of that river."

"And ladies don't take the plunge till they've had time to think what may come after it. Perhaps you were a little too sudden with our cousin Clara?"

"Of course I was. Of course I was a fool, and a brute too."

"I know you were not a brute, and I don't think you were a fool; but yet you were too sudden. You see a lady cannot always make up her mind to love a man, merely because she is asked, all in a moment. She should have a little time to think about it before she is called upon for an answer."

"And I didn't give her two minutes."

"You never do give two minutes to any one;—do you, Will? But you'll be back there at Christmas, and then she will have had time to turn you and it over in her mind."

"And you think that I may have a chance?"

"Certainly you may have a chance."

"Although she was so sure about it?"

"She spoke of her own mind and her own heart as she knew them then. But it depends chiefly on this, Will,—whether there is any one else. For anything we know, she may be engaged now."

"Of course she may." Then Belton speculated on the extreme probability of such a contingency; arguing within his own heart that of course every unmarried man who might see Clara would want to marry her, and that there could not but be some one whom even she would be able to love.

When he had been home about a fortnight, there came a letter to him from Clara, which was a great treasure to him. In truth it simply told him of the completion of the cattle-shed, of her father's health, and of the milk which the little cow gave; but she signed herself his affectionate cousin, and the letter was very gratifying to him. There were two lines of a postscript, which could not but flatter him:—"Papa is so anxious for Christmas, that you may be here again;—and so, indeed, am I also." Of course it will be understood that this was written before Clara's visit to Perivale, and before Mrs. Winterfield's death. Indeed, much happened in Clara's history between the writing of that letter and Will Belton's winter visit to the Castle.

But Christmas came at last, all too slowly for Will;—and he started on his journey. On this occasion he arranged to stay a week in London, having a lawyer there whom he desired to see; and thinking, perhaps, that a short time spent among the theatres might assist him in his love troubles.

CHAPTER XIV.

MR. WILLIAM BELTON TAKES A WALK IN LONDON.

AT the time of my story there was a certain Mr. Green, a worthy attorney, who held chambers in Stone Buildings, Lincoln's Inn, much to the profit of himself and family,—and to the profit and comfort also of a numerous body of clients,—a man much respected in the neighbourhood of Chancery Lane, and beloved, I do not doubt, in the neighbourhood of Bushey, in which delightfully rural parish he was possessed of a genteel villa and ornamental garden. With Mr. Green's private residence we shall, I believe, have no further concern; but to him at his chambers in Stone Buildings I must now introduce the reader of these memoirs. He was a man not yet forty years of age, with still much of the salt of youth about him, a pleasant companion as well as a good lawyer, and one who knew men and things in London, as it is given to pleasant clever fellows, such as Joseph Green, to know them. Now Mr. Green, and his father before him, had been the legal advisers of the Amedroz family, and our Mr. Joseph Green had had but a bad time of it with Charles Amedroz in the last years of that unfortunate young man's life. But lawyers endure these troubles, submitting themselves to the extravagances, embarrassments, and even villany of the bad subjects among their clients' families, with a good-humoured patience that is truly wonderful. That, however, was all over now as regarded Mr. Green and the Amedrozes, and he had nothing further to do but to save for the father what relics of the property he might secure. And he was also legal adviser to our friend Will Belton, there having been some old family connection among them, and had often endeavoured to impress upon his old client at Belton Castle his own strong conviction that the heir

was a generous fellow who might be trusted in everything.
But this had been taken amiss by the old squire, who,
indeed, was too much disposed to take all things amiss
and to suspect everybody. " I understand," he had said
to his daughter. " I know all about it. Belton and Mr.
Green have been dear friends always. I can't trust my
own lawyer any longer." In all which the old squire
showed much ingratitude. It will, however, be understood that these suspicions were rife before the time of
Belton's visit to the family estate.

Some four or five days before Christmas there came a
visitor to Mr. Green with whom the reader is acquainted,
and who was no less a man than the Member for Perivale.
Captain Aylmer, when Clara parted from him on the
morning of her return to Belton Castle, had resolved that
he would repeat his offer of marriage by letter. A month
had passed by since then, and he had not as yet repeated
it. But his intention was not altered. He was a deli-
berate man, who did not do such things quite as quickly
as his rival, and who upon this occasion had thought it
prudent to turn over more than once in his mind all that
he proposed to do. Nor had he as yet taken any definite
steps as to that fifteen hundred pounds which he had
promised to Clara in her aunt's name, and which Clara had
been, and was, so unwilling to receive. He had now
actually paid it over, having purchased government stock
in Clara's name for the amount, and had called upon Mr.
Green, in order that that gentleman, as Clara's lawyer,
might make the necessary communication to her.

" I suppose there's nothing further to be done ?" asked
Captain Aylmer.

" Nothing further by me," said the lawyer. " Of course
I shall write to her, and explain that she must make arrangements as to the interest. I am very glad that her
aunt thought of her in her last moments."

" Mrs. Winterfield would have provided for her before,
had she known that everything had been swallowed up by
that unfortunate young man."

" All's well that ends well. Fifteen hundred pounds is
better than nothing."

" Is it not enough ?" said the Captain, blushing.

" It isn't for me to have an opinion about that, Captain

Aylmer. It depends on the nature of the claim; and that again depends on the relative position of the aunt and niece when they were alive together."

" You are aware that Miss Amedroz was not Mrs. Winterfield's niece."

" Do not think for a moment that I am criticising the amount of the legacy. I am very glad of it, as, without it, there was literally no provision,—no provision at all."

" You will write to herself?"

" Oh yes, certainly to herself. She is a better man of business than her father :—and then this is her own, to do as she likes with it."

" She can't refuse it, I suppose ?"

" Refuse it !"

" Even though she did not wish to take it, it would be legally her property, just as though it had been really left by the will ?"

" Well; I don't know. I dare say you could have resisted the payment. But that has been made now, and there seems to be an end of it."

At this moment a clerk entered the room and handed a card to his employer. " Here's the heir himself," said Mr. Green.

" What heir ?"

" Will Belton;—the heir of the property which Mr. Amedroz holds." Captain Aylmer had soon explained that he was not personally acquainted with Mr. William Belton ; but, having heard much about him, declared himself anxious to make the acquaintance. Our friend Will, therefore, was ushered into the room, and the two rivals for Clara's favour were introduced to each other. Each had heard much of the other, and each had heard of the other from the same person. But Captain Aylmer knew much more as to Belton, than Belton knew in respect to him. Aylmer knew that Belton had proposed to Clara, and had been rejected; and he knew also that Belton was now again going down to Somersetshire.

" You are to spend your Christmas, I believe, with our friends at Belton Castle ?" said the Captain.

" Yes;—and am now on my way there. I believe you know them also—intimately." Then there was some explanation as to the Winterfield connection, a few remarks

as to the precarious state of the old squire's health, a message
or two from Captain Aylmer, which of course were of no
importance, and the Captain took his leave.

Then Green and Belton became very comfortably intimate in their conversation, calling each other Will and Joe,
—for they were old and close friends. And they discussed
matters in that cozy tone of confidential intercourse which
is so directly at variance with the tones used by men when
they ordinarily talk of business. " He has brought me
good news for your friend, Miss Amedroz," said the lawyer.

" What good news ?"

" That aunt of hers left her fifteen hundred pounds,
after all. Or rather, she did not leave it, but desired on
her death-bed that it might be given."

" That's the same thing, I suppose ?"

" Oh, quite;—that is to say, it's the same thing, if the
person who has to hand over the money does not dispute
the legacy. But it shows how the old lady's conscience
pricked her at last. And after all it was a shabby sum,
and should have been three times as much."

" Fifteen hundred pounds ! And that is all she will have
when her father dies."

" Every farthing, Will. You'll take all the rest."

" I wish she wasn't going to have that."

" Why ? Why on earth should you of all men grudge
her such a moderate maintenance, seeing that you have not
got to pay it ?"

" It isn't a maintenance. How could it be a maintenance
for such as her ? What sort of maintenance would it be ?"

" Much better than nothing. And so you would feel, if
she were your daughter."

" She shall be my daughter, or my sister, or whatever
you like to call her. You don't think that I'll take the
whole estate, and leave her to starve on the interest of
fifteen hundred pounds a year !"

" You'd better make her your wife at once, Will."

Will Belton blushed as he answered, " That, perhaps,
would be easier said than done. That is not in my power,
—even if I should wish it. But the other is in my
power."

" Will, take my advice, and don't make any romantic
promises when you are down at Belton. You'll be sure to

regret them if you do. And you should remember that in truth Miss Amedroz has no greater claim on you than any other lady in the land."

"Isn't she my cousin?"

"Well;—yes. She is your cousin, but a distant one only; and I'm not aware that cousinship gives any claim."

"Who is she to have a claim on? I'm the nearest she has got. Besides, am not I going to take all the property which ought to be hers?"

"That's just it. There's no such ought in the case. The property is as much your own as this poker is mine. That's exactly the mistake I want you to guard against. If you liked her, and chose to marry her, that would be all very well;—presuming that you don't want to get money in marriage."

"I hate the idea of marrying for money."

"All right. Then marry Miss Amedroz if you please. But don't make any rash undertakings to be her father, or her brother, or her uncle, or her aunt. Such romance always leads a man into trouble."

"But I've done it already."

"What do you mean?"

"I've told her that I would be her brother, and that as long as I had a shilling she should never want sixpence. And I mean it. And as for what you say about romance and repenting it, that simply comes from your being a lawyer."

"Thank ye, Will."

"If one goes to a chemist, of course one gets physic, and has to put up with the bad smells."

"Thank you again."

"But the chemist may be a very good sort of fellow at home all the same, and have a cupboard full of sweetmeats and a garden full of flowers. However, the thing is done as far as I am concerned, and I can almost find it in my heart to be sorry that Clara has got this driblet of money. Fifteen hundred pounds! It would keep her out of the workhouse, and that is about all."

"If you knew how many ladies in her position would think that the heaven had rained wealth upon them if some one would give them fifteen hundred pounds!"

"Very well. At any rate I won't take it away from her

And now I want you to tell me something else. Do you remember a fellow we used to know, named Berdmore?"

" Philip Berdmore?"

" He may have been Philip, or Daniel, or Jeremiah, for anything I know. But the man I mean was very much given to taking his liquor freely."

" That was Jack Berdmore, Philip's brother. Oh yes, I remember him. He's dead now. He drank himself to death at last, out in India."

" He was in the army."

" Yes;—and what a pleasant fellow he was at times! I see Phil constantly, and Phil's wife, but they never speak of Jack."

" He got married, didn't he, after we used to see him?"

" Oh yes;—he and Phil married sisters. It was a sad affair, that."

" I remember being with him and her,—and the sister too, after they were engaged, and he got so drunk that we were obliged to take him away. There was a large party of us at Richmond, but I don't think you were there."

" But I heard of it."

" And she was a Miss Vigo."

" Exactly. I see the younger sister constantly. Phil isn't very rich, and he's got a lot of children,—but he's very happy."

" What became of the other sister?"

" Of Jack's wife?"

" Yes. What became of her?"

" I haven't an idea. Something bad, I suppose, as they never speak of her."

" And how long is he dead?"

" He died about three years since. I only knew it from Phil's telling me that he was in mourning for him. Then he did speak of him for a moment or two, and I came to know that he had carried on to the end in the same way. If a fellow takes to drink in this country, he'll never get cured in India."

" I suppose not."

" Never."

" And now I want to find out something about his widow."

" And why?"

" Ah ;—I'm not sure that I can tell you why. Indeed I'm sure that I cannot. But still you might be able to assist me."

" There were heaps of people who used to know the Vigos," said the lawyer.

" No end of people,—though I couldn't for the life of me say who any of them were."

" They used to come out in London with an aunt, but nobody knew much about her. I fancy they had neither father nor mother."

" They were very pretty."

" And how well they danced ! I don't think I ever knew a girl who danced so pleasantly,—giving herself no airs, you know,—as Mary Vigo."

"Her name was Mary," said Belton, remembering that Mrs. Askerton's name was also Mary.

" Jack Berdmore married Mary."

" Well now, Joe, you must find out for me what became of her. Was she with her husband when he died?"

" Nobody was with him. Phil told me so. No one, that is, but a young lieutenant and his own servant. It was very sad. He had D. T., and all that sort of thing."

" And where was she?"

" At Jericho, for anything that I know."

"Will you find out?" Then Mr. Joseph Green thought for a moment of his capabilities in that line, and having made an engagement to dine with his friend at his club on the evening before Will left London, said at last that he thought he could find out through certain mutual friends who had known the Berdmores in the old days. " But the fact is," said the lawyer, " that the world is so good-natured,—instead of being ill-natured, as people say,—that it always forgets those who want to be forgotten."

We must now go back for a few moments to Captain Aylmer and his affairs. Having given a full month to the consideration of his position as regarded Miss Amedroz, he made up his mind to two things. In the first place, he would at once pay over to her the money which was to be hers as her aunt's legacy, and then he would renew his offer. To that latter determination he was guided by mixed motives,—by motives which, when joined together, rarely fail to be operative. His conscience told him that he ought to do so,—and then the fact of her having, as it were, taken herself away from him, made him again wish to possess her.   And there was another cause which, perhaps, operated in the same direction.   He had consulted his mother, and she had strongly advised him to have nothing further to do with Miss Amedroz.   Lady Aylmer abused her dead sister heartily for having interfered in the matter, and endeavoured to prove to her son that he was released from his promise by having in fact performed it. But on this point his conscience interfered,—backed by his wishes,—and he made his resolve as has been above stated. On leaving Mr. Green's chambers he went to his own lodgings, and wrote his letter, as follows:—

"Mount Street, December, 186—

"DEAREST CLARA,

"When you parted from me at Perivale you said certain things about our engagement which I have come to understand better since then, than I did at the time. It escaped from me that my dear aunt and I had had some conversation about you, and that I had told her what was my intention.   Something was said about a promise, and I think it was that word which made you unhappy.   At such a time as that, when I and my aunt were talking together, and when she was, as she well knew, on her deathbed, things will be said which would not be thought of in other circumstances.   I can only assure you now, that the promise I gave her was a promise to do that which I had previously resolved upon doing.   If you can believe what I say on this head, that ought to be sufficient to remove the feeling which induced you to break our engagement.

"I now write to renew my offer to you, and to assure you that I do so with my whole heart.   You will forgive me if I tell you that I cannot fail to remember, and always to bear in my mind, the sweet assurances which you gave me of your regard for myself.   As I do not know that anything has occurred to alter your opinion of me, I write this letter in strong hope that it may be successful.   I believe that your fear was in respect to my affection for you, not as to yours for me.   If this was so, I can assure you that there is no necessity for such fear.

" I need not tell you that I shall expect your answer with great anxiety.

" Yours most affectionately,

" F. F. AYLMER.

"P.S. I have to-day caused to be bought in your name bank stock to the amount of fifteen hundred pounds, the amount of the legacy coming to you from my aunt."

This letter, and that from Mr. Green respecting the money, both reached Clara on the same morning. Now, having learned so much as to the position of affairs at Belton Castle, we may return to Will and his dinner engagement with Mr. Joseph Green.

" And what have you heard about Mrs. Berdmore ?" Belton asked, almost as soon as the two men were together.

" I wish I knew why you want to know."

" I don't want to do anybody any harm."

" Do you want to do anybody any good ?"

" Any good! I can't say that I want to do any particular good. The truth is, I think I know where she is, and that she is living under a false name."

" Then you know more of her than I do."

" I don't know anything. I'm only in doubt. But as the lady I mean lives near to friends of mine, I should like to know."

" That you may expose her."

" No ;—by no means. But I hate the idea of deceit. The truth is, that any one living anywhere under a false name should be exposed,—or should be made to assume their right name."

" I find that Mrs. Berdmore left her husband some years before he died. There was nothing in that to create wonder, for he was a man with whom a woman could hardly continue to live. But I fear she left him under protection that was injurious to her character."

" And how long ago is that ?"

" I do not know. Some years before his death."

" And how long ago did he die ?"

" About three years since. My informant tells me that he believes she has since married. Now you know all that I know." And Belton also knew that Mrs. Askerton of the cottage was the Miss Vigo with whom he had been acquainted in earlier years.

After that they dined comfortably, and nothing passed between them which need be recorded as essential to our story till the time came for them to part. Then, when they were both standing at the club door, the lawyer said a word or two which is essential. "So you're off to-morrow?" said he.

"Yes; I shall go down by the express."

"I wish you a pleasant journey. By-the-by, I ought to tell you that you won't have any trouble in being either father or mother, or uncle or aunt to Miss Amedroz."

"Why not?"

"I suppose it's no secret."

"What's no secret?"

"She's going to be married to Captain Aylmer."

Then Will Belton started so violently, and assumed on a sudden so manifest a look of anger, that his tale was at once told to Mr. Green. "Who says so?" he asked. "I don't believe it."

"I'm afraid it's true all the same, Will."

"Who says it?"

"Captain Aylmer was with me to-day and he told me. He ought to be good authority on such a subject."

"He told you that he was going to marry Clara Amedroz?"

"Yes, indeed."

"And what made him come to you, to tell you?"

"There was a question about some money which he had paid to her, and which, under existing circumstances, he thought it as well that he should not pay. Matters of that kind are often necessarily told to lawyers. But I should not have told it to you, Will, if I had not thought that it was good news."

"It is not good news," said Belton, moodily.

"At any rate, old fellow, my telling it will do no harm. You must have learned it soon." And he put his hand kindly,—almost tenderly, on the other's arm. But Belton moved himself away angrily. The wound had been so lately inflicted that he could not as yet forgive the hand that had seemed to strike him.

"I'm sorry that it should be so bad with you, Will."

" What do you mean by bad ? It is not bad with me.
It is very well with me. Keep your pity for those who
want it." Then he walked off by himself across the broad
street before the club door, leaving his friend without a
word of farewell, and made his way up into St. James's
Square, choosing, as was evident to Mr. Green, the first
street that would take him out of sight.

" He's hit, and hit hard," said the lawyer, looking after
him. " Poor fellow! I might have guessed it from what he
said. I never knew of his caring for any woman before."
Then Mr. Green put on his gloves and went away home.

We will now follow Will Belton into St. James's Square,
and we shall follow a very unhappy gentleman. Doubtless
he had hitherto known and appreciated the fact that Miss
Amedroz had refused his offer, and had often declared,
both to himself and to his sister, his conviction that that
refusal would never be reversed. But in spite of that
expressed conviction, he had lived on hope. Till she
belonged to another man she might yet be his. He might
win her at last by perseverance. At any rate, he had it in
his power to work towards the desired end, and might
find solace even in that working. And the misery of his
loss would not be so great to him,—as he found himself
forced to confess to himself before he had completed his
wanderings on this night,—in not having her for his own,
as it would be in knowing that she had given herself to
another man. He had often told himself that of course she
would become the wife of some man, but he had never yet
realized to himself what it would be to know that she was
the wife of any one specified rival. He had been sad
enough on that moonlight night in the avenue at Plaistow,
—when he had leaned against the tree, striking his hands
together as he thought of his great want; but his unhappiness then had been as nothing to his agony now. Now it
was all over,—and he knew the man who had supplanted
him!

How he hated him! With what an unchristian spirit
did he regard that worthy captain as he walked across St.
James's Square, across Jermyn Street, across Piccadilly, and
up Bond Street, not knowing whither he was going. He
thought with an intense regret of the laws of modern
society which forbid duelling.—forgetting altogether that

even had the old law prevailed, the conduct of the man
whom he so hated would have afforded him no *casus belli*.
But he was too far gone in misery and animosity to be
capable of any reason on the matter. Captain Aylmer had
interfered with his dearest wishes, and during this now
passing hour he would willingly have crucified Captain .
Aylmer had it been within his power to do so. Till he had
gone beyond Oxford Street, and had wandered away into
the far distance of Portman Square and Baker Street, he
had not begun to think of any interest which Clara Amedroz might have in the matter on which his thoughts were
employed. He was sojourning at an hotel in Bond Street,
and had gone thitherwards more by habit than by thought;
but he had passed the door of his inn, feeling it to be
impossible to render himself up to his bed in his present
disturbed mood. As he was passing the house in Bond
Street he had been intent on the destruction of Captain
Aylmer,—and had almost determined that if Captain
Aylmer could not be made to vanish into eternity, he must
make up his mind to go that road himself.

It was out of the question that he should go down to
Belton. As to that he had come to a very decided opinion
by the time that he had crossed Oxford Street. Go down
to see her, when she had treated him after this fashion!
No, indeed. She wanted no brother now. She had chosen
to trust herself to this other man, and he, Will Belton,
would not interfere further in her affairs. Then he drew
upon his imagination for a picture of the future, in which
he portrayed Captain Aylmer as a ruined man, who would
probably desert his wife, and make himself generally odious
to all his acquaintance,—a picture as to the realisation of
which I am bound to say that Captain Aylmer's antecedents gave no probability. But it was the looking at this
self-drawn picture which first softened the artist's heart
towards the victim whom he had immolated on his ima-
ginary canvas. When Clara should be ruined by the base-
ness and villany and general scampishness of this man
whom she was going to marry,—to whom she was about to
be weak enough and fool enough to trust herself,—then he
would interpose and be her brother once again,—a broken-
hearted brother, no doubt, but a brother efficacious to keep
the wolf from the door of this poor woman and her—

children. Then, as he thus created Captain Aylmer's em-
bryo family of unprovided orphans,—for after awhile he
killed the captain, making him to die some death that was
very disgraceful, but not very distinct even to his own
imagination,—as he thought of those coming pledges of a
love which was to him so bitter, he stormed about the
streets, performing antics of which no one would have believed him capable, who had known him as the thriving
Mr. William Belton, of Plaistow Hall, among the fens of
Norfolk.

But the character of a man is not to be judged from the
pictures which he may draw, or from the antics which he
may play in his solitary hours. Those who act generally
with the most consummate wisdom in the affairs of the
world, often meditate very silly doings before their wiser
resolutions form themselves. I beg, therefore, that Mr.
Belton may be regarded and criticised in accordance with
his conduct on the following morning,—when his midnight
rambles, which finally took him even beyond the New
Road, had been followed by a few tranquil hours in his
Bond Street bedroom ;—for at last he did bring himself to
return thither, and put himself to bed after the usual
fashion. He put himself to bed in a spirit somewhat tran-
quillised by the exercise of the night, and at last—wept
himself to sleep like a baby.

But he was by no means like a baby when he took him
early on the following morning to the Paddington Station,
and booked himself manfully for Taunton. He had had
time to recognise the fact that he had no ground of quarrel
with his cousin because she had preferred another man to
him. This had happened to him as he was recrossing the
New Road about two o'clock, and was beginning to find
that his legs were weary under him. And, indeed, he had
recognised one or two things before he had gone to sleep,
with his tears dripping on to his pillow. In the first place,
he had ill-treated Joe Green, and had made a fool of himself in his friend's presence. As Joe Green was a sensible,
kind-hearted fellow, this did not much signify ;—but not
on that account did he omit to tell himself of his own fault.
Then he discovered that it would ill become him to break
his word to Mr. Amedroz and to his daughter, and to do so
without a word of excuse, because Clara had exercised a

right which was indisputably her own. He had undertaken certain work at Belton which required his presence, and he would go down and do his work as though nothing had occurred to disturb him. To remain away because of this misfortune would be to show the white feather. It would be unmanly. All this he recognised as the pictures he had painted faded away from their canvases. As to Captain Aylmer himself, he hoped that he might never be called upon to meet him. He still hoped that, even as he was resolutely cramming his shirts into his portmanteau before he began his journey. His cousin Clara he thought he could meet, and tender to her some expression of good wishes as to her future life, without giving way under the effort. And to the old squire he could endeavour to make himself pleasant, speaking of the relief from all trouble which this marriage with Captain Aylmer would afford,— for now in his cooler moments he could perceive that Captain Aylmer was a man not apt to ruin himself, or his wife and children. But to Captain Aylmer himself, he could not bring himself to say pleasant things, or to express pleasant wishes. She who was to be Captain Aylmer's wife, who loved him, would of course have told him what had occurred up among the rocks in Belton Park; and if that was so, any meeting between Will and Captain Aylmer would be death to the former.

Thinking of all this he journeyed down to Taunton, and thinking of all this, he made his way from Taunton across to Belton Park.

CHAPTER XV.

EVIL WORDS.

CLARA AMEDROZ had received her two letters together,— that, namely, from the attorney, and that from Captain Aylmer,—and the result of those letters is already known. She accepted her lover's renewed offer of marriage, acknowledging the force of his logic, and putting faith in the strength of his assurances. This she did without seeking advice from any one. Who was there from whom she could seek advice on such a matter as that?—who, at least, was there at Belton? That her father would, as a matter of course, bid her accept Captain Aylmer, was, she thought, certain; and she knew well that Mrs. Askerton would do the same. She asked no counsel from any one, but taking the two letters up to her own room, sat down to consider them. That which referred to her aunt's money, together with the postscript in Captain Aylmer's letter on the same subject, would be of the least possible moment, if she could bring herself to give a favourable answer to the other proposition. But should she not be able to do this,—should she hesitate as to doing so at once,—then she must write to the lawyer in very strong terms, refusing altogether to have anything to do with the money. And in such a case as this, not a word could she say to her father either on one subject or on the other.

But why should she not accept the offer made to her? Captain Aylmer declared that he had determined to ask her to be his wife before he had made any promise to Mrs. Winterfield. If this were in truth so, then the very ground on which she had separated herself from him would be removed. Why should she hesitate in acknowledging to herself that she loved the man and believed him to be true? So she sat herself down and answered both the letters,—writing to the lawyer first. To him she said that nothing need be done about the money or the interest till he should see or hear from Captain Aylmer again. Then to Captain Aylmer she wrote very shortly, but very openly, —with the same ill-judged candour which her spoken words to him had displayed. Of course she would be his; his without hesitation, now that she knew that he expressed his own wishes, and not merely those of his aunt. "As to the money," she said, "it would be simply nonsense now for us to have any talk of money. It is yours in any way, and you had better manage about it as you please. I have written an ambiguous letter to Mr. Green, which will simply plague him, and which you may go and see if you like." Then she added her postscript, in which she said that she should now at once tell her father, as the news would remove from his mind all solicitude as to her future position. That Captain Aylmer did go to Mr. Green, we already know, and we know also that he told Mr. Green of his intended marriage.

Nothing was said by Captain Aylmer as to any proposed period for their marriage; but that was only natural. It was not probable that any man would name a day till he knew whether or not he was accepted. Indeed, Clara, on thinking over the whole affair, was now disposed to find fault rather with herself than with her lover, and forgetting his coldness and formality at Perivale, remembered only the fact of his offer to her, and his assurance now received that he had intended to make it before the scene which had taken place between him and his aunt. She did find fault with herself, telling herself that she had quarrelled with him without sufficient cause;—and the eager, loving candour of her letter to him was attributable to those self-accusations.

"Papa," she said, after the postman had gone away from Belton, so that there might be no possibility of any recall of her letter, "I have something to tell you, which I hope will give you pleasure."

"It isn't often that I hear anything of that kind," said he.

"But I think that this will give you pleasure. I do indeed. I am going to be married."

"Going to what?"

"Going to be married, papa. That is, if I have your leave. Of course any offer of that kind that I have accepted is subject to your approval."

"And I have been told nothing about it?"

"It began at Perivale, and I could not tell you then. You do not ask me who is to be my husband."

"It is not Will Belton?"

"Poor Will! No; it is not Will. It is Frederic Aylmer. I think you would prefer him as a son-in-law even to my cousin Will."

"No I shouldn't. Why should I prefer a man whom I don't even know, who lives in London, and who will take you away, so that I shall never see you again?"

"Dear papa;—don't speak of it in that way. I thought you would be glad to know that I was to be so—so—so happy."

"But why is it to be done this way,—of a sudden? Why didn't he come to me? Will came to me the very first thing."

" He couldn't come all the way to Belton very well;—particularly as he does not know you."

" Will came here."

" Oh, papa, don't make difficulties. Of course that was different. He was here when he first thought of it. And even then he didn't think very much about it."

" He did all that he could, I suppose."

" Well ;—yes. I don't know how that might be." And Clara almost laughed as she felt the difficulties into which she was creeping. " Dear Will. He is much better as a cousin than as a husband."

" I don't see that at all. Captain Aylmer will not have the Belton estate, or Plaistow Hall."

" Surely he is well enough off to take care of a wife. He will have the whole of the Perivale estate, you know."

" I don't know anything about it. According to my ideas of what is proper he should have spoken to me first. If he could not come, he might have written. No doubt my ideas may be old-fashioned, and I'm told that Captain Aylmer is a fashionable young man."

" Indeed he is not, papa. He is a hard-working member of Parliament."

" I don't know that he is any the better for that. People seem to think that if a man is a member of Parliament he may do what he pleases. There is Thompson, the member for Minehead, who has bought some sort of place out by the moors. I never saw so vulgar, pig-headed a fellow in my life. Being in Parliament used to be something, when I was young, but it won't make a man a gentleman now-a-days. It seems to me that none but brewers, and tallow-chandlers, and lawyers go into Parliament now. Will Belton could go into Parliament if he pleased, but he knows better than that. He won't make himself such a fool."

This was not comfortable to Clara ; but she knew her father, and allowed him to go on with his grumbling. He would come round by degrees, and he would appreciate, if he could not be induced to acknowledge, the wisdom of the step she was about to take.

" When is it to be ?" he asked.

" Nothing of that kind has ever been mentioned, papa."

" It had better be soon, if I am to have anything to do

with it." Now it was certainly the case that the old man
was very ill. He had not been out of the house since Clara
had returned home ; and though he was always grumbling
about his food, he could hardly be induced to eat anything
when the morsels for which he expressed a wish were got
for him.

" Of course you will be consulted, papa, before anything
is settled."

" I don't want to be in anybody's way, my dear."

" And may I tell Frederic that you have given your
consent ?"

" What's the use of my consenting or not consenting ?
If you had been anxious to oblige me you would have taken
your cousin Will."

" Oh, papa, how could I accept a man I didn't love ?"

" You seemed to me to be very fond of him at first ; and
I must say, I thought he was ill-treated."

" Papa, papa ; do not say such things as that to me !"

" What am I to do ? You tell me, and I can't altogether
hold my tongue." Then there was a pause. " Well, my
dear, as for my consent, of course you may have it,—if it's
worth anything. I don't know that I ever heard anything
bad about Captain Aylmer."

He had heard nothing bad about Captain Aylmer!
Clara, as she left her father, felt that this was very
grievous. Whatever cause she might have had for dis-
content with her lover, she could not but be aware that he
was a man whom any father might be proud to welcome
as a suitor for his daughter. He was a man as to whom
no ill tales had ever been told ;—who had never been
known to do anything wrong or imprudent ; who had
always been more than respectable, and as to whose
worldly position no exception could be taken. She had
been entitled to expect her father's warmest congratulations ; and her tidings had been received as though she had
proposed to give her hand to one whose character and
position only just made it not imperative on the father to
withhold his consent ! All this was hard, and feeling it to
be so, she went upstairs, all alone, and cried bitterly as
she thought of it.

On the next day she went down to the cottage and saw
Mrs. Askerton. She went there with the express purpose

of telling her friend of her engagement,—desirous of obtaining in that quarter the sympathy which her father declined to give her. Had her communication to him been accepted in a different spirit, she might probably have kept her secret from Mrs. Askerton till something further had been fixed about her marriage; but she was in want of a few kind words, and pined for some of that encouragement which ladies in love usually wish to receive, at any rate from some one chosen friend. But when she found herself alone with Mrs. Askerton she hardly knew how to tell her news; and at first could not tell it at all, as that lady was eager in speaking on another subject.

"When do you expect your cousin?" Mrs. Askerton asked, almost as soon as Clara was seated.

"The day after to-morrow."

"And he is in London now?"

"He may be. I dare say he is. But I don't know anything about it."

"I can tell you then that he is. Colonel Askerton has heard of his being there."

"You seem to speak of it as though there were some offence in it. Is there any reason why he should not be in London if he pleases?"

"None in the least. I would much rather that he should be there than here."

"Why so? Will his coming hurt you?"

"I don't like him. I don't like him at at all;—and now you know the truth. You believe in him;—I don't. You think him to be a fine fellow and a gentleman, whereas I don't think him to be either."

"Mrs. Askerton!"

"This is strong language, I know."

"Very strong language."

"Yes, my dear; but the truth is, Clara, that you and I, living together here this sort of hermit's life, each seeing so much of the other and seeing nothing of anybody else, must either be real friends, telling each other what we think, or we must be nothing. We can't go on with the ordinary make-believes of society, saying little civil speeches and not going beyond them. Therefore I have made up my mind to tell you in plain language that I don't like your cousin, and don't believe in him."

"I dont know what you mean by believing in a man."

"I believe in you. Sometimes I have thought that you believe in me, and sometimes I have feared that you do not. I think that you are good, and honest, and true; and therefore I like to see your face and hear your voice, —though it is not often that you say very pleasant things to me."

"Do I say unpleasant things?"

"I am not going to quarrel with you,—not if I can help it. What business has Mr. Belton to go about London making inquiries as to me? What have I done to him that he should honour me so far?"

"Has he made inquiries?"

"Yes; he has. If you have been contented with me as I am,—if you are satisfied, why should he want to learn more? If you have any question to ask me I will answer it. But what right can he have to be asking questions among strangers?"

Clara had no question to ask, and yet she could not say that she was satisfied. She would have been better satisfied to have known more of Mrs. Askerton, but yet she had never condescended to make inquiries about her friend. But her curiosity was now greatly raised; and, indeed, Mrs. Askerton's manner was so strange, her vehemence so unusual, and her eagerness to rush into dangerous subjects so unlike her usual tranquillity in conversation, that Clara did not know how to answer her.

"I know nothing of any questioning," she said.

"I am sure you don't. Had I thought you did, much as I love you,—valuable as your society is to me down in this desert,—I would never speak to you again. But remember,—if you want to ask any questions, and will ask them of me,—of me,—I will answer them, and will not be angry."

"But I don't want to ask any questions."

"You may some day; and then you can remember what I say."

"And am I to understand that you are determined to quarrel with my cousin Will?"

"Quarrel with him! I don't suppose that I shall see him. After what I have said it is not probable that you will bring him here; and the servant will have orders to say that I am not at home if he should call. Luckily he and Colonel Askerton did not meet when he was here before."

"This is the most strange thing I ever heard in my life."

"You will understand it better, my dear, when he makes his communication to you."

"What communication?"

"You'll find that he'll have a communication to make. He has been so diligent and so sharp that he'll have a great deal to tell, I do not doubt. Only, remember, Clara, that if anything that he tells you makes any difference in your feelings towards me, I shall expect you to come to me and say so openly. If he makes his statement, let me make mine. I have a right to ask for that, after what I have promised."

"You may be sure that I will."

"I want nothing more. I have no distrust in you,— none in the least. I tell you that I believe in you. If you will do that, and will keep Mr. William Belton out of my way during his visit to these parts, I shall be satisfied." For some time past Mrs. Askerton had been walking about the room, but, as she now finished speaking, she sat herself down as though the subject was fully discussed and completed. For a minute or two she made an effort to resume her usual tranquillity of manner, and in doing so attempted to smile as though ridiculing her own energy. "I knew I should make a fool of myself when you came," she said; "and now I have done it."

"I don't think you have been a fool at all, but you may have been mistaken."

"Very well, my dear, we shall see. It's very odd what a dislike I took to that man the first time I saw him."

"And I am so fond of him!"

"Yes; he has cozened you as he has your father. I am only glad that he did not succeed in cozening you further than he did. But I ought to have known you better than to suppose you could give your heart of hearts to one who is——"

"Do not abuse him any more."

"—Who is so very unlike the sort of people with whom you have lived. I may, at any rate, say that."

"I don't know that. I haven't lived much with any one yet—except papa, and my aunt, and you."

"But you know a gentleman when you see him."

"Come, Mrs. Askerton, I will not stand this. I thought you had done with the subject, and now you begin again. I had come here on purpose to tell you something of real importance,—that is, to me; but I must go away without telling you, unless you will give over abusing my cousin."

"I will not say a word more about him,—not at present."

"I feel so sure that you are mistaken, you know."

"Very well;—and I feel sure that you are mistaken. We will leave it so, and go to this matter of importance." But Clara felt it to be very difficult to tell her tidings after such a conversation as that which had just occurred. When she had entered the room her mind had been tuned to the subject, and she could have found fitting words without much difficulty to herself; but now her thoughts had been scattered and her feelings hurt, and she did not know how to bring herself back to the subject of her engagement. She paused, therefore, and sat with a doubtful, hesitating look, meditating some mode of escape. "I am all ears," said Mrs. Askerton; and Clara thought that she discovered something of ridicule, or of sarcasm, in the tone of her friend's voice.

"I believe I'll put it off till another day," she said.

"Why so? You don't think that anything really important to you will not be important to me also?"

"I'm sure of that, but somehow——"

"You mean to say that I have ruffled you?"

"Well;—perhaps; a little."

"Then be unruffled again, like my own dear, honest Clara. I have been ruffled too, but I'll be as tranquil now as a drawing-room cat." Then Mrs. Askerton got up from her chair, and seated herself by Clara's side on the sofa. "Come; you can't go till you've told me; and if you hesitate, I shall think that you mean to quarrel with me."

"I'll come to you to-morrow."

"No, no; you shall tell me to-day. All to-morrow you'll be preparing for your cousin."

"What nonsense!"

"Or else you'll come prepared to vindicate him, and then we shan't get on any further. Tell me what it is to-day. You can't leave me in curiosity after what you have said."

"You've heard of Captain Aylmer, I think?"

"Of course I've heard of him."

"But you've never seen him?"

"You know I never have."

"I told you that he was at Perivale when Mrs. Winterfield died."

"And now he has proposed, and you are going to accept him? That will indeed be important. Is it so?—say. But don't I know it is so? Why don't you speak?"

"If you know it, why need I speak?"

"But it is so? Oh, Clara, I am so glad. I congratulate you with all my heart,—with all my heart. My dearest, dearest Clara! What a happy arrangement! What a success! It is just as it should be. Dear, good man! to come forward in that sensible way, and put an end to all the little family difficulties!"

"I don't know so much about success. Who is it that is successful?"

"You, to be sure."

"Then by the same measurement he must be unsuccessful."

"Don't be a fool, Clara."

"Of course I have been successful if I've got a man that I can love as my husband."

"Now, my dear, don't be a fool. Of course all that is between you and him, and I don't in the least doubt that it is all as it should be. If Captain Aylmer had been the elder brother instead of the younger, and had all the Aylmer estates instead of the Perivale property, I know you would not accept him if you did not like him."

"I hope not."

"I am sure you would not. But when a girl with nothing a year has managed to love a man with two or three thousand a year, and has managed to be loved by him in return, —instead of going through the same process with the curate or village doctor,—it is a success, and her friends will always think so. And when a girl marries a gentleman, and a member of Parliament, instead of——; well, I'm not going to say anything personal,—her friends will congratulate her upon his position. It may be **very** wicked, and mercenary, and all that; but it's the way of the world."

" I hate hearing about the world."

" Yes, my dear; all proper young ladies like you do hate it. But I observe that such girls as you never offend its prejudices. You can't but know that you would have done a wicked as well as a foolish thing to marry a man without an adequate income."

"But I needn't marry at all."

"And what would you live on then? Come, Clara, we needn't quarrel about that. I've no doubt he's charming, and beautiful, and——"

" He is not beautiful at all; and as for charming——"

" He has charmed you at any rate."

" He has made me believe that I can trust him without doubt, and love him without fear."

" An excellent man! And the income will be an additional comfort; you'll allow that."

" I'll allow nothing."

" And when is it to be ?"

" Oh,—perhaps in six or seven years."

" Clara !"

"Perhaps sooner; but there's been no word said about time."

" Is not Mr. Amedroz delighted ?"

" Not a bit. He quite scolded me when I told him."

" Why ;—what did he want?"

" You know papa."

" I know he scolds at everything, but I shouldn't have thought he would have scolded at that. And when does he come here ?"

" Who come here ?"

" Captain Aylmer."

" I don't know that he is coming at all."

" He must come to be married."

" All that is in the clouds as yet. I did not like not to tell you; but you mustn't suppose that because I've told you, everything is settled. Nothing is settled."

" Nothing except the one thing ?"

" Nothing else."

It was more than an hour after that before Clara went away, and when she did so she was surprised to find that she was followed out of the house by Colonel Askerton. It was quite dusk at this time, the days being just at their shortest, and Colonel Askerton, according to his custom, would have been riding, or returning from his ride. Clara had been over two hours at the cottage, and had been aware when she reached it that he had not as yet gone out. It appeared now that he had not ridden at all, and, as she remembered to have seen his horse led before the window, it at once occurred to her that he had remained at home with the view of catching her as she went away. He came up to her just as she was passing through the gate, and offered her his right hand as he raised his hat with his left. It sometimes happens to all of us in life that we become acquainted with persons intimately,—that is, with an assumed intimacy,—whom in truth we do not know at all. We meet such persons frequently, often eating and drinking in their company, being familiar with their appearance, and well-informed generally as to their concerns; but we never find ourselves holding special conversations with them, or in any way fitting the modes of our life to the modes of their life. Accident has brought us together, and in one sense they are our friends. We should probably do any little kindness for them, or expect the same from them; but there is nothing in common between us, and there is generally a mutual though unexpressed agreement that there shall be nothing in common. Miss Amedroz was intimately acquainted with Colonel Askerton after this fashion. She saw him very frequently, and his name was often on her tongue; but she rarely, if ever, conversed with him, and knew of his habits only from his wife's words respecting them. When, therefore, he followed her through the garden gate into the park, she was driven to suppose that he had something special to say to her.

"I'm afraid you'll have a dark walk, Miss Amedroz," he said.

"It's only just across the park, and I know the way so well."

"Yes,—of course. I saw you coming out, and as I want to say a word or two, I have ventured to follow you. When Mr. Belton was down here I did not have the pleasure of meeting him."

"I remember that you missed each other."

" Yes, we did. I understand from my wife that he will be here again in a day or two."

" He will be with us the day after to-morrow."

" I hope you will excuse my saying that it will be very desirable that we should miss each other again." Clara felt that her face became red with anger as she listened to Colonel Askerton's words. He spoke slowly, as was his custom, and without any of that violence of expression which his wife had used; but on that very account there was more, if possible, of meaning in his words than in hers. William Belton was her cousin, and such a speech as that which Colonel Askerton had made, spoken with deliberation and unaccompanied by any previous explanation, seemed to her almost to amount to insult. But as she did not know how to answer him at the spur of the moment, she remained silent. Then he continued, "You may be sure, Miss Amedroz, that I should not make so strange a request to you if I had not good reason for making it."

" I think it a very strange request."

" And nothing but a strong conviction of its propriety on my part would have induced me to make it."

" If you do not want to see my cousin, why cannot you avoid him without saying anything to me on the subject ?"

" Because you would not then have understood as thoroughly as I wish you to do why I kept out of his way. For my wife's sake,—and for yours, if you will allow me to say so,—I do not wish to come to any open quarrel with him; but if we met, a quarrel would, I think, be inevitable. Mary has probably explained to you the nature of his offence against us ?"

" Mrs. Askerton has told me something as to which I am quite sure that she is mistaken."

" I will say nothing about that, as I have no wish at all to set you against your cousin. I will bid you good-night now, as you are close at home." Then he turned round and left her.

Clara, as she thought of all this, could not but call to mind her cousin's remembrances about Miss Vigo and Mr. Berdmore. What if he had made some inquiry as to the correctness of his old recollections ? Nothing, she thought, could be more natural. And then she reflected that, in the ordinary way of the world, persons feel none of that violent objection to the asking of questions about their antecedents which was now evinced by both Colonel and Miss Askerton. But of one thing she felt quite assured,—that her cousin, Will Belton, would make no inquiry which he ought not to make; and would make no improper use of any information which he might obtain.

CHAPTER XVI.

THE HEIR'S SECOND VISIT TO BELTON.

CLARA began to doubt whether any possible arrangement of the circumstances of her life could be regarded as fortunate. She was very fond, in a different degree and after a different fashion, of both Captain Aylmer and Mr. Belton. As regarded both, her position was now exactly what she herself would have wished. The man that she loved was betrothed to her, and the other man, whom she loved indeed also as a brother, was coming to her in that guise, —with the understanding that that was to be his position. And yet everything was going wrong! Her father, though he did not actually say anything against Captain Aylmer, showed by a hundred little signs, of which he was a skilful master, that the Aylmer alliance was distasteful to him, and that he thought himself to be aggrieved in that his daughter would not marry her cousin; whereas, over at the cottage, there was a still more bitter feeling against Mr. Belton,—a feeling so bitter, that it almost induced Clara to wish that her cousin was not coming to them.

But the cousin did come, and was driven up to the door in the gig from Taunton, just as had been the case on his previous visit. Then, however, he had come in the full daylight, and the hay-carts had been about, and all the prettiness and warmth of summer had been there; now it was mid-winter, and there had been some slight beginnings of snow, and the wind was moaning about the old tower, and the outside of the house looked very unpleasant from the hall-door. As it had become dusk in the afternoon, the old squire had been very careful in his orders as to prepa-- rations for Will's comfort,—as though Clara would have forgotten all those things in the preoccupation of her mind, caused by the constancy of her thoughts towards Will's rival. He even went so far as to creep across the upstairs landing-place to see that the fire was lighted in Will's room, this being the first time that he had left his chamber for many days,—and had given special orders as to the food which was to be prepared for Will's dinner,—in a very different spirit from that which had dictated some former orders when Will was about to make his first visit, and when his coming had been regarded by the old man as a heartless, indelicate, and almost hostile proceeding.

"I wish I could go down to receive him," said Mr. Amedroz, plaintively. "I hope he won't take it amiss."

"You may be sure he won't do that."

"Perhaps I can to-morrow."

"Dear papa, you had better not think of it till the weather is milder."

"Milder! how is it to get milder at this time of the year?"

"Of course he'll come up to you, papa."

"He's very good. I know he's very good. No one else would do as much."

Clara understood accurately what all this meant. Of course she was glad that her father should feel so kindly towards her cousin, and think so much of his coming; but every word said by the old man in praise of Will Belton implied an equal amount of dispraise as regarded Captain Aylmer, and contained a reproach against his daughter for having refused the former and accepted the latter.

Clara was in the hall when Belton arrived, and received him as he entered, enveloped in his damp great-coats. "It is so good of you to come in such weather," she said.

"Nice seasonable weather, I call it," he said. It was the same comfortable, hearty, satisfactory voice which had done so much towards making his way for him on his first arrival at Belton Castle. The voices to which Clara was most accustomed were querulous,—as though the world had been found by the owners of them to be but a bad place. But Belton's voice seemed to speak of cheery days, and happy friends, and a general state of things which made life worth having. Nevertheless, forty-eight hours had not yet passed over his head since he was walking about

London in such misery that he had almost cursed the hour in which he was born. His misery still remained with him, as black now as it had been then;—and yet his voice was cheery. The sick birds, we are told, creep into holes, that they may die alone and unnoticed; and the wounded beasts hide themselves that their grief may not be seen of their fellows. A man has the same instinct to conceal the weakness of his sufferings; but, if he be a man, he hides it in his own heart, keeping it for solitude and the watches of the night, while to the outer world he carries a face on which his care has made no marks.

"You will be sorry to hear that papa is too ill to come downstairs."

"Is he, indeed? I am truly sorry. I had heard he was ill; but did not know he was so ill as that."

"Perhaps he fancies himself weaker than he is."

"We must try and cure him of that. I can see him, I hope?"

"Oh dear, yes. He is most anxious for you to go to him. As soon as ever you can come upstairs I will take you." He had already stripped himself of his wrappings, and declaring himself ready, at once followed Clara to the squire's room.

"I'm sorry, sir, to find you in this way," he said.

"I'm very poorly, Will;—very," said the squire, putting out his hand, as though he were barely able to lift it above his knee. Now it certainly was the fact that half an hour before he had been walking across the passage.

"We must see if we can't soon make you better among us," said Will.

The squire shook his head with a slow, melancholy movement, not raising his eyes from the ground. I don't think you'll ever see me much better, Will," he said. And yet half an hour since he had been talking of being down in the dining-room on the next day. "I shan't trouble you much longer," said the squire. "You'll soon have it all without paying rent for it."

This was very unpleasant, and almost frustrated Belton's attempts to be cheery. But he persevered nevertheless. "It'll be a long time yet before that day comes, sir."

"Ah; that's easily said. But never mind. Why should 1 want to remain when I shall have once seen her properly settled. I've nothing to live for except that she may have a home."

On this subject it was quite impossible that Belton should say anything. Clara was standing by him, and she, as he knew, was engaged to Captain Aylmer. So circumstanced, what could he say as to Clara's settlement in life? That something should be said between him and the old man, and something also between him and Clara, was a matter of course; but it was quite out of the question that he should discuss Clara's prospects in life in presence of them both together.

"Papa's illness makes him a little melancholy," said Clara.

"Of course—of course. It always does," said Will.

"I think he will be better when the weather becomes milder," said Clara.

"I suppose I may be allowed to know how I feel myself," said the squire. "But don't keep Will up here when he wants his dinner. There; that'll do. You'd better leave me now." Then Will went out to his old room, and a quarter of an hour afterwards he found himself seated with Clara at the dinner-table; and a quarter of an hour after that the dinner was over, and they had both drawn their chairs to the fire.

Neither of them knew how to begin with the other. Clara was under no obligation to declare her engagement to her cousin, but yet she felt that it would be unhandsome in her not to do so. Had Will never made the mistake of wanting to marry her himself, she would have done so as a matter of course. Had she supposed him to cherish any intention of renewing that mistake, she would have felt herself bound to tell him,—so that he might save himself from unnecessary pain. But she gave him credit for no such intention, and yet she could not but remember that scene among the rocks. And then was she, or was she not, to say anything to him about the Askertons? With him also the difficulty was as great. He did not in truth believe that the tidings which he had heard from his friend, the lawyer, required corroboration; but yet it was necessary that he should know from herself that she had disposed of her hand; and it was necessary also that he should say some word to her as to their future standing and friendship.

"You must be very anxious to see how your farm goes on," said she.

He had not thought much of his agricultural venture at Belton for the last three or four days, and would hardly have been vexed had he been told that every head of cattle about the place had died of the murrain. Some general idea of the expediency of going on with a thing which he had commenced still actuated him; but it was the principle involved, and not the speculation itself, which interested him. But he could not explain all this, and he therefore was driven to some cold agreement with her. "The farm!—you mean the stock. Yes; I shall go and have a look at them early to-morrow. I suppose they're all alive?"

"Pudge says that they are doing uncommonly well." Pudge was a leading man among the Belton labourers, whom Will had hired to look after his concerns.

"That's all right. I dare say Pudge knows quite as much about it as I do."

"But the master's eye is everything."

"Pudge's eye is quite as good as mine; and probably much better, as he knows the country."

"You used to say that it was everything for a man to look after his own interests."

"And I do look after them. Pudge and I will go and have a look at every beast to-morrow, and I shall look very wise and pretend to know more about it than he does. In stock-farming the chief thing is not to have too many beasts. They used to say that half-stocking was whole profit, and whole-stocking was half profit. If the animals have plenty to eat, and the rent isn't too high, they'll take care of their owner."

"But then there is so much illness."

"I always insure."

Clara perceived that the subject of the cattle didn't suit the present occasion. When he had before been at Belton he had liked nothing so much as talking about the cattle-sheds, and the land, and the kind of animals which would suit the place; but now the novelty of the thing was gone, —and the farmer did not wish to talk of his farm. In her anxiety to find a topic which would not be painful, she went from the cattle to the cow   "You can't think what a

pet Bessy has been with us. And she seems to think that
she is privileged to go everywhere, and do anything."

" I hope they have taken care that she has had winter
food."

" Winter food!   Why Pudge, and all the Pudges, and all
the family in the house, and all your cattle would have to
want, before Bessy would be allowed to miss a meal.
Pudge always says, with his sententious shake of the head,
that the young squire was very particular about Bessy."

"Those Alderneys want a little care,—that's all."

Bessy was of no better service to Clara in her present
difficulty than the less aristocratic herd of common cattle.
There was a pause for a moment, and then she began
again. "How did you leave your sister, Will?"

" Much the same as usual. I think she has borne the
first of the cold weather better than she did last year."

" I do so wish that I knew her."

"Perhaps you will some day. But I don't suppose that
you ever will."

" Why not?"

" It's not likely that you'll ever come to Plaistow now;
—and Mary never leaves it except to go to my uncle's."

Clara instantly knew that he had heard of her engagement, though she could not imagine from what source he
had heard it. There was something in the tone of his
voice,—something especially in the expression of that word
" now," which told her that it must be so. " I should be so
glad to go there, if I could," she said, with that special
hypocrisy which belongs to women, and is allowed to
them; " but, of course, I cannot leave papa in his present
state."

"And if you did leave him you would not go to
Plaistow."

" Not unless you and Mary asked me."

" And you wouldn't if we did. How could you?"

" What do you mean, Will? It seems as though you
were almost savage to me."

" Am I? Well;—I feel savage, but not to you."

" Nor to any one, I hope, belonging to me." She
knew that it was all coming; that the whole subject of her
future life must now be discussed; and she began to fear
that the discussion might not be easy. But she did not

know how to give it a direction. She feared that he would become angry, and yet she knew not why. He had accepted his own rejection tranquilly, and could hardly take it as an offence that she should now be engaged to Captain Aylmer.

"Mr. Green has told me," said he, "that you are going to be married."

"How could Mr. Green have known?"

"He did know;—at least I suppose he knew, for he told me."

"How very odd."

"I suppose it is true?" Clara did not make any immediate answer, and then he repeated the question. "I suppose it is true?"

"It is true that I am engaged."

"To Captain Aylmer?"

"Yes; to Captain Aylmer. You know that I had known him very long. I hope you are not angry with me because I did not write and tell you. Strange as it may seem, seeing that you had heard it already, it is not a week yet since it was settled; and had I written to you, I could only have addressed my letter to you here."

"I wasn't thinking about that. I didn't specially want you to write to me. What difference would it make?"

"But I should have felt that I owed it to your kindness and your—regard for me."

"My regard! What's the use of regard?"

"You are not going to quarrel with me, Will, because—because—because——. If you had really been my brother, as you once said you would be, you could not but have approved of what I have done."

"But I am not your brother."

"Oh, Will, that sounds so cruel!"

"I am not your brother, and I have no right to approve or disapprove."

"I will not say that I could make my engagement with Captain Aylmer dependent on your approval. It would not be fair to him to do so, and it would put me into a false position."

"Have I asked you to make any such absurd sacrifice?"

"Listen to me, Will. I say that I could not do that. But, short of that, there is nothing I would not do to satisfy you. I think so much of your judgment and goodness, and so very much of your affection ; I love you so dearly, that——. Oh, Will, say a kind word to me!"

"A kind word ; yes, but what sort of kindness ?"

"You must know that Captain Aylmer——"

"Don't talk to me of Captain Aylmer. Have I said anything against him ? Have I ventured to make any objection ? Of course, I know his superiority to myself. I know that he is a man of the world, and that I am not ; that he is educated, and that I am ignorant; that he has a position, and that I have none ; that he has much to offer, and that I have nothing. Of course, I see the difference ; but that does not make me comfortable."

"Will, I had learned to love him before I had ever seen you.",

"Why didn't you tell me so, that I might have known there was no hope, and have gone away utterly,—out of the kingdom ? If it was all settled then, why didn't you tell me, and save me from breaking my heart with false hopes ?"

"Nothing was settled then. I hardly knew my own mind ; but yet I loved him. There; cannot you understand it ? Have I not told you enough ?"

"Yes ; I understand it."

"And do you blame me ?"

He paused awhile before he answered her. "No ; I do not blame you. I suppose I must blame no one but myself. But you should bear with me. I was so happy, and now I am so wretched."

There was nothing that she could say to comfort him. She had altogether mistaken the nature of the man's regard, and had even mistaken the very nature of the man. So much she now learned, and could tell herself that had she known him better she would either have prevented this second visit, or would have been careful that he should have learned the truth from herself before he came. Now she could only wait till he should again have got strength to hide his suffering under the veil of his own manliness.

"I have not a word to say against what you are doing," he said at last ; "not a word. But you will understand what I mean when I tell you that it is not likely that you will come to Plaistow."

"Some day, Will, when you have a wife of your own ——"

"Very well; but we won't talk about that at present, if you please. When I have, things will be different. In the meantime your course and mine will be separate. You, I suppose, will be with him in London, while I shall be,-- at the devil as likely as not."

"How can you speak to me in that way? Is that like being my brother?"

"I don't feel like being your brother. However, I beg your pardon, and now we will have done with it. Spilt milk can't be helped, and my milk pans have got themselves knocked over. That's all. Don't you think we ought to go up to your father again?"

On the following day, Belton and Mr. Amedroz discussed the same subject, but the conversation went off very quietly. Will was determined not to exhibit his weakness before the father as he had done before the daughter. When the squire with a maundering voice drawled out some expression of regret that his daughter's choice had not fallen in another place, Will was able to say that bygones must be bygones. He regretted it also, but that was now over. And when the squire endeavoured to say a few ill-natured words about Captain Aylmer, Will stopped him at once by asserting that the Captain was all that he ought to be.

"And it would have made me so happy to think that my daughter's child should come to live in his grandfather's old house," murmured Mr. Amedroz.

"And there's no knowing that he mayn't do so yet," said Will.

"But all these things are so doubtful that a man is wrong to fix his happiness upon them." After that he went out to ramble about the place, and before the third day was over Clara was able to perceive that, in spite of what he had said, he was as busy about the cattle as though his bread depended on them.

Nothing had been said as yet about the Askertons, and Clara had resolved that their name should not first be mentioned by her. Mrs. Askerton had prophesied that Will would have some communication to make about herself, and Clara would at any rate see whether her cousin would,

of his own accord, introduce the subject. But three days
passed by, and he had made no allusion to the cottage or
its inhabitants. This in itself was singular, as the Askertons were the only local friends whom Clara knew, and as
Belton had become personally acquainted with Mrs. Askerton. But such was the case; and when Mr. Amedroz once
said something about Mrs. Askerton in the presence of
both Clara and Belton, they both of them shrank from the
subject in a manner that made Clara understand that any
conversation about the Askertons was to be avoided. On
the fourth day Clara saw Mrs. Askerton, but then Will
Belton's name was not mentioned. There was therefore,
among them all, a sense of some mystery which made them
uncomfortable, and which seemed to admit of no solution.
Clara was more sure than ever that her cousin had made
no inquiries that he should not have made, and that he
would put no information that he might have to an improper use. But of such certainty on her part she could
say nothing.

Three weeks passed by, and it seemed as though Belton's
visit were come to an end without any further open trouble.
Now and then something was said about Captain Aylmer;
but it was very little, and Belton made no further reference
to his own feelings. It had come to be understood that his
visit was to be limited to a month, and to both him and
Clara the month wore itself away slowly, neither of them
having much pleasure in the society of the other. The old
squire came down stairs once for an hour or two, and spent
the whole time in bitter complaints. Everything was
wrong, and everybody was ill-treating him. Even with
Will he quarrelled, or did his best to quarrel, in regard to
everything about the place, though at the same time he did
not cease to grumble at his visitor for going away and
leaving him. Belton bore it all so well that the grumbling
and quarrelling did not lead to much; but it required all
his good humour and broad common sense to prevent serious
troubles and misunderstanding.

During the period of her cousin's visit at Belton, Clara
received two letters from Captain Aylmer, who was spending the Christmas holidays with his father and mother, and
on the day previous to that of her cousin's departure there
came a third. In neither of these letters was there much

said about Sir Anthony, but they were all very full of Lady Aylmer. In the first he wrote with something of the personal enthusiasm of a lover, and therefore Clara hardly felt the little drawbacks to her happiness which were contained in certain innuendoes respecting Lady Aylmer's ideas, and Lady Aylmer's hopes, and Lady Aylmer's fears. Clara was not going to marry Lady Aylmer, and did not fear but that she could hold her own against any mother-in-law in the world when once they should be brought face to face. And as long as Captain Aylmer seemed to take her part rather than that of his mother, it was all very well. The second letter was more trying to her temper, as it contained one or two small morsels of advice as to conduct which had evidently originated with her ladyship. Now there is nothing, I take it, so irritating to an engaged young lady as counsel from her intended husband's mamma. An engaged young lady, if she be really in love, will take almost anything from her lover as long as she is sure that it comes altogether from himself. He may take what liberties he pleases with her dress. He may prescribe high church or low church,—if he be not, as is generally the case, in a condition to accept, rather than to give, prescriptions on that subject. He may order almost any course of reading, —providing that he supply the books. And he may even interfere with the style of dancing, and recommend or prohibit partners. But he may not thrust his mother down his future wife's throat. In answer to the second letter, Clara did not say much to show her sense of objection. Indeed she said nothing. But in saying nothing she showed her objection, and Captain Aylmer understood it. Then came the third letter, and as it contained matter touching upon our story, it shall be given entire,—and I hope it may be taken by gentlemen about to marry as a fair specimen of the sort of letter they ought not to write to the girls of their hearts:—

"Aylmer Castle, 19th January, 186—.

"DEAREST CLARA,—I got 'your letter of the 16th yesterday, and was sorry you said nothing in reference to my mother's ideas as to the house at Perivale. Of course she knew that I heard from you, and was disappointed when I was obliged to tell her that you had not alluded to the subject.

She is very anxious about you, and, having now given her assent to our marriage, is of course desirous of knowing that her kindly feeling is reciprocated. I assured her that my own Clara was the last person to be remiss in such a matter, and reminded her that young ladies are seldom very careful in their mode of answering letters. Remember, therefore, that I am now your guarantee, and send some message to relieve me from my liability.

"When I told her of your father's long illness, which she laments greatly, and of your cousin's continued presence at Belton Castle, she seemed to think that Mr. Belton's visit should not be prolonged. When I told her that he was your nearest relative, she remarked that cousins are the same as any other people,—which indeed they are. I know that my Clara will not suppose that I mean more by this than the words convey. Indeed I mean less. But not having the advantage of a mother of your own, you will not be sorry to know what are my mother's opinions on matters which so nearly concern you.

"And now I come to another subject, as to which what I shall say will surprise you very much. You know, I think, that my aunt Winterfield and I had some conversation about your neighbours, the Askertons; and you will remember that my aunt, whose ideas on such matters were always correct, was a little afraid that your father had not made sufficient inquiry respecting them before he allowed them to settle near him as tenants. It now turns out that she is,—very far, indeed, from what she ought to be. My mother at first thought of writing to you about this; but she is a little fatigued, and at last resolved that under all the circumstances it might be as well that I should tell you. It seems that Mrs. Askerton was married before to a certain Captain Berdmore, and that she left her first husband during his lifetime under the protection of Colonel Askerton. I believe they, the Colonel and Mrs. Askerton, have been since married. Captain Berdmore died about four years ago in India, and it is probable that such a marriage has taken place. But under these circumstances, as Lady Aylmer says, you will at once perceive that all acquaintance between you and the lady should be brought to an end. Indeed your own sense of what is becoming to you, either as an unmarried girl or as my future wife, or indeed as a woman at all, will at once make you feel that this must be so. I think, if I were you, I would tell the whole to Mr. Amedroz; but this I will leave to your own discretion. I can assure you that Lady Aylmer has full proof as to the truth of what I tell you.

"I go up to London in February. I suppose I may hardly hope to see you before the recess in July or August; but I trust that before that we shall have fixed the day when you will make me the happiest of men.

"Yours with truest affection,

"F. F. AYLMER."

It was a disagreeable, nasty letter from the first line to the last. There was not a word in it which did not grate against Clara's feelings,—not a thought expressed which did not give rise to fears as to her future happiness. But the information which it contained about the Askertons,— "the communication," as Mrs. Askerton herself would have called it,—made her for the moment almost forget Lady Aylmer and her insolence. Could this story be true? And if true, how far would it be imperative on her to take the hint, or rather obey the order which had been given her? What steps should she take to learn the truth? Then she remembered Mrs. Askerton's promise—"If you want to ask any questions, and will ask them of me, I will answer them." The communication, as to which Mrs. Askerton had prophesied, had now been made;—but it had been made, not by Will Belton whom Mrs. Askerton had reviled, but by Captain Aylmer whose praises Mrs. Askerton had so loudly sung. As Clara thought of this, she could not analyse her own feelings, which were not devoid of a cer tain triumph. She had known that Belton would not put on his armour to attack a woman. Captain Aylmer had done so, and she was hardly surprised at his doing it. Yet Captain Aylmer was the man she loved! Captain Aylmer was the man she had promised to marry. But, in truth, she hardly knew which was the man she loved!

This letter came on a Sunday morning, and on that day she and Belton went to church together. On the following morning early he was to start for Taunton. At church they saw Mrs. Askerton, whose attendance there was not very frequent. It seemed, indeed, as though she had come

with the express purpose of seeing Belton once during his
visit. As they left the church she bowed to him, and that
was all they saw of each other throughout the month that
he remained in Somersetshire.

"Come to me to-morrow, Clara," Mrs. Askerton said as
they all passed through the village together. Clara muttered some reply, having not as yet made up her mind as
to what her conduct must be. Early on the next morning
Will Belton went away, and again Clara got up to give
him his breakfast. On this occasion he had no thought of
kissing her. He went away without having had a word
said to him about Mrs. Askerton, and then Clara settled
herself down to the work of deliberation. What should
she do with reference to the communication that had been
made to her by Captain Aylmer?

CHAPTER XVII.

AYLMER PARK.

AYLMER PARK and the great house of the Aylmers together
formed an important, and, as regarded some minds, an imposing, country residence. The park was large, including
some three or four hundred acres, and was peopled, rather
thinly, by aristocratic deer. It was surrounded by an
aristocratic paling, and was entered, at three different
points, by aristocratic lodges. The sheep were more numerous than the deer, because Sir Anthony, though he had
a large income, was not in very easy circumstances. The
ground was quite flat; and though there were thin belts of
trees, and some ornamental timber here and there, it was
not well wooded. It had no special beauty of its own, and
depended for its imposing qualities chiefly on its size, on
its three sets of double lodges, and on its old-established
character as an important family place in the county. The
house was of stone, with a portico of Ionic columns which
looked as though it hardly belonged of right to the edifice,
and stretched itself out grandly, with two pretentious
wings, which certainly gave it a just claim to be called a
mansion. It required a great many servants to keep it in

order, and the numerous servants required an experienced duenna, almost as grand in appearance as Lady Aylmer herself, to keep them in order. There was an open carriage and a close carriage, and a butler and two footmen and three gamekeepers and four gardeners, and there was a coachman and there were grooms, and sundry inferior men and boys about the place to do the work which the gardeners and gamekeepers and grooms did not choose to do themselves. And they all became fat, and lazy, and stupid, and respectable together; so that, as the reader will at once perceive, Aylmer Park was kept up in the proper English style. Sir Anthony very often discussed with his steward the propriety of lessening the expenditure of his residence, and Lady Aylmer always attended and probably directed these discussions; but it was found that nothing could be done. Any attempt to remove a gamekeeper or a gardener would evidently throw the whole machinery of Aylmer Park out of gear. If retrenchment was necessary Aylmer Park must be abandoned, and the glory of the Aylmers must be allowed to pale. But things were not so bad as that with Sir Anthony. The gardeners, grooms, and gamekeepers were maintained; ten domestic servants sat down to four heavy meals in the servants' hall every day, and Lady Aylmer contented herself with receiving little or no company, and with stingy breakfasts and bad dinners for herself and her husband and daughter. By all this it must be seen that she did her duty as the wife of an English country gentleman, and properly maintained his rank as a baronet.

He was a heavy man, over seventy years of age, much afflicted with gout, and given to no pursuit on earth which was now available for his comfort. He had been a hunting man, and he had shot also; but not with that energy which induces a sportsman to carry on those amusements in opposition to the impediments of age. He had been, and still was, a county magistrate; but he had never been very successful in the justice-room, and now seldom troubled the county with his judicial incompetence. He had been fond of good dinners and good wine, and still, on occasions, would make attempts at enjoyment in that line; but the gout and Lady Aylmer together were too many for him and he had but small opportunity for filling up the blanks of his existence out of the kitchen or cellar. He was a big man, with a broad chest, and a red face, and a quantity of white hair,—and was much given to abusing his servants. He took some pleasure in standing, with two sticks on the top of the steps before his own front door, and railing at any one who came in his way. But he could not do this when Lady Aylmer was by ; and his dependents, knowing his habits, had fallen into an ill-natured way of deserting the side of the house which he frequented. With his eldest son, Anthony Aylmer, he was not on very good terms ; and though there was no positive quarrel, the heir did not often come to Aylmer Park. Of his son Frederic he was proud, —and the best days of his life were probably those which Captain Aylmer spent at the house. The table was then somewhat more generously spread, and this was an excuse for having up the special port in which he delighted. Altogether his life was not very attractive; and though he had been born to a baronetcy, and eight thousand a year, and the possession of Aylmer Park, I do not think that he was, or had been, a happy man.

Lady Aylmer was more fortunate. She had occupations of which her husband knew nothing, and for which he was altogether unfit. Though she could not succeed in making retrenchments, she could and did succeed in keeping the household books. Sir Anthony could only blow up the servants when they were thoughtless enough to come in his way, and in doing that was restricted by his wife's presence. But Lady Aylmer could get at them day and night. She had no gout to impede her progress about the house and grounds, and could make her way to places which the master never saw ; and then she wrote many letters daily, whereas Sir Anthony hardly ever took a pen in his hand. And she knew the cottages of all the poor about the place, and knew also all their sins of omission and commission. She was driven out, too, every day, summer and winter, wet and dry, and consumed enormous packets of wool and worsted, which were sent to her monthly from York. And she had a companion in her daughter, whereas Sir Anthony had no companion. Wherever Lady Aylmer went Miss Aylmer went with her, and relieved what might otherwise have been the tedium of her life. She had been a beauty on a large scale, and was still

aware that she had much in her personal appearance which
justified pride. She carried herself uprightly, with a com-
manding nose and broad forehead; and though the graces
of her own hair had given way to a front, there was something even in the front which added to her dignity, if it
did not make her a handsome woman.

Miss Aylmer, who was the eldest of the younger genera-
tion, and who was now gently descending from her fortieth
year, lacked the strength of her mother's character, but
admired her mother's ways, and followed Lady Aylmer in
all things,—at a distance. She was very good,—as indeed
was Lady Aylmer,—entertaining a high idea of duty, and
aware that her own life admitted but of little self-indul-
gence. She had no pleasures, she incurred no expenses;
and was quite alive to the fact that, as Aylmer Park required
a regiment of lazy, gormandizing servants to maintain its
position in the county, the Aylmers themselves should not
be lazy, and should not gormandize. No one was more
careful with her few shillings than Miss Aylmer. She had,
indeed, abandoned a life's correspondence with an old friend
because she would not pay the postage on letters to Italy.
She knew that it was for the honour of the family that one
of her brothers should sit in Parliament, and was quite
willing to deny herself a new dress because sacrifices must
be made to lessen electioneering expenses. She knew that
it was her lot to be driven about slowly in a carriage, with
a livery servant before her and another behind her, and
then eat a dinner which the cook-maid would despise. She
was aware that it was her duty to be snubbed by her
mother, and to encounter her father's ill-temper, and to
submit to her brother's indifference, and to have, so to say,
the slightest possible modicum of personal individuality.
She knew that she had never attracted a man's love, and
might hardly hope to make friends for the comfort of her
coming age. But still she was contented, and felt that she
had consolation for it all in the fact that she was an
Aylmer. She read many novels, and it cannot but be supposed that something of regret would steal over her as she
remembered that nothing of the romance of life had ever,
or could ever, come in her way. She wept over the loves
of many women, though she had never been happy or unhappy in her own. She read of gaiety, though she never

encountered it, and must have known that the world elsewhere was less dull than it was at Aylmer Park. But she
took her life as it came without a complaint, and prayed that
God would make her humble in the high position to which
it had pleased Him to call her. She hated Radicals, and
thought that Essays and Reviews, and Bishop Colenso,
came direct from the Evil One. She taught the little
children in the parish, being specially urgent to them
always to curtsey when they saw any of the family;—and
was as ignorant, meek, and stupid a poor woman as you
shall find anywhere in Europe.

It may be imagined that Captain Aylmer, who knew the
comforts of his club, and was accustomed to life in London,
would feel the dulness of the paternal roof to be almost
unendurable. In truth, he was not very fond of Aylmer
Park, but he was more gifted with patience than most men
of his age and position, and was aware that it behoved him
to keep the Fifth Commandment if he expected to have his
own days prolonged in the land. He therefore made his
visits periodically, and contented himself with clipping a
few days at both ends from the length prescribed by family
tradition, which his mother was desirous of exacting. September was always to be passed at Aylmer Park because of
the shooting. In September, indeed, the eldest son himself
was wont to be there,—probably with a friend or two,—
and the fat old servants bestirred themselves, and there was
something of life about the place. At Christmas, Captain
Aylmer was there as the only visitor, and Christmas was
supposed to extend from the middle of December to the
opening of Parliament. It must, however, be explained,
that on the present occasion his visit had been a matter of
treaty and compromise. He had not gone to Aylmer Park
at all till his mother had in some sort assented to his marriage with Clara Amedroz. To this Lady Aylmer had been
very averse, and there had been many serious letters.
Belinda Aylmer, the daughter of the house, had had a bad
time in pleading her brother's cause,—and some very harsh
words had been uttered;—but ultimately the matter had
been arranged, and, as is usual in such contests, the mother
had yielded to the son. Captain Aylmer had therefore
gone down a few days before Christmas with a righteous
feeling that he owed much to his mother for her conde-

scension, and almost prepared to make himself very dis
agreeable to Clara, by way of atoning to his family for his
folly in desiring to marry her.

Lady Aylmer was very plain-spoken on the subject of all
Clara's shortcomings,—very plain-spoken, and very inqui-
sitive. "She will never have one shilling, I suppose?" she
said.

"Yes, ma'am." Captain Aylmer always called his mother
ma'am. "She will have that fifteen hundred pounds that I
told you of."

"That is to say, you will have back the money which
you yourself have given her, Fred. I suppose that is the
English of it." Then Lady Aylmer raised her eyebrows
and looked very wise.

"Just so, ma'am."

"You can't call that having anything of her own. In
point of fact, she is penniless."

"It is no good harping on that," said Captain Aylmer,
somewhat sharply.

"Not in the least, my dear; no good at all. Of course
you have looked it all in the face. You will be a poor man
instead of a rich man, but you will have enough to live on,
—that is, if she doesn't have a large family;—which of
course she will."

"I shall do very well, ma'am."

"You might do pretty well, I dare say, if you could live
privately,—at Perivale, keeping up the old family house
there, and having no expenses; but you'll find even that
close enough with your seat in Parliament, and the necessity there is that you should be half the year in London.
Of course, she won't go to London. She can't expect it.
All that had better be made quite clear at once." Hence
had come the letter about the house at Perivale, containing
Lady Aylmer's advice on that subject, as to which Clara
had made no reply.

Lady Aylmer, though she had given in her assent, was
still not altogether without hope. It might be possible
that the two young people could be brought to see the folly
and error of their ways before it would be too late; and
that Lady Aylmer, by a judicious course of constant advice,
might be instrumental in opening the eyes, if not of the
lady, at any rate of the gentleman. She had great reliance

on her own powers, and knew well that a falling drop will hollow a stone. Her son manifested no hot eagerness to complete his folly in a hurry, and to cut the throat of his prospects out of hand. Time, therefore, would be allowed to her, and she was a woman who could use time with patience. Having, through her son, despatched her advice about the house at Perivale,—which simply amounted to this, that Clara should expressly state her willingness to live there alone whenever it might suit her husband to be in London or elsewhere,—she went to work on other points connected with the Amedroz family, and eventually succeeded in learning something very much like the truth as to poor Mrs. Askerton and her troubles. At first she was so comfortably horror-stricken by the iniquity she had unravelled,—so delightfully shocked and astounded,—as to believe that the facts as they then stood would suffice to annul the match.

" You don't tell me," she said to Belinda, " that Frederic's wife will have been the friend of such a woman as that!" And Lady Aylmer, sitting upstairs with her household books before her, put up her great fat hands and her great fat arms, and shook her head,—front and all,— in most satisfactory dismay.

" But I suppose Clara did not know it." Belinda had considered it to be an act of charity to call Miss Amedroz Clara since the family consent had been given.

" Didn't know it! They have been living in that sort of way that they must have been confidantes in everything. Besides, I always hold that a woman is responsible for her female friends."

" I think if she consents to drop her at once,—that is, absolutely to make a promise that she will never speak to her again,—Frederic ought to take that as sufficient. That is, of course, mamma, unless she has had anything to do with it herself."

" After this I don't know how I'm to trust her. I don't indeed. It seems to me that she has been artful throughout. It has been a regular case of catching."

" I suppose, of course, that she has been anxious to marry Frederic ;—but perhaps that was natural."

" Anxious ;—look at her going there just when he had to meet his constituents. How young women can do such things passes me! And how it is that men don't see it all when it's going on just under their noses, I can't understand. And then her getting my poor, dear sister to speak to him when she was dying! I didn't think your aunt would have been so weak." It will be thus seen that there was entire confidence on this subject between Lady Aylmer and her daughter.

We know what were the steps taken with reference to the discovery, and how the family were waiting for Clara's reply. Lady Aylmer, though in her words she attributed so much mean cunning to Miss Amedroz, still was disposed to believe that that lady would show rather a high spirit on this occasion, and trusted to that high spirit as the means for making the breach which she still hoped to accomplish. It had been intended,—or rather desired,—that Captain Aylmer's letter should **have** been much sharper and authoritative than he had really made it ; but the mother could not write the letter herself, and had felt that to write in her own name would not have served to create anger on Clara's part against her betrothed. But she had quite succeeded in inspiring her son with a feeling of horror against the iniquity of the Askertons. He was prepared to be indignantly moral ; and perhaps,—perhaps,—the misguided Clara might be silly enough to say a word for her lost friend! Such being the present position of affairs, there was certainly ground for hope.

And now they were all waiting for Clara's answer. Lady Aylmer had well calculated the course of post, and knew that a letter might reach them by Wednesday morning. " Of course she will not write on Sunday," she had said to her son ; " but you have a right to expect that not another day should go by." Captain Aylmer, who felt that they were putting Clara on her trial, shook his head impatiently, and made no immediate answer. Lady Aylmer, triumphantly feeling that she had the culprit on the hip, did not care to notice this. She was doing the best she could for his happiness,—as she had done for his health, when in days gone by she had administered to him his infantine rhubarb and early senna ; but as she had never then expected him to like her doses, neither did she now expect that he should be well pleased at the remedial measures to which he was to be subjected.

No letter came on the Wednesday, nor did any come on the Thursday, and then it was thought by the ladies at the Park that the time had come for speaking a word or two. Belinda, at her mother's instance, began the attack,—not in her mother's presence,—but when she only was with her brother.

"Isn't it odd, Frederic, that Clara shouldn't write about those people at Belton?"

"Somersetshire is the other side of London, and letters take a long time."

"But if she had written on Monday, her answer would have been here on Wednesday morning;—indeed, you would have it Tuesday evening, as mamma sent over to Whitby for the day-mail letters." Poor Belinda was a bad lieutenant, and displayed too much of her senior officer's tactics in thus showing how much calculation and how much solicitude there had been as to the expected letter.

"If I am contented I suppose you may be," said the brother.

"But it does seem to me to be so very important! If she hasn't got your letter, you know, it would be so necessary that you should write again, so that the—the—contamination should be stopped as soon as possible." Captain Aylmer shook his head and walked away. He was, no doubt, prepared to be morally indignant,—morally very indignant,—at the Askerton iniquity; but he did not like the word contamination as applied to his future wife.

"Frederic," said his mother, later on the same day,—when the hardly-used groom had returned from his futile afternoon's inquiry at the neighbouring post town,—"I think you should do something in this affair."

"Do what, ma'am? Go off to Belton myself?"

"No, no. I certainly would not do that. In the first place it would be very inconvenient to you, and in the next place it would not be fair upon us. I did not mean that at all. But I think that something should be done. She should be made to understand."

"You may be sure, ma'am, that she understands as well as anybody."

"I dare say she is clever enough at these kind of things."

"What kind of things?"

" Don't bite my nose off, Frederic, because I am anxious about your wife."

"What is it that you wish me to do? I have written to her, and can only wait for her answer."

" It may be that she feels a delicacy in writing to you on such a subject; though I own—— However, to make a long story short, if you like, I will write to her myself."

" I don't see that that would do any good. It would only give her offence."

" Give her offence, Frederic, to receive a letter from her future mother-in-law;—from me! Only think, Frederic, what you are saying."

" If she thought she was being bullied about this, she would turn rusty at once."

" Turn rusty! What am I to think of a young lady who is prepared to turn rusty,—at once, too, because she is cautioned by the mother of the man she professes to love against an improper acquaintance,—against an acquaintance so very improper?" Lady Aylmer's eloquence should have been heard to be appreciated. It is but tame to say that she raised her fat arms and fat hands, and wagged her front,—her front that was the more formidable as it was the old one, somewhat rough and dishevelled, which she was wont to wear in the morning. The emphasis of her words should have been heard, and the fitting solemnity of her action should have been seen. " If there were any doubt," she continued to say,—" but there is no doubt. There are the damning proofs." There are certain words usually confined to the vocabularies of men, which women such as Lady Aylmer delight to use on special occasions, when strong circumstances demand strong language. As she said this she put her hand below the table, pressing it apparently against her own august person; but she was in truth indicating the position of a certain valuable correspondence which was locked up in the drawer of her writing-table.

" You can write if you like it, of course; but I think you ought to wait a few more days."

" Very well, Frederic; then I will wait. I will wait till Sunday. I do not wish to take any step of which you do not approve. If you have not heard by Sunday morning, then I will write to her—on Monday."

On the Saturday afternoon life was becoming inexpressibly disagreeable to Captain Aylmer, and he began to meditate an escape from the Park. In spite of the agreement between him and his mother, which he understood to signify that nothing more was to be said as to Clara's wickedness, at any rate till Sunday after post-hour, Lady Aylmer had twice attacked him on the Saturday, and had expressed her opinion that affairs were in a very frightful position. Belinda went about the house in melancholy guise, with her eyes rarely lifted off the ground, as though she were prophetically weeping the utter ruin of her brother's respectability And even Sir Anthony had raised his eyes and shaken his head when on opening the post-bag at the breakfast table,—an operation which was always performed by Lady Aylmer in person,—her ladyship had exclaimed, " Again no letter !" Then Captain Aylmer thought that he would fly, and resolved that, in the event of such flight, he would give special orders as to the re-direction of his own letters from the post-office at Whitby.

That evening, after dinner, as soon as his mother and sister had left the room, he began the subject with his father. " I think I shall go up to town on Monday, sir," said he.

" So soon as that? I thought you were to stop till the 9th."

" There are things I must see to in London, and I believe I had better go at once."

" Your mother will be greatly disappointed."

" I shall be sorry for that ;—but business is business, you know." Then the father filled his glass, and passed the bottle. He himself did not at all like the idea of his son's going before the appointed time, but he did not say a word of himself. He looked at the red-hot coals, and a hazy glimmer of a thought passed through his mind, that he too would escape from Aylmer Park,—if it were possible.

" If you'll allow me, I'll take the dog-cart over to Whitby on Monday, for the express train."

" You can do that certainly, but——"

" Sir ?"

" Have you spoken to your mother yet ?"

" Not yet. I will to-night."

" I think she'll be a little angry, Fred." There was a

sudden tone of subdued confidence in the old man's voice
as he made this suggestion, which, though it was by no
means a customary tone, his son well understood. "Don't
you think she will be ;—eh, a little ?"

"She shouldn't go on as she does with me about Clara,"
said the Captain.

"Ah,—I supposed there was something of that. Are
you drinking port ?"

"Of course I know that she means all that is good," said
the son, passing back the bottle.

"Oh yes ;—she means all that is good.'

"She is the best mother in the world."

"You may say that, Fred ;—and the best wife."

"But if she can't have her own way altogether——"
Then the son paused, and the father shook his head.

"Of course she likes to have her own way," said Sir
Anthony.

"It's all very well in some things."

"Yes ;—it's very well in some things."

"But there are things which a man must decide for
himself."

"I suppose there are," said Sir Anthony, not venturing
to think what those things might be as regarded himself.

"Now with reference to marrying——"

"I don't know what you want with marrying at all,
Fred. You ought to be very happy as you are. By heavens,
I don't know any one who ought to be happier. If I were
you, I know——"'

"But you see, sir, that's all settled."

"If it's all settled, I suppose there's an end of it."

"It's no good my mother nagging at one."

"My dear boy, she's been nagging at me, as you call it,
for forty years. That's her way. The best woman in the
world, as we were saying ;—but that's her way. And it's
the way with most of them. They can do anything if they
keep it up ;—anything. The best thing is to bear it if
you've got it to bear. But why on earth you should go
and marry, seeing that you're not the eldest son, and that
you've got everything on earth that you want as a bachelor,
I can't understand. I can't indeed, Fred. By heaven, I
can't !" Then Sir Anthony gave a long sigh, and sat
musing awhile, thinking of the club in London to which

he belonged, but which he never entered;—of the old days
in which he had been master of a bedroom near St. James's
Street,—of his old friends whom he never saw now, and of
whom he never heard except as one and another, year after
year, shuffled away from their wives to that world in which
there is no marrying or giving in marriage. " Ah, well,"
he said, " I suppose we may as well go into the drawing-
room. If it is settled, I suppose it is settled. But it really
seems to me that your mother is trying to do the best she
can for you. It really does."

Catain Aylmer did not say anything to his mother that
night as to his going, but as he thought of his prospects in
the solitude of his bedroom, he felt really grateful to his
father for the solicitude which Sir Anthony had displayed
on his behalf. It was not often that he received paternal
counsel, but now that it had come he acknowledged its
value. That Clara Amedroz was a self-willed woman he
thought that he was aware. She was self-reliant, at any
rate,—and by no means ready to succumb with that pretty
feminine docility which he would like to have seen her
evince. He certainly would not wish to be "nagged" by
his wife. Indeed he knew himself well enough to assure
himself that he would not stand it for a day. In his own
house he would be master, and if there came tempests he
would rule them. He could at least promise himself that.
As his mother had been strong, so had his father been
weak. But he had,—as he felt thankful in knowing,—inherited his mother's strength rather than his father's weakness. But, for all that, why have a tempest to rule at all?
Even though a man do rule his domestic tempests, he
cannot have a very quiet house with them. Then again
he remembered how very easily Clara had been won. He
wished to be just to all men and women, and to Clara
among the number. He desired even to be generous to
her,—with a moderate generosity. But above all things
he desired not to be duped. What if Clara had in truth
instigated her aunt to that deathbed scene, as his mother
had more than once suggested! He did not believe it.
He was sure that it had not been so. But what if it were
so? His desire to be generous and trusting was moderate;
—but his desire not to be cheated, not to be deceived, was
immoderate. Upon the whole, might it not be well for

him to wait a little longer, and ascertain how Clara really intended to behave herself in this emergency of the Askertons? Perhaps, after all, his mother might be right.

On the Sunday the expected letter came;—but before its contents are made known, it will be well that we should go back to Belton, and see what was done by Clara in reference to the tidings which her lover had sent her.

CHAPTER XVIII.

MRS. ASKERTON'S STORY.

WHEN Clara received the letter from Captain Aylmer on which so much is supposed to hang, she made up her mind to say nothing of it to any one,—not to think of it if she could avoid thinking of it,—till her cousin should have left her. She could not mention it to him; for, though there was no one from whom she would sooner have asked advice than from him, even on so delicate a matter as this, she could not do so in the present case, as her informant was her cousin's successful rival. When, therefore, Mrs. Askerton on leaving the church had spoken some customary word to Clara, begging her to come to the cottage on the following day, Clara had been unable to answer,—not having as yet made up her mind whether she would or would not go to the cottage again. Of course the idea of consulting her father occurred to her,—or rather the idea of telling him; but any such telling would lead to some advice from him which she would find it difficult to obey, and to which she would be unable to trust. And, moreover, why should she repeat this evil story against her neighbours?

She had a long morning by herself after Will had started, and then she endeavoured to arrange her thoughts and lay down for herself a line of conduct. Presuming this story to be true, to what did it amount? It certainly amounted to very much. If, in truth, this woman had left her own husband and gone away to live with another man, she had by doing so,—at any rate while she was doing so,—fallen in such a way as to make herself unfit for the society of an unmarried young woman who meant

to keep her name unblemished before the world. Clara
would not attempt any further unravelling of the case,
even in her own mind;—but on that point she could not
allow herself to have a doubt. Without condemning the
unhappy victim, she understood well that she would owe
it to all those who held her dear, if not to herself, to
eschew any close intimacy with one in such a position.
The rules of the world were too plainly written to allow
her to guide herself by any special judgment of her own in
such a matter. But if this friend of hers,—having been
thus unfortunate,—had since redeemed, or in part redeemed, her position by a second marriage, would it be
then imperative upon her to remember the past for ever,
and to declare that the stain was indelible? Clara felt
that with a previous knowledge of such a story she would
probably have avoided any intimacy with Mrs. Askerton.
She would then have been justified in choosing whether
such intimacy should or should not exist, and would so
have chosen out of deference to the world's opinion. But
now it was too late for that. Mrs. Askerton had for years
been her friend; and Clara had to ask herself *this* question;
was it now needful,—did her own feminine purity demand,—that she should throw her friend over because in
past years her life had been tainted by misconduct?

It was clear enough at any rate that this was expected
from her,—nay, imperatively demanded, by him who was
to be her lord,—by him to whom her future obedience
would be due. Whatever might be her immediate decision, he would have a right to call upon her to be guided
by his judgment as soon as she would become his wife.
And indeed, she felt that he had such right now,—unless
she should decide that no such right should be his, now
or ever. It was still within her power to say that she
could not submit herself to such a rule as his,—but having
received his commands she must do that or obey them.
Then she declared to herself, not following the matter out
logically, but urged to her decision by sudden impulse,
that at any rate she would not obey Lady Aylmer. She
would have nothing to do, in any such matter, with Lady
Aylmer. Lady Aylmer should be no god to her. That
question about the house at Perivale had been very painful
to her. She felt that she could have endured the dreary

solitude of Perivale without complaint, if, after her marriage, her husband's circumstances had made such a mode of living expedient. But to have been asked to pledge her consent to such a life before her marriage, to feel that he was bargaining for the privilege of being rid of her, to know that the Aylmer people were arranging that he, if he would marry her, should be as little troubled with his wife as possible;—all this had been very grievous to her. She had tried to console herself by the conviction that Lady Aylmer,—not Frederic,—had been the sinner; but even in that consolation there had been the terrible flaw that the words had come to her written by Frederic's hand. Could Will Belton have written such a letter to his future wife?

In her present emergency she must be guided by her own judgment or her own instincts,—not by any edicts from Aylmer Park! If in what she might do she should encounter the condemnation of Captain Aylmer, she would answer him,—she would be driven to answer him,—by counter-condemnation of him and his mother. Let it be so. Anything would be better than a mean, truckling subservience to the imperious mistress of Aylmer Park.

But what should she do as regarded Mrs. Askerton? That the story was true she was beginning to believe. That there was some such history was made certain to her by the promise which Mrs. Askerton had given her. " If you want to ask any questions, and will ask them of me, I will answer them." Such a promise would not have been volunteered, unless there was something special to be told. It would be best, perhaps, to demand from Mrs. Askerton the fulfilment of this promise. But then in doing so she must own from whence her information had come. Mrs. Askerton had told her that the " communication" would be made by her cousin Will. Her cousin Will had gone away without a word of Mrs. Askerton, and now the " communication" had come from Captain Aylmer!

The Monday and Tuesday were rainy days, and the rain was some excuse for her not going to the cottage. On the Wednesday her father was ill, and his illness made a further excuse for her remaining at home. But on the Wednesday evening there came a note to her from Mrs. Askerton. " You naughty girl, why do you not come to

me? Colonel Askerton has been away since yesterday
morning, and I am forgetting the sound of my own voice.
I did not trouble you when your divine cousin was here,—
for reasons; but unless you come to me now, I shall think
that his divinity has prevailed. Colonel Askerton is in
Ireland, about some property, and will not be back till
next week."

Clara sent back a promise by the messenger, and on the
following morning she put on her hat and shawl, and
started on her dreaded task. When she left the house she
had not even yet quite made up her mind what she would
do. At first she put her lover's letter into her pocket, so
that she might have it for reference; but, on second
thoughts, she replaced it in her desk, dreading lest she
might be persuaded into showing or reading some part of
it. There had come a sharp frost after the rain, and the
ground was hard and dry. In order that she might gain
some further last moment for thinking, she walked round,
up among the rocks, instead of going straight to the
cottage; and for a moment,—though the air was sharp
with frost,—she sat upon the stone where she had been
seated when her cousin Will blurted out the misfortune of
his heart. She sat there on purpose that she might think
of him, and recall his figure, and the tones of his voice, and
the look of his eyes, and the gesture of his face. What a
man he was;—so tender, yet so strong; so thoughtful of
others, and yet so self-sufficient! She had, unconsciously,
imputed to him one fault, that he had loved and then forgotten his love;—unconsciously, for she had tried to think
that this was a virtue rather than a fault;—but now,—
with a full knowledge of what she was doing, but without
any intention of doing it,—she acquitted him of that one
fault. Now that she could acquit him, she owned that it
would have been a fault. To have loved, and so soon to
have forgotten it! No; he had loved her truly; and alas!
he was one who could not be made to forget it. Then she
went on to the cottage, exercising her thoughts rather on
the contrast between the two men, than on the subject to
which she should have applied them.

"So you have come at last," said Mrs. Askerton. "Till
I got your message I thought there was to be some dreadful
misfortune."

"What misfortune?"

"Something dreadful! One often anticipates something very bad without exactly knowing what. At least, I do. I am always expecting a catastrophe;—when I am alone that is;—and then I am so often alone."

"That simply means low spirits, I suppose."

"It's more than that, my dear."

"Not much more, I take it."

"Once when we were in India we lived close to the powder magazine, and we were always expecting to be blown up. You never lived near a powder magazine."

"No, never;—unless there's one at Belton. But I should have thought that was exciting."

"And then there was the gentleman who always had the sword hanging over him by the horse's hair."

"What do you mean, Mrs. Askerton?"

"Don't look so innocent, Clara. You know what I mean. What were the results at last of your cousin's diligence as a detective officer?"

"Mrs. Askerton, you wrong my cousin greatly. He never once mentioned your name while he was with us. He did not make a single allusion to you, or to Colonel Askerton, or to the cottage."

"He did not?"

"Never once."

"Then I beg his pardon. But not the less has he been busy making inquiries."

"But why should you say that there is a powder magazine, or a sword hanging over your head?"

"Ah, why?"

Here was the subject ready opened to her hand, and yet Clara did not know how to go on with it. It seemed to her now that it would have been easier for her to commence it, if Mrs. Askerton had made no commencement herself. As it was, she knew not how to introduce the subject of Captain Aylmer's letter, and was almost inclined to wait, thinking that Mrs. Askerton might tell her own story without any such introduction. But nothing of the kind was forthcoming. Mrs. Askerton began to talk of the frost, and then went on to abuse Ireland, complaining of the hardship her husband endured in being forced to go thither in winter to look after his tenants.

"What did you mean?" said Clara, at last, "by the sword hanging over your head?"

"I think I told you what I meant pretty plainly. If you did not understand me, I cannot tell you more plainly."

"It is odd that you should say so much, and not wish to say more."

"Ah;—you are making your inquiries now."

"In my place, would you not do so too? How can I help it when you talk of a sword? Of course you make me ask what the sword is."

"And am I bound to satisfy your curiosity?"

"You told me just before my cousin came here, that if I asked any question you would answer me."

"And I am to understand that you are asking such a question now?"

"Yes;—if it will not offend you."

"But what if it will offend me,—offend me greatly? Who likes to be inquired into?"

"But you courted such inquiry from me."

"No, Clara, I did not do that. I'll tell you what I did. I gave you to understand that if it was needful that you should hear about me and my antecedents, certain matters as to which Mr. Belton had been inquiring in a manner that I thought to be most unjustifiable, I would tell you that story."

"And do so without being angry with me for asking."

"I meant, of course, that I would not make it a ground for quarrelling with you. If I wished to tell you I could do so without any inquiry."

"I have sometimes thought that you did wish to tell me."

"Sometimes I have,—almost."

"But you have no such wish now."

"Can't you understand? It may well be that one so much alone as I am,—living here without a female friend, or even acquaintance, except yourself,—should often feel a longing for that comfort which full confidence between us would give me."

"Then why not——"

"Stop a moment. Can't you understand that I may feel this, and yet entertain the greatest horror against inquiry? We all like to tell our own sorrows, but who likes to be

inquired into? Many a woman burns to make a full con-
fession, who would be as mute as death before a policeman."

" I am no policeman."

" But you are determined to ask a policeman's questions."

To this Clara made no immediate reply. She felt that
she was acting almost falsely in going on with such questions, while she was in fact aware of all the circumstances
which Mrs. Askerton could tell;—but she did not know
how to declare her knowledge and to explain it. She sincerely wished that Mrs. Askerton should be made acquainted with the truth; but she had fallen into a line of
conversation which did not make her own task easy. But
the idea of her own hypocrisy was distressing to her, and
she rushed at the difficulty with hurried, eager words,
resolving that, at any rate, there should be no longer any
doubt between them.

"Mrs. Askerton," she said, "I know it all. There is
nothing for you to tell. I know what the sword is."

" What is it that you know?"

" That you were married long ago to—Mr. Berdmore."

" Then Mr. Belton did do me the honour of talking about
me when he was here." As she said this she rose from her
chair, and stood before Clara with flashing eyes.

" Not a word. He never mentioned your name, or the
name of any one belonging to you. I have heard it from
another."

" From what other?"

" I do not know that that signifies,—but I have learned it."

" Well;—and what next?"

" I do not know what next. As so much has been told
me, and as you had said that I might ask you, I have come
to you, yourself. I shall believe your own story, more
thoroughly from yourself than from any other teller."

" And suppose I refuse to answer you?"

" Then I can say nothing further."

" And what will you do?"

" Ah;—that I do not know. But you are harsh to
me, while I am longing to be kind to you. Can you not
see that this has been all forced upon me,—partly by
yourself?"

"And the other part;—who has forced that upon you? Who
is your informant? If you mean to be generous, be generous

altogether. Is it a man or a woman that has taken the trouble
to rip up old sorrows that my name may be blackened?
But what matters? There; I was married to Captain
Berdmore. I left him, and went away with my present
husband. For three years I was a man's mistress, and not
his wife. When that poor creature died we were married,
and then came here. Now you know it all;—all;—all,—
though doubtless your informant has made a better story of
it. After that perhaps I have been very wicked to sully
the air you breathe by my presence."

" Why do you say that,—to me?"

" But no;—you do not know it all. No one can ever
know it all. No one can ever know how I suffered before I
was driven to escape, or how good to me has been he who
—who—who——" Then she turned her back upon Clara,
and, walking off to the window, stood there, hiding the
tears which clouded her eyes, and concealing the sobs
which choked her utterance.

For some moments,—for a space which seemed long to
both of them,—Clara kept her seat in silence. She hardly
dared to speak, and though she longed to show her sympathy, she knew not what to say. At last she too rose and
followed the other to the window. She uttered no words,
however, but gently putting her arm around Mrs. Askerton's waist, stood there close to her, looking out upon the
cold wintry flower-beds,—not venturing to turn her eyes
upon her companion. The motion of her arm was at first
very gentle, but after a while she pressed it closer, and
thus by degrees drew her friend to her with an eager,
warm, and enduring pressure. Mrs. Askerton made some
little effort towards repelling her, some faint motion of
resistance; but as the embrace became warmer the poor
woman yielded herself to it, and allowed her face to fall
upon Clara's shoulder. So they stood, speaking no word,
making no attempt to rid themselves of the tears which
were blinding their eyes, but gazing out through the mois-
ture on the bleak wintry scene before them. Clara's mind
was the more active at the moment, for she was resolving
that in this episode of her life she would accept no lesson
whatever from Lady Aylmer's teaching;—no, nor any lesson
whatever from the teaching of any Aylmer in existence. And
as for the world's rules, she would fit herself to them as best

she could; but no such fitting should drive her to the un-womanly cruelty of deserting this woman whom she had known and loved,—and whom she now loved with a fervour which she had never before felt towards her.

"You have heard it all now," said Mrs. Askerton at last.

"And is it not better so?"

"Ah;—I do not know. How should I know?"

"Do you not know?" And as she spoke Clara pressed her arm still closer. "Do you not know yet?" Then, turning herself half round, she clasped the other woman full in her arms and kissed her forehead, and her lips. "Do you not know yet?"

"But you will go away, and people will tell you that you are wrong."

"What people?" said Clara, thinking as she spoke of the whole family at Aylmer Castle.

"Your husband will tell you so."

"I have no husband,—as yet,—to order me what to think or what not to think."

"No;—not quite as yet. But you will tell him all this."

"He knows it. It was he who told me."

"What!—Captain Aylmer?"

"Yes; Captain Aylmer."

"And what did he say?"

"Never mind. Captain Aylmer is not my husband,—not as yet. If he takes me, he must take me as I am, not as he might possibly have wished me to be. Lady Aylmer——"

"And does Lady Aylmer know it?"

"Yes. Lady Aylmer is one of those hard, severe women who never forgive."

"Ah, I see it all now. I understand it all. Clara, you must forget me, and come here no more. You shall not be ruined because you are generous."

"Ruined! If Lady Aylmer's displeasure can ruin me, I must put up with ruin. I will not accept her for my guide. I am too old, and have had my own way too long. Do not let that thought trouble you. In this matter I shall judge for myself. I have judged for myself already."

"And your father?"

"Papa knows nothing of it."

"But you will tell him?"

"I do not know. Poor papa is very ill. If he were well I would tell him, and he would think as I do."

"And your cousin?"

"You say that he has heard it all."

"I think so. Do you know that I remembered him the first moment that I saw him. But what could I do? When you mentioned to me my old name, my real name, how could I be honest? I have been driven to do that which has made honesty to me impossible. My life has been a lie; and yet how could I help it? I must live somewhere,—and how could I live anywhere without deceit?"

"And yet that is so sad."

"Sad indeed! But what could I do? Of course I was wrong in the beginning. Though how am I to regret it, when it has given me such a husband as I have? Ah!— if you could know it all, I think,—I think you would forgive me."

Then by degrees she told it all, and Clara was there for hours listening to her story. The reader will not care to hear more of it than he has heard. Nor would Clara have desired any closer revelation; but as it is often difficult to obtain a confidence, so is it impossible to stop it in the midst of its effusion. Mrs. Askerton told the history of her life,—of her first foolish engagement, her belief, her half-belief, in the man's reformation, of the miseries which resulted from his vices, of her escape and shame, of her welcome widowhood, and of her second marriage. And as she told it, she paused at every point to insist on the goodness of him who was now her husband. "I shall tell him this," she said at last, "as I do everything; and then he will know that I have in truth got a friend."

She asked again and again about Mr. Belton, but Clara could only tell her that she knew nothing of her cousin's knowledge. Will might have heard it all, but if so he had kept his information to himself.

"And now what shall you do?" Mrs. Askerton asked of Clara, at length prepared to go.

"Do? in what way? I shall do nothing."

" But you will write to Captain Aylmer ?"

" Yes ;—I shall write to him."

" And about this ?"

" Yes ;—I suppose I must write to him."

" And what will you say ?"

" That I cannot tell. I wish I knew what to say. If it were to his mother I could write my letter easily enough."

" And what would you say to her ?"

" I would tell her that I was responsible for my own friends. But I must go now. Papa will complain that I am so long away." Then there was another embrace, and at last Clara found her way out of the house and was alone again in the park.

She clearly acknowledged to herself that she had a great difficulty before her. She had committed herself altogether to Mrs. Askerton, and could no longer entertain any thought of obeying the very plainly-expressed commands which Captain Aylmer had given her. The story as told by Captain Aylmer had been true throughout ; but, in the teeth of that truth, she intended to maintain her acquaintance with Mrs. Askerton. From that there was now no escape. She had been carried away by impulse in what she had done and said at the cottage ; but she could not bring herself to regret it. She could not believe that it was her duty to throw over and abandon a woman whom she loved, because that woman had once, in her dire extremity, fallen away from the path of virtue. But how was she to write the letter ?

When she reached her father he complained of her absence and almost scolded her for having been so long at the cottage. " I cannot see," said he, " what you find in that woman to make so much of her."

" She is the only neighbour I have, papa."

" And better none than her, if all that people say of her is true."

" All that people say is never true, papa."

" There is no smoke without fire. I am not at all sure that it's good for you to be so much with her."

" Oh, papa,—don't treat me like a child."

" And I'm sure it's not good for me that you should be so much away. For anything I have seen of you all day you might have been at Perivale. But you are going soon,

altogether, so I suppose I may as well make up my mind
to it."

" I am not going for a long time yet, papa."

" What do you mean by that ?"

" I mean that there's nothing to take me away from here
at present."

" You are engaged to be married."

" But it will be a long engagement. It is one of those
engagements in which neither party is very anxious for an
immediate change." There was something bitter in Clara's
tone as she said this, which the old man perceived, but
could only half understand. Clara remained with him
then for the rest of the day, going down stairs for five
minutes, to her dinner, and then returning to him and
reading aloud while he dozed. Her winter evenings at Belton
Castle were not very bright, but she was used to them, and
made no complaint.

When she left her father for the night she got out her
desk and prepared herself for her letter to her lover. She
was determined that it should be finished that night before
she went to bed. And it was so finished; though the
writing of it gave her much labour, and occupied her till
the late hours had come upon her. When completed it was
as follows :—

"Belton Castle, Thursday Night.

" DEAR FREDERIC,—I received your letter last Sunday
but I could not answer it sooner, as it required much consideration, and also some information which I have only
obtained to-day. About the plan of living at Perivale I
will not say much now, as my mind is so full of other
things. I think, however, I may promise that I will never
make any needless difficulty as to your plans. My cousin
Will left us on Monday, so your mother need not have any
further anxiety on that head. It does papa good to have
him here, and for that reason I am sorry that he has gone.
I can assure you that I don't think what you said about
him meant anything at all particular. Will is my nearest
cousin, and of course you would be glad that I should like
him,—which I do, very much.

"And now about the other subject, which I own has
distressed me, as you supposed it would ;—I mean about

Mrs. Askerton. I find it very difficult in your letter to divide what comes from your mother and what from yourself. Of course I want to make the division, as every word from you has great weight with me. At present I don't know Lady Aylmer personally, and I cannot think of her as I do of you. Indeed, were I to know her ever so well, I could not have the same deference for her that I have for the man who is to be my husband. I only say this, as I fear that Lady Aylmer and I may not perhaps agree about Mrs. Askerton.

"I find that your story about Mrs. Askerton is in the main true. But the person who told it you does not seem to have known any of the provocations which she received. She was very badly treated by Captain Berdmore, who, I am afraid, was a terrible drunkard; and at last she found it impossible to stay with him. So she went away. I cannot tell you how horrid it all was, but I am sure that if I could make you understand it, it would go a long way in inducing you to excuse her. She was married to Colonel Askerton as soon as Captain Berdmore died, and this took place before she came to Belton. I hope you will remember that. It all occurred out in India, and I really hardly know what business we have to inquire about it now.

"At any rate, as I have been acquainted with her a long time, and very intimately, and as I am sure that she has repented of anything that has been wrong, I do not think that I ought to quarrel with her now. Indeed I have promised her that I will not. I think I owe it you to tell you the whole truth, and that is the truth.

"Pray give my regards to your mother, and tell her that I am sure she would judge differently if she were in my place. This poor woman has no other friend here; and who am I, that I should take upon myself to condemn her? I cannot do it. Dear Frederic, pray do not be angry with me for asserting my own will in this matter. I think you would wish me to have an opinion of my own. In my present position I am bound to have one, as I am, as yet, responsible for what I do myself. I shall be very, very sorry, if I find that you differ from me; but still I cannot be made to think that I am wrong. I wish you were here that we might talk it over together, as I think that, in that case, you would agree with me.

" If you can manage to come to us at Easter, or any
other time when Parliament does not keep you in London,
we shal' be so delighted to see you.

"Dear Frederic,

"Yours very affectionately,

"Clara Amedroz."

CHAPTER XIX.

MISS AMEDROZ HAS ANOTHER CHANCE.

It was on a Sunday morning that Clara's letter reached
Aylmer Park, and that Frederick Aylmer found it on his
plate as he took his place at the breakfast-table. Domestic
habits at Aylmer Castle had grown with the growth of
years till they had become adamantine, and domestic
habit required prayers every morning at a quarter before
nine o'clock. At twenty minutes before nine Lady Aylmer
would always be in the dining-room to make the tea and
open the post-bag, and as she was always there alone, she
knew more about other people's letters than other people
ever knew about hers. When these operations were over
Lady Aylmer rang the bell; and the servants of the family,
who by that time had already formed themselves into
line in the hall, would march in, and settle themselves
on benches prepared for them near the side-board,—which
benches were afterwards carried away by the retiring pro-
cession. Lady Aylmer herself always read prayers, as
Sir Anthony never appeared till the middle of breakfast.
Belinda would usually come down in a scurry as she heard
her mother's bell, in such a way as to put the army in the
hall to some confusion; but Frederic Aylmer, when he was
at home, rarely entered the room till after the service was
over. At Perivale no doubt he was more strict in his conduct; but then at Perivale he had special interest and
influences which were wanting to him at Aylmer Park.
During those five minutes Lady Aylmer would deal round
the letters to the several plates of the inmates of her house,
—not without looking at the post-office marks upon them;

and on this occasion she had dealt a letter from Clara to her son.

The arrival of the letter was announced to Frederic Aylmer before he took his seat.

"Frederic," said her ladyship in her most portentous voice, "I am glad to say that at last there is a letter from Belton."

He made no immediate reply, but making his way slowly to his place, took up the little packet, turned it over in his hand, and then put it into his pocket. Having done this, he began very slowly with his tea and egg. For three minutes his mother was contented to make, or to pretend to make, some effort in the same direction. Then her impatience became too much for her, and she began to question him.

"Will you not read it, Frederic?"

"Of course I shall, ma'am."

"But why not do so now, when you know how anxious we are?"

"There are letters which one would sooner read in private."

"But when a matter is of so much importance——" said Belinda.

"The importance, Bel, is to me, and not to you," said her brother.

"All we want to know is," continued the sister, "that she promises to be guided by you in this matter; and of course we feel quite sure that she will."

"If you are quite sure, that must be sufficient for you."

"I really think you need not quarrel with your sister," said Lady Aylmer, "because she is anxious as to the—the respectability, I must say, for there is no other word, of a young lady whom you propose to make your wife. I can assure you that I am very anxious myself,—very anxious indeed."

Captain Aylmer made no answer to this; but he did not take the letter from his pocket. He drank his tea in silence, and in silence sent up his cup to be refilled. In silence also was it returned to him. He ate his two eggs and his three bits of toast according to his custom, and, when he had finished, sat out his three or four minutes as was usual. Then he got up to retire to his room, with the envelope still unbroken in his pocket.

"You will go to church with us, I suppose?" said Lady Aylmer.

"I won't promise, ma'am; but if I do, I'll walk across the park,—so that you need not wait for me."

Then both the mother and sister knew that the member for Perivale did not intend to go to church on that occasion. To morning service Sir Anthony always went, the habits of Aylmer Park having in them more of adamant in reference to him than they had as regarded his son.

When the father, mother, and daughter returned, Captain Aylmer had read his letter, and had, after doing so, received further tidings from Belton Park,—further tidings which for the moment prevented the necessity of any reference to the letter, and almost drove it from his own thoughts. When his mother entered the library, he was standing before the fire with a scrap of paper in his hand.

"Since you have been at church there has come a telegraph message," he said.

"What is it, Frederic? Do not frighten me,—if you can avoid it!"

"You need not be frightened, ma'am, for you did not know him. Mr. Amedroz is dead."

"No!" said Lady Aylmer, seating herself.

"Dead!" said Belinda, holding up her hands.

"God bless my soul!" said the baronet, who had now followed the ladies into the room. "Dead! Why, Fred, he was five years younger than I am!"

Then Captain Aylmer read the words of the message:—

"Mr. Amedroz died this morning at five o'clock. I have sent word to the lawyer and to Mr. Belton."

"Who does it come from?" asked Lady Aylmer.

"From Colonel Askerton."

Lady Aylmer paused, and shook her head, and moved her foot uneasily upon the carpet. The tidings, as far as they went, might be unexceptionable, but the source from whence they had come had evidently polluted them in her ladyship's judgment. Then she uttered a series of inter-ejaculations, expressions of mingled sorrow and anger.

"There was no one else near her," said Captain Aylmer, apologetically.

" Is there no clergyman in the parish ?"

" He lives a long way off. The message had to be sent at once."

" Are there no servants in the house ? It looks,—it looks—— But I am the last person in the world to form a harsh judgment of a young woman at such a moment as this. What did she say in her letter, Fred ?"

Captain Aylmer had devoted two hours of consideration to the letter before the telegram had come to relieve his mind by a fresh subject, and in those two hours he had not been able to extract much of comfort out of the document. It was, as he felt, a stubborn, stiff-necked, disobedient, almost rebellious letter. It contained a manifest defiance of his mother, and exhibited doctrines of most questionable morality. It had become to him a matter of doubt whether he could possibly marry a woman who could entertain such ideas and write such a letter. If the doubt was to be decided in his own mind against Clara, he had better show the letter at once to his mother, and allow her ladyship to fight the battle for him ;—a task which, as he well knew, her ladyship would not be slow to undertake. But he had not succeeded in answering the question satisfactorily to himself, when the telegram arrived and diverted all his thoughts. Now that Mr. Amedroz was dead, the whole thing might be different. Clara would come away from Belton and Mrs. Askerton, and begin life, as it were, afresh. It seemed as though in such an emergency she ought to have another chance ; and therefore he did not hasten to pronounce his judgment. Lady Aylmer also felt something of this, and forbore to press her question when it was not answered.

" She will have to leave Belton now, I suppose ?" said Sir Anthony.

" The property will belong to a distant cousin,—a Mr. William Belton."

" And where will she go ?" said Lady Aylmer. " I suppose she has no place that she can call her home ?"

" Would it not be a good thing to ask her here ?" said Belinda. Such a question as that was very rash on the part of Miss Aylmer. In the first place, the selection of guests for Aylmer Park was rarely left to her ; and in this special case she should have understood that such a proposal should have been fully considered by Lady Aylmer, before it reached Frederic's ears.

"I think it would be a very good plan," said Captain Aylmer, generously.

Lady Aylmer shook her head. "I should like much to know what she has said about that unfortunate connection before I offer to take her by the hand myself. I'm sure Fred will feel that I ought to do so."

But Fred retreated from the room without showing the letter. He retreated from the room and betook himself to solitude, that he might again endeavour to make up his mind as to what he would do. He put on his hat and his great-coat and gloves, and went off,—without his luncheon, that he might consider it all. Clara Amedroz had now no home,—and, indeed, very little means of providing one. If he intended that she should be his-wife, he must furnish her with a home at once. It seemed to him that three houses might possibly be open to her,—of which one, the only one which under such circumstances would be proper, was Aylmer Park. The other two were Plaistow Hall, and Mrs. Askerton's cottage at Belton. As to the latter,— should she ever take shelter there, everything must be over between him and her. On that point there could be no doubt. He could not bring himself to marry a wife out of Mrs. Askerton's drawing-room, nor could he expect his mother to receive a young woman brought into the family under such circumstances. And Plaistow Hall was almost as bad. It was as bad to him, though it would, perhaps, be less objectionable in the eyes of Lady Aylmer. Should Clara go to Plaistow Hall, there must be an end to everything. Of that also he taught himself to be quite certain. Then he took out Clara's letter and read it again. She acknowledged the story about the woman to be true,—such a story as it was too,—and yet refused to quarrel with the woman; had absolutely promised the woman not to quarrel with her! Then he read and re-read the passage in which Clara claimed the right of forming her own opinion in such matters. Nothing could be more indelicate;—nothing more unfit for his wife. He began to think that he had better show the letter to his mother, and acknowledge that the match must be broken off. That softening of his heart which had followed upon the receipt of the tele-

graph message departed from him as he dwelt upon the
stubborn, stiff-necked, unfeminine obstinacy of the latter.
Then he remembered that nothing had as yet been done
towards putting his aunt's fifteen hundred pounds absolutely into Clara's hands, and he remembered also that she
might at the present moment be in great want. William
Belton might not, improbably, assist her in her want, and
this idea was wormwood to him in spite of his almost
formed resolution to give up his own claims. He calculated that the income arising from fifteen hundred pounds
would be very small, and he wished that he had counselled
his aunt to double the legacy. He thought very much
about the amount of the money and the way in which it
might be best expended, and was, after his cold fashion,
really solicitous as to Clara's welfare. If he could have
fashioned her future life, and his own too, in accordance
with his own now existing wishes, I think he would have
arranged that neither of them should marry at all, and that
to him should be assigned the duty and care of being
Clara's protector,—with full permission to tell her his
mind as often as he pleased on the subject of Mrs.
Askerton. Then he went in and wrote a note to Mr.
Green, the lawyer, desiring that the interest of the fifteen
hundred pounds for one year might be at once remitted to
Miss Amedroz. He knew that he ought to write to her
himself immediately, without loss of a post; but how was
he to write while things were in their present position?
Were he now to condole with her on her father's death,
without any reference to the great Askerton iniquity, he
would thereby be condoning all that was past, and acknowledging the truth and propriety of her arguments.
And he would be doing even worse than that; he would
be cutting the ground absolutely from beneath his own
feet as regarded that escape from his engagement which he
was contemplating.

What a cold-hearted, ungenerous wretch he must have
been! That will be the verdict against him. But the
verdict will be untrue. Cold-hearted and ungenerous he
was; but he was no wretch,—as men and women are
now-a-days called wretches. He was chilly-hearted, but
yet quite capable of enough love to make him a good son,
a good husband, and a good father. And though he was

ungenerous from the nature of his temperament, he **was** not close-fisted or over-covetous. And he was a just man, desirous of obtaining nothing that was not fairly his own. But, in truth, the artists have been so much in the habit of painting for us our friends' faces without any of those flaws and blotches with which work and high living are apt to disfigure us, that we turn in disgust from a portrait in which the roughnesses and pimples are made apparent.

But it was essential that he should now do something, and before he sat down to dinner he did show Clara's letter to his mother. "Mother," he said, as he sat himself down in her little room upstairs ;—and she knew well by the tone of his voice, and by the mode of his address, that there was to be a solemn occasion, and a serious deliberative council on the present existing family difficulty,—"mother, of course I have intended to let you know what is the nature of Clara's answer to my letter."

"I am glad there is to be no secret between us, Frederic. You know how I dislike secrets in families." As she said this she took the letter out of her son's hands with an eagerness that was almost greedy. As she read it, he stood over her, watching her eyes, as they made their way down the first page and on to the second, and across to the third, and so, gradually on, till the whole reading was accomplished. What Clara had written about her cousin Will, Lady Aylmer did not quite understand ; and on this point now she was so little anxious that she passed over that portion of the letter readily. But when she came to Mrs. Askerton and the allusions to herself, she took care to comprehend the meaning and weight of every word. "Divide your words and mine ! Why should we want to divide them ? Not agree with me about Mrs. Askerton ! How is it possible that any decent young woman should not agree with me ! It is a matter in which there is no room for a doubt. True ;—the story true ! Of course it is true. Does she not know that it would not have reached her from Aylmer Park if it were not true ? Provocation ! Badly treated ! Went away. Married to Colonel Askerton as soon as Captain Berdmore died ! Why, Frederic, she cannot have been taught to understand the first principle of morals in life ! And she that was so much with my poor sister ! Well, well !" The reader should understand that the late Mrs. Winterfield and Lady Aylmer had never been able to agree with each other on religious subjects. "Remember that they are married. Why should we remember anything of the kind? It does not make an atom of difference as to the woman's character. Repented! How can Clara say whether she has repented or not? But that has nothing to do with it. Not quarrel with her,—as she calls it! Not give her up! Then, Frederic, of course it must be all over as far as you are concerned." When she had finished her reading, she returned the letter still open to her son, shaking her head almost triumphantly. "As far as I am a judge of a young woman's character, I can only give you one counsel," said Lady Aylmer solemnly.

"I think that she should have another chance," said Captain Aylmer.

"What other chance can you give her? It seems to me that she is obstinately bent on her own destruction."

"You might ask her to come here, as Belinda suggested."

"Belinda was very foolish to suggest anything of the kind without more consideration."

"I suppose that my future wife would be made welcome here?"

"Yes, Frederic, certainly. I do not know who could be more welcome. But is she to be your wife?"

"We are engaged."

"But does not that letter break any engagement? Is there not enough in that to make such a marriage quite out of the question? What do you think about it yourself, Frederic?"

"I think that she should have another chance."

What would Clara have thought of all this herself, if he could have heard the conversation between Lady Aylmer and her betrothed husband, and have known that her lover was proposing to give her "another chance?" But it is lucky for us that we seldom know what our best friends say on our behalf, when they discuss us and our faults behind our backs.

"What chance, Frederic, can she have? She knows all about this horrid woman, and yet refuses to give her up! What chance can she have after that?"

"I think that you might have her here,—and talk to

her." Lady Aylmer in answer to this simply shook her head. And I think she was right in supposing that such shaking of her head was a sufficient reply to her son's proposition. What talking could possibly be of service to such a one as this Miss Amedroz? Why should she throw her pearls before swine? "We must either ask her to come here, or else I must go to her," said Captain Aylmer.

"I don't see that at all, Frederic."

"I think it must be so. As she is situated at present, she has got no home; and I think it would be very horrid that she should be driven into that woman's house, simply because she has no other shelter for her head."

"I suppose she can remain where she is for the present?"

"She is all alone, you know; and it must be very gloomy; —and her cousin can turn her out at a moment's notice."

"But all that would not entitle her to come here, unless——"

"No;—I quite understand that. But you cannot wonder that I should feel the hardship of her position."

"Who is to be blamed if it be hard? You see, Frederic, I take my standing upon that letter;—her own letter. How am I to ask a young woman into my house who declares openly that my opinion on such a matter goes for nothing with her? How am I to do it? That's what I ask you. How am I to do it? It's all very well for Belinda to suggest this and that. But how am I to do it? That's what I want to know."

But at last Lady Aylmer managed to answer the question for herself, and did do it. But this was not done on that Sunday afternoon; nor on the Monday, nor on the Tuesday. The question was closely debated, and at last the anxious mother perceived that the giving of the invitation would be more safe than the withholding it. Captain Aylmer at last expressed his determination to go to Belton unless the invitation were given; and then should he do that, there might be danger that he would never be again seen at Aylmer Park till he brought Clara Amedroz with him as his wife. The position was one of great difficulty, but the interests at stake were so immense that something must be risked. It might be that Clara would not come when invited, and in that case her obstinacy would be a great point gained. And if she did come——! Well; Lady

Aylmer admitted to herself that the game would be difficult, —difficult and very troublesome; but yet it might be played, and perhaps won. Lady Aylmer was a woman who had great confidence in herself. Not so utterly had victory in such contests deserted her hands, that she need fear to break a lance with Miss Amedroz beneath her own roof, when the occasion was so pressing.

The invitation was therefore sent in a note written by herself, and was enclosed in a letter from her son. After much consultation and many doubts on the subject, it was at last agreed that nothing further should now be urged about Mrs. Askerton. "She shall have her chance," said Lady Aylmer over and over again, repeating her son's words. "She shall have her chance." Lady Aylmer, therefore, in her note, confined herself strictly to the giving of the invitation, and to a suggestion that as Clara had now no settled home of her own, a temporary sojourn at Aylmer Park might be expedient. And Captain Aylmer in his letter hardly said much more. He knew, as he wrote the words, that they were cold and comfortless, and that he ought on such an occasion to have written words that should have been warm at any rate, even though they might not have contained comfort. But, to have written with affection, he should have written at once; and he had postponed his letter from the Sunday till the Wednesday. It had been absolutely necessary that that important question as to the invitation should be answered before he could write at all.

When all this was settled he went up to London; and there was an understanding between him and his mother that he should return to Aylmer Park with Clara, in the event of her acceptance of the invitation.

"You won't go down to Belton for her?" said the mother.

"No;—I do not think that will be necessary," said the son.

"I should think not," said the mother.

CHAPTER XX.

WILLIAM BELTON DOES NOT GO OUT HUNTING

WE will now follow the other message, which was sent down into Norfolk, and which did not get into Belton's hands till the Monday morning. He was sitting with his sister at breakfast, and was prepared for hunting, when the paper was brought into the room. Telegraph messages were not very common at Plaistow Hall, and on the arrival of any that had as yet reached that house, something of that awe had been felt with which such missives were always accompanied in their earliest days. "A telegruff message, mum, for Mr. William," said the maid, looking at her mistress with eyes opened wide, as she handed the important bit of paper to her master. Will opened it rapidly, laying down the knife and fork with which which he was about to operate upon a ham before him. He was dressed in boots and breeches, and a scarlet coat,—in which garb he was, in his sister's eyes, the most handsome man in Norfolk.

"Oh, Mary!" he exclaimed.

"What is it, Will?"

"Mr. Amedroz is dead."

Miss Belton put out her hand for the paper before she spoke again, as though she could better appreciate the truth of what she heard when reading it herself on the telegraph slip, than she had done from her brother's words. "How sudden! how terribly sudden!" she said.

"Sudden indeed! When I left him he was not well, certainly, but I should have said that he might have lived for twenty years. Poor old man! I can hardly say why it was so, but I had taken a liking to him."

"You take a liking to everybody, Will."

"No I don't. I know people I don't like." Will Belton as he said this was thinking of Captain Aylmer, and he pressed the heel of his boot hard against the floor.

"And Mr. Amedroz is dead! It seems to be so terribly sudden. What will she do, Will?"

"That's what I'm thinking about."

"Of course you are, my dear. I can see that. I wish—I wish——"

"It's no good wishing anything, Mary. I don't think wishing ever did any good yet. If I might have my wish, I shouldn't know how to have it."

"I was wishing that you didn't think so much about it."

"You need not be troubled about me. I shall do very well. But what is to become of her,—now at once? Might she not come here? You are now the nearest female relation that she has." Mary looked at him with her anxious, painful eyes, and he knew by her look that she did not approve of his plan. "I could go away," he continued. "She could come to you without being troubled by seeing me."

"And where would you go, Will?"

"What does it matter? To the devil, I suppose."

"Oh, Will, Will!"

"You know what I mean. I'd go anywhere. Where is she to find a home till,—till she is married?" He had paused at the word; but was determined not to shrink from it, and bolted it out in a loud, sharp tone, so that both he and she recognised all the meaning of the word, —all that was conveyed in the idea. He hated himself when he endeavoured to conceal from his own mind any of the misery that was coming upon him. He loved her. He could not get over it. The passion was on him,—like a palsy, for the shaking off of which no sufficient physical energy was left to him. It clung to him in his goings out and comings in with a painful, wearing tenacity, against which he would now and again struggle, swearing that it should be so no longer,—but against which he always struggled in vain. It was with him when he was hunting. He was ever thinking of it when the bird rose before his gun. As he watched the furrow, as his men and horses would drive it straight and deep through the ground, he was thinking of her,—and not of the straightness and depth of the furrow, as had been his wont in former years. Then he would turn away his face, and stand alone in his field, blinded by the salt drops in his eyes, weeping at his own weakness. And when he was quite alone, he would stamp his foot on the ground, and throw abroad his arms, and

curse himself. What Nessus's shirt was this that had fallen
upon him and unmanned him from the sole of his foot to the
top of his head? He went through the occupations of the
week; he hunted, and shot, and gave his orders, and paid
his men their wages;—but he did it all with a palsy of
love upon him as he did it. He wanted her, and he could not
overcome the want. He could not bear to confess to himself that the thing by which he had set so much store could
never belong to him. His sister understood it all, and
sometimes he was almost angry with her because of her
understanding it. She sympathised with him in all his
moods, and sometimes he would shake away her sympathy
as though it scalded him. " Where is she to find a home
till,—till she is married?" he said.

Not a word had as yet been said between them about
the property which was now his estate. He was now
Belton of Belton, and it must be supposed that both he and
she had remembered that it was so. But hitherto not a
word had been said between them on that point. Now
she was compelled to allude to it. " Can not she live at
the Castle for the present?"

" What!—all alone?"

" Of course she is remaining there now."

"Yes," said he, " of course she is there now. Now!
Why, remember what these telegraph messages are. He
died only on yesterday morning. Of course she is there,
but I do not think it can be good that she should remain
there. There is no one near her where she is but that Mrs.
Askerton. It can hardly be good for her to have no other
female friend at such a time as this."

" I do not think that Mrs. Askerton will hurt her."

" Mrs. Askerton will not hurt her at all,—and as long as
Clara does not know the story, Mrs. Askerton may serve
as well as another. But yet——"

" Can I go to her, Will?"

" No, dearest. The journey would kill you in winter.
And he would not like it. We are bound to think of that
for her sake, — cold-hearted, thankless, meagre-minded
creature as I know he is."

" I do not know why he should be so bad."

" No, nor I. But I know that he is. Never mind.
Why should we talk about him? I suppose she'll have to

go there,—to Aylmer Park. I suppose they'll send for
her, and keep her there till it's all finished. I'll tell you
what, Mary,—I shall give her the place."

" What,—Belton Castle?"

" Why not? Will it ever be of any good to you or me?
Do you want to go and live there?"

" No, indeed;—not for myself."

" And do you think that I could live there. Besides,
why should she be turned out of her father's house?"

" He would not be mean enough to take it."

" He would be mean enough for anything. Besides, I
should take very good care that it should be settled upon her."

" That's nonsense, Will;—it is indeed. You are now
William Belton of Belton, and you must remain so."

" Mary,—I would sooner be Will Belton with Clara
Amedroz by my side to get through the world with me,
and not the interest of an acre either at Belton Castle or
at Plaistow Hall! And I believe I should be the richer
man at the end,—if there were any good in that." Then
he went out of the room, and she heard him go through
the kitchen, and knew that he passed out into the farm-
yard, towards the stable, by the back door. He intended,
it seems, to go on with his hunting in spite of this death
which had occurred. She was sorry for it, but she could
not venture to stop him. And she was sorry also that
nothing had been settled as to the writing of any letter to
Clara. She, however, would take upon herself to write
while he was gone.

He went straight out towards the stables, hardly conscious of what he was doing or where he was going, and
found his hack ready saddled for him in the stall. Then
he remembered that he must either go, or come to some
decision that he would not go. The horse that he intended
to ride had been sent on to the meet, and if he were not to
be used, some message must be despatched as to the
animal's return. But Will was half inclined to go, although
he knew that the world would judge him to be heartless if
he were to go hunting immediately on the receipt of the
tidings which had reached him that morning. He thought
that he would like to set the world at defiance in this
matter. Let Frederic Aylmer go into mourning for the old
man who was dead. Let Frederic Aylmer be solicitous for

the daughter who was left lonely in the old house. No doubt he, Will Belton, had inherited the dead man's estate, and should therefore, in accordance with all the ordinary rules of the world on such matters, submit himself at any rate to the decency of funereal reserve. An heir should not be seen out hunting on the day on which such tidings as to his heritage had reached him. But he did not wish, in his present mood, to be recognised as the heir. He did not want the property. He would have preferred to rid himself altogether of any of the obligations which the ownership of the estate entailed upon him. It was not permitted to him to have the custody of the old squire's daughter, and therefore he was unwilling to meddle with any of the old squire's concerns.

Belton had gone into the stable, and had himself loosed the animal, leading him out into the yard as though he were about to mount him. Then he had given the reins to a stable-boy, and had walked away among the farm-buildings, not thinking of what he was doing. The lad stood staring at him with open mouth, not at all understanding his master's hesitation. The meet, as the boy knew, was fourteen miles off, and Belton had not allowed himself above an hour and a half for the journey. It was his practice to jump into the saddle and bustle out of the place, as though seconds were important to him. He would look at his watch with accuracy, and measure his pace from spot to spot, as though minutes were too valuable to be lost. But now he wandered away like one distraught, and the stable-boy knew that something was wrong. "I thout he was a thinken of the white cow as choked 'erself with the tunnup that was skipped in the chopping," said the boy, as he spoke of his master afterwards to the old groom. At last, however, a thought seemed to strike Belton. "Do you get on Brag," he said to the boy, "and ride off to Goldingham Corner, and tell Daniel to bring the horse home again. I shan't hunt to-day. And I think I shall go away from home. If so, tell him to be sure the horses are out every morning;—and to tell him to stop their beans. I mightn't hunt again for the next month." Then he returned into the house, and went to the parlour in which his sister was sitting. "I shan't go out to-day," he said.

" I thought you would not, Will," she answered.

" Not that I see any harm in it."

" I don't say that there is any harm, but it is as well on such occasions to do as others do."

" That's humbug, Mary."

" No, Will; I do not think that. When any practice has become the fixed rule of the society in which we live, it is always wise to adhere to that rule, unless it call upon us to do something that is actually wrong. One should not offend the prejudices of the world, even if one is quite sure that they are prejudices."

" It hasn't been that that has brought me back, Mary. I'll tell you what. I think I'll go down to Belton—after all."

His sister did not know what to say in answer to this. Her chief anxiety was, of course, on behalf of her brother. That he should be made to forget Clara Amedroz, if that were only possible, was her great desire; and his journey at such a time as this down to Belton was not the way to accomplish such forgetting. And then she felt that Clara might very possibly not wish to see him. Had Will simply been her cousin, such a visit might be very well; but he had attempted to be more than her cousin, and therefore it would probably not be well. Captain Aylmer might not like it; and Mary felt herself bound to consider even Captain Aylmer's likings in such a matter. And yet she could not bear to oppose him in anything. " It would be a very long journey," she said.

" What does that signify?"

" And then it might so probably be for nothing."

" Why should it be for nothing?"

" Because——"

" Because what? Why don't you speak out? You need not be afraid of hurting me. Nothing that you can say can make it all worse than it is."

" Dear Will, I wish I could make it better."

" But you can't. Nobody can make it either better or worse. I promised her once before that I would go to her when she might be in trouble, and I will be as good as my word. I said I would be a brother to her;—and so I will. So help me God, I will!" Then he rushed out of the room, striding through the door as though he would knock it down, and hurried upstairs to his own chamber. When there he stripped himself of his hunting things, and dressed himself again with all the expedition in his power; and then he threw a heap of clothes into a large portmanteau, and set himself to work packing as though everything in the world were to depend on his catching a certain train. And he went to a locked drawer, and taking out a cheque-book, folded it up and put it into his pocket. Then he rang the bell violently; and as he was locking the portmanteau, pressing down the lid with all his weight and all his strength, he ordered that a certain mare might be put into a certain dog-cart, and that somebody might be ready to drive over with him to the Downham station. Within twenty minutes of the time of his rushing upstairs he appeared again before his sister with a great-coat on, and a railway rug hanging over his arm. "Do you mean that you are going to-day?" said she.

"Yes. I'll catch the 11·40 up-train at Downham. What's the good of going unless I go at once? If I can be of any use it will be at the first. It may be that she will have nobody there to do anything for her."

"There is the clergyman and Colonel Askerton,—even if Captain Aylmer has not gone down."

"The clergyman and Colonel Askerton are nothing to her. And if that man is there, I can come back again."

"You will not quarrel with him?"

"Why should I quarrel with him? What is there to quarrel about. I am not such a fool as to quarrel with a man because I hate him. If he is there I shall see her for a minute or two, and then I shall come back."

"I know it is no good my trying to dissuade you."

"None on earth. If you knew it all you would not try to dissuade me. Before I thought of asking her to be my wife,—and yet I thought of that very soon;—but before I ever thought of that, I told her that when she wanted a brother's help, I would give it her. Of course I was thinking of the property,—that she shouldn't be turned out of her father's house like a beggar. I hadn't any settled plan then;—how could I? But I meant her to understand that when her father died I would be the same to her that I am to you. If you were alone, in distress, would I not go to you?"

"But I have no one else, Will," said she, stretching out her hand to him where he stood.

"That makes no difference," he replied, almost roughly. "A promise is a promise, and I resolved from the first that my promise should hold good in spite of my disappointmeet. Dear, dear;—it seems but the other day when I made it,—and now, already, everything is changed." As he was speaking the servant entered the room, and told him that the horse and gig were ready for him. "I shall just do it nicely," said he, looking at his watch. "I have over an hour. God bless you, Mary. I shan't be away long. You may be sure of that."

"I don't suppose you can tell as yet, Will."

"What should keep me long? I shall see Green as I go by, and that is half of my errand. I dare say I shan't stay above a night down in Somersetshire."

"You'll have to give some orders about the estate."

"I shall not say a word on the subject,—to anybody; that is, not to anybody there. I am going to look after her, and not the estate." Then he stooped down and kissed his sister, and in another minute was turning the corner out of the farm-yard on to the road, at a quick pace, not losing a foot of ground in the turn, in that fashion of rapidity which the horses at Plaistow Hall soon learned from their master. The horse is a closely sympathetic beast, and will make his turns, and do his trottings, and comport himself generally in strict unison with the pulsations of his master's heart. When a horse won't jump it is generally the case that the inner man is declining to jump also, let the outer man seem ever so anxious to accomplish the feat.

Belton, who was generally very communicative with his servants, always talking to any man he might have beside him in his dog-cart about the fields and cattle and tillage around him, said not a word to the boy who accompanied him on this occasion. He had a good many things to settle in his mind before he got to London, and he began upon the work as soon as he had turned the corner out of the farmyard. As regarded this Belton estate, which was now altogether his own, he had always had doubts and qualms, —qualms of feeling rather than of conscience; and he had, also, always entertained a strong family ambition. His

people, ever so tar back, had been Beltons of Belton. They
told him that his family could be traced back to very early
days,—before the Plantagenets, as he believed, though on
this point of the subject he was very hazy in his information,
—and he liked the idea of being the man by whom the
family should be reconstructed in its glory. Worldly circumstances had been so kind to him, that he could take up the
Belton estate with more of the prestige of weath than had belonged to any of the owners of the place for many years past.
Should it come to pass that living there would be desirable,
he could rebuild the old house, and make new gardens, and
fit himself out with all the pleasant braveries of a well-to-
do English squire. There need be no pinching and scrap-
ing, no question whether a carriage would be possible, no
doubt as to the prudence of preserving game. All this had
given much that was delightful to his prospects. And he had,
too, been instigated by a somewhat weak desire to emerge
from that farmer's rank into which he knew that many connected with him had supposed him to have sunk. It was
true that he farmed land that was half his own,—and that,
even at Plaistow, he was a wealthy man; but Plaistow
Hall, with all its comforts, was a farm-house; and the
ambition to be more than a farmer had been strong upon
him.

But then there had been the feeling that in taking the
Belton estate he would be robbing his cousin Clara of all that
should have been hers. It must be remembered that he
had not been brought up in the belief that he would ever
become the owner of Belton. All his high ambition in
that matter had originated with the wretched death of
Clara's brother. Could he bring himself to take it all with
pleasure, seeing that it came to him by so sad a chance,—
by a catastrophe so deplorable? When he would think
of this, his mind would revolt from his own desires, and
he would declare to himself that its inheritance would
come to him with a stain of blood upon it. He, indeed,
would have been guiltless; but how could he take his
pleasure in the shades of Belton without thinking of the
tragedy which had given him the property? Such had
been the thoughts and desires, mixed in their nature and
militating against each other, which had induced him to offer
his first visit to his cousin's house. We know what was

the effect of that visit, and by what pleasant scheme he
had endeavoured to overcome all his difficulties, and so to
become master of Belton that Clara Amedroz should also be
its mistress.   There had been a way which, after two days'
intimacy with Clara, seemed to promise him comfort and
happiness on all sides.   But he had come too late, and that
way was closed against him!   Now the estate was his, and
what was he to do with it?   Clara belonged to his rival,
and in what way would it become him to treat her?   He
was still thinking simply of the cruelty of the circumstances which had thrown Captain Aylmer between him
and his cousin, when he drove himself up to the railway
station at Downham.

"'Take her back steady, Jem," he said to the boy.

" I'll be sure to take her wery steady," Jem answered.

" And tell Compton to have the samples of barley ready
for me.   I may be back any day, and we shall be sowing
early this spring."

Then he left his cart, followed the porter who had taken
his luggage eagerly, knowing that Mr. Belton was always
good for sixpence, and in five minutes' time he was again
in motion.

On his arrival in London he drove at once to the chambers of his friend, Mr. Green, and luckily found the
lawyer there.   Had he missed doing this, it was his intention to go out to his friend's house; and in that case he
could not have gone down to Taunton till the next morning; but now he would be able to say what he wished to
say, and hear what he wished to hear, and would travel
down by the night-mail train.   He was anxious that Clara
should feel that he had hurried to her without a moment's
delay.   It would do no good.   He knew that.   Nothing
that he could do would alter her, or be of any service to
him.   She had accepted this man, and had herself no
power of making a change, even if she should wish it.   But
still there was to him something of gratification in the
idea that she should be made to feel that he, Belton, was
more instant in his affection, more urgent in his good
office, more anxious to befriend her in her difficulties, than
the man whom she had consented to take for her husband.
Aylmer would probably go down to Belton, but Will was
very anxious to be the first on the ground,—very anxious,
—though his doing so could be of no use.   All this was

wrong on his part. He knew that it was wrong, and he abused himself for his own selfishness. But such self-abuse gave him no aid in escaping from his own wickedness. He would, if possible, be at Belton before Captain Aylmer; and he would, if possible, make Clara feel that, though he was not a member of Parliament, though he was not mnch given to books, though he was only a farmer, yet he had at any rate as much heart and spirit as the fine gentleman whom she preferred to him.

"I thought I should see you," said the lawyer; "but I hardly expected you so soon as this."

"I ought to have been a day sooner, only we don't get our telegraph messages on a Sunday." He still kept his great-coat on; and it seemed by his manner that he had no intention of staying where he was above a minute or two.

"You'll come out and dine with me to-day?" said Mr. Green.

"I can't do that, for I shall go down by the mail train."

"I never saw such a fellow in my life. What good will that do? It is quite right that you should be there in time for the funeral; but I don't suppose he will be buried before this day week."

But Belton had never thought about the funeral. When he had spoken to his sister of saying but a few words to Clara, and then returning, he had forgotten that there would be any such ceremony, or that he would be delayed by any such necessity.

"I was not thinking about the funeral," said Belton.

"You'll only find yourself uncomfortable there."

"Of course I shall be uncomfortable."

"You can't do anything about the property, you know."

"What do you mean by doing anything?" said Belton in an angry tone.

"You can't very well take possession of the place, at any rate, till after the funeral. It would not be considered the proper thing to do."

"You think, then, that I am a bird of prey, smelling the feast from afar off, and hurrying at the dead man's carcase as soon as the breath is out of his body?"

"I don't think anything of the kind, my dear fellow."

"Yes, you do, or you wouldn't talk to me about doing the proper thing! I don't care a straw about the proper thing! If I find that there's anything to be done to-morrow that can be of any use, I shall do it, though all Somersetshire should think it improper! But I am not going to look after my own interests!"

"Take off your coat and sit down, Will, and don't look so angry at me. I know that you're not greedy, well enough. Tell me what you are going to do, and let me see if I can help you."

Belton did as he was told; he pulled off his coat and sat himself down by the fire. "I don't know that you can do anything to help me,—at least, not as yet. But I must go and see after her. Perhaps she may be all alone."

"I suppose she is all alone."

"He hasn't gone down, then?"

"Who?—Captain Aylmer? No;—he hasn't gone down, certainly. He is in Yorkshire."

"I'm glad of that!"

"He won't hurry himself. He never does, I fancy. I had a letter from him this morning about Miss Amedroz."

"And what did he say?"

"He desired me to send her seventy-five pounds,—the interest of her aunt's money."

"Seventy-five pounds!" said Will Belton, contemptuously.

"He thought she might want money at once; and I sent her the cheque to-day. It will go down by the same train that carries you."

"Seventy-five pounds! And you are sure that he has not gone himself?"

"It isn't likely that he should have written to me, and passed through London himself at the same time;—but it is possible, no doubt. I don't think he even knew the old squire; and there is no reason why he should go to the funeral."

"No reason at all," said Belton,—who felt that Captain Aylmer's presence at the Castle would be an insult to himself. "I don't know what on earth he should do there,—except that I think him just the fellow to intrude where he is not wanted." And yet Will was in his heart despising Captain Aylmer because he had not already hurried down to the assistance of the girl whom he professed to love.

"He is engaged to her, you know," said the lawyer in a low voice.

" What difference does that make with such a fellow as he is,—a cold-blooded fish of a man, who thinks of nothing in the world but being respectable? Engaged to her! Oh, damn him!"

" I've not the slightest objection. I don't think, how-ever, that you'll find him at Belton before you. No doubt she will have heard from him; and it strikes me as very possible that she may go to Aylmer Park."

" What should she go there for?"

" Would it not be the best place for her?"

" No. My house would be the best place for her. I am her nearest relative. Why should she not come to us?"

Mr. Green turned round his chair, and poked the fire, and fidgeted about for some moments before he answered. " My dear fellow, you must know that that wouldn't do," he then said. " You ought to feel that it wouldn't do;—you ought, indeed."

" Why shouldn't my sister receive Miss Amedroz as well as that old woman down in Yorkshire?"

" If I may tell you, I will."

" Of course you may tell me."

" Because Miss Amedroz is engaged to be married to that old woman's son, and is not engaged to be married to your sister's brother. The thing is done, and what is the good of interfering. As far as she is concerned, a great burden is off your hands."

" What do you mean by a burden?"

" I mean that her engagement to Captain Aylmer makes it unnecessary for you to suppose that she is in want of any pecuniary assistance. You told me once before that you would feel yourself called upon to see that she wanted nothing."

" So I do now."

" But Captain Aylmer will look after that."

" I tell you what it is, Joe; I mean to settle the Belton property in such a way that she shall have it, and that he shan't be able to touch it. And it shall go to some one who shall have my name,—William Belton. That's what I want you to arrange for me."

" After you are dead, you mean."

" I mean now at once. I won't take the estate from her.

I hate the place and everything belonging to it. I don't mean her. There is no reason for hating her."

" My dear Will, you are talking nonsense."

" Why is it nonsense? I may give what belongs to me to whom I please."

" You can do nothing of the kind ;—at any rate, not by my assistance. You talk as though the world were all over with you,—as though you were never to be married or have any children of your own."

" I never shall marry."

" Nonsense, Will. Don't make such an ass of yourself as to suppose that you'll not get over such a thing as this. You'll be married and have a dozen children yet to provide for. Let the eldest have Belton Castle, and everything will go on then in the proper way."

Belton had now got the poker into his hands, and sat silent for some time knocking the coals about. Then he got up, and took his hat, and put on his coat. " Of course I can't make you understand me," he said ; " at any rate not all at once. I'm not such a fool as to want to give up my property just because a girl is going to be married to a man I don't like. I'm not such an ass as to give him my estate for such a reason as that ;—for it will be giving it to him, let me tie it up as I may. But I've a feeling about it which makes it impossible for me to take it. How would you like to get a thing by another fellow having destroyed himself ?"

" You can't help that. It's yours by law."

" Of course it is. I know that. And as it's mine I can do what I like with it. Well ;—good-bye. When I've got anything to say, I'll write." Then he went down to his cab and had himself driven to the Great Western Railway Hotel.

Captain Aylmer had sent to his betrothed seventy-five pounds ; the exact interest at five per cent. for one year of the sum which his aunt had left her. This was the first subject of which Belton thought when he found himself again in the railway-carriage, and he continued thinking of it half the way down to Taunton. Seventy-five pounds! As though this favoured lover were prepared to give her exactly her due, and nothing more than her due! Had he been so placed, he, Will Belton, what would he have done?

Seventy-five pounds might have been more money than she
would have wanted, for he would have taken her to his
own house,—to his own bosom as soon as she would have
permitted, and would have so laboured on her behalf,
taking from her shoulders all money troubles, that there
would have been no question as to principal or interest between them. At any rate he would not have confined
himself to sending to her the exact sum which was her due.
But then Aylmer was a cold-blooded man,—more like a
fish than a man. Belton told himself over and over again
that he had discovered that at the single glance which he
had had when he saw Captain Aylmer in Green's chambers.
Seventy-five pounds indeed! He himself was prepared to
give his whole estate to her, if she would take it,—even
though she would not marry him, even though she was
going to throw herself away upon that fish! Then he felt
somewhat as Hamlet did when he jumped upon Laertes at
the grave of Ophelia. Send her seventy-five pounds indeed,
while he was ready to drink up Esil for her, or to make
over to her the whole Belton estate, and thus abandon the
idea for ever of being Belton of Belton!

He reached Taunton in the middle of the night,—during
the small hours of the morning in a winter night; but yet
he could not bring himself to go to bed. So he knocked up
an ostler at the nearest inn, and ordered out a gig. He
would go down to the village of Redicote, on the Minehead
road, and put up at the public-house there. He could not
now have himself driven at once to Belton Castle, as he
would have done had the old squire been alive. He fancied
that his presence would be a nuisance if he did so. So he
went to the little inn at Redicote, reaching that place
between four and five o'clock in the morning; and very
uncomfortable he was when he got there. But in his present
frame of mind he preferred discomfort. He liked being
tired and cold, and felt when he was put into a chill room,
without fire, and with a sanded floor, that things with him
were quite as they ought to be.

Yes,—he could have a fly over to Belton Castle after
breakfast. Having learned so much, and ordered a dish of
eggs and bacon for his morning's breakfast, he went up-
stairs to a miserable little bed-room, to dress himself after
his night's journey.

CHAPTER XXI.

MRS. ASKERTON'S GENEROSITY.

THE death of the old man at Belton Castle had been very sudden. At three o'clock in the morning Clara had been called into his room, and at five o'clock she was alone in the world,—having neither father, mother, nor brother; without a home, without a shilling that she would call her own; with no hope as to her future life, if,—as she had so much reason to suppose,—Captain Aylmer should have chosen to accept her last letter as a ground for permanent separation. But at this moment, on this saddest morning, she did not care much for that chance. It seemed to be almost indifferent to her, that question of Lady Aylmer and her anger. The more that she was absolutely in need of external friendship, the more disposed was she to reject it, and to declare to herself that she was prepared to stand alone in the world.

For the last week she had understood from the doctor that her father was in truth sinking, and that she might hardly hope ever to see him again convalescent. She had therefore in some sort prepared herself for her loneliness, and anticipated the misery of her position. As soon as it was known to the women in the room that life had left the old man, one of them had taken her by the hand and led her back to her own chamber. "Now, Miss Clara, you had better lay down on the bed again;—you had indeed; you can do nothing sitting up." She took the old woman's advice, and allowed them to do with her as they would. It was true that there was no longer any work by which she could make herself useful in that house,—in that house, or, as far as she could see, in any other. Yes; she would go to bed, and lying there would feel how convenient it would be for many persons if she also could be taken away to her long rest, as her father, and aunt, and brother had been taken before her. Her name and family had been unfortunate, and it would be well that there should be no

Amedroz left to trouble those more fortunate persons who were to come after them. In her sorrow and bitterness she included both her cousin Will and Captain Aylmer among those more fortunate ones for whose sake it might be well that she should be made to vanish from off the earth. She had read Captain Aylmer's letter over and over again since she had answered it, and had read nearly as often the copy of her own reply,—and had told herself as she read them that of course he would not forgive her. He might perhaps pardon her, if she would submit to him in everything, but that she would not submit to his commands respecting Mrs. Askerton she was fully resolved,—and, therefore, there could be no hope. Then, when she remembered how lately her dear father's spirit had fled, she hated herself for having allowed her mind to dwell on anything beyond her loss in him.

She was still in her bedroom, having fallen into that half-waking slumber which the numbness of sorrow so often produces, when word was brought to her that Mrs. Askerton was in the house. It was the first time that Mrs. Askerton had ever crossed the door, and the remembrance that it was so came upon her at once. During her father's lifetime it had seemed to be understood that their neighbour should have no admittance there ;—but now,—now that her father was gone,—the barrier was to be overthrown. And why not? Why should not Mrs. Askerton come to her? Why, if Mrs. Askerton chose to be kind to her, should she not altogether throw herself into her friend's arms? Of course her doing so would give mortal offence to everybody at Aylmer Park ; but why need she stop to think of that? She had already made up her mind that she would not obey orders from Aylmer Park on this subject.

She had not seen Mrs. Askerton since that interview between them, which was described some few chapters back. Then everything had been told between them, so that there was no longer any mystery either on the one side or on the other. Then Clara had assured her friend of her loving friendship in spite of any edicts to the contrary which might come from Aylmer Park ; and after that what could be more natural than that Mrs. Askerton should come to her in her sorrow. "She says she'll come up to you if you'll let her," said the servant. But Clara declined this proposition, and in a few minutes went down to the small parlour in which she had lately lived, and where she found her visitor.

" My poor dear, this has been very sudden," said Mrs. Askerton.

" Very sudden;—very sudden. And yet, now that he has gone, I know that I expected it."

" Of course I came to you as soon as I heard of it, because I knew you were all alone. If there had been any one else I should not have come."

" It is very good of you."

" Colonel Askerton thought that perhaps he had better come. I told him of all that which we said to each other the other day. He thought at first that it would be better that I should not see you."

" It was very good of you to come," said Clara again, and as she spoke she put out her hand and took Mrs. Askerton's,—continuing to hold it for awhile; " very good indeed."

" I told him that I could not but go down to you,—that I thought you would not understand it if I stayed away."

" At any rate it was good of you to come to me."

" I don't believe," said Mrs. Askerton, " that what people call consolation is ever of any use. It is a terrible thing to lose a father."

" Very terrible. Ah, dear, I have hardly yet found out how sad it is. As yet I have only been thinking of myself, and wishing that I could be with him."

" Nay, Clara."

" How can I help it? What am I to do, or where am I to go? Of what use is life to such a one as me? And for him,—who would dare to wish him back again? When people have fallen and gone down in the world it is bad for them to go on living. Everything is a trouble, and there is nothing but vexation."

" Think what I have suffered, dear."

" But you have had somebody to care for you,—somebody whom you could trust."

" And have not you ?"

" No; no one."

' What do you mean, Clara?"

" I mean what I say. I have no one. It is no use
asking questions,—not now, at such a time as this. And I
did not mean to complain. Complaining is weak and
foolish. I have often told myself that I could bear anything,
and so I will. When I can bring myself to think of what
I have lost in my father I shall be better, even though I
shall be more sorrowful. As it is, I hate myself for being
so selfish."

" You will let me come and stay with you to-day, will
you not ?"

" No, dear ; not to-day."

" Why not to-day, Clara ?"

" I shall be better alone. I have so many things to
think of."

" I know well that it would be better that you should
not be alone,—much better. But I will not press it. I
cannot insist with you, as another woman would."

" You are wrong there ; quite wrong. I would be led
by you sooner than by any woman living. What other
woman is there to whom I would listen for a moment?"
As she said this, even in the depth of her sorrow, she
thought of Lady Aylmer, and strengthened herself in her
resolution to rebel against her lover's mother. Then she
continued, " I wish I knew my cousin Mary, — Mary
Belton : but I have never seen her."

" Is she nice ?"

" So Will tells me ; and I know that what he says must
be true,—even about his sister."

" Will, Will ! You are always thinking of your cousin
Will. If he be really so good he will show it now."

" How can he show it ? What can he do ?"

" Does he not inherit all the property ?"

" Of course he does. And what of that? When 1
say that I have no friend I am not thinking of my
poverty."

" If he has that regard for you which he pretends, he can
do much to assist you. Why should he not come here at
once ?"

" God forbid."

" Why? Why do you say so ? He is your nearest
relative."

" If you do not understand I cannot explain."

"Has he been told what has happened?" Mrs. Askerton asked.

"Colonel Askerton sent a message to him, I believe."

"And to Captain Aylmer also?"

"Yes; and to Captain Aylmer. It was Colonel Askerton who sent it."

"Then he will come, of course?"

"I think not. Why should he come? He did not even know poor papa."

"But, my dear Clara, has he not known you?"

"You will see that he will not come. And I tell you beforehand that he will be right to stay away. Indeed, I do not know how he could come;—and I do not want him here."

"I do not understand you, Clara."

"I suppose not. I cannot very well understand myself."

"I should not be at all surprised if Lady Aylmer were to come herself."

"Oh heavens! How little you can know of Lady Aylmer's position and character!"

"But if she is to be your mother-in-law?"

"And even if she were! The idea of Lady Aylmer coming away from Aylmer Park, all the way from Yorkshire, to such a house as this! If they told me that the Queen was coming it would hardly disconcert me more. But, dear, there is no danger of that at least."

"I do not know what may have passed between you and him; but unless there has been some quarrel he will come. That is, he will do so if he is at all like any men whom I have known."

"He will not come."

Then Mrs. Askerton made some half-whispered offers of services to be rendered by Colonel Askerton, and soon afterwards took her leave, having first asked permission to come again in the afternoon, and when that was declined, having promised to return on the following morning. As she walked back to the cottage she could not but think more of Clara's engagement to Captain Aylmer than she did of the squire's death. As regarded herself, of course she could not grieve for Mr. Amedroz; and as regarded Clara, Clara's father had for some time past been apparently so insignificant even in his own house that it was difficult to acknowledge the fact that the death of such a one as he might leave a great blank in the world. But what had Clara meant by declaring so emphatically that Captain Aylmer would not visit Belton, and by speaking of herself as one who had neither position nor friends in the world? If there had been a quarrel, indeed, then it was sufficiently intelligible; and if there was any such quarrel, from what source must it have arisen? Mrs. Askerton felt the blood rise to her cheeks as she thought of this, and told herself that there could be but one such source. Mrs. Askerton knew that Clara had received orders from Aylmer Castle to discontinue all acquaintance with herself, and, therefore, there could be no doubt as to the cause of the quarrel. It had come to this, then, that Clara was to lose her husband because she was true to her friend; or rather because she would not consent to cast an additional stone at one who for some years past had become a mark for many stones.

I am not prepared to say that Mrs. Askerton was a high-minded woman. Misfortunes had come upon her in life of a sort which are too apt to quench high nobility of mind in women. There are calamities which by their natural tendencies elevate the character of women and add strength to the growth of feminine virtue;—but then, again, there are other calamities which few women can bear without some degradation, without some injury to that delicacy and tenderness which is essentially necessary to make a woman charming,—as a woman. In this, I think, the world is harder to women than to men, that a woman often loses much by the chance of adverse circumstances which a man only loses by his own misconduct. That there are women whom no calamity can degrade is true enough;—and so it is true that there are some men who are heroes; but such are exceptions both among men and women. Not such a one had Mrs. Askerton been. Calamity had come upon her;—partly, indeed, by her own fault, though that might have been pardoned;—but the weight of her misfortunes had been too great for her strength, and she had become in some degree hardened by what she had endured; if not unfeminine, still she was feminine in an inferior degree, with womanly feelings of a lower order. And she had learned to intrigue, not being desirous of gaining aught by dishonest intriguing, but believing that she could only hold her own by carrying on her battle after that fashion. In all this I am speaking of the general character of the woman, and am not alluding to the one sin which she had committed. Thus, when she had first become acquainted with Miss Amedroz, her conscience had not rebuked her, in that she was deceiving her new friend. When asked casually in conversation as to her maiden name, she had not blushed as she answered the question with a falsehood. When, unfortunately, the name of her first husband had in some way made itself known to Clara she had been ready again with some prepared fib. And when she had recognised William Belton she had thought that the danger to herself of having any one near her who might know her, quite justified her in endeavouring to create ill-will between Clara and her cousin. " Self-preservation is the first law of nature," she would have said, and would have failed to remember,—as she did always fail to remember,— that nature does not require by any of its laws that self-preservation should be aided by falsehood.

But though she was not high-minded, so also was she not ungenerous; and now, as she began to understand that Clara was sacrificing herself because of that promise which had been given when they two had stood together at the window in the cottage drawing-room, she was capable of feeling more for her friend than for herself. She was capable even of telling herself that it was cruel on her part even to wish for any continuance of Clara's acquaintance. " I have made my bed, and I must lie upon it," she said to herself ; and then she resolved that instead of going up to the house on the following day, she would write to Clara, and put an end to the intimacy which existed between them. " The world is hard, and harsh, and unjust," she said, still speaking to herself. " But that is not her fault ; I will not injure her because I have been injured myself."

Colonel Askerton was up at the house on the same day ; but he did not ask for Miss Amedroz, nor did she see him. Nobody else came to the house then, or on the following morning,—or on that afternoon, though Clara did not fail to tell herself that Captain Aylmer might have been there if he had chosen to take the journey and to leave home as soon as he had received the message ; and she made the same calculation as to her cousin Will,—though in that calculation, as we know, she was wrong. These two days had been very desolate with her, and she had begun to look forward to Mrs. Askerton's coming,—when instead of that there came a messenger with a letter from the cottage.

"You can do as you like, my dear," Colonel Askerton had said on the previous evening to his wife. He had listened to all she had been saying without taking his eyes from off his newspaper, though she had spoken with much eagerness.

"But that is not enough. You should say more to me than that."

"Now I think you are unreasonable. For myself, I do not care how this matter goes; nor do I care one straw what any tongues may say. They cannot reach me, excepting so far as they may reach me through you."

"But you should advise me."

"I always do,—copiously when I think that I know better than you; but in this matter I feel so sure that you know better than I, that I don't wish to suggest anything." Then he went on with his newspaper, and she sat for a while looking at him, as though she expected that something more would be said. But nothing more was said, and she was left entirely to her own guidance.

Since the days in which her troubles had come upon Mrs. Askerton, Clara Amedroz was the first female friend who had come near her to comfort her, and she was very loth to abandon such comfort. There had, too, been something more than comfort, something almost approaching to triumph, when she found that Clara had clung to her with affection after hearing the whole story of her life. Though her conscience had not pricked her while she was exercising all her little planned deceits, she had not taken much pleasure in them. How should any one take pleasure in such work! Many of us daily deceive our friends, and are so far gone in deceit, that the deceit alone is hardly painful to us. But the need of deceiving a friend is always painful. The treachery is easy; but to be treacherous to those we love is never easy,—never easy, even though it be so common. There had been a double delight to this poor woman in the near neighbourhood of Clara Amedroz since there had ceased to be any necessity for falsehood on her part. But now, almost before her joy had commenced, almost before she had realised the sweetness of her triumph, had come upon her this task of doing that herself which Clara in her generosity had refused to do. " I have made my bed and I must lie upon it," she said. And then, instead of going down to the house as she had promised, she wrote the following letter to Miss Amedroz :—

' *The Cottage, Monday.*

" Dearest Clara,—I need not tell you that I write as I do now with a bleeding heart. A few days since I should have laughed at any woman who used such a phrase of herself, and declared her to be an affected fool ; but now I know how true such a word may be   My heart is bleeding, and I feel myself to be overcome by my disgrace. You told me that I did not understand you yesterday. Of course I understood you. Of course I know how it all is, and why you spoke as you did of Captain Aylmer. He has chosen to think that you could not know me without pollution, and has determined that you must give up either me or him. Though he has judged me I am not going to judge him. The world is on his side ; and, perhaps, he is right. He knows nothing of my trials and difficulties,—and why should he? I do not blame him for demanding that his future wife shall not be intimate with a woman who is supposed to have lost her fitness for the society of women.

" At any rate, dearest, you must obey him,—and we will see each other no more. I am quite sure that I should be very wicked were I to allow you to injure your position in life on my account. You at any rate love him, and would be happy with him, and as you are engaged to him, you have no just ground for resenting his interference.

" You will understand me now as well as though I were to fill sheets and sheets of paper with what I could say on the subject. The simple fact is, that you and I must forget each other, or simply remember one another as past friends. You will know in a day or two what your plans are. If you remain here, we will go away. If you go away, we will remain here ;—that is, if your cousin will keep us as tenants. I do not of course know what you may have

written to Captain Aylmer since our interview up here, but
I beg that you will write to him now, and make him
understand that he need have no fears in respect of me.
You may send him this letter if you will. Oh, dear! if
you could know what I suffer as I write this.

"I feel that I owe you an apology for harassing you on
such a subject at such a time; but I know that I ought not
to lose a day in telling you that you are to see nothing
more of the friend who has loved you.

"MARY ASKERTON."

Clara's first impulse on receiving this letter was to go off
at once to the cottage, and insist on her privilege of
choosing her own friends. If she preferred Mrs. Askerton
to Captain Aylmer, that was no one's business but her own.
And she would have done so had she not been afraid of
meeting with Colonel Askerton. To him she would not
have known how to speak on such a subject;—nor would
she have known how to conduct herself at the cottage without speaking of it. And then, after a while, she felt that
were she to do so,—should she now deliberately determine
to throw herself into Mrs. Askerton's arms,—she must at
the same time give up all idea of becoming Captain
Aylmer's wife. As she thought of this she asked herself
various questions concerning him, which she did not find it
easy to answer. Did she wish to be his wife? Could she
assure herself that if they were married they would make
each other happy? Did she love him? She was still able
to declare to herself that the answer to the last question
should be an affirmative; but, nevertheless, she thought
that she could give him up without great unhappiness.
And when she began to think of Lady Aylmer, and to
remember that Frederic Aylmer's imperative demands upon
her obedience had, in all probability, been dictated by his
mother, she was again anxious to go at once to the cottage,
and declare that she would not submit to any interference
with her own judgment.

On the next morning the postman brought to her a letter
which was of much moment to her,—but he brought to her
also tidings which moved her more even than the letter.
The letter was from the lawyer, and enclosed a cheque for
seventy-five pounds, which he had been instructed to pay

to her, as the interest of the money left to her by-her aunt.
What should be her answer to that letter she knew very
well,—and she instantly wrote it, sending back the cheque
to Mr. Green.   The postman's news, more important than
the letter, told her that William Belton was at the inn at
Redicote.

CHAPTER XXII.

PASSIONATE PLEADING.

CLARA wrote her letter to the lawyer, returning the cheque,
before she would allow herself a moment to dwell upon the
news of her cousin's arrival.   She felt that it was necessary to do that before she should even see her cousin,—
thus providing against any difficulty which might arise
from adverse advice on his part; and as soon as the letter
was written she sent it to the post-office in the village.
She would do almost anything that Will might tell her to
do, but Captain Aylmer's money she would not take, even
though Will might so direct her.   They would tell her, no
doubt, among them, that the money was her own,—that
she might take it without owing any thanks for it to
Captain Aylmer.   But she knew better than that,—as she
told herself over and over again.   Her aunt had left her
nothing, and nothing would she have from Captain Aylmer,
—unless she had all that Captain Aylmer had to give,
after the fashion in which women best love to take such
gifts.

Then, when she had done that, she was able to think of
her cousin's visit.   " I knew he would come," she said to
herself, as she sat herself in one of the old chairs in the
hall, with a large shawl wrapped round her shoulders.
She had just been to the front door, with the nominal purpose of despatching her messenger thence to the post-office;
but she had stood for a minute or two under the portico
looking in the direction by which Belton would come
from Redicote, expecting, or rather hoping, that she might
see his figure or hear the sound of his gig.   But she saw
nothing and heard nothing, and so returned into the hall,

slowly shutting the door. " I knew that he would come,"
she said, repeating to herself the same words, over and
over again. Yet when Mrs. Askerton had told her that
he would do this thing which he had now done, she had
expressed herself as almost frightened by the idea. " God
forbid," she had said. Nevertheless, now that he was
there at Redicote, she assured herself that his coming was
a thing of which she had been certain; and she took a joy
in the knowledge of his nearness to her which she did not
attempt to define to herself. Had he not said that he
would be a brother to her, and was it not a brother's part
to go to a sister in affliction? "I knew that he would
come. I was sure of it. He is so true." As to Captain
Aylmer's not coming she said nothing, even to herself;
but she felt that she had been equally sure on that subject.
Of course, Captain Aylmer would not come! He had sent
her seventy-five pounds in lieu of coming, and in doing so
was true to his character. Both men were doing exactly
that which was to have been expected of them. So at
least Clara Amedroz now assured herself. She did not
ask herself how it was that she had come to love the
thinner and the meaner of the two men, but she knew well
that such had been her fate.

On a sudden she rose from her chair, as though remembering a duty to be performed, and went to the kitchen
and directed that breakfast might be got ready for Mr.
Belton. He would have travelled all night,—and would
be in want of food. Since the old squire's death there had
been no regular meal served in the house, and Clara had
taken such scraps of food and cups of tea as the old
servant of the house had brought to her. But now the
cloth must be spread again, and as she did this with her
own hands she remembered the dinners which had been
prepared for Captain Aylmer at Perivale after his aunt's
death. It seemed to her that she was used to be in the
house with death, and that the sadness and solemn ceremonies of woe were becoming things familiar to her.
There grew upon her a feeling that it must be so with her
always. The circumstances of her life would ever be sad.
What right had she to expect any other fate after such a
catastrophe as that which her brother had brought upon
the family? It was clear to her that she had done wrong

in supposing that she could marry and live with a prosperous man of the world like Captain Aylmer. Their natures
were different, and no such union could lead to any good.
So she told herself with much misery of spirit as she was
preparing the breakfast-table for William Belton.

But William Belton did not come to eat the breakfast.
He got what he wanted in that way at the inn at Redicote,
and even then hesitated, loitering at the bar, before he
would go over. What was he to say, and how would he
be received? After all had he not done amiss in coming
to a house at which he probably might not be wanted?
Would it not be thought that his journey had been made
solely with a view to his own property? He would be
regarded as the heir pouncing upon the inheritance before
as yet the old owner was under the ground. At any rate
it would be too early for him to make his visit yet a
while; and, to kill time, he went over to a carpenter who
had been employed by him about the place at Belton.
The carpenter spoke to him as though everything were his
own, and was very intent upon future improvements.
This made Will more disgusted with himself than ever,
and before he could get out of the carpenter's yard, he
thoroughly wished himself back at Plaistow. But having
come so far, he could hardly return without seeing his
cousin, and at last he had himself driven over, reaching
the house between eleven and twelve o'clock in the day.

Clara met him in the hall, and at once led him into the
room which she had prepared for him. He had given her
his hand in the hall, but did not speak to her till she had
spoken to him after the closing of the room door behind
them. "I thought that you would come," she said, still
holding him by the hand.

"I did not know what to do," he answered. "I couldn't
say which was best. Now I am here, I shall only be in
your way." He did not dare to press her hand, nor could
he bring himself to take his away from her.

"In my way;—yes; as an angel, to tell me what to do
in my trouble. I knew you would come, because you are
so good. But you will have breakfast;—see, I have got it
ready for you."

"Oh no; I breakfasted at Redicote. I would not trouble you."

"Trouble me, Will! Oh, Will, if you knew!" Then there came tears in her eyes, and at the sight of them both his own were filled. How was he to stand it? To take her to his bosom and hold her there for always, to wipe away her tears so that she should weep no more, to devote himself and all his energy and all that was his to comfort her,—this he could have done; but he knew not how to do anything short of this. Every word that she spoke to him was an encouragement to this, and yet he knew that it could not be so. To say a word of his love, or even to look it, would now be an unmanly insult. And yet, how was he not to look it,—not to speak of it? "It is such a comfort that you should be here with me," she said.

"Then I am glad I am here, though I do not know what I can do. Did he suffer much, Clara?"

"No, I think not; very little. He sank at last quicker than I expected, but just as I thought he would go. He used to speak of you so often, and always with regard and esteem!"

"Dear old man!"

"Yes, Will; he was, in spite of his little faults. No father ever loved his daughter better than he loved me."

After a while the servant brought in tea, explaining to Belton that Miss Clara had neither eaten nor drank that morning. "She wouldn't take anything till you came, sir." Then Will added his entreaties, and Clara was persuaded, and by degrees there grew between them more ease of manner and capability for talking than had been within their reach when they first met. And during the morning many things were explained, as to which Clara would a few hours previously have thought it to be almost impossible that she should speak to her cousin. She had told him of her aunt's money, and the way in which she had on that very morning sent back the cheque to the lawyer; and she had said something also as to Lady Aylmer's views, and her own views as to Lady Aylmer. With Will this subject was one most difficult of discussion, and he blushed and fidgeted in his chair, and walked about the room, and found himself unable to look Clara in the face as she spoke to him. But she went on, goading him with the name which of a names was the most distasteful to him; and mentioning that name almost in terms of reproach,—of reproach which he felt it would be ungenerous to reciprocate, but which he would have exaggerated to unmeasured abuse if he had given his tongue licence to speak his mind.

"I was right to send back the money;—wasn't I, Will? Say that I was right. Pray tell me that you think so!"

"I don't understand it at present, you see; I am no lawyer."

"But it doesn't want a lawyer to know that I couldn't take the money from him. I am sure you feel that."

"If a man owes money, of course he ought to pay it."

"But he doesn't owe it, Will. It is intended for generosity."

"You don't want anybody's generosity, certainly." Then he reflected that Clara must, after all, depend entirely on the generosity of some one till she was married, and he wanted to explain to her that everything he had in the world was at her service,—was indeed her own. Or he would have explained, if he knew how, that he did not intend to take advantage of the entail,—that the Belton estate should belong to her as the natural heir of her father. But he conceived that the moment for explaining this had hardly as yet arrived, and that he had better confine himself to some attempt at teaching her that no extraneous assistance would be necessary to her. "In money matters," said he, "of course you are to look to me. That is a matter of course. I'll see Green about the other affairs. Green and I are friends. We'll settle it."

"That's not what I meant, Will."

"But it's what I mean. This is one of those things in which a man has to act on his own judgment. Your father and I understood each other."

"He did not understand that I was to accept your bounty."

"Bounty is a nasty word, and I hate it. You accepted me,—as your brother, and as such I mean to act." The word almost stuck in his throat, but he brought it out at last in a fierce tone, of which she understood accurately the cause and meaning. "All money matters about the place must be settled by me. Indeed, that's why I came down."

"Not only for that, Will."

"Just to be useful in that way, I mean.

"You came to see me,—because you know I should want

you." Surely this was malice prepense! Knowing what was his want, how could she exasperate it by talking thus of her own? "As for money, I have no claim on any one. No creature was ever more forlorn. But I will not talk of that."

"Did you not say that you would treat me as a brother?"

"I did not mean that I was to be a burden on you."

"I know what I meant, and that is sufficient."

Belton had been at the house some hours before he made any sign of leaving her, and when he did so he had to explain something of his plans. He would remain, he said, for about a week in the neighbourhood. She of course was obliged to ask him to stay at the house,—at the house which was in fact his own; but he declined to do this, blurting out his reason at last very plainly. "Captain Aylmer would not like it, and I suppose you are bound to think of what he likes and dislikes." "I don't know what right Captain Aylmer would have to dislike any such thing," said Clara. But, nevertheless, she allowed the reason to pass as current, and did not press her invitation. Will declared that he would stay at the inn at Redicote, striving to explain in some very unintelligible manner that such an arrangement would be very convenient. He would remain at Redicote, and would come over to Belton every day during his sojourn in the country. Then he asked one question in a low whisper as to the last sad ceremony, and, having received an answer, started off with the declared intention of calling on Colonel Askerton.

The next two or three days passed uncomfortably enough with Will Belton. He made his head-quarters at the little inn of Redicote, and drove himself backwards and forwards between that place and the estate which was now his own. On each of these days he saw Colonel Askerton, whom he found to be a civil pleasant man, willing enough to rid himself of the unpleasant task he had undertaken, but, at the same time, willing also to continue his services if any further services were required of him. But of Mrs. Askerton on these occasions Will saw nothing, nor had he ever spoken to her since the time of his first visit to the Castle. Then came the day of the funeral, and after that rite was over he returned with his cousin to the house. There was

no will to be read. The old squire had left no will, nor
was there anything belonging to him at the time of his
death that he could bequeath. The furniture in the house,
the worn-out carpets and old-fashioned chairs, belonged to
Clara ; but, beyond that, property had she none, nor had it
been in her father's power to endow her with anything.
She was alone in the world, penniless, with a conviction on
her own mind that her engagement with Frederic Aylmer
must of necessity come to an end, and with a feeling about
her cousin which she could hardly analyse, but which told
her that she could not go to his house in Norfolk, nor live
with him at Belton Castle, nor trust herself into his hands
as she would into those of a real brother.

On the afternoon of the day on which her father had
been buried, she brought to him a letter, asking him to
read it, and tell her what she should do. The letter was
from Lady Aylmer, and contained an invitation to
Aylmer Castle. It had been accompanied, as the reader
may possibly remember, by a letter from Captain Aylmer
himself. Of this she of course informed her cousin ;
but she did not find it to be necessary to show the letter of
one rival to the other. Lady Aylmer's letter was cold in
its expression of welcome, but very dictatorial in pointing
out the absolute necessity that Clara should accept the
invitation so given. " I think you will not fail to agree
with me, dear Miss Amedroz," the letter said, " that under
these strange and perplexing circumstances, this is the
only roof which can, with any propriety, afford you a shelter." " And why not the poor-house ?" she said aloud to
her cousin, when she perceived that his eye had descended
so far on the page. He shook his head angrily, but said
nothing ; and when he had finished the letter he folded it
and gave it back still in silence. " And what am I to do ?"
she said. " You tell me that I am to come to you for advice
in everything."

" You must decide for yourself here."

" And you won't advise me. You won't tell me whether
she is right ?"

" I suppose she is right."

" Then I had better go ?"

" If you mean to marry Captain Aylmer, you had better
go."

"I am engaged to him."

"Then you had better go."

"But I will not submit myself to her tyranny."

"Let the marriage take place at once, and you will have to submit only to his. I suppose you are prepared for that?"

"I do not know. I do not like tyranny."

Again he stood silent for awhile, looking at her, and then he answered: "I should not tyrannize over you, Clara."

"Oh, Will, Will, do not speak like that. Do not destroy everything."

"What am I to say?"

What would you say if your sister, your real sister, asked advice in such a strait? If you had a sister, who came to you, and told you all her difficulty, you would advise her. You would not say words to make things worse for her."

"It would be very different."

"But you said you would be my brother."

"How am I to know what you feel for this man? It seems to me that you half hate him, half fear him, and sometimes despise him."

"Hate him!—no, I never hate him."

"Go to him, then, and ask him what you had better do. Don't ask me." Then he hurried out of the room, slamming the door behind him. But before he had half gone down the stairs he remembered the ceremony at which he had just been present, and how desolate she was in the world, and he returned to her. "I beg your pardon, Clara," he said, "I am passionate; but I must be a beast to show my passion to you on such a day as this. If I were you I should accept Lady Aylmer's invitation,—merely thanking her for it in the ordinary way. I should then go and see how the land lay. That is the advice I should give my sister."

"And I will,—if it is only because you tell me."

"But as for a home,—tell her you have one of your own, —at Belton Castle, from which no one can turn you out, and where no one can intrude on you. This house belongs to you." Then, before she could answer him, he had left the room; and she listened to his heavy quick footsteps as he went across the hall and out of the front door.

He walked across the park and entered the little gate of

Colonel Askerton's garden, as though it were his habit to go to the cottage when he was at Belton. There had been various matters on which the two men had been brought into contact concerning the old squire's death and the tenancy of the cottage, so that they had become almost intimate. Belton had nothing new that he specially desired to say to Colonel Askerton, whom, indeed, he had seen only a short time before at the funeral; but he wanted the relief of speaking to some one before he returned to the solitude of the inn at Redicote. On this occasion, however, the Colonel was out, and the maid asked him if he would see Mrs. Askerton. When he said something about not troubling her, the girl told him that her mistress wished to speak to him, and then he had no alternative but to allow himself to be shown into the drawing-room.

"I wanted to see you a minute," said Mrs. Askerton, bowing to him without putting out her hand, "that I might ask you how you find your cousin."

"She is pretty well, I think."

"Colonel Askerton has seen more of her than I have since her father's death, and he says that she does not bear it well. He thinks that she is ill."

"I do not think her ill. Of course she is not in good spirits."

"No; exactly. How should she be? But he thinks she seems so worn. I hope you will excuse me, Mr. Belton, but I love her so well that I cannot bear to be quite in the dark as to her future. Is anything settled yet?"

"She is going to Aylmer Castle."

"To Aylmer Castle! Is she indeed? At once?"

"Very soon. Lady Aylmer has asked her."

"Lady Aylmer! Then I suppose——"

"You suppose what?" Will Belton asked.

"I did not think she would have gone to Aylmer Castle, —though I dare say it is the best thing she could do. She seemed to me to dislike the Aylmers, — that is, Lady Aylmer,— so much! But I suppose she is right."

"She is right to go if she likes it."

"She is circumstanced so cruelly! Is she not? Where else could she go? I do so feel for her. I believe I need hardly tell you, Mr. Belton, that she would be as welcome here as flowers in May,—but that I do not dare to ask her

to come to us." She said this in a low voice, turning her
eyes away from him, looking first upon the ground, and
then again up at the window,—but still not daring to meet
his eye.

"I don't exactly know about that," said Belton awkwardly.

"You know, I hope, that I love her dearly."

"Everybody does that," said Will.

"You do, Mr. Belton."

"Yes;—I do; just as though she were——my sister."

"And as your sister would you let her come here,—to
us?" He sat silent for awhile, thinking, and she waited
patiently for his answer. But she spoke again before he
answered her. "I am well aware that you know all my
history, Mr. Belton."

"I shouldn't tell it her, if you mean that, though she
were my sister. If she were my wife I should tell her."

"And why your wife?"

"Because then I should be sure it would do no harm."

"Then I find that you can be generous, Mr. Belton.
But she knows it all as well as you do."

"I did not tell her."

"Nor did I;—but I should have done so had not Captain Aylmer been before me. And now tell me whether I
could ask her to come here."

"It would be useless, as she is going to Aylmer Castle."

"But she is going there simply to find a home,—having
no other."

"That is not so, Mrs. Askerton. She has a home as
perfectly her own as any woman in the land. Belton
Castle is hers to do what she may please with it. She can
live here if she likes it, and nobody can say a word to her.
She need not go to Aylmer Castle to look for a home."

"You mean you would lend her the house."

"It is hers."

"I do not understand you, Mr. Belton."

"It does not signify;—we will say no more about it."

"And you think she likes going to Lady Aylmer's?"

"How should I say what she likes?"

Then there was another pause before Mrs. Askerton
spoke again. "I can tell you one thing," she said: "she
does not like him."

" That is her affair."

" But she should be taught to know her own mind
before she throws herself away altogether. You would not
wish your cousin to marry a man whom she does not love
because at one time she had come to think that she loved
him. That is the truth of it, Mr. Belton. If she goes to
Aylmer Castle she will marry him,—and she will be an
unhappy woman always afterwards. If you would sanction her coming here for a few days, I think all that would
be cured. She would come in a moment, if you advised
her."

Then he went away, allowing himself to make no further
answer at the moment, and discussed the matter with
himself as he walked back to Redicote, meditating on it
with all his mind, and all his heart, and all his strength.
And, as he meditated, it came on to rain bitterly,—a cold
piercing February rain,—and the darkness of night came
upon him, and he floundered on through the thick mud of
the Somersetshire lanes, unconscious of the weather and of
the darkness. There was a way open to him by which he
might even yet get what he wanted. He thought he saw
that there was a way open to him through the policy
of this woman, whom he perceived to have become friendly
to him. He saw, or thought that he saw, it all. No
day had absolutely been fixed for this journey to Yorkshire; and if Clara were induced to go first to the cottage,
and stay there with Mrs. Askerton, no such journey might
ever be taken. He could well understand that such a
visit on her part would give a mortal offence to all the
Aylmers. That tyranny of which Clara spoke with so
much dread would be exhibited then without reserve,
and so there would be an end altogether of the Aylmer
alliance. But were she once to start for Aylmer Park,
then there would be no hope for him. Then her fate
would be decided,—and his. As far as he could see too,—
as far as he could see then, there would be no dishonesty
in this plan. Why should Clara not go to Mrs. Askerton's
house? What could be more natural than such a visit at
such a time? If she were in truth his sister he would not
interfere to prevent it if she wished it. He had told
himself that the woman should be forgiven her offence,
and had thought that that forgiveness should be complete.

If the Aylmers were so unreasonable as to quarrel with her on this ground, let them quarrel with her. Mrs. Askerton had told him that Clara did not really like Captain Aylmer. Perhaps it was so; and if so, what greater kindness could he do her than give her an opportunity for escaping from such a union?

The whole of the next day he remained at Redicote thinking, doubting, striving to reconcile his wishes and his honesty. It rained all day, and as he sat alone, smoking in the comfortless inn, he told himself that the rain was keeping him;—but in truth it was not the rain. Had he resolved to do his best to prevent this visit to Yorkshire, or had he resolved to further it, I think he would have gone to Belton without much fear of the rain. On the second day after the funeral he did go, and he had then made up his mind. Clara, if she would listen to him, should show her independence of Lady Aylmer by staying a few days with the Askertons before she went to Yorkshire, and by telling Lady Aylmer that such was her intention. "If she really loves the man," he said to himself, "she will go at once, in spite of anything that I can say. If she does not, I shall be saving her."

"How cruel of you not to come yesterday!" Clara said, as soon as she saw him.

"It rained so hard," he answered.

"But men like you care so little for rain; but that is when you have business to take you out,—or pleasure."

"You need not be so severe. The truth is I had things to trouble me."

"What troubled you, Will? I thought all the trouble was mine."

"I suppose everybody thinks that his own shoe pinches the hardest."

"Your shoe can't pinch you very bad, I should think. Sometimes when I think of you it seems that you are an embodiment of prosperity and happiness."

"I don't see it myself;—that's all. Did you write to Lady Aylmer, Clara?"

"I wrote; but I didn't send it. I would not send any letter till I had shown it to you, as you are my confessor and adviser. There; read it. Nothing, I think, could be more courteous or less humble." He took the letter and

read it. Clara had simply expressed herself willing to
accept Lady Aylmer's invitation, and asked her ladyship to
fix a day. There was no mention of Captain Aylmer's
name in the note.

"And you think this is best?" he said. His voice was
hardly like his own as he spoke. There was wanting to it
that tone of self-assurance which his voice almost always possessed, even when self-assurance was lacking to his words.

"I thought it was your own advice," she said.

"Well;—yes; that is, I don't quite know. You
couldn't go for a week or so yet, I suppose."

"Perhaps in about a week."

"And what will you do till then?"

"What will I do!"

"Yes; where do you mean to stay?"

"I thought, Will, that perhaps you would let me—
remain here."

"Let you!—Oh, heavens! Look here, Clara."

"What is it, Will?"

"Before heaven I want to do for you what may be the
best for you,—without thinking of myself;—without thinking of myself, if I could only help it."

"I have never doubted you. I never will doubt you.
I believe in you next to my God. I do, Will; I do." He
walked up and down the room half-a-dozen times before
he spoke again, while she stood by the table watching him.
"I wish," she said, "I knew what it is that troubles you."
To this he made no answer, but went on walking till she
came up to him, and putting both her hands upon his arm
said, "It will be better, Will, that I should go;—will it
not? Speak to me and say so. I feel that it will be
better." Then he stopped in his walk and looked down
upon her, as her hands still rested upon his shoulder. He
gazed upon her for some few seconds, remaining quite motionless, and then, opening his arms, he surrounded her with
his embrace, and pressing her with all his strength close
to his bosom, kissed her forehead, and her cheeks, and her
lips, and her eyes. His will was so masterful, his strength
so great, and his motion so quick, that she was powerless
to escape from him till he relaxed his hold. Indeed she
hardly struggled, so much was she surprised and so soon
released. But the moment that he left her he saw that

her face was burning red, and that the tears were stream-
ing from her eyes. She stood for a moment trembling,
with her hands clenched, and with a look of scorn upon
her lips and brow that he had never seen before; and then
she threw herself on a sofa, and, burying her face, sobbed
aloud, while her whole body was shaken as with convul-
sions. He leaned over her repentant, not knowing what
to do, not knowing how to speak. All ideas of his scheme
had gone from him now. He had offended her for ever,—
past redemption. What could be the use now of any
scheme? And as he stood there he hated himself because
of his scheme. The utter misery and disgrace of the
present moment had come upon him because he had
thought more of himself than of her. It was but a few
moments since she had told him that she trusted him next
to her God; and yet, in those few moments, he had shown
himself utterly unworthy of that trust, and had destroyed
all her confidence. But he could not leave her without
speaking to her. "Clara," he said;—"Clara." But she
did not answer him. "Clara; will you not speak to me?
Will you not let me ask you to forgive me?" But still she
only sobbed. For her, at that moment, we may say that
sobbing was easier than speech. How was she to pardon
so great an offence? How was she to resent such passionate love?

But he could not continue to stand there motionless, all
but speechless, while she lay with her face turned away
from him. He must at any rate in some manner take him
self away out of the room; and this he could not do, even
in his present condition of unlimited disgrace, without a
word of farewell. "Perhaps I had better go and leave
you," he said.

Then at last there came a voice, "Oh, Will, why have
you done this? Why have you treated me so badly?"
When he had last seen her face her mouth had been
full of scorn, but there was no scorn now in her voice.
"Why—why—why?"

Why indeed;—except that it was needful for him that
she should know the depth of his passion. "If you will
forgive me, Clara I will not offend you so again," he said.

"You have offended me. What am I to say? What
am I to do? I have no other friend."

"I am a wretch. I know that I am a wretch."

"I did not suspect that you would be so cruel. Oh, Will!"

But before he went she told him that she had forgiven him, and she had preached to him a solemn, sweet sermon on the wickedness of yielding to momentary impulses. Her low, grave words sank into his ears as though they were divine; and when she said a word to him, blushing as she spoke, of the sin of his passion, and of what her sin would be if she were to permit it, he sat by her weeping like an infant, tears which were certainly tears of innocence. She had been very angry with him; but I think she loved him better when her sermon was finished, than she had ever loved him before.

There was no further question as to her going to Aylmer Castle, nor was any mention made of Mrs. Askerton's invitation to the cottage. The letter for Lady Aylmer was sent, and it was agreed between them that Will should remain at Redicote till the answer from Yorkshire should come, and should then convey Clara as far as London on her journey. And when he took leave of her that afternoon, she was able to give him her hand in her old hearty, loving way, and to call him Will with the old hearty, loving tone. And he,—he was able to accept these tokens of her graciousness, as though they were signs of a pardon which she had been good to give, but which he certainly had not deserved.

As he went back to Redicote, he swore to himself that he would never love any woman but her,—even though she must be the wife of Captain Aylmer.

CHAPTER XXIII.

THE LAST DAY AT BELTON.

IN course of post there came an answer from Lady Aylmer, naming a day for Clara's journey to Yorkshire, and also a letter from Captain Aylmer, in which he stated that he would meet her in London and convey her down to Aylmer Park. "The House is sitting," he said, "and

therefore I shall be a little troubled about my time; but I
cannot allow that your first meeting with my mother
should take place in my absence." This was all very
well, but at the end of the letter there was a word of
caution that was not so well. " I am sure, my dear Clara,
that you will remember how much is due to my mother's
age, and character and position. Nothing will be wanted
to the happiness of our marriage if you can succeed in
gaining her affection, and therefore I make it my first
request to you that you should endeavour to win her good
cpinion." There was nothing perhaps really amiss,
certainly nothing unreasonable, in such words from a
future husband to his future wife; but Clara, as she read
them, shook her head and pressed her foot against the
ground in anger. It would not do. Sorrow would come,
and trouble and disappointment. She did not say so, even
to herself, in words; but the words, though not spoken,
were audible enough to herself. She could not, would not,
bend to Lady Aylmer, and she knew that trouble would
come of this visit.

I fear that many ladies will condemn Miss Amedroz
when I tell them that she showed this letter to her cousin
Will. It does not promise well for any of the parties
concerned when a young woman with two lovers can bring
herself to show the love-letters of him to whom she is
engaged to the other lover whom she has refused! But I
have two excuses to put forward in Clara's defence. In
the first place, Captain Aylmer's love-letters were not in
truth love-letters, but were letters of business; and in the
next place, Clara was teaching herself to regard Will
Belton as her brother, and to forget that he had ever
assumed the part of a lover.

She was so teaching herself, but I cannot say that the
lesson was one easily learned; nor had the outrage upon
her of which Will had been guilty, and which was described in the last chapter, made the teaching easier. But
she had determined, nevertheless, that it should be so.
When she thought of Will her heart would become very
soft towards him; and sometimes, when she thought of
Captain Aylmer, her heart would become anything but
soft towards him. Unloving feelings would be very strong
within her bosom as she re-read his letters, and remem-

bered that he had not come to her, but had sent her
seventy-five pounds to comfort her in her trouble !
Nevertheless, he was to be her husband, and she would
do her duty. What might have happened had Will Belton
come to Belton Castle before she had known Frederic
Aylmer,—of that she stoutly resolved that she would
never think at all ; and consequently the thought was
always intruding upon her.

" You will sleep one night in town, of course," said
Will.

" I suppose so. You know all about that. I shall do as
I'm told."

" You can't go down to Yorkshire from here in one day.
Where would you like to stay in London ?"

" How on earth should I know ? Ladies do sleep at
hotels in London sometimes, I suppose ?"

" Oh, yes. I can write and have rooms ready for you."

" Then that difficulty is over," said Clara.

But in Belton's estimation the difficulty was not exactly
over. Captain Aylmer would, of course, be in London
that night, and it was a question with Will whether or no
Clara was not bound in honour to tell the—accursed beast,
I am afraid Mr. Belton called him in his soliloquies—
where she would lodge on the occasion. Or would it
suffice that he, Will, should hand her over to the enemy
at the station of the Great Northern Railway on the
following morning? All the little intricacies of the question presented themselves to Will's imagination. How
careful he would be with her, that the inn accommodation
should suffice for her comfort ! With what pleasure would
he order a little dinner for them two, making something of
a gentle *fête* of the occasion! How sedulously would he
wait upon her with those little attentions, amounting
almost to worship, with which such men as Will Belton
are prone to treat all women in exceptionable circumstances,
when the ordinary routine of life has been disturbed ! If
she had simply been his cousin, and if he had never regarded
her otherwise, how happily could he have done all this !
As things now were, if it was left to him to do, he should
do it, with what patience and grace might be within his
power ; he would do it, though he would be mindful
every moment of the bitterness of the transfer which he

would so soon be obliged to make; but he doubted whether it would not be better for Clara's sake that the transfer should be made over-night. He would take her up to London, because in that way he would be useful; and then he would go away and hide himself. "Has Captain Aylmer said where he would meet you?" he asked after a pause.

"Of course I must write and tell him."

"And is he to come to you,—when you reach London?"

"He has said nothing about that. He will probably be at the House of Commons, or too busy somewhere to come to me then. But why do you ask? Do you want to hurry through town?"

"Oh dear, no."

"Or perhaps you have friends you want to see. Pray don't let me be in your way. I shall do very well, you know."

Belton rebuked her by a look before he answered her. "I was only thinking," he said, "of what would be most convenient for yourself. I have nobody to see, and nothing to do, and nowhere to go to." Then Clara understood it all, and said that she would write to Captain Aylmer and ask him to join them at the hotel.

She determined that she would see Mrs. Askerton before she went; and as the lady did not come to the Castle, Clara called upon her at the cottage. This she did the day before she left, and she took her cousin with her. Belton had been at the cottage once or twice since the day on which Mrs. Askerton had explained to him how the Aylmer alliance might be extinguished, but Colonel Askerton had always been there, and no reference had been made to the former conversation. Colonel Askerton was not there now, and Belton was almost afraid that words would be spoken to which he would hardly know how to listen.

"And so you are really going?" said Mrs. Askerton.

"Yes; we start to-morrow," said Clara.

"I am not thinking of the journey to London," said Mrs. Askerton, "but of the danger and privations of your subsequent progress to the North."

"I shall do very well. I am not afraid that any one will eat me."

" There are so many different ways of eating people!
Are there not, Mr. Belton ?"

" I don't know about eating, but there are a great many
ways of boring people," said he.

" And I should think they will be great at that kind of
thing at Aylmer Castle.   One never hears of Sir Anthony,
but I can fancy Lady Aylmer to be a terrible woman."

" I shall manage to hold my own, I dare say," said Clara.

" I hope you will ; I do hope you will," said Mrs. Askerton.   " I don't know whether you will be powerful to
do so, or whether you will fail ; my heart is not absolute ;
but I do know what will be the result if you are successful."

" It is much more then than I know myself."

" That I can believe too.   Do you travel down to Yorkshire alone ?"

"No ; Captain Aylmer will meet me in town."

Then Mrs. Askerton looked at Mr. Belton, but made no
immediate reply ; nor did she say anything further about
Clara's journey.   She looked at Mr. Belton, and Will
caught her eye, and understood that he was being rebuked
for not having carried out that little scheme which had
been prepared for him.   But he had come to hate the
scheme, and almost hated Mrs. Askerton for proposing it.
He had declared to himself that her welfare, Clara's welfare, was the one thing which he should regard ; and he
had told himself that he was not strong enough, either in
purpose or in wit, to devise schemes for her welfare.   She
was better able to manage things for herself than he was
to manage them for her.   If she loved this " accursed
beast," let her marry him ; only,—for that was now his
one difficulty,—only he could not bring himself to think
it possible that she should love him.

" I suppose you will never see this place again ?" said
Mrs. Askerton after a long pause.

" I hope I shall, very often," said Clara.   " Why should
I not see it again ?   It is not going out of the family."

" No ; not exactly out of the family.   That is, it will
belong to your cousin."

" And cousins may be as far apart as strangers, you
mean ; but Will and I am not like that ; are we, Will ?"

" I hardly know what we are like," said he.

" You do not mean to say that you will throw me over ?

But the truth is, Mrs. Askerton, that I do not mean to be thrown over. I look upon him as my brother, and I intend to cling to him as sisters do cling."

"You will hardly come back here before you are married," said Mrs. Askerton. It was a terrible speech for her to make, and could only be excused on the ground that the speaker was in truth desirous of doing that which she thought would benefit both of those whom she addressed. "Of course you are going to your wedding now?"

"I am doing nothing of the kind," said Clara. "How can you speak in that way to me so soon after my father's death? It is a rebuke to me for being here at all."

"I intend no rebuke, as you well know. What I mean is this; if you do not stay in Yorkshire till you are married, let the time be when it may, where do you intend to go in the meantime?"

"My plans are not settled yet."

"She will have this house if she pleases," said Will. "There will be no one else here. It will be her own to do as she likes with it."

"She will hardly come here,—to be alone."

"I will not be inquired into, my dear," said Clara, speaking with restored good-humour. "Of course I am an unprotected female, and subject to disadvantages. Perhaps I have no plans for the future; and if I have plans perhaps I do not mean to divulge them."

"I had better come to the point at once," said Mrs. Askerton. "If—if—if it should ever suit you, pray come here to us. Flowerss hall not be more welcome in May. It is difficult to speak of it all, though you both understand everything as well as I do. I cannot press my invitation as another woman might."

"Yes, you can," said Clara with energy. "Of course you can."

"Can I? Then I do. Dear Clara, do come to us." And then as she spoke Mrs. Askerton knelt on the ground at her visitor's knees. "Mr. Belton, do tell her that when she is tired with the grandeur of Aylmer Park she may come to us here."

"I don't know anything about the grandeur of Aylmer Park," said Will, sullenly.

" But she may come here ;—may she not ?"

" She will not ask my leave," said he.

" She says that you are her brother. Whose leave should she ask ?"

" He knows that I should ask his rather than that of any living person," said Clara.

" There, Mr. Belton. Now you must say that she may come ;—or that she may not."

" I will say nothing. She knows what to do much better than I can tell her."

Mrs. Askerton was still kneeling, and again appealed to Clara. " You hear what he says. What do you say yourself ? Will you come to us ?—that is, if such a visit will suit you,—in point of convenience ?"

" I will make no promise ; but I know no reason why I should not."

" And I must be content with that ? Well ; I will be content." Then she got up. " For such a one as I am, that is a great deal. And, Mr. Belton, let me tell you this ;—I can be grateful to you; though you cannot be gracious to me."

" I hope I have not been ungracious," said he.

" Upon my word, I cannot compliment you. But there is something so much better than grace, that I can forgive you. You know, at any rate, how thoroughly I wish you well."

Upon this Clara got up to take her leave, and the demonstrative affection of an embrace between the two women afforded a remedy for the awkwardness of the previous conversation. " God bless you, dearest," said Mrs. Askerton. " May I write to you ?"

" Certainly," said Clara.

" And you will answer my letters ?"

" Of course I will. You must tell me everything about the place ;—and especially as to Bessy. Bessy is never to be sold ;—is she, Will ?" Bessy was the cow which Belton had given her.

" Not if you choose to keep her."

" I will go down and see to her myself," said Mrs. Askerton, " and will utter little prayers of my own over her horns,—that certain events that I desire may come to pass. Good-bye, Mr. Belton. You may be as ungracious as you please, but it will not make any difference."

When Clara and her cousin left the cottage they did not return to the house immediately, but took a last walk round the park, and through the shrubbery, and up to the rocks on which a remarkable scene had once taken place between them. Few words were spoken as they were walking, and there had been no agreement as to the path they would take. Each seemed to understand that there was much of melancholy in their present mood, and that silence was more fitting than speech. But when they reached the rocks Belton sat himself down, asking Clara's leave to stop there for a moment. "I don't suppose I shall ever come to this place again," said he.

"You are as bad as Mrs. Askerton," said Clara.

"I do not think I shall ever come to this place again," said he, repeating his words very solemnly. "At any rate, I will never do so willingly, unless——"

"Unless what?"

"Unless you are either my wife, or have promised to become so."

"Oh, Will! you know that that is impossible."

"Then it is impossible that I should come here again."

"You know that I am engaged to another man."

"Of course I do. I am not asking you to break your engagement. I am simply telling you that in spite of that engagement I love you as well as I did love you before you had made it. I have a right to let you know the truth." As if she had not known it without his telling it to her now! "It was here that I told you that I loved you. I now repeat it here; and will never come here again unless I may say the same thing over and over and over. That is all. We might as well go on now." But when he got up she sat down as though unwilling to leave the spot. It was still winter, and the rock was damp with cold drippings from the trees, and the moss around was wet, and little pools of water had formed themselves in the shallow holes upon the surface. She did not speak as she seated herself; but he was of course obliged to wait till she should be ready to accompany him. "It is too cold for you to sit there," he said. "Come, Clara; I will not have you loiter here. It is cold and wet."

"It is not colder for me than for you."

"You are not used to that sort of thing as I am."

"Will," she said, "you must never speak to me again as you spoke just now. Promise me that you will not."

"Promises will do no good in such a matter."

"It is almost a repetition of what you did before;—though of course it is not so bad as that."

"Everything I do is bad."

"No, Will;—dear Will! Almost everything you do is good. But of what use can it be to either of us for you to be thinking of that which can never be? Cannot you think of me as your sister,—and only as your sister?"

"No; I cannot."

"Then it is not right that we should be together."

"I know nothing about right. You ask me a question, and I suppose you don't wish that I should tell you a lie."

"Of course I do not wish that."

"Therefore I tell you the truth. I love you,—as any other man loves the girl that he does love; and, as far as I know myself now, I never can be happy unless you are my own."

"Oh, Will, how can that be, when I am engaged to marry another man?"

"As to your engagement I should care nothing. Does he love you as I love you? If he loves you, why is he not here? If he loves you, why does he let his mother ill-use you, and treat you with scorn? If he loves you as I love you, how could he write to you as he does write? Would I write you such a letter as that? Would I let you be here without coming to you,—to be looked after by any one else? If you had said that you would be my wife, would I leave you in solitude and sorrow, and then send you seventy-five pounds to console you. If you think he loves you, Clara——"

"He thought he was doing right when he sent me the money."

"But he shouldn't have thought it right, Never mind. I don't want to accuse him; but this I know,—and you know; he does not love you as I love you."

"What can I say to answer you?"

"Say that you will wait till you have seen him. Say that I may have a hope,—a chance; that if he is cold, and hard, and,—and,—and, just what we know he is, then I may have a chance."

" How can I say that when I am engaged to him? Cannot you understand that I am wrong to let you speak of him as you do?"

" How else am I to speak of him? Tell me this. Do you love him?"

" Yes;—I do."

" I don't believe it!"

" Will!"

" I don't believe it. Nothing on earth shall make me believe it. It is impossible;—impossible!"

" Do you mean to insult me, Will?"

" No; I do not mean to insult you, but I mean to tell you the truth. I do not think you love that man as you ought to love the man whom you are going to marry. I should tell you just the same thing if I were really your brother. Of course it isn't that I suppose you love any one else,—me for instance. I'm not such a fool as that. But I don't think you love him; and I'm quite sure he doesn't love you. That's just what I believe; and if I do believe it, how am I to help telling you?"

" You've no right to have such beliefs."

" How am I to help it? Well;—never mind. I won't let you sit there any longer. At any rate you'll be able to understand now that I shall never come to this place any more." Clara, as she got up to obey him, felt that she also ought never to see it again;—unless, indeed,—unless——

They passed that evening together without any reference to the scene on the rock, or any allusion to their own peculiar troubles. Clara, though she would not admit to Mrs. Askerton that she was going away from the place for ever, was not the less aware that such might very probably be the case. She had no longer any rights of ownership at Belton Castle, and all that had taken place between her and her cousin tended to make her feel that under no circumstances could she again reside there. Nor was it probable that she would be able to make to Mrs. Askerton the visit of which they had been talking. If Lady Aylmer were wise,—so Clara thought,—there would be no mention of Mrs. Askerton at Aylmer Park; and, if so, of course she would not outrage her future husband by proposing to go to a house of which she knew that he disapproved. If

Lady Aylmer were not wise;—if she should take upon herself the task of rebuking Clara for her friendship,—then, in such circumstances as those, Clara believed that the visit to Mrs. Askerton might be possible.

But she determined that she would leave the home in which she had been born, and had passed so many happy and so many unhappy days, as though she were never to see it again. All her packing had been done, down to the last fragment of an old letter that was stuffed into her writing-desk; but, nevertheless, she went about the house with a candle in her hand, as though she were still looking that nothing had been omitted, while she was in truth saying farewell in her heart to every corner which she knew so well. When at last she came down to pour out for her desolate cousin his cup of tea, she declared that everything was done. "You may go to work now, Will," she said, "and do what you please with the old place. My jurisdiction in it is over."

"Not altogether," said he. He no longer spoke like a despairing lover. Indeed there was a smile round his mouth, and his voice was cheery.

"Yes;—altogether. I give over my sovereignty from this moment;—and a dirty, dilapidated sovereignty it is."

"That's all very well to say."

"And also very well to do. What best pleases me in going to Aylmer Castle just now is the power it gives me of doing at once that which otherwise I might have put off till the doing of it had become much more unpleasant. Mr. Belton, there is the key of the cellar,—which I believe gentlemen always regard as the real sign of possession. I don't advise you to trust much to the contents." He took the key from her, and without saying a word chucked it across the room on to an old sofa. "If you won't take it, you had better, at any rate, have it tied up with the others," she said.

"I dare say you'll know where to find it when you want it," he answered.

"I shall never want it."

"Then it's as well there as anywhere else."

"But you won't remember, Will."

"I don't suppose I shall have occasion for remembering."
Then he paused a moment before he went on. "I have

told you before that I do not intend to take possession of the place. I do not regard it as mine at all."

"And whose is it then ?"

"Yours."

"No, dear Will; it is not mine. You know that."

"I intend that it shall be so, and therefore you might as well put the keys where you will know how to find them."

After he had gone she did take up the key, and tied it with sundry others, which she intended to give to the old servant who was to be left in charge of the house. But after a few moments' consideration she took the cellar key again off the bunch, and put it back upon the sofa,—in the place to which he had thrown it.

On the following morning they started on their journey. The old fly from Redicote was not used on this occasion, as Belton had ordered a pair of post-horses and a comfortable carriage from Taunton. "I think it such a shame," said Clara, "going away for the last time without having Jerry and the grey horse." Jerry was the man who had once driven her to Taunton when the old horse fell with her on the road. "But Jerry and the grey horse could not have taken you and me too, and all our luggage," said Will. "Poor Jerry! I suppose not," said Clara; "but still there is an injury done in going without him."

There were four or five old dependents of the family standing round the door to bid her adieu, to all of whom she gave her hand with a cordial pressure. They at least seemed to regard her departure as final. And of course it was final. She had assured herself of that during the night. And just as they were about to start, both Colonel and Mrs. Askerton walked up to the door. "He wouldn't let you go without bidding you farewell," said Mrs. Askerton. "I am so glad to shake hands with him," Clara answered. Then the Colonel spoke a word to her, and, as he did so, his wife contrived to draw Will Belton for a moment behind the carriage. "Never give it up, Mr. Belton," said she, eagerly. "If you persevere, she'll be yours yet." "I fear not," he said. "Stick to her like a man," said she, pressing his hand in her vehemence. "If you do, you'll live to thank me for having told you so." Will had not a word to say for himself, but he thought that ne would stick to her. Indeed, he thought that he had stuck to her pretty well.

At last they were off, and the village of Belton was behind them. Will, glancing into his cousin's face, saw that her eyes were laden with tears, and refrained from speaking. As they passed the ugly red-brick rectory-house, Clara for a moment put her face to the window, and then withdrew it. "There is nobody there," she said, "who will care to see me. Considering that I have lived here all my life, is it not odd that there should be so few to bid me good-bye?"

"People do not like to put themselves forward on such occasions," said Will.

"People!—there are no people. No one ever had so few to care for them as I have. And now——. But never mind; I mean to do very well, and I shall do very well." Belton would not take advantage of her in her sadness, and they reached the station at Taunton almost without another word.

Of course they had to wait there for half an hour, and of course the waiting was very tedious. To Will it was very tedious indeed, as he was not by nature good at waiting. To Clara, who on this occasion sat perfectly still in the waiting-room, with her toes on the fender before the fire, the evil of the occasion was not so severe. "The man would take two hours for the journey, though I told him an hour and a half would be enough," said Will, querulously.

"But we might have had an accident."

"An accident! What accident? People don't have accidents every day."

At last the train came and they started. Clara, though she had with her her best friend,—I may almost say the friend whom in the world she loved the best,—did not have an agreeable journey. Belton would not talk; but as he made no attempt at reading, Clara did not like to have recourse to the book which she had in her travelling-bag. He sat opposite to her, opening the window and shutting it as he thought she might like it, but looking wretched and forlorn. At Swindon he brightened up for a moment under the excitement of getting her something to eat, but that relaxation lasted only for a few minutes. After that he relapsed again into silence till the train had passed Slough, and he knew that in another half-hour they would be in London. Then he leant over her and spoke.

"This will probably be the last opportunity I shall have of saying a few words to you,—alone."

"I don't know that at all, Will."

"It will be the last for a long time at any rate. And as I have got something to say, I might as well say it now. I have thought a great deal about the property,—the Belton estate I mean; and I don't intend to take it as mine."

"That is sheer nonsense, Will. You must take it, as it is yours, and can't belong to any one else."

"I have thought it over, and I am quite sure that all the business of the entail was wrong,—radically wrong from first to last. You are to understand that my special regard for you has nothing whatever to do with it. I should do the same thing if I felt that I hated you."

"Don't hate me, Will!"

"You know what I mean. I think the intent was all wrong, and I shan't take advantage of it. It's not common sense that I should have everything because of poor Charley's misfortune."

"But it seems to me that it does not depend upon you or upon me, or upon anybody. It is yours,—by law, you know."

"And therefore it won't be sufficient for me to give it up without making it yours by law also,—which I intend to do. I shall stay in town to-morrow and give instructions to Mr. Green. I have thought it proper to tell you this now, in order that you may mention it to—Captain Aylmer."

They were leaning over in the carriage one towards the other; her face had been slightly turned away from him; but now she slowly raised her eyes till they met his, and looking into the depth of them, and seeing there all his love and all his suffering, and the great nobility of his nature, her heart melted within her. Gradually, as her tears came,—would come, in spite of all her constraint, she again turned her face towards the window. "I can't talk now," she said; "indeed I can't."

"There is no need for any more talking about it," he replied. And there was no more talking between them on that subject, or on any other, till the tickets had been taken and the train was again in motion. Then he referred to it again for a moment. "You will tell Captain Aylmer, my dear."

"I will tell him what you say, that he may know your generosity. But of course he will agree with me that no such offer can be accepted. It is quite,—quite,—quite out of the question."

"You had better tell him and say nothing more; or you can ask him to see Mr Green,—after to-morrow. He, as a man who understands business, will know that this arrangement must be made, if I choose to make it. Come; here we are. Porter, a four-wheel cab. Do you go with him, and I'll look after the luggage."

Clara as she got into the cab, felt that she ought to have been more stout in her resistance to his offer. But it would be better, perhaps, that she should write to him from Aylmer Park, and get Frederic to write also.

CHAPTER XXIV.

THE GREAT NORTHERN RAILWAY HOTEL.

AT the door of the hotel of the Great Northern Railway Station they met Captain Aylmer. Rooms had been taken there because they were to start by an early train on that line in the morning, and Captain Aylmer had undertaken to order dinner. There was nothing particular in the meeting to make it unpleasant to our friend Will. The fortunate rival could do no more in the hall of the inn than give his hand to his affianced bride, as he might do to any other lady, and then suggest to her that she should go upstairs and see her room. When he had done this, he also offered his hand to Belton; and Will, though he would almost sooner have cut off his own, was obliged to take it. In a few minutes the two men were standing alone together in the sitting-room.

"I suppose you found it cold coming up?" said the Captain.

"Not particularly," said Will.

" It's rather a long journey from Belton."

" Not very long," said Will.

"Not for you, perhaps ; but Miss Amedroz must be tired."

Belton was angry at having his cousin called Miss Amedroz,—feeling that the reserve of the name was intended to keep him at a distance. But he would have been equally angry had Aylmer called her Clara.

" My cousin," said Will stoutly, " is able to bear slight fatigue of that kind without suffering."

" I didn't suppose she suffered ; but journeys are always tedious, especially where there was so much road work. I believe you are twenty miles from the station ?"

" Belton Castle is something over twenty miles from Taunton."

" We are seven from our station at Aylmer Park, and we think that a great deal."

" I am more than that at Plaistow," said Will.

" Oh, indeed. Plaistow is in Norfolk, I believe ?"

" Yes ;—Plaistow is in Norfolk."

" I suppose you will leave it now and go into Somersetshire," suggested Captain Aylmer.

" Certainly not. Why should I leave it ?"

" I thought, perhaps,—as Belton Castle is now your own——"

" Plaistow Hall is more my own than Belton Castle, if that signifies anything,—which it doesn't." This he said in an angry tone, which, as he became conscious of it, he tried to rectify. " I've a deal of stock and all that sort of thing at Plaistow, and couldn't very well leave it, even if I wished it," he said.

" You've pretty good shooting too, I suppose," said Aylmer.

" As far as partridges go, I'll back it against most properties of the same extent in any county."

" I'm too busy a man myself," " said the Captain, " to do much at partridges. We think more of pheasants down with us."

" I dare say."

" But a Norfolk man like you is of course keen about birds."

" We are obliged to put up with what we've got, you

know ;—not but what I believe there is a better general
head of game in Norfolk than in any other county in
England."

"That's what makes your hunting rather poor."

"Our hunting poor! Why do you say it's poor?"

"So many of you are against preserving foxes."

"I'll tell you what, Captain Aylmer; I don't know
what pack you hunt with, but I'll bet you a five-pound
note that we killed more foxes last year than you did ;—
that is, taking three days a week. Nine-and-twenty brace
and a half in a short season I don't call poor at all."

Captain Aylmer saw that the man was waxing angry,
and made no further allusion either to the glories or
deficiencies of Norfolk. As he could think of no other
subject on which to speak at the spur of the moment, he
sat himself down and took up a paper; Belton took up
another, and so they remained till Clara made her appearance. That Captain Aylmer read his paper is probable
enough. He was not a man easily disconcerted, and there
was nothing in his present position to disconcert him.
But I feel sure that Will Belton did not read a word.
He was angry with this rival, whom he hated, and was
angry with himself for showing his anger. He would
have wished to appear to the best advantage before this
man, or rather before Clara in this man's presence ; and he
knew that in Clara's absence he was making such a fool of
himself that he would be unable to recover his prestige.
He had serious thoughts within his own breast whether it
would not be as well for him to get up from his seat and
give Captain Aylmer a thoroughly good thrashing ;—" drop
into him and punch his head," as he himself would have
expressed it. For the moment such an exercise would
give him immense gratification. The final results would,
no doubt, be disastrous ; but then, all future results, as far
as he could see them, were laden with disaster. He was
still thinking of this, eyeing the man from under the
newspaper, and telling himself that the feat would probably
be too easy to afford much enjoyment, when Clara re-
entered the room. Then he got up acting on the spur of
the moment,—got up quickly and suddenly, and began to
bid her adieu.

"But you are going to dine here, Will?" she said.

"No; I think not."

"You promised you would. You told me you had nothing to do to-night." Then she turned to Captain Aylmer. "You expect my cousin to dine with us to-day?"

"I ordered dinner for three," said Captain Aylmer.

"Oh, very well; it's all the same thing to me," said Will.

"And to me," said Captain Aylmer.

"It's not at all the same thing to me," said Clara. "I don't know when I may see my cousin again. I should think it very bad of you, Will, if you went away this evening."

"I'll go out just for half an hour," said he, "and be back to dinner."

"We dine at seven," said the Captain. Then Belton took his hat and left the two lovers together.

"Your cousin seems to be a rather surly sort of gentleman." Those were the first words which Captain Aylmer spoke when he was alone with the lady of his love. Nor was he demonstrative of his affection by any of the usual signs of regard which are permitted to accepted lovers. He did not offer to kiss her, nor did he attempt to take her hand with a warmer pressure now that he was alone with her. He probably might have gone through some such ceremony had he first met Clara in a position propitious to such purposes; but, as it was, he had been a little ruffled by Will Belton's want of good breeding, and had probably forgotten that any such privileges might have been his. I wonder whether any remembrance flashed across Clara's mind at this moment of her cousin Will's great iniquity in the sitting-room at Belton Castle. She thought of it very often, and may possibly have thought of it now.

"I don't believe that he is surly, Frederic," she said. "He may, perhaps, be out of humour."

"And why should he be out of humour with me? I only suggested to him that it might suit him to live at Belton instead of at that farm of his, down in Norfolk."

"He is very fond of Plaistow, I fancy."

"But that's no reason why he should be cross with me. I don't envy him his taste, that's all. If he can't under-stand that he, with his name, ought to live on the family property which belongs to him, it isn't likely that anything that I can say will open his eyes upon the subject."

" The truth is, Frederic, he has some romantic notion about the Belton estate."

" What romantic notion ?"

" He thinks it should not be his at all."

" Whose then ?   Who does he think should have it ?"

" Of course there can be nothing in it, you know ; of course it's all nonsense."

" But what is his idea?   Who does he think should be the owner ?"

" He means—that it should be—mine.   But of course, Frederic, it is all nonsense ; we know that."

It did not seem to be quite clear at the moment that Frederic had altogether made up his mind upon the subject. As he heard these tidings from Clara there came across his face a puzzled, dubious look, as though he did not quite understand the proposition which had been suggested to him ;—as though some consideration were wanted before he could take the idea home to himself and digest it, so as to enable himself to express an opinion upon it.   There might be something in it,—some show of reason which did not make itself clear to Clara's feminine mind.   " I have never known what was the precise nature of your father's marriage settlement," said he.

Then Clara began to explain with exceeding eagerness that there was no question as to the accuracy of the settle-ment, or the legality of the entail ;—that indeed there was no question as to anything.   Her cousin Will was romantic. and that was the end of it.   Of course,—quite as a matter of course, this romance would lead to nothing ; and she had only mentioned the subject now to show that her cousin's mind might possibly be disturbed when the question of his future residence was raised.   " I quite feel with you," she said, " that it will be much nicer that he should live at the old family place ; but just at present I do not speak about it."

" If he is thinking of not claiming Belton, it is quite another thing," said Aylmer.

" It is his without any claiming," said Clara.

" Ah, well ; it will all be settled before long," said Aylmer.

"It is settled already," said Clara.

At seven the three met again, and when the dinner was on the table there was some little trouble as to the helping of the fish. Which of the two men should take the lead on the occasion? But Clara decided the question by asking her cousin to make himself useful. There can be little doubt but that Captain Aylmer would have distributed the mutton chops with much more grace, and have carved the roast fowl with much more skill; but it suited Clara that Will should have the employment, and Will did the work. Captain Aylmer throughout the dinner, endeavoured to be complaisant, and Clara exerted herself to talk as though all matters around them were easy. Will, too, made his effort, every now and then speaking a word, and restraining himself from snapping at his rival; but the restraint was in itself evident, and there were symptoms throughout the dinner that the untamed man was longing to fly at the throat of the man that was tamed.

"Is it supposed that I ought to go away for a little while?" said Clara, as soon as she had drank her own glass of wine.

"Oh dear, no," said the Captain. "We'll have a cup of coffee;—that is, if Mr. Belton likes it."

"It's all the same to me," said Will.

"But won't you have some more wine?" Clara asked.

"No more for me," said Captain Aylmer. "Perhaps Mr. Belton——"

"Who; I? No; I don't want any more wine," said Will; and then they were all silent.

It was very hard upon Clara. After a while the coffee came, and even that was felt to be a comfort. Though there was no pouring out to be done, no actual employment enacted, still the manœuvring of the cups created a diversion. "If either of you like to smoke," she said, "I shan't mind it in the least." But neither of them would smoke. "At what hour shall we get to Aylmer Park to-morrow?" Clara asked.

"At half-past four," said the Captain.

"Oh indeed;—so early as that." What was she to say next? Will, who had not touched his coffee, and who was sitting stiffly at the table as though he were bound in duty not to move, was becoming more and more grim every

moment. She almost repented that she had asked him to
remain with them. Certainly there was no comfort in his
company, either to them or to himself. "How long shall
you remain in town, Will, before you go down to Plaistow?"
she asked.

"One day," he replied.

"Give my kind love,—my very kindest love to Mary.
I wish I knew her. I wish I could think that I might
soon know her."

"You'll never know her," said Belton. The tone of his
voice was actually savage as he spoke; so much so that Aylmer
turned in his chair to look at him, and Clara did not dare to
answer him. But now that he had been made to speak, it
seemed that he was determined to persevere. "How should
you ever know her? Nothing will ever bring you into
Norfolk, and nothing will ever take her out of it."

"I don't quite see why either of those assertions should
be made."

"Nevertheless they're both true. Had you ever meant
to come to Norfolk you would have come now." He had
not even asked her to come, having arranged with his sister
that in their existing circumstances any such asking would
not be a kindness; and yet he rebuked her now for not
coming!

"My mother is very anxious that Miss Amedroz should
pay her a visit at Aylmer Park," said the Captain.

"And she's going to Aylmer Park, so your mother's
anxiety need not disturb her any longer."

"Come, Will, don't be out of temper with us," said Clara.
"It is our last night together. We, who are so dear to each
other, ought not to quarrel."

"I'm not quarrelling with you," said he.

"I can hardly suppose that Mr. Belton wants to quarrel
with me," said Captain Aylmer smiling.

"I'm sure he does not," said Clara. Belton sat silent,
with his eyes fixed upon the table, with a dark frown upon
his brow. He did long to quarrel with Captain Aylmer;
but was still anxious, if it might be possible, to save himself from what he knew would be a transgression.

"To use a phrase common with us down in Yorkshire,"
said Aylmer, "I should say that Mr. Belton had got out
of bed the wrong side this morning."

" What the d—— does it matter to you, sir, what side
I got out of bed?" said Will, clenching both his fists.   Oh
—if he might only have been allowed to have a round of
five minutes with Aylmer, he would have been restored
to good temper for that night, let the subsequent results
have been what they might.   He moved his feet impatiently on the floor, as though he were longing to kick
something; and then he pushed his coffee-cup away from
him, upsetting half the contents upon the table, and knocking down a wine-glass, which was broken.

" Will;—Will!" said Clara, looking at him with implor
ing eyes.

" Then he shouldn't talk to me about getting out of
bed on the wrong side.   I didn't say anything to him."

" It is unkind of you, Will, to quarrel with Captain
Aylmer because he is my friend."

" I don't want to quarrel with him; or, rather, as I won't
quarrel with him because you don't wish it, I'll go away. I
can't do more than that.   I didn't want to dine with him
here.   There's my cousin Clara, Captain Aylmer; I love
her better than all the world besides.   Love her!   It
seems to me that there's nothing else in the world for me
to love.   I'd give my heart for her this minute.   All
that I have in the world is hers.   Oh,—love her!   I
don't believe that it's in you to know what I mean when
I say that I love her!   She tells me that she's going to
be your wife.   You can't suppose that I can be very
comfortable under those circumstances,—or that I can
be very fond of you.   I'm not very fond of you.   Now I'll
go away, and then I shan't trouble you any more.   But
look here,—if ever you should ill-treat her, whether you
marry her or whether you don't, I'll crush every bone
in your skin."   Having so spoken he went to the door,
but stopped himself before he left the room.   " Good-bye,
Clara.   I've got a word or two more to say to you, but I'll
write you a line down-stairs.   You can show it to him
if you please.   It'll only be about business.   Good-night."

She had got up and followed him to the door, and he
had taken her by the hand.   " You shouldn't let your
passion get the better of you in this way," she said; but
the tone of her voice was very soft, and her eyes were
full of love.

"I suppose not," said he.

"I can forgive him," said Captain Aylmer.

"Damn your forgiveness," said Will Belton. Then Clara dropped the hand and started back, and the door was shut, and Will Belton was gone.

"Your cousin seems to be a nice sort of a young man," said Aylmer.

"Cannot you understand it all, Frederic, and pardon him?"

"I can pardon him easily enough; but one doesn't like men who are given to threatening. He's not the sort of man that I took him to be."

"Upon my word I think he's as nearly perfect as a man can be."

"Then you like men to swear at you, and to swagger like Bobadils, and to misbehave themselves, so that one has to blush for them if a servant chances to hear them. Do you really think that he has conducted himself to-day like a gentleman?"

"I know that he is a gentleman," said Clara.

"I must confess I have no reason for supposing him to be so but your assurance."

"And I hope that is sufficient, Frederic."

Captain Aylmer did not answer her at once, but sat for awhile silent, considering what he would say. Clara, who understood his moods, knew that he did not mean to drop the subject, and resolved that she would defend her cousin, let Captain Aylmer attack him as he would. "Upon my word, I hardly know what to say about it," said Aylmer.

"Suppose then that we say nothing more. Will not that be best?"

"No, Clara. I cannot now let the matter pass by in that way. You have asked me whether I do not think Mr. Belton to be a gentleman, and I must say that I doubt it. Pray hear me out before you answer me. I do not want to be harder upon him than I can help; and I would have borne, and I did bear from him, a great deal in silence. But he said that to me which I cannot allow to pass without notice. He had the bad taste to speak to me of his—his regard for you."

"I cannot see what harm he did by that;—except to himself."

" I believe that it is understood among gentlemen that one man never speaks to another man about the lady the other man means to marry, unless they are very intimate friends indeed. What I mean is, that if Mr. Belton had understood how gentlemen live together, he would never have said anything to me about his affection for you. He should at any rate have supposed me to be ignorant of it. There is something in the very idea of his doing so that is in the highest degree indelicate. I wonder, Clara, that you do not see this yourself."

" I think he was indiscreet."

" Indiscreet! Indiscreet is not the word for such conduct. I must say, that as far as my opinion goes, it was ungentlemanlike."

" I don't believe that there is a nobler-minded gentleman in all London than my cousin Will."

" Perhaps it gratified you to hear from him the assurance of his love," said Captain Aylmer.

" If it is your wish to insult me, Frederic, I will leave you."

" It is my wish to make you understand that your judgment has been wrong."

" That is simply a matter of opinion, and as I do not wish to argue with you about it, I had better go. At any rate, I am very tired. Good-night, Frederic." He then told her what arrangements he had made for the morrow, at what hour she would be called, and when she would have her breakfast. After that he let her go without making any further allusion to Will Belton.

It must be admitted that the meeting between the lovers had not been auspicious; and it must be acknowledged, also, that Will Belton had behaved very badly. I am not aware of the existence of that special understanding among gentlemen in respect to the ladies they are going to marry which Captain Aylmer so eloquently described; but, nevertheless, I must confess that Belton would have done better had he kept his feelings to himself. And when he talked of crushing his rival's bones, he laid himself justly open to severe censure. But, for all that, he was no Bobadil. He was angry, sore, and miserable; and in his anger, soreness, and misery he had allowed himself to be carried away. He felt very keenly his own folly, even as he was leaving the room, and as he made his way out of the hotel he hated himself for his own braggadocio. " I wish some one would crush my bones," he said to himself almost audibly. " No one ever deserved to be crushed better than I do."

Clara, when she got to her own room, was very serious and very sad. What was to be the end of it all? This had been her first meeting after her father's death with the man whom she had promised to marry; indeed, it was the first meeting after her promise had been given; and they had only met to quarrel. There had been no word of love spoken between them. She had parted from him now almost in anger, without the slightest expression of confidence between them,—almost as those part who are constrained by circumstances to be together, but who yet hate each other, and know that they hate each other. Was there in truth any love between him and her? And if there was none, could there be any advantage, any good either to him or to her, in this journey of hers to Aylmer Park? ' Would it not be better that she should send for him and tell him that they were not suited for each other, and that thus she should escape from all the terrors of Lady Aylmer? As she thought of this, she could not but think of Will Belton also. Not a gentleman! If Will Belton was not a gentleman, she desired to know nothing further of gentlemen. Women are so good and kind that those whom they love they love almost the more when they commit offences, because of the offences so committed. Will Belton had been guilty of great offences,—of offences for which Clara was prepared to lecture him in the gravest manner should opportunities for such lectures ever come; —but I think that they had increased her regard for him rather than diminished it. She could not, however, make up her mind to send for Captain Aylmer, and when she went to bed she had resolved that the visit to Yorkshire must be made.

Before she left her room the following morning, a letter was brought to her from her cousin, which had been written that morning. She asked the maid to inquire for him, and sent down word to him that if he were in the house she specially wished to see him; but the tidings came from the hall porter that he had gone out very early, and had expressly said that he should not breakfast at the inn.

The letter was as follows :—

" DEAR CLARA,

" I meant to have handed to you the enclosed in person, but I lost my temper last night,—like a fool as I am,—and so I couldn't do it. You need not have any scruple about the money which I send,—£100 in ten ten-pound notes,—as it is your own. There is the rent due up to your father's death, which is more than what I now enclose, and there will be a great many other items, as to all of which you shall have a proper account. When you want more, you had better draw on me, till things are settled. It shall all be done as soon as possible. It would not be comfortable for you to go away without money of your own, and I suppose you would not wish that he should pay for your journeys and things before you are married.

" Of course I made a fool of myself yesterday. I believe that I usually do. It is not any good my begging your pardon, for I don't suppose I shall ever trouble you any more. Good-bye, and God bless you.

" Your ever-affectionate Cousin,

" WILLIAM BELTON.

" It was a bad day for me when I made up my mind to go to Belton Castle last summer."

Clara, when she had read the letter, sat down and cried, holding the bundle of notes in her hand. What would she do with them? Should she send them back? Oh no;—she would do nothing to displease him, or to make him think that she was angry with him. Besides, she had none of that dislike to taking his money which she had felt as to receiving money from Captain Aylmer. He had said that she would be his sister, and she would take from him any assistance that a sister might properly take from a brother.

She went down-stairs, and met Captain Aylmer in the sitting-room. He stepped up to her as soon as the door was closed, and she could at once see that he had determined to forget the unpleasantnesses of the previous even-

ing. He stepped up to her, and, gracefully taking her by
one hand, and passing the other behind her waist, saluted
her in a becoming and appropriate manner.   She did not
like it.   She especially disliked it, believing in her heart of
hearts that she would never become the wife of this man
whom she had professed to love,—and whom she really had
once loved. But she could only bear it. And, to say the truth,
there was not much suffering of that kind to be borne.

Their journey down to Yorkshire was very prosperous.
He maintained his good-humour throughout the day, and
never once said a word about Will Belton. Nor did he say
a word about Mrs. Askerton. " Do your best to please my
mother, Clara," he said, as they were driving up from the
park lodges to the house.   This was fair enough, and she
therefore promised him that she would do her best.

CHAPTER XXV.

MISS AMEDROZ HAS SOME HASHED CHICKEN.

CLARA felt herself to be a coward as the Aylmer Park
carriage which had been sent to meet her at the station,
was drawn up at Sir Anthony Aylmer's door. She had
made up her mind that she would not bow down to Lady
Aylmer, and yet she was afraid of the woman.   As she
got out of the carriage, she looked up, expecting to see her
in the hall ; but Lady Aylmer was too accurately acquainted with the weights and measures of society for any
such movement as that.   Had her son brought Lady
Emily to the house as his future bride, Lady Aylmer
would probably have been in the hall when the arrival
took place ; and had Clara possessed ten thousand pounds
of her own, she would probably have been met at the
drawing-room door ; but as she had neither money nor title,
—as she in fact brought with her no advantages of any
sort, Lady Aylmer was found stitching a bit of worsted, as
though she had expected no one to come to her.   And
Belinda Aylmer was stitching also,—by special order
from her mother. The reader will remember that Lady
Aylmer was not without strong hope that the engagement

might even yet be broken off. Snubbing, she thought, might probably be efficacious to this purpose, and so Clara was to be snubbed.

Clara, who had just promised to do her best to gain Lady Aylmer's good opinion, and who desired to be in some way true to her promise, though she thoroughly believed that her labour would be in vain, put on her pleasantest smile as she entered the room. Belinda, under the pressure of the circumstances forgetting somewhat of her mother's injunctions, hurried to the door to welcome the stranger. Lady Aylmer kept her chair, and even maintained her stitch, till Clara was half across the room. Then she got up, and, with great mastery over her voice, made her little speech,

" We are delighted to see you, Miss Amedroz," she said, putting out her hand,—of which Clara, however, felt no more than the finger.

" Quite delighted," said Belinda, yielding a fuller grasp. Then there were affectionate greetings between Frederic and his mother and Frederic and his sister, during which Clara stood by, ill at ease. Captain Aylmer said not a word as to the footing on which his future wife had come to his father's house. He did not ask his mother to receive her as another daughter, or his sister to take his Clara to her heart as a sister. There had been no word spoken of recognised intimacy. Clara knew that the Aylmers were cold people. She had learned as much as that from Captain Aylmer's words to herself, and from his own manner. But she had not expected to be so frozen by them as was the case with her now. In ten minutes she was sitting down with her bonnet still on, and Lady Aylmer was again at her stitches.

" Shall I show you your room ?" said Belinda.

" Wait a moment, my dear," said Lady Aylmer. " Frederic has gone to see if Sir Anthony is in his study."

Sir Anthony was found in his study, and now made his appearance.

" So this is Clara Amedroz," he said. " My dear, you are welcome to Aylmer Park." This was so much better, that the kindness expressed,—though there was nothing special in it,—brought a tear into Clara's eye, and almost made her love Sir Anthony.

" By-the-by, Sir Anthony, have you seen Darvel? Darvel was wanting to see you especially about Nuggins. Nuggins says that he'll take the bullocks now." This was said by Lady Aylmer, and was skilfully arranged by her to put a stop to anything like enthusiasm on the part of Sir Anthony. Clara Amedroz had been invited to Aylmer Park, and was to be entertained there, but it would not be expedient that she should be made to think that anybody was particularly glad to see her, or that the family was at all proud of the proposed connection. Within five minutes after this she was up in her room, and had received from Belinda tenders of assistance as to her lady's maid. Both the mother and daughter had been anxious to learn whether Clara would bring her own maid. Lady Aylmer, thinking that she would do so, had already blamed her for her extravagance. " Of course Fred will have to pay for the journey and all the rest of it," she had said. But as soon as she had perceived that Clara had come without a servant, she had perceived that any young woman who travelled in that way must be unfit to be mated with her son. Clara, whose intelligence in such matters was sharp enough, assured Belinda that she wanted no assistance. " I dare say you think it very odd," she said, " but I really can dress myself." And when the maid did come to unpack the things, Clara would have sent her away at once had she been able. But the maid, who was not a young woman, was obdurate. " Oh no, miss; my lady wouldn't be pleased. If you please, miss, I'll do it." And so the things were unpacked.

Clara was told that they dined at half-past seven, and she remained alone in her room till dinner-time, although it had not yet struck five when she had gone up-stairs. The maid had brought her a cup of tea, and she seated herself at her fire, turning over in her mind the different members of the household in which she found herself. It would never do. She told herself over and over again that it would never come to pass that that woman should be her mother-in-law, or that that other woman should be her sister. It was manifest to her that she was distasteful to them; and she had not lost a moment in assuring herself that they were distasteful to her. What purpose

could it answer that she should strive,—not to like them,
for no such strife was possible,—but to appear to like
them? The whole place and everything about it was
antipathetic to her. Would it not be simply honest to
Captain Aylmer that she should tell him so at once, and
go away? Then she remembered that Frederic had not
spoken to her a single word since she had been under his
father's roof. What sort of welcome would have been
accorded to her had she chosen to go down to Plaistow
Hall?

At half-past seven she made her way by herself down-
stairs. In this there was some difficulty, as she remembered nothing of the rooms below, and she could not at
first find a servant. But a man at last did come to her in
the hall, and by him she was shown into the drawing-room.
Here she was alone for a few minutes. As she looked
about her, she thought that no room she had ever seen had
less of the comfort of habitation. It was not here that she
had met Lady Aylmer before dinner. There had, at any
rate, been in that other room work-things, and the look of
life which life gives to a room. But here there was no
life. The furniture was all in its place, and everything
was cold and grand and comfortless. They were making
company of her at Aylmer Park! Clara was intelligent in
such matters, and understood it all thoroughly.

Lady Aylmer was the first person to come to her. " I
hope my maid has been with you," said she;—to which
Clara muttered something intended for thanks. " You'll
find Richards a very clever woman, and quite a proper
person."

" I don't at all doubt that.'

" She has been here a good many years, and has perhaps
little ways of her own,—but she means to be obliging."

" I shall give her very little trouble, Lady Aylmer. I
am used to dress myself." I am afraid this was not exactly
true as to Clara's past habits; but she could dress herself,
and intended to do so in future, and in this way justified
the assertion to herself.

" You had better let Richards come to you, my dear,
while you are here," said Lady Aylmer, with a slight smile
on her countenance which outraged Clara more even than
the words. " We like to see young ladies nicely dressed

here." To be told that she was to be nicely dressed
because she was at Aylmer Park! Her whole heart was
already up in rebellion. Do her best to please Lady
Aylmer! It would be utterly impossible to her to make
any attempt whatever in that direction. There was something in her ladyship's eye,—a certain mixture of cunning,
and power, and hardness in the slight smile that would
gather round her mouth, by which Clara was revolted.
She already understood much of Lady Aylmer; but in one
thing she was mistaken. She thought that she saw simply
the natural woman; but she did, in truth, see the woman
specially armed with an intention of being disagreeable,
made up to give offence, and prepared to create dislike and
enmity. At the present moment nothing further was said,
as Captain Aylmer entered the room, and his mother
immediately began to talk to him in whispers.

The two first days of Clara's sojourn at Aylmer Park
passed by without the occurrence of anything that was
remarkable. That which most surprised and annoyed her,
as regarded her own position, was the coldness of all the
people around her, as connected with the actual fact of her
engagement. Sir Anthony was very courteous to her, but
had never as yet once alluded to the fact that she was to
become one of his family as his daughter-in-law. Lady
Aylmer called her Miss Amedroz,—using the name with a
peculiar emphasis, as though determined to show that Miss
Amedroz was to be Miss Amedroz as far as any one at
Aylmer Park was concerned,—and treated her almost as
though her presence in the house was intrusive. Belinda
was as cold as her mother in her mother's presence; but
when alone with Clara would thaw a little. She, in her
difficulty, studiously avoided calling the new-comer by any
name at all. As to Captain Aylmer, it was manifest to
Clara that he was suffering almost more than she suffered
herself. His position was so painful that she absolutely
pitied him for the misery to which he was subjected by his
own mother. They still called each other Frederic and
Clara, and that was the only sign of special friendship
which manifested itself between them. And Clara, though
she pitied him, could not but learn to despise him. She
had hitherto given him credit at any rate for a will of his
own. She had believed him to be a man able to act in

accordance with the dictates of his own conscience. But now
she perceived him to be so subject to his mother that he
did not dare to call his heart his own. What was to be the
end of it all? And if there could only be one end, would
it not be well that that end should be reached at once so
that she might escape from her purgatory?

But on the afternoon of the third day there seemed to
have come a change over Lady Aylmer. At lunch she was
especially civil,—civil to the extent of picking out herself
for Clara, with her own fork, the breast of a hashed fowl
from a dish that was before her. This she did with considerable care,—I may say, with a show of care; and then,
though she did not absolutely call Clara by her Christian
name, she did call her "my dear." Clara saw it all, and
felt that the usual placidity of the afternoon would be
broken by some special event. At three o'clock, when the
carriage as usual came to the door, Belinda was out of the
way, and Clara was made to understand that she and Lady
Aylmer were to be driven out without any other companion.
"Belinda is a little busy, my dear. So, if you don't mind,
we'll go alone." Clara of course assented, and got into the
carriage with a conviction that now she would hear her
fate. She was rather inclined to think that Lady Aylmer
was about to tell her that she had failed in obtaining the
approbation of Aylmer Park, and that she must be returned
as goods of a description inferior to the order given. If
such were the case, the breast of the chicken had no doubt
been administered as consolation. Clara had endeavoured,
since she had been at Aylmer Park, to investigate her own
feelings in reference to Captain Aylmer; but had failed,
and knew that she had failed. She wished to think that
she loved him, as she could not endure the thought of
having accepted a man whom she did not love. And she
told herself that he had done nothing to forfeit her love.
A woman who really loves will hardly allow that her love
should be forfeited by any fault. True love breeds forgiveness for all faults. And, after all, of what fault had
Captain Aylmer been guilty? He had preached to her out
of his mother's mouth. That had been all! She had first
accepted him, and then rejected him, and then accepted
him again; and now she would fain be firm, if firmness
were only possible to her. Nevertheless, if she were told

that she was to be returned as inferior, she would hold up her head under such disgrace as best she might, and would not let the tidings break her heart.

"My dear," said Lady Aylmer, as soon as the trotting horses and rolling wheels made noise enough to prevent her words from reaching the servants on the box, " I want to say a few words to you;—and I think that this will be a good opportunity."

"A very good opportunity," said Clara.

"Of course, my dear, you are aware that I have heard of something going on between you and my son Frederic. Now that Lady Aylmer had taught herself to call Clara "my dear," it seemed that she could hardly call her so often enough.

"Of course I know that Captain Aylmer has told you of our engagement.   But for that, I should not be here."

"I don't know how that might be," said Lady Aylmer ; "but at any rate, my dear, he has told me that since the day of my sister's death there has been——in point of fact, a sort of engagement."

"I don't think Captain Aylmer has spoken of it in that way."

"In what way?   Of course he has not said a word that was not nice and lover-like, and all that sort of thing.   I believe he would have done anything in the world that his aunt had told him ; and as to his——

"Lady Aylmer !" said Clara, feeling that her voice was almost trembling with anger, "I am sure you cannot intend to be unkind to me?"

"Certainly not."

"Or to insult me ?"

"Insult you, my dear !   You should not use such strong words, my dear ; indeed you should not.   Nothing of the kind is near my thoughts."

"If you disapprove of my marrying your son, tell me so at once, and I shall know what to do."

"It depends, my dear ;—it depends on circumstances, and that is just why I want to speak to you."

"Then tell me the circumstances,—though indeed I think it would have been better if they could have been told to me by Captain Aylmer himself."

"There, my dear, you must allow me to judge.   As a

mother, of course I am anxious for my son. Now Frederic is a poor man. Considering the kind of society in which he has to live, and the position which he must maintain as a Member of Parliament, he is a very poor man."

This was an argument which Clara certainly had not expected that any of the Aylmer family would condescend to use. She had always regarded Captain Aylmer as a rich man since he had inherited Mrs. Winterfield's property, knowing that previously to that he had been able to live in London as rich men usually do live. "Is he?" said she. "It may seem odd to you, Lady Aylmer, but I do not think that a word has ever passed between me and your son as to the amount of his income."

"Not odd at all, my dear. Young ladies are always thoughtless about those things, and when they are looking to be married think that money will come out of the skies."

"If you mean that I have been looking to be married——"

"Well;—expecting. I suppose you have been expecting it." Then she paused; but as Clara said nothing she went on. "Of course, Frederic has got my sister's moiety of the Perivale property;—about eight hundred a year, or something of that sort, when all deductions are made. He will have the other moiety when I die, and if you and he can be satisfied to wait for that event,—which may not perhaps be very long——" Then there was another pause, indicative of the melancholy natural to such a suggestion, during which Clara looked at Lady Aylmer, and made up her mind that her ladyship would live for the next twenty-five years at least. "If you can wait for that," she continued, "it may be all very well, and though you will be poor people, in Frederic's rank of life, you will be able to live."

"That will be so far fortunate," said Clara.

"But you'll have to wait," said Lady Aylmer, turning upon her companion almost fiercely. "That is, you certainly will have to do so if you are to depend upon Frederic's income alone."

"I have nothing of my own,—as he knows; absolutely nothing."

"That does not seem to be quite so clear," said Lady Aylmer, speaking now very cautiously,—or rather with a

purpose of great caution; "I don't think that that is quite
so clear. Frederic has been telling me that there seems to
be some sort of a doubt about the settlement of the Belton
estate."

"There is no sort of doubt whatsoever;—no shadow of
a doubt. He is quite mistaken."

"Don't be in such a hurry, my dear. It is not likely
that you yourself should be a very good lawyer."

"Lady Aylmer, I must be in a hurry lest there should
be any mistake about this. There is no question here for
lawyers. Frederic must have been misled by a word or
two which I said to him with quite another purpose.
Everybody concerned knows that the Belton estate goes to
my cousin Will. My poor father was quite aware of it."

"That is all very well; and pray remember, my dear,
that you need not attack me in this way. I am endeavouring, if possible, to arrange the accomplishment of your
own wishes. It seems that Mr. Belton himself does not
claim the property."

"There is no question of claiming. Because he is a
man more generous than any other person in the world,—
romantically generous, he has offered to give me the
property which was my father's for his lifetime; but I do
not suppose that you would wish, or that Captain Aylmer
would wish, that I should accept such an offer as that."
There was a tone in her voice as she said this, and a
glance in her eye as she turned her face full upon her
companion, which almost prevailed against Lady Aylmer's
force of character.

"I really don't know, my dear," said Lady Aylmer.
"You are so violent."

"I certainly am eager about this. No consideration on
earth would induce me to take my cousin's property from
him."

"It always seemed to me that that entail was a most
unfair proceeding."

"What would it signify even if it were,—which it was
not? Papa got certain advantages on those conditions.
But what can all that matter? It belongs to Will
Belton."

Then there was another pause, and Clara thought that
that subject was over between them. But Lady Aylmer

had not as yet completed her purpose. "Shall I tell you, my dear, what I think you ought to do?"

"Certainly, Lady Aylmer; if you wish it."

"I can at any rate tell you what it would become any young lady to do under such circumstances. I suppose you will give me credit for knowing as much as that. Any young lady placed as you are would be recommended by her friends,—if she had friends able and fit to give her advice,—to put the whole matter into the hands of her natural friends and her lawyer together. Hear me out, my dear, if you please. At least you can do that for me, as I am taking a great deal of trouble on your behalf. You should let Frederic see Mr. Green. I understand that Mr. Green was your father's lawyer. And then Mr. Green can see Mr. Belton. And so the matter can be arranged. It seems to me, from what I hear, that in this way, and in this way only, something can be done as to the proposed marriage. In no other way can anything be done."

Then Lady Aylmer had finished her argument, and throwing herself back into the carriage, seemed to intimate that she desired no reply. She had believed and did believe that her guest was so intent upon marrying her son, that no struggle would be regarded as too great for the achievement of that object. And such belief was natural on her part. Mothers always so think of girls engaged to their sons, and so think especially when the girls are penniless, and the sons are well to do in the world. But such belief, though it is natural, is sometimes wrong;—and it was altogether wrong in this instance. "Then," said Clara, speaking very plainly, "nothing can be done."

"Very well, my dear."

After that there was not a word said between them till the carriage was once more within the park. Then Lady Aylmer spoke again. "I presume you see, my dear, that under these circumstances any thought of marriage between you and my son must be quite out of the question,—at any rate for a great many years."

"I will speak to Captain Aylmer about it, Lady Aylmer."

"Very well, my dear. So do. Of course he is his own

master. But he is my son as well, and I cannot see him
sacrificed without an effort to save him."

When Clara came down to dinner on that day she
was again Miss Amedroz, and she could perceive,—from
Belinda's manner quite as plainly as from that of her ladyship,—that she was to have no more tit-bits of hashed
chicken specially picked out for her by Lady Aylmer's
own fork. That evening and the two next days passed,
just as had passed the two first days, and everything was
dull, cold, and uncomfortable. Twice she had walked out
with Frederic, and on each occasion had thought that he
would refer to what his mother had said; but he did not
venture to touch upon the subject. Clara more than once
thought that she would do so herself; but when the
moments came she found that it was impossible. She
could not bring herself to say anything that should have
the appearance of a desire on her part to hurry on a
marriage. She could not say to him, " If you are too poor
to be married,—or even if you mean to put forward that
pretence, say so at once." He still called her Clara, and
still asked her to walk with him, and still talked, when
they were alone together, in a distant cold way, of the
events of their future combined life. Would they live
at Perivale? Would it be necessary to refurnish the
house? Should he keep any of the land on his own hands?
These are all interesting subjects of discussion between an
engaged man and the girl to whom he is engaged; but the
man, if he wish to make them thoroughly pleasant to the
lady, should throw something of the urgency of a determined and immediate purpose into the discussion. Something should be said as to the actual destination of the
rooms. A day should be fixed for choosing the furnishing.
Or the gentleman should declare that he will at once buy
the cows for the farm. But with Frederic Aylmer all
discussions seemed to point to some cold, distant future,
to which Clara might look forward as she did to the
joys of heaven. Will Belton would have bought the
ring long since, and bespoken the priest, and arranged
every detail of the honeymoon tour,—and very probably
would have stood looking into a cradle shop with longing
eyes.

At last there came an absolute necessity for some plain

speaking. Captain Aylmer declared his intention of return
ing to London that he might resume his parliamentary
duties. He had purposed to remain till after Easter, but it
was found to be impossible. " I find I must go up to-
morrow," he said at breakfast. " They are going to make
a stand about the Poor-rates, and I must be in the House
in the evening." Clara found herself to be very cold and
uncomfortable. As things were at present arranged she
was to be left at Aylmer Park without a friend. And how
long was she to remain there ? No definite ending had been
proposed for her visit. Something must be said and something settled before Captain Aylmer went away.

" You will come down for Easter, of course," said his
mother.

" Yes ; I shall come down for Easter, I think,—or at any
rate at Whitsuntide."

" You must come at Easter, Frederic," said his mother.

" I don't doubt but I shall," said he.

" Miss Amedroz should lay her commands upon him,"
said Sir Anthony gallantly.

" Nonsense," said Lady Aylmer.

" I have commands to lay upon him all the same," said
Clara ; " and if he will give me half an hour this morning
he shall have them." To this Captain Aylmer, of course,
assented, —as how could he escape from such assent?—and
a regular appointment was made. Captain Aylmer and
Miss Amedroz were to be closeted together in the little
back drawing-room immediately after breakfast. Clara
would willingly have avoided any such formality could she
have done so compatibly with the exigencies of the occasion. She had been obliged to assert herself when Lady
Aylmer had rebuked Sir Anthony, and then Lady Aylmer
had determined that an air of business should be assumed.
Clara, as she was marched off into the back drawing-room,
followed by her lover with more sheep-like gait even than
her own, felt strongly the absurdity and the wretchedness
of her position. But she was determined to go through
with her purpose.

" I am very sorry that I have to leave you so soon," said
Captain Aylmer as soon as the door was shut and they
were alone together.

" Perhaps it may be better as it is, Frederic ; as in this

way we shall all come to understand each other, and something will be settled."

"Well, yes; perhaps that will be best."

"Your mother has told me that she disapproves of our marriage."

"No; not that, I think. I don't think she can have quite said that."

"She says that you cannot marry while she is alive,— that is, that you cannot marry me because your income would not be sufficient."

"I certainly was speaking to her about my income."

"Of course I have got nothing." Here she paused. "Not a penny piece in the world that I can call my own."

"Oh yes, you have."

"Nothing. Nothing!"

"You have your aunt's legacy?"

"No I have not. She left me no legacy. But as that is between you and me, if we think of marrying each other that would make no difference."

"None at all, of course."

"But in truth I have got nothing. Your mother said something to me about the Belton estate; as though there was some idea that possibly it might come to me."

"Your cousin himself seemed to think so."

"Frederic, do not let us deceive ourselves. There can be nothing of the kind. I could not accept any portion of the property from my cousin,—even though our marriage were to depend upon it."

"Of course it does not."

"But if your means are not sufficient for your wants, I am quite ready to accept that reason as being sufficient for breaking our engagement."

"There need be nothing of the kind."

"As for waiting for the death of another person,— for your mother's death, I should think it very wrong. Of course, if our engagement stands there need be no hurry; but— some time should be fixed." Clara as she said this felt that her face and forehead were suffused with a blush; but she was determined that it should be said, and the words were pronounced.

"I quite think so too," said he.

"I am glad that we agree. Of course, I will leave it to you to fix the time."

"You do not mean at this very moment?" said Captain Aylmer, almost aghast.

"No; I did not mean that."

"I'll tell you what. I'll make a point of coming down at Easter. I wasn't sure about it before, but now I will be. And then it shall be settled."

Such was the interview; and on the next morning Captain Aylmer started for London. Clara felt aware that she had not done or said all that should have been done and said; but, nevertheless, a step in the right direction had been taken.

CHAPTER XXVI.

THE AYLMER PARK HASHED CHICKEN COMES TO AN END.

Easter in this year fell about the middle of April, and it still wanted three weeks of that time when Captain Aylmer started for London. Clara was quite alive to the fact that the next three weeks would not be a happy time for her. She looked forward, indeed, to so much wretchedness during this period, that the days as they came were not quite so bad as she had expected them to be. At first Lady Aylmer said little or nothing to her. It seemed to be agreed between them that there was to be war, but that there was no necessity for any of the actual operations of war during the absence of Captain Aylmer. Clara had become Miss Amedroz again; and though an offer to be driven out in the carriage was made to her every day, she was in general able to escape the infliction; so that at last it came to be understood that Miss Amedroz did not like carriage exercise. "She has never been used to it," said Lady Aylmer to her daughter. "I suppose not," said Belinda; "but if she wasn't so very cross she'd enjoy it just for that reason." Clara sometimes walked about the grounds with Belinda, but on such occasions there was hardly anything that could be called conversation between them, and Frederic Aylmer's name was never mentioned.

Captain Aylmer had not been gone many days before she received a letter from her cousin, in which he spoke with absolute certainty of his intention of giving up the estate. He had, he said, consulted Mr. Green, and the thing was to be done. " But it will be better, I think," he went on to say, " that I should manage it for you till after your marriage. I simply mean what I say. You are not to suppose that I shall interfere in any way afterwards. Of course there will be a settlement, as to which I hope you will allow me to see Mr. Green on your behalf." In the first draught of his letter he had inserted a sentence in which he expressed a wish that the property should be so settled that it might at last come to some one bearing the name of Belton. But as he read this over, the condition,— for coming from him it would be a condition,—seemed to him to be ungenerous, and he expunged it. " What does it matter who has it," he said to himself bitterly, " or what he is called? I will never set my eyes upon his children, nor yet upon the place when he has become the master of it." Clara wrote both to her cousin and to the lawyer, repeating her assurance,—with great violence, as Lady Aylmer would have said,—that she would have nothing to do with the Belton estate. She told Mr. Green that it would be useless for him to draw up any deeds. "It can't be made mine unless I choose to have it," she said ; " and I don't choose to have it." Then there came upon her a terrible fear. What if she should marry Captain Aylmer after all ; and what if he, when he should be her husband, should take the property on her behalf ! Something must be done before her marriage to prevent the possibility of such results,—something as to the efficacy of which for such prevention she could feel altogether certain.

But could she marry Captain Aylmer at all in her present mood? During these three weeks she was unconsciously teaching herself to hope that she might be relieved from her engagement. She did not love him. She was becoming aware that she did not love him. She was beginning to doubt whether, in truth, she had ever loved him. But yet she felt that she could not escape from her engagement if he should show himself to be really actuated by any fixed purpose to carry it out ; nor could she bring herself to be so weak before Lady

Aylmer as to seem to yield. The necessity of not striking
her colours was forced upon her by the warfare to which
she was subjected. She was unhappy, feeling that her
present position in life was bad, and unworthy of her.
She could have brought herself almost to run away from
Aylmer Park, as a boy runs away from a school, were it not
that she had no place to which to run. She could not
very well make her appearance at Plaistow Hall, and say
that she had come there for shelter and succour. She
could, indeed, go to Mrs. Askerton's cottage for awhile ;
and the more she thought of the state of her affairs, the
more did she feel sure that that would, before long, be her
destiny. It must be her destiny,—unless Captain Aylmer
should return at Easter with purposes so firmly fixed that
even his mother should not be able to prevail against
them.

And now, in these days, circumstances gave her a new
friend,—or perhaps, rather, a new acquaintance, where
she certainly had looked neither for the one nor for the
other. Lady Aylmer and Belinda and the carriage and
the horses used, as I have said, to go off without her.
This would take place soon after luncheon. Most of us
know how the events of the day drag themselves on
tediously in such a country house as Aylmer Park,—a
country house in which people neither read, nor flirt, nor
gamble, nor smoke, nor have resort to the excitement of
any special amusement. Lunch was on the table at half-
past one, and the carriage was at the door at three. Eating
and drinking and the putting on of bonnets occupied the
hour and a half. From breakfast to lunch Lady Aylmer,
with her old " front," would occupy herself with her household accounts. For some days after Clara's arrival she put
on her new " front " before lunch; but of late,—since the
long conversation in the carriage,—the new " front " did
not appear till she came down for the carriage. According
to the theory of her life, she was never to be seen by any
but her own family in her old " front." At breakfast she
would appear with her head so mysteriously enveloped,—
with such a bewilderment of morning caps, that old
" front " or new " front " was all the same. When Sir
Anthony perceived this change,—when he saw that Clara
was treated as though she belonged to Aylmer Park, then

he told himself that his son's marriage with Miss Amedroz
was to be; and, as Miss Amedroz seemed to him to be a
very pleasant young woman, he would creep out of his
own quarters when the carriage was gone and have a little
chat with her,—being careful to creep away again before
her ladyship's return. This was Clara's new friend.

"Have you heard from Fred since he has been gone?"
the old man asked one day, when he had come upon Clara
still seated in the parlour in which they had lunched. He
had been out, at the front of the house, scolding the under-
gardener: but the man had taken away his barrow and
left him, and Sir Anthony had found himself without
employment.

"Only a line to say that he is to be here on the six-
teenth."

"I don't think people write so many love-letters as they
did when I was young," said Sir Anthony.

"To judge from the novels, I should think not. The
old novels used to be full of love-letters."

"Fred was never good at writing, I think."

"Members of Parliament have too much to do, I suppose," said Clara.

"But he always writes when there is any business.
He's a capital man of business. I wish I could say as
much for his brother,—or for myself."

"Lady Aylmer seems to like work of that sort."

"So she does. She's fond of it,—I am not. I sometimes think that Fred takes after her. Where was it you
first knew him?"

"At Perivale. We used, both of us, to be staying with
Mrs. Winterfield."

"Yes, yes; of course. The most natural thing in life.
Well, my dear, I can assure you that I am quite satisfied."

"Thank you, Sir Anthony. I'm glad to hear you say
even as much as that."

"Of course money is very desirable for a man situated
like Fred; but he'll have enough, and if he is pleased, I
am. Personally, as regards yourself, I'm more than
pleased. I am indeed."

"It's very good of you to say so."

Sir Anthony looked at Clara, and his heart was softened
towards her as he saw that there was a tear in her eye,

A man's heart must be very hard when it does not become softened by the trouble of a woman with whom he finds himself alone. "I don't know how you and Lady Aylmer get on together," said he; "but it will not be my fault if we are not friends."

"I am afraid that Lady Aylmer does not like me," said Clara.

"Indeed. I was afraid there was something of that. But you must remember she is hard to please. You'll find she'll come round in time."

"She thinks that Captain Aylmer should not marry a woman without money."

"That's all very well; but I don't see why Fred shouldn't please himself. He's old enough to know what he wants."

"Is he, Sir Anthony? That's just the question. I'm not quite sure that he does know what he wants."

"Fred doesn't know, do you mean?"

"I don't quite think he does, sir. And the worst of it is, I am in doubt as well as he."

"In doubt about marrying him?"

"In doubt whether it will be good for him or for any of us. I don't like to come into a family that does not desire to have me."

"You shouldn't think so much of Lady Aylmer as all that, my dear."

"But I do think a great deal of her."

"I shall be very glad to have you as a daughter-in-law. And as for Lady Aylmer——between you and me, my dear, you shouldn't take every word she says so much to heart. She's the best woman in the world, and I'm sure I'm bound to say so. But she has her temper, you know; and I don't think you ought to give way to her altogether. There's the carriage. It won't do you any good if we're found together talking over it all; will it?" Then the baronet hobbled off, and Lady Aylmer, when she entered the room, found Clara sitting alone.

Whether it was that the wife was clever enough to extract from her husband something of the conversation that had passed between him and Clara, or whether she had some other source of information,—or whether her conduct might proceed from other grounds, we need not inquire;

but from that afternoon Lady Aylmer's manner and words to Clara became much less courteous than they had been before. She would always speak as though some great iniquity was being committed, and went about the house with a portentous frown, as though some terrible measure must soon be taken with the object of putting an end to the present extremely improper state of things. All this was so manifest to Clara, that she said to Sir Anthony one day that she could no longer bear the look of Lady Aylmer's displeasure,—and that she would be forced to leave Aylmer Park before Frederic's return, unless the evil were mitigated. She had by this time told Sir Anthony that she much doubted whether the marriage would be possible, and she really believed that it would be best for all parties that the idea should be abandoned. Sir Anthony when he heard this, could only shake his head and hobble away. The trouble was too deep for him to cure.

But Clara still held on; and now there wanted but two days to Captain Aylmer's return, when, all suddenly, there arose a terrible storm at Aylmer Park, and then came a direct and positive quarrel between Lady Aylmer and Clara,—a quarrel direct and positive, and, on the part of both the ladies, very violent.

Nothing had hitherto been said at Aylmer Park about Mrs. Askerton,—nothing, that is, since Clara's arrival. And Clara had been thankful for this silence. The letter which Captain Aylmer had written to her about Mrs. Askerton will perhaps be remembered, and Clara's answer to that letter. The Aylmer Park opinion as to this poor woman, and as to Clara's future conduct towards the poor woman, had been expressed very strongly; and Clara had as strongly resolved that she would not be guided by Aylmer Park opinions in that matter. She had anticipated much that was disagreeable on this subject, and had therefore congratulated herself not a little on the absence of all allusion to it. But Lady Aylmer had, in truth, kept Mrs. Askerton in reserve, as a battery to be used against Miss Amedroz if all other modes of attack should fail,—as a weapon which would be powerful when other weapons had been powerless. For awhile she had thought it possible that Clara might be the owner of the Belton estate, and then it had been worth the careful mother's while to be prepared to accept a daughter-in-law so dowered. We have seen how the question of such ownership had enabled her to put forward the plea of poverty which she had used on her son's behalf. But since that Frederic had declared his intention of marrying the young woman in spite of his poverty, and Clara seemed to be equally determined. " He has been fool enough to speak the word, and she is determined to keep him to it," said Lady Aylmer to her daughter. Therefore the Askerton battery was brought to bear,—not altogether unsuccessfully.

The three ladies were sitting together in the drawing-room, and had been as mute as fishes for half an hour. In these sittings they were generally very silent, speaking only in short little sentences. " Will you drive with us to-day, Miss Amedroz?" "Not to-day, I think, Lady Aylmer." " As you are reading, perhaps you wont mind our leaving you?" "Pray do not put yourself to inconvenience for me, Miss Aylmer." Such and such like was their conversation ; but on a sudden, after a full half-hour's positive silence, Lady Aylmer asked a question altogether of another kind. " I think, Miss Amedroz, my son wrote to you about a certain Mrs. Askerton ?"

Clara put down her work and sat for a moment almost astonished. It was not only that Lady Aylmer had asked so very disagreeable a question, but she had asked it with so peculiar a voice,—a voice as it were a command, in a manner that was evidently intended to be taken as serious, and with a look of authority in her eye, as though she were resolved that this battery of hers should knock the enemy absolutely into the dust ! Belinda gave a little spring in her chair, looked intently at her work, and went on stitching faster than before. " Yes he did," said Clara, finding that an answer was imperatively demanded from her.

" It was quite necessary that he should write. I believe it to be an undoubted fact that Mrs. Askerton is,—is,—is, —not at all what she ought to be."

" Which of us is what we ought to be ?" said Clara.

" Miss Amedroz, on this subject I am not at all inclined to joke. Is it not true that Mrs. Askerton——"

" You must excuse me, Lady Aylmer, but what I know

of Mrs. Askerton, I know altogether in confidence; so that I cannot speak to you of her past life."

"But, Miss Amedroz, pray excuse me if I say that I must speak of it. When I remember the position in which you do us the honour of being our visitor here, how can I help speaking of it?" Belinda was stitching very hard, and would not even raise her eyes. Clara, who still held her needle in her hand, resumed her work, and for a moment or two made no further answer. But Lady Aylmer had by no means completed her task. "Miss Amedroz," she said, "you must allow me to judge for myself in this matter. The subject is one on which I feel myself obliged to speak to you."

"But I have got nothing to say about it."

"You have, I believe, admitted the truth of the allegations made by us as to this woman." Clara was becoming very angry. A red spot showed itself on each cheek, and a frown settled upon her brow. She did not as yet know what she would say or how she would conduct herself. She was striving to consider how best she might assert her own independence. But she was fully determined that in this matter she would not bend an inch to Lady Aylmer. "I believe we may take that as admitted?" said her ladyship.

"I am not aware that I have admitted anything to you, Lady Aylmer, or said anything that can justify you in questioning me on the subject."

"Justify me in questioning a young woman who tells me that she is to be my future daughter-in-law!"

"I have not told you so. I have never told you anything of the kind."

"Then on what footing, Miss Amedroz, do you do us the honour of being with us here at Aylmer Park?"

"On a very foolish footing."

"On a foolish footing! What does that mean?"

"It means that I have been foolish in coming to a house in which I am subjected to such questioning."

"Belinda, did you ever hear anything like this? Miss Amedroz, I must persevere, however much you may dislike it. The story of this woman's life,—whether she be Mrs. Askerton or not, I don't know——"

"She is Mrs. Askerton," said Clara.

"As to that I do not profess to know, and I dare say

that you are no wiser than myself. But what she has been we do know." Here Lady Aylmer raised her voice and continued to speak with all the eloquence which assumed indignation could give her. " What she has been we do know, and I ask you, as a duty which I owe to my son, whether you have put an end to your acquaintance with so very disreputable a person,—a person whom even to have known is a disgrace ?"

" I know her, and——"

" Stop one minute, if you please. My questions are these—Have you put an end to that acquaintance ? And are you ready to give a promise that it shall never be resumed ?"

" I have not put an end to that acquaintance,—or rather that affectionate friendship, as I should call it; and I am ready to promise that it shall be maintained with all my heart."

" Belinda, do you hear her ?"

" Yes, mamma." And Belinda slowly shook her head, which was now bowed lower than ever over her lap.

" And that is your resolution ?"

" Yes, Lady Aylmer; that is my resolution."

" And you think that becoming to you, as a young woman ?"

" Just so; I think that becoming to me,—as a young woman."

" Then let me tell you, Miss Amedroz, that I differ from you altogether,—altogether." Lady Aylmer, as she repeated the last word, raised her folded hands as though she was calling upon heaven to witness how thoroughly she differed from the young woman !

" I don't see how I am to help that, Lady Aylmer. I dare say we may differ on many subjects."

" I dare say we do. I dare say we do. And I need not point out to you how very little that would be a matter of regret to me, but for the hold you have upon my unfortunate son."

" Hold upon him, Lady Aylmer! How dare you insult me by such language ?" Hereupon Belinda again jumped in her chair; but Lady Aylmer looked as though she enjoyed the storm.

" You undoubtedly have a hold upon him, Miss Amedroz,

and I think that it is a great misfortuue. Of course,
when he hears what your conduct is with reference to
this—person, he will release himself from his entanglement."

"He can release himself from his entanglement whenever he chooses," said Clara, rising from her chair. "Indeed, he is released. I shall let Captain Aylmer know
that our engagement must be at an end, unless he will
promise that I shall never in future be subjected to the
unwarrantable insolence of his mother." Then she walked
off to the door, not regarding, and indeed not hearing, the
parting shot that was fired at her.

And now what was to be done! Clara went up to her
own room, making herself strong and even comfortable,
with an inward assurance that nothing should ever induce
her even to sit down to table again with Lady Aylmer.
She would not willingly enter the same room with Lady
Aylmer, or have any speech with her. But what should
she at once do? She could not very well leave Aylmer
Park without settling whither she would go; nor could
she in any way manage to leave the house on that afternoon. She almost resolved that she would go to Mrs.
Askerton. Everything was of course over between her
and Captain Aylmer, and therefore there was no longer
any hindrance to her doing so on that score. But what
would be her cousin Will's wish? He, now, was the only
friend to whom she could trust for good council. What
would be his advice? Should she write and ask him?
No;—she could not do that. She could not bring herself
to write to him, telling him that the Aylmer "entanglement" was at an end. Were she to do so, he, with his
temperament, would take such letter as meaning much
more than it was intended to mean. But she would write
a letter to Captain Aylmer. This she thought that she
would do at once, and she began it. She got as far as
"My dear Captain Aylmer," and then she found that the
letter was one which could not be written very easily.
And she remembered, as the greatness of the difficulty of
writing the letter became plain to her, that it could not
now be sent so as to reach Captain Aylmer before he
would leave London. If written at all, it must be
addressed to him at Aylmer Park, and the task might be

done to-morrow as well as to-day.   So that task was given up for the present.

But she did write a letter to Mrs. Askerton,—a letter which she would send or not on the morrow, according to the state of her mind as it might then be.   In this she declared her purpose of leaving Aylmer Park on the day after Captain Aylmer's arrival, and asked to be taken in at the cottage.   An answer was to be sent to her, addressed to the Great Northern Railway Hotel.

Richards, the maid, came up to her before dinner, with offers of assistance for dressing,—offers made in a tone which left no doubt on Clara's mind that Richards knew all about the quarrel.   But Clara declined to be dressed, and sent down a message saying that she would remain in her room, and begging to be supplied with tea.   She would not even condescend to say that she was troubled with a headache.   Then Belinda came up to her, just before dinner was announced, and with a fluttered gravity advised Miss Amedroz to come down-stairs.   "Mamma thinks it will be much better that you should show yourself, let the final result be what it may."

"But I have not the slightest desire to show myself."

"There are the servants, you know."

"But, Miss Aylmer, I don't care a straw for the servants; —really not a straw."

"And papa will feel it so."

"I shall be sorry if Sir Anthony is annoyed; but I cannot help it.   It has not been my doing."

"And mamma says that my brother would of course wish it."

"After what your mother has done, I don't see what his wishes would have to do with it,—even if she knew them, —which I don't think she does."

"But if you will think of it, I'm sure you'll find it is the proper thing to do.   There is nothing to be avoided so much as an open quarrel, that all the servants can see."

"I must say, Miss Aylmer, that I disregard the servants. After what passed down-stairs, of course I have had to consider what I should do.   Will you tell your mother that I will stay here, if she will permit it?"

"Of course.   She will be delighted."

" I will remain, if she will permit it, till the morning after Captain Aylmer's arrival. Then I shall go."

" Where to, Miss Amedroz?"

" I have already written to a friend, asking her to receive me."

Miss Aylmer paused a moment before she asked her next question;—but she did ask it, showing by her tone and manner that she had been driven to summon up all her courage to enable her to do so. " To what friend, Miss Amedroz? Mamma will be glad to know."

" That is a question which Lady Aylmer can have no right to ask," said Clara.

" Oh; very well. Of course, if you don't like to tell, there's no more to be said."

" I do not like to tell, Miss Aylmer."

Clara had her tea in her room that evening, and lived there the whole of the next day. The family down-stairs was not comfortable. Sir Anthony could not be made to understand why his guest kept her room,—which was not odd, as Lady Aylmer was very sparing in the information she gave him; and Belinda found it to be impossible to sit at table, or to say a few words to her father and mother, without showing at every moment her consciousness that a crisis had occurred. By the next day's post the letter to Mrs. Askerton was sent, and at the appointed time Captain Aylmer arrived. About an hour after he entered the house, Belinda went up-stairs with a message from him;—would Miss Amedroz see him? Miss Amedroz would see him, but made it a condition of doing so that she should not be required to meet Lady Aylmer. " She need not be afraid," said Lady Aylmer. " Unless she sends me a full apology, with a promise that she will have no further intercourse whatever with that woman, I will never willingly see her again." A meeting was therefore arranged between Captain Aylmer and Miss Amedroz in a sitting-room up-stairs.

" What is all this, Clara?" said Captain Aylmer, at once.

" Simply this,—that your mother has insulted me most wantonly."

" She says that it is you who have been uncourteous to her."

" Be it so;—you can of course believe whichever you

please, and it is desirable, no doubt, that you should prefer to believe your mother."

" But I do not wish there to be any quarrel."

" But there is a quarrel, Captain Aylmer, and I must leave your father's house. I cannot stay here after what has taken place. Your mother told me——; I cannot tell you what she told me, but she made against me just those accusations which she knew it would be the hardest for me to bear."

" I'm sure you have mistaken her."

" No ; I have not mistaken her."

" And where do you propose to go ?"

" To Mrs. Askerton."

" Oh, Clara !"

" I have written to Mrs. Askerton to ask her to receive me for awhile. Indeed, I may almost say that I had no other choice."

" If you go there, Clara, there will be an end to every-thing."

" And there must be an end of what you call every-thing, Captain Aylmer," said she smiling. " It cannot be for your good to bring into your family a wife of whom your mother would think so badly as she thinks of me."

There was a great deal said, and Captain Aylmer walked very often up and down the room, endeavouring to make some arrangement which might seem in some sort to appease his mother. Would Clara only allow a telegram to be sent to Mrs. Askerton, to explain that she had changed her mind ? But Clara would allow no such telegram to be sent, and on that evening she packed up all her things. Captain Aylmer saw her again and again, sending Belinda backwards and forwards, and making different appointments up to midnight ; but it was all to no purpose, and on the next morning she took her departure alone in the Aylmer Park carriage for the railway station. Captain Aylmer had proposed to go with her ; but she had so stoutly declined his company that he was obliged to abandon his intention. She saw neither of the ladies on that morning, but Sir Anthony came out to say a word of farewell to her in the hall. " I am very sorry for all this," said he. " It is a pity," said Clara, " but it cannot be helped. Good-bye, Sir Anthony." " I hope we may meet again under pleasanter circumstances," said the baronet. To this Clara made no reply, and was then handed into the carriage by Captain Aylmer.

" I am so bewildered," said he, " that I cannot now say anything definite, but I shall write to you, and probably follow you."

" Do not follow me, pray, Captain Aylmer," said she. Then she was driven to the station; and as she passed through the lodges of the park entrance she took what she intended to be a final farewell of Aylmer Park.

CHAPTER XXVII.

ONCE MORE BACK TO BELTON.

WHEN the carriage was driven away, Sir Anthony and Captain Aylmer were left standing alone at the hall door of the house. The servants had slunk off, and the father and son, looking at each other, felt that they also must slink away, or else have some words together on the subject of their guest's departure. The younger gentleman would have preferred that there should be no words, but Sir Anthony was curious to know something of what had passed in the house during the last few days. " I'm afraid things are not going quite comfortable," he said.

" It seems to me, sir," said his son, " that things very seldom do go quite comfortable."

" But, Fred,—what is it all about? Your mother says that Miss Amedroz is behaving very badly."

" And Miss Amedroz says that my mother is behaving very badly."

" Of course ;—that's only natural. And what do you say ?"

" I say nothing, sir. The less said the soonest mended."

"That's all very well; but it seems to me that you, in your position, must say something. The long and the short of it is this—Is she to be your wife ?"

" Upon my word, sir, I don't know."

They were still standing out under the portico, and as Sir Anthony did not for a minute or two ask any further questions, Captain Aylmer turned as though he were going into the house. But his father had still a word or two to say. " Stop a moment, Fred. I don't often trouble you with advice."

" I'm sure I'm always glad to hear it when you offer any."

" I know very well that in most things your opinion is better than mine. You've had advantages which I never had. But I've had more experience than you, my dear boy. It stands to reason that in some things I must have had more experience than you." There was a tone of melancholy in the father's voice as he said this which quite touched his son, and which brought the two closer together out in the porch. " Take my word for it," continued Sir Anthony, " that you are much better off as you are than you could be with a wife."

" Do you mean to say that no man should marry ?"

" No ;—I don't mean to say that. An eldest son ought to marry, so that the property may have an heir. And poor men should marry, I suppose, as they want wives to do for them. And sometimes, no doubt, a man must marry, —when he has got to be very fond of a girl, and has compromised himself, and all that kind of thing. I would never advise any man to sully his honour." As Sir Anthony said this he raised himself a little with his two sticks and spoke out in a bolder voice. The voice, however, sank again as he descended from the realms of honour to those of prudence. " But none of these cases are yours, Fred. To be sure you'll have the Perivale property ; but that is not a family estate, and you'll be much better off by turning it into money. And in the way of comfort, you can be a great deal more comfortable without a wife than you can with one. What do you want a wife for ? And then, as to Miss Amedroz,—for myself I must say that I like her uncommonly. She has been very pleasant in her ways with me. But,—somehow or another I don't think you are so much in love with her but what you can do without her." Hereupon he paused and looked his son full in the face. Fred had also been thinking of the matter in his own way, and asking himself the same question,—whether he was in truth so much in love with Clara that he could not live without her. " Of course I don't know." continued Sir Anthony, " what has

taken place just now between you and her, or what
between her and your mother ; but I suppose the whole
thing might fall through without any further trouble to
you,—or without anything unhandsome on your part?"
But Captain Aylmer still said nothing. The whole thing
might, no doubt, fall through, but he wished to be neithei
unjust nor ungenerous,—and he specially wished to avoid
anything unhandsome. After a further pause of a few
minutes, Sir Anthony went on again, pouring forth the
words of experience. "Of course marriage is all very
well. I married rather early in life, and have always
found your mother to be a most excellent woman. A
better woman doesn't breathe. I'm as sure of that as I
am of anything, But God bless me,—of course you can
see. I can't call anything my own. I'm tied down here
and I can't move. I've never got a shilling to spend,
while all these lazy hounds about the place are eating me
up. There isn't a clerk with a hundred a year in London
that isn't better off than I am as regards ready money.
And what comfort have I in a big house, and no end of
gardens, and a place like this ? What pleasures do I get
out of it ? That comes of marrying and keeping up one's
name in the county respectably ! What do I care for the
county ?   D—— the county ! I often wish that I'd
been a younger son,—as you are."

Captain Aylmer had no answer to make to all this. It
was, no doubt, the fact that age and good living had made
Sir Anthony altogether incapable of enjoying the kind of
life which he desiderated, and that he would probably
have eaten and drank himself into his grave long since had
that kind of life been within his reach. This, however,
the son could not explain to the father. But in fitting, as
he endeavoured to do, his father's words to his own case,
Captain Aylmer did perceive that a bachelor's life
might perhaps be the most suitable to his own peculiar
case. Only he would do nothing unhandsome. As to
that he was quite resolved. Of course Clara must show
herself to bo in some degree amenable to reason and to
the ordinary rules of the world ; but he was aware that
his mother was hot-tempered, and he generously made up
his mind that he would give Miss Amedroz even yet
another chance.

At the hotel in London Clara found a short note from Mrs. Askerton, in which she was warmly assured that everything should be done to make her comfortable at the cottage as long as she should please to stay there. But the very warmth of affection thus expressed made her almost shrink from what she was about to do. Mrs. Askerton was no doubt anxious for her coming; but would her cousin Will Belton approve of the visit; and what would her cousin Mary say about it? If she was being driven into this step against her own approval, by the insolence of Lady Aylmer,—if she was doing this thing simply because Lady Aylmer had desired her not to do it, and was doing it in opposition to the wishes of the man she had promised to marry as well as to her own judgment, there could not but be cause for shrinking. And yet she believed that she was right. If she could only have had some one to tell her,—some one in whom she could trust implicitly to direct her! She had hitherto been very much prone to rebel against authority. Against her aunt she had rebelled, and against her father, and against her lover. But now she wished with all her heart that there might be some one to whom she could submit with perfect faith. If she could only know what her cousin Will would think. In him she thought she could have trusted with that perfect faith;—if only he would have been a brother to her.

But it was too late now for doubting, and on the next day she found herself getting out of the old Redicote fly, at Colonel Askerton's door. He came out to meet her, and his greeting was very friendly. Hitherto there had been no great intimacy between him and her, owing rather to the manner of life adopted by him than to any cause of mutual dislike between them. Mrs. Askerton had shown herself desirous of some social intercourse since she had been at Belton, but with Colonel Askerton there had been nothing of this. He had come there intending to live alone, and had been satisfied to carry out his purpose. But now Clara had come to his house as a guest, and he assumed towards her altogether a new manner. "We are so glad to have you," he said, taking both her hands. Then she passed on into the cottage, and in a minute was in her friend's arms.

"Dear Clara;—dearest Clara, I am so glad to have you here."

"It is very good of you."

"No, dear; the goodness is with you to come. But we won't quarrel about that. We will both be ever so good. And he is so happy that you should be here. You'll get to know him now. But come up-stairs. There's a fire in your room, and I'll be your maid for the occasion,—because then we can talk." Clara did as she was bid, and went up-stairs; and as she sat over the fire while her friend knelt beside her,—for Mrs. Askerton was given to such kneelings,—she could not but tell herself that Belton Cottage was much more comfortable than Aylmer Park. During the whole time of her sojourn at Aylmer Park no word of real friendship had once greeted her ears. Everything there had been cold and formal, till coldness and formality had given way to violent insolence.

"And so you have quarrelled with her ladyship," said Mrs. Askerton. "I knew you would."

"I have not said anything about quarrelling with her."

"But of course you have. Come, now; don't make yourself disagreeable. You have had a downright battle; —have you not?"

"Something very like it, I'm afraid."

"I am so glad," said Mrs. Askerton, rubbing her hands.

"That is ill-natured."

"Very well. Let it be ill-natured. One isn't to be good-natured all round, or what would be the use of it. And what sort of woman is she?"

"Oh dear; I couldn't describe her. She is very large, and wears a great wig, and manages everything herself, and I've no doubt she's a very good woman in her own way."

"I can see her at once; and a very pillar of virtue as regards morality and going to church. Poor me! Does she know that you have come here?"

"I've no doubt she does. I did not tell her, nor would I tell her daughter; but I told Captain Aylmer."

"That was right. That was very right. I'm so glad of that. But who would doubt that you would show a proper spirit. And what did he say?"

"Not much, indeed."

"I won't trouble you about him. I don't in the least doubt but all that will come right. And what sort of a man is Sir Anthony?"

"A commonplace sort of a man; very gouty, and with none of his wife's strength. I liked him the best of them all."

"Because you saw the least of him, I suppose."

"He was kind in his manner to me."

"And they were like she-dragons. I understand it all, and can see them just as though I had been there. I felt that I knew what would come of it when you first told me that you were going to Aylmer Park. I did indeed. I could have prophesied it all."

"What a pity you did not."

"It would have done no good;—and your going there has done good. It has opened your eyes to more than one thing, I don't doubt. But tell me,—have you told them in Norfolk that you were coming here?"

"No;—I have not written to my cousin."

"Don't be angry with me if I tell you something. I have."

"Have what?"

"I have told Mr. Belton that you were coming here. It was in this way. I had to write to him about our continuing in the cottage. Colonel Askerton always makes me write if it's possible, and of course we were obliged to settle something as to the place."

"I'm sorry you said anything about me."

"How could I help it? What would you have thought of me, or what would he have thought, if, when writing to him, I had not mentioned such a thing as your visit? Besides, it's much better that he should know."

"I am sorry that you said anything about it."

"You are ashamed that he should know that you are here," said Mrs. Askerton, in a tone of reproach.

"Ashamed! No; I am not ashamed. But I would sooner that he had not been told,—as yet. Of course he would have been told before long."

"But you are not angry with me?"

"Angry! How can I be angry with any one who is so kind to me?"

That evening passed by very pleasantly, and when sho

went again to her own room, Clara was almost surprised to
find how completely she was at home. On the next day
she and Mrs. Askerton together went up to the house, and
roamed through all the rooms, and Clara seated herself in
all the accustomed chairs. On the sofa, just in the spot to
which Belton had thrown it, she found the key of the cellar. She took it up in her hand, thinking that she would
give it to the servant; but again she put it back upon the
sofa. It was his key, and he had left it there, and if ever
there came an occasion she would remind him where he
had put it. Then they went out to the cow, who was at
her ease in a little home paddock. " Dear Bessy," said
Clara. " See how well she knows me." But I think the
tame little beast would have known any one else as well
who had gone up to her as Clara did, with food in her
hand. "She is quite as sacred as any cow that ever was
worshipped among the cow-worshippers," said Mrs. Askerton. " I suppose they milk her and sell the butter, but
otherwise she is not regarded as an ordinary cow at all."

"Poor Bessy," said Clara. " I wish she had never
come here. What is to be done with her?" " Done with
her! She'll stay here till she dies a natural death, and
then a romantic pair of mourners will follow her to her
grave, mixing their sympathetic tears comfortably as they
talk of the old days; and in future years, Bessy will grow
to be a divinity of the past, never to be mentioned without
tenderest reminiscences. I have not the slightest difficulty
in prophesying as to Bessy's future life and posthumous
honours." They roamed about the place the whole morning, through the garden and round the farm buildings, and
in and out of the house; and at every turn something was
said about Will Belton. But Clara would not go up to the
rocks, although Mrs. Askerton more than once attempted
to turn in that direction. He had said that he never would
go there again except under certain circumstances. She
knew that those circumstances would never come to pass;
but yet neither would she go there. She would never go
there till her cousin was married. Then, if in those days
she should ever be present at Belton Castle, she would
creep up to the spot all alone, and allow herself to think of
the old days.

On the following morning there came to her a letter

bearing the Downham post-mark,—but at the first glance she knew that it was not from her cousin Will. Will wrote with a bold round hand, that was extremely plain and caligraphic when he allowed himself time for the work in hand, as he did with the commencement of his epistles, but which would become confused and altogether anti-caligraphic when he fell into a hurry towards the end of his performance,—as was his wont. But the address of this letter was written in a pretty, small, female hand,—very careful in the perfection of every letter, and very neat in every stroke. It was from Mary Belton, between whom and Clara, there had never hitherto been occasion for corre spondence. The letter was as follows :—

"Plaistow Hall, April, 186—.

" MY DEAR COUSIN CLARA,

"William has heard from your friends at Belton, who are tenants on the estate, and as to whom there seems to be some question whether they are to remain. He has written, saying, I believe, that there need be no difficulty if they wish to stay there. But we learn, also, from Mrs. Askerton's letter, that you are expected at the cottage, and therefore I will address this to Belton, supposing that it may find you there.

" You and I have never yet known each other ;—which has been a grief to me; but this grief, I hope, may be cured some day before long. I myself, as you know, am such a poor creature that I cannot go about the world to see my friends as other people do ;—at least, not very well; and therefore I write to you with the object of asking you to come and see me here. This is an interesting old house in its way; and though I must not conceal from you that life here is very, very quiet, I would do my best to make the days pass pleasantly with you. I had heard that you were gone to Aylmer Park. Indeed, William told me of his taking you up to London. Now it seems you have left Yorkshire, and I suppose you will not return there very soon. If it be so, will it not be well that you should come to me for a short time ?

" Both William and I feel that just for the present,—for a little time,—you would perhaps prefer to be alone with

me. He must go to London for awhile, and then on to
Belton, to settle your affairs and his. He intends to be
absent for six weeks. If you would not be afraid of the
dulness of this house for so long a time, pray come to us.
The pleasure to me would be very great, and I hope that
you have some of that feeling, which with me is so strong,
that we ought not to be any longer personally strangers to
each other. You could then make up your mind as to
what you would choose to do afterwards. I thing that by
the end of that time,—that is, when William returns,—my
uncle and aunt from Sleaford will be with us. He is a
clergyman, you know; and if you then like to remain,
they will be delighted to make your acquaintance.

"It seems to be a long journey for a young lady to
make alone, from Belton to Plaistow; but travelling is so
easy now-a-days, and young ladies seem to be so independent, that you may be able to manage it. Hoping to
see you soon, I remain

"Your affectionate Cousin,

"MARY BELTON."

This letter she received before breakfast, and was therefore able to read it in solitude, and to keep its receipt from
the knowledge of Mrs. Askerton, if she should be so
minded. She understood at once all that it intended to
convey,—a hint that Plaistow Hall would be a better
resting-place for her than Mrs. Askerton's cottage; and an
assurance that if she would go to Plaistow Hall for her
convenience, no advantage should be taken of her presence
there by the owner of the house for his convenience. As
she sat thinking of the offer which had been made to her,
she fancied that she could see and hear her cousin Will as
he discussed the matter with his sister, and with a half
assumption of surliness declared his own intention of
going away. Captain Aylmer after that interview in
London had spoken of Belton's conduct as being unpardon-
able; but Clara had not only pardoned him, but had, in
her own mind, pronounced his virtues to be so much
greater than his vices as to make him almost perfect.
"But I will not drive him out of his own house," she said.
"What does it matter where I go?"

" Colonel Askerton has had a letter from your cousin,"
said Mrs. Askerton as soon as the two ladies were alone
together.

" And what does he say ?"

" Not a word about you."

" So much the better. I have given him trouble enough,
and am glad to think that he should be free of me for awhile.
Is Colonel Askerton to stay at the cottage ?"

" Now, Clara, you are a hypocrite. You know that you
are a hypocrite."

" Very likely,—but I don't know why you should accuse
me just now."

" Yes, you do. Have not you heard from Norfolk
also ?

" Yes ;—I have."

" I was sure of it. I knew he would never have written
in that way, in answer to my letter, ignoring your visit
here altogether, unless he had written to you also."

" But he has not written to me. My letter is from his
sister. There it is." Whereupon she handed the letter to
Mrs. Askerton, and waited patiently while it was being
read. Her friend returned it to her without a word, and
Clara was the first to speak again. " It is a nice letter, is
it not ? I never saw her you know."

" So she says."

" But is it not a kind letter ?"

" I suppose it is meant for kindness. It is not very
complimentary to me. It presumes that such a one as I
may be treated without the slightest consideration. And
so I may. It is only fit that I should be so treated. If
you ask my advice, I advise you to go at once ;—at
once."

" But I have not asked your advice, dear; nor do I
intend to ask it."

" You would not have shown it me if you had not
intended to go."

" How unreasonable you are ! You told me just now
that I was a hypocrite for not telling you of my letter, and
now you are angry with me because I have shown it you."

" I am not angry. I think you have been quite right to
show it me. I don't know how else you could have acted
upon it."

" But I do not mean to act upon it. I shall not go to Plaistow. There are two reasons against it, each sufficient. I shall not leave you quite yet,—unless you send me away; and I shall not cause my cousin to be turned out of his own house."

" Why should he be turned out? Why should you not go to him? You love him;—and as for him, he is more in love than any man I ever knew. Go to Plaistow Hall, and everything will run smooth."

" No, dear; I shall not do that."

" Then you are foolish. I am bound to tell you so, as I have inveigled you here."

" I thought I had invited myself."

" No; I asked you to come, and when I asked you I knew that I was wrong. Though I meant to be kind, I knew that I was unkind. I saw that my husband disapproved it, though he had not the heart to tell me so. I wish he had. I wish he had."

" Mrs. Askerton, I cannot tell you how much you wrong yourself, and how you wrong me also. I am more than contented to be here."

" But you should not be contented to be here. It is just that. In learning to love me,—or rather, perhaps, to pity me, you lower yourself. Do you think that I do not see it all, and know it all? Of course it is bad to be alone, but I have no right not to be alone." There was nothing for Clara to do but to draw herself once again close to the poor woman, and to embrace her with protestations of fair, honest, equal regard and friendship. " Do you think I do not understand that letter?" continued Mrs. Askerton. " If it had come from Lady Aylmer I could have laughed at it, because I believe Lady Aylmer to be an overbearing virago, whom it is good to put down in every way possible. But this comes from a pure-minded woman, one whom I believe to be little given to harsh judgments on her fellow-sinners; and she tells you in her calm wise way that it is bad for you to be here with me."

" She says nothing of the kind."

" But does she not mean it? Tell me honestly;—do you not know that she means it?"

" I am not to be guided by what she means."

" But you are to be guided by what her brother means.

It is to come to that, and you may as well bend your neck
at once. It is to come to that, and the sooner the better
for you. It is easy to see that you are, badly off for
guidance when you take up me as your friend." When she
had so spoken Mrs. Askerton got up and went to the door.
"No, Clara, do not come with me; not now," she said,
turning to her companion, who had risen as though to
follow her. "I will come to you soon, but I would rather
be alone now. And, look here, dear; you must answer
your cousin's letter. Do so at once, and say that you will
go to Plaistow. In any event it will be better for you."

Clara, when she was alone, did answer her cousin's letter,
but she did not accept the invitation that had been given
her. She assured Miss Belton that she was most anxious
to know her, and hoped that she might do so before long
either at Plaistow or at Belton; but that at present she was
under an engagement to stay with her friend Mrs. Askerton.
In an hour or two Mrs. Askerton returned, and Clara
handed to her the note to read. "Then all I can say is you
are very silly, and don't know on which side your bread is
buttered." It was evident from Mrs. Askerton's voice that
she had recovered her mood and tone of mind. "I don't
suppose it will much signify, as it will all come right at
last," she said afterwards. And then, after luncheon, when
she had been for a few minutes with her husband in his
own room, she told Clara that the Colonel wanted to speak
to her. "You'll find him as grave as a judge, for he has
got something to say to you in earnest. Nobody can be so
stern as he is when he chooses to put on his wig and gown."
So Clara went into the Colonel's study, and seated herself
in a chair which he had prepared for her.

She remained there for over an hour, and during the
hour the conversation became very animated. Colonel
Askerton's assumed gravity had given way to ordinary
eagerness, during which he had walked about the room in
the vehemence of his argument; and Clara, in answering
him, had also put forth all her strength. She had expected
that he also was going to speak to her on the propriety of
her going to Norfolk; but he made no allusion to that
subject, although all that he did say was founded on Will
Belton's letter to himself. Belton, in speaking of the
cottage, had told Colonel Askerton that Miss Amedroz

would be his future landlord, and had then gone on to
explain that it was his, Belton's, intention to destroy the
entail, and allow the property to descend from the father
to the daughter. "As Miss Amedroz is with you now,"
he said, "may I beg you to take the trouble to explain the
matter to her at length, and to make her understand that
the estate is now, at this moment, in fact her own. Her
possession of it does not depend on any act of hers,—or,
indeed, upon her own will or wish in the matter." On this
subject Colonel Askerton had argued, using all his skill to
make Clara in truth perceive that she was her father's
heiress,—through the generosity undoubtedly of her cousin,
—and that she had no alternative but to assume the possession which was thus thrust upon her.

And so eloquent was the Colonel that Clara was staggered,
though she was not convinced. "It is quite impossible,"
she said. "Though he may be able to make it over to me,
I can give it back again."

"I think not. In such a matter as this a lady in your
position can only be guided by her natural advisers,—her
father's lawyer and other family friends."

"I don't know why a young lady should be in any way
different from an old gentleman."

"But an old gentleman would not hesitate under such
circumstances. The entail in itself was a cruelty, and the
operation of it on your poor brother's death was additionally
cruel."   ·

"It is cruel that any one should be poor," argued Clara;
"but that does not take away the right of a rich man to his
property."

There was much more of this sort said between them,
till Clara was at any rate convinced that Colonel Askerton
believed that she ought to be the owner of the property.
And then at last he ventured upon another argument which
soon drove Clara out of the room. "There is, I believe,
one way in which it can all be made right," said he.

"What way?" said Clara, forgetting in her eagerness the
obviousness of the mode which her companion was about
to point out.

"Of course, I know nothing of this myself," he said
smiling; "but Mary thinks that you and your cousin
might arrange it between you if you were together."

"You must not listen to what she says about that, Colonel Askerton."

"Must I not? Well; I will not listen to more than I can help; but Mary, as you know, is a persistent talker. I, at any rate, have done my commission." Then Clara left him, and was alone for what remained of the afternoon.

It could not be, she said to herself, that the property ought to be hers. It would make her miserable, were she once to feel that she had accepted it. Some small allowance out of it, coming to her from the brotherly love of her cousin,—some moderate stipend sufficient for her livelihood, she thought she could accept from him. It seemed to her that it was her destiny to be dependent on charity, —to eat bread given to her from the benevolence of a friend; and she thought that she could endure his benevolence better than that of any other. Benevolence from Aylmer Park or from Perivale would be altogether unendurable.

But why should it not be as Colonel Askerton had proposed? That this cousin of hers loved her with all his heart,—with a constancy for which she had at first given him no credit, she was well aware. And as regarded herself, she loved him better than all the world beside. She had at last become conscious that she could not now marry Captain Aylmer without sin,—without false vows, and fatal injury to herself and him. To the prospect of that marriage, as her future fate, an end must be put at any rate,—an end, if that which had already taken place was not to be regarded as end enough. But yet she had been engaged to Captain Aylmer,—was engaged to him even now. When last her cousin had mentioned to her Captain Aylmer's name she had declared that she loved him still. How then could she turn round now, and so soon accept the love of another man? How could she bring herself to let her cousin assume to himself the place of a lover, when it was but the other day that she had rebuked him for expressing the faintest hope in that direction?

But yet,—yet——! As for going to Plaistow, that was quite out of the question.

"So you are to be the heiress after all," said Mrs. Askerton to her that night in her bed-room.

"No ; I am not to be the heiress after all," said Clara, rising against her friend impetuously.

"You'll have to be lady of Belton in one way or the other, at any rate," said Mrs. Askerton.

CHAPTER XXVIII.

MISS AMEDROZ IS PURSUED.

"I suppose now, my dear, it may be considered that everything is settled about that young lady," said Lady Aylmer to her son, on the same day that Miss Amedroz left Aylmer Park.

"Nothing is settled, ma'am," said the Captain.

"You don't mean to tell me that after what has passed you intend to follow her up any further?"

"I shall certainly endeavour to see her again."

"Then, Frederic, I must tell you that you are very wrong indeed;—almost worse than wrong. I would say wicked, only I feel sure that you will think better of it. You cannot mean to tell me that you would—marry her after what has taken place?"

"The question is whether she would marry me."

"That is nonsense, Frederic. I wonder that you, who are generally so clear-sighted, cannot see more plainly than that. She is a scheming, artful young woman, who is playing a regular game to catch a husband."

"If that were so, she would have been more humble to you, ma'am."

"Not a bit, Fred. That's just it. That has been her cleverness. She tried that on at first, and found that she could not get round me. Don't allow yourself to be deceived by that, I pray. And then there is no knowing how she may be bound up with those horrid people, so that she cannot throw them over even if she would.".

"I don't think you understand her, ma'am."

"Oh ;—very well. But I understand this, and you had better understand it too ;—that she will never again enter a house of which I am the mistress ; nor can I ever enter

a house in which she is received. If you choose to make
her your wife after that, I have done." Lady Aylmer had
not done, or nearly done; but we need hear no more of
her threats or entreaties.   Her son left Aylmer Park
immediately after Easter Sunday, and as he went, the
mother, nodding her head, declared to her daughter that
that marriage would never come off, let Clara Amedroz be
ever so sly, or ever so clever.

"Think of what I have said to you, Fred," said Sir
Anthony, as he took his leave of his son.

"Yes, sir, I will."

"You can't be better off than you are ;—you can't,
indeed."   With these words in his ears Captain Aylmer
started for London, intending to follow Clara down to
Belton.   He hardly knew his own mind on this matter of
his purposed marriage.   He was almost inclined to agree
with his father that he was very well off as he was.   He
was almost inclined to agree with his mother in her
condemnation of Clara's conduct.   He was almost inclined
to think that he had done enough towards keeping the
promise made to his aunt on her deathbed,—but still he
was not quite contented with himself.   He desired to be
honest and true, as far as his ideas went of honesty and
truth, and his conscience told him that Clara had been
treated with cruelty by his mother.   I am inclined to think
that Lady Aylmer, in spite of her high experience and
character for wisdom, had not fought her battle altogether
well.   No man likes to be talked out of his marriage by
his mother, and especially not so when the talking takes
the place of threats.   When she told him that under no
circumstances would she again know Clara Amedroz, he
was driven by his spirit of manhood to declare to himself
that that menace from her should not have the slightest
influence on him.   The word or two which his father said
was more effective.   After all it might be better for him in
his peculiar position to have no wife at all.   He did begin
to believe that he had no need for a wife.   He had never
before thought so much of his father's example as he did
now.   Clara was manifestly a hot-tempered woman,—a
very hot-tempered woman indeed!   Now, his mother was
also a hot-tempered woman, and he could not but see the
result in the present condition of his father's life.   He re-

solved that he would follow Clara to Belton, so that some final
settlement might be made between them; but in coming
to this resolution he acknowledged to himself that should
she decide against him he would not break his heart. She,
however, should have her chance. Undoubtedly it was
only right that she should have her chance.

But the difficulty of the circumstances in which he was
placed was so great, that it was almost impossible for him
to make up his mind fixedly to any purpose in reference
to Clara. As he passed through London on his way to
Belton he called at Mr. Green's chambers with reference
to that sum of fifteen hundred pounds, which it was now
absolutely necessary that he should make over to Miss
Amedroz, and from Mr. Green he learned that William
Belton had given positive instructions as to the destination
of the Belton estate. He would not inherit it, or have
anything to do with it under the entail,—from the effects
of which he desired to be made entirely free. Mr. Green,
who knew that Captain Aylmer was engaged to marry
his client, and who knew nothing of any interruption to
that agreement, felt no hesitation in explaining all this to
Captain Aylmer. "I suppose you had heard of it before,"
said Mr. Green. Captain Aylmer certainly had heard
of it, and had been very much struck by the idea; but
up to this moment he had not quite believed in it. Coming
simply from William Belton to Clara Amedroz, such an
offer might be no more than a strong argument used in
love-making. "Take back the property, but take me
with it, of course." That Captain Aylmer thought might
have been the correct translation of Mr. William Belton's
romance. But he was forced to look at the matter differently when he found that it had been put into a lawyer's
hands. "Yes," said he, "I have heard of it. Mr. Belton
mentioned it to me himself." This was not strictly true.
Clara had mentioned it to him; but Belton had come into
the room immediately afterwards, and Captain Aylmer
might probably have been mistaken.

"He's quite in earnest," said Mr. Green.

"Of course, I can say nothing, Mr. Green, as I am
myself so nearly interested in the matter. It is a great
question no doubt how far such an entail as that should
be allowed to operate."

"I think it should stand as a matter of course. I think Belton is wrong," said Mr. Green.

"Of course I can give no opinion," said the other.

"I'll tell you what you can do, Captain Aylmer. You can suggest to Miss Amedroz that there should be a compromise. Let them divide it. They are both clients of mine, and in that way I shall do my duty to each. Let them divide it. Belton has money enough to buy up the other moiety, and in that way would still be Belton of Belton.

Captain Aylmer had not the slightest objection to such a plan. Indeed, he regarded it as in all respects a wise and salutary arrangement. The moiety of the Belton estate might probably be worth twenty-five thousand pounds, and the addition of such a sum as that to his existing means would make all the difference in the world as to the expedience of his marriage. His father's arguments would all fall to the ground if twenty-five thousand pounds were to be obtained in this way; and he had but little doubt that such a change in affairs would go far to mitigate his mother's wrath. But he was by no means mercenary in his views;—so, at least, he assured himself. Clara should have her chance with or without the Belton estate,—or with or without the half of it. He was by no means mercenary. Had he not made his offer to her, —and repeated it almost with obstinacy, when she had no prospect of any fortune? He could always remember that of himself at least; and remembering that now, he could take a delight in these bright money prospects without having to accuse himself in any degree of mercenary motives. This fortune was a godsend which he could take with clean hands;—if only he should ultimately be able to take the lady who possessed the fortune!

From London he wrote to Clara, telling her that he proposed to visit her at Belton. His letter was written before he had seen Mr. Green, and was not very fervent in its expressions; but, nevertheless, it was a fair letter, written with the intention of giving her a fair chance. He had seen with great sorrow,—"with heartfelt grief," that quarrel between his mother and his own Clara. Thinking, as he felt himself obliged to think, about Mrs. Askerton, he could not but feel that his mother had cause for her anger. But he himself was unprejudiced, and was ready, and anxious also,—the word anxious was underscored,—to carry out his engagement. A few words between them might probably set everything right, and therefore he proposed to meet her at the Belton Castle house, at such an hour, on such a day. He should run down to Perivale on his journey, and perhaps Clara would let him have a line addressed to him there. Such was his letter.

"What do you think of that ?" said Clara, showing it to Mrs. Askerton on the afternoon of the day on which she had received it.

"What do you think of it?" said Mrs Askerton. " I can only hope that he will not come within the reach of my hands."

" You are not angry with me for showing it to you ?"

" No;—why should I be angry with you? Of course I knew it all without any showing. Do not tell Colonel Askerton, or they will be killing each other."

" Of course I shall not tell Colonel Askerton; but I could not help showing this to you."

"And you will meet him ?"

" Yes; I shall meet him. What else can I do?"

" Unless, indeed, you were to write and tell him that it would do no good."

" It will be better that he should come."

" If you allow him to talk you over you will be a wretched woman all your life."

" It will be better that he should come," said Clara again. And then she wrote to Captain Aylmer at Perivale, telling him that she would be at the house at the hour he had named, on the day he had named.

When that day came she walked across the park a little before the time fixed, not wishing to meet Captain Aylmer before she had reached the house. It was now nearly the middle of April, and the weather was soft and pleasant. It was almost summer again, and as she felt this, she thought of all the events which had occurred since the last summer,—of their agony of grief at the catastrophe which had closed her brother's life, of her aunt's death first, and then of her father's following so close upon the other, and of the two offers of marriage made to her,—as to which

she was now aware that she had accepted the wrong man
and rejected the wrong man. She was steadily minded,
now, at this moment, that before she parted from Captain
Aylmer, her engagement with him should be brought to a
close. Now, at this coming interview, so much at any
rate should be done. She had tried to make herself
believe that she felt for him that sort of affection which a
woman should have for the man she is to marry, but she
had failed. She hardly knew whether she had in truth
ever loved him; but she was quite sure that she did not
love him now. No;—she had done with Aylmer Park,
and she could feel thankful, amidst all her troubles, that
that difficulty should vex her no more. In showing
Captain Aylmer's letter to Mrs. Askerton she had made no
such promise as this, but her mind had been quite made
up. " He certainly shall not talk me over," she said to
herself as she walked across the park.

But she could not see her way so clearly out of that
further difficulty with regard to her cousin. It might be
that she would be able to rid herself of the one lover with
comparative ease ; but she could not bring herself to
entertain the idea of accepting the other. It was true
that this man longed for her,—desired to call her his own,
with a wearing, anxious, painful desire which made his
heart grievously heavy as though with lead hanging to its
strings ; and it was true that Clara knew that it was so.
It was true also that his spirit had mastered her spirit, and
that his persistence had conquered her resistance,—the
resistance, that is, of her feelings. But there remained
with her a feminine shame, which made it seem to her to
be impossible that she should now reject Captain Aylmer,
and, as a consequence of that rejection, accept Will Belton's
hand. As she thought of this, she could not see her way
out of her trouble in that direction with any of that
clearness which belonged to her in reference to Captain
Aylmer.

She had been an hour in the house before he came, and
never did an hour go so heavily with her. There was no
employment for her about the place, and Mrs. Bunce, the
old woman who now lived there, could not understand why
her late mistress chose to remain seated among the unused
furniture. Clara had of course told her that a gentleman

was coming. " Not Mr. Will," said the woman. " No ;
it is not Mr. Will," said Clara; " his name is Captain
Aylmer." " Oh, indeed." And then Mrs. Bunce looked
at her with a mystified look. Why on earth should not
the gentleman call on Miss Amedroz at Mrs. Askerton's
cottage. " I'll be sure to show 'un up, when a comes, at
any rate," said the old woman solemnly ;—and Clara felt
that it was all very uncomfortable.

At last the gentleman did come, and was shown up
with all the ceremony of which Mrs. Bunce was capable.
" Here he be, mum." Then Mrs. Bunce paused a moment
before she retreated, anxious to learn whether the new
comer was a friend or a foe. She concluded from the
Captain's manner that he was a very dear friend, and then
she departed.

" I hope you are not surprised at my coming," said
Captain Aylmer, still holding Clara by the hand.

" A little surprised," she said, smiling.

" But not annoyed ?"

" No ;—not annoyed."

" As soon as you had left Aylmer Park I felt that it was the
right thing to do ;—the only thing to do,—as I told my
mother."

" I hope you have not come in opposition to her
wishes," said Clara, unable to control a slight tone of
banter as she spoke.

" In this matter I found myself compelled to act in
accordance with my own judgment," said he, untouched by
her sarcasm.

" Then I suppose that Lady Aylmer is,—is vexed with
you for coming here. I shall be so sorry for that ;—so very
sorry, as no good can come of it."

" Well ;—I am not so sure of that. My mother is a
most excellent woman, one for whose opinion on all matters I have the highest possible value ;—a value so high,
that—that—that——"

" That you never ought to act in opposition to it. That
is what you really mean, Captain Aylmer ; and upon my
word I think that you are right."

" No, Clara ; that is not what I mean,—not exactly that.
Indeed, just at present I mean the reverse of that. There
are some things on which a man must act on his

own judgment, irrespectively of the opinions of any one else."

"Not of a mother, Captain Aylmer."

"Yes;—of a mother. That is to say, a man must do so. With a lady of course it is different. I was very, very sorry that there should have been any unpleasantness at Aylmer Park."

"It was not pleasant to me, certainly."

"Nor to any of us, Clara."

"At any rate it need not be repeated."

"I hope not."

"No;—it certainly need not be repeated. I know now that I was wrong to go to Aylmer Park. I felt sure beforehand that there were many things as to which I could not possibly agree with Lady Aylmer, and I ought not to have gone."

"I don't see that at all, Clara."

"I do see it now."

"I can't understand you. What things? Why should you be determined to disagree with my mother? Surely you ought at any rate to endeavour to think as she thinks."

"I cannot do that, Captain Aylmer."

"I am sorry to hear you speak in this way. I have come here all the way from Yorkshire to try to put things straight between us; but you receive me as though you would remember nothing but that unpleasant quarrel."

"It was so unpleasant,—so very unpleasant! I had better speak out the truth at once. I think that Lady Aylmer ill-used me cruelly. I do. No one can talk me out of that conviction. Of course I am sorry to be driven to say as much to you,—and I should never have said it, had you not come here. But when you speak of me and your mother together, I must say what I feel. Your mother and I, Captain Aylmer, are so opposed to each other, not only in feelings, but in opinions also, that it is impossible that we should be friends;—impossible that we should not be enemies if we are brought together."

This she said with great energy, looking intently into his face as she spoke. He was seated near her, on a chair, from which he was leaning over towards her, holding his hat in both hands between his legs. Now, as he listened

to her, he drew his chair still nearer, ridding himself of
his hat, which he left upon the carpet, and keeping his
eyes upon hers as though he were fascinated. "I am
sorry to hear you speak like this," he said.

"It is best to say the truth."

"But, Clara, if you intend to be my wife——"

"Oh, no ;—that is impossible now."

"What is impossible ?"

"Impossible that I should become your wife. Indeed I
have convinced myself that you do not wish it."

"But I do wish it."

"No ;—no. If you will question your heart about it
quietly, you will find that you do not wish it."

"You wrong me, Clara."

"At any rate it cannot be so."

"I will not take that answer from you," he said, getting
up from his chair and walking once up and down the
room. Then he returned to it, and repeated his words.
"I will not take that answer from you. An engagement
such as ours cannot be put aside like an old glove. You
do not mean to tell me that all that has been between us is
to mean nothing?" There was something now like feeling
in his tone, something like passion in his gesture, and
Clara, though she had no thought of changing her purpose, was becoming unhappy at the idea of his unhappiness.

"It has meant nothing," she said. "We have been like
children together, playing at being in love. It is a game
from which you will come out scatheless, but I have been
scalded."

"Scalded !"

"Well ;—never mind. I do not mean to complain, and
certainly not of you."

"I have come here all the way from Yorkshire in order
that things may be put right between us."

"You have been very good,—very good to come, and I
will not say that I regret your trouble. It is best, I think,
that we should meet each other once more face to face, so
that we may understand each other. There was no understanding anything during those terrible days at Aylmer
Park." Then she paused, but as he did not speak at once
she went on. "I do not blame you for anything that has

taken place, but I am quite sure of this,—that you and I
could never be happy together as man and wife."

" I do not know why you say so; I do not indeed."

" You would disapprove of everything that I should do.
You do disapprove of what I am doing now."

" Disapprove of what ?"

" I am staying with my friend, Mrs. Askerton."

He felt that this was hard upon him. As she had shown
herself inclined to withdraw herself from him, he had
become more resolute in his desire to follow her up, and to
hold by his engagement. He was not employed now in
giving her another chance,—as he had proposed to himself
to do,—but was using what eloquence he had to obtain
another chance for himself. Lady Aylmer had almost
made him believe that Clara would be the suppliant, but
now he was the suppliant himself. In his anxiety to keep
her he was willing even to pass over her terrible iniquity
in regard to Mrs. Askerton,—that great sin which had led
to all these troubles. He had once written to her about
Mrs. Askerton, using very strong language, and threatening
her with his mother's full displeasure. At that time Mrs.
Askerton had simply been her friend. There had been no
question then of her taking refuge under that woman's roof.
Now she had repelled Lady Aylmer's counsels with scorn,
was living as a guest in Mrs. Askerton's house; and yet he
was willing to pass over the Askerton difficulty without a
word. He was willing not only to condone past offences,
but to wink at existing iniquity ! But she,—she who was
the sinner, would not permit of this. She herself dragged
up Mrs. Askerton's name, and seemed to glory in her own
shame.

" I had not intended," said he, " to speak of your friend."

" I only mention her to show how impossible it is that
we should ever agree upon some subjects,—as to which a
husband and wife should always be of one mind. I knew
this from the moment in which I got your letter,—and only
that I was a coward I should have said so then."

" And you mean to quarrel with me altogether."

" No ;—why should we quarrel ?"

" Why, indeed ?" said he.

" But I wish it to be settled,—quite settled, as from the
nature of things it must be, that there shall be no attempt

at renewal of our engagement. After what has passed, how could I enter your mother's house?"

"But you need not enter it." Now in his emergency he was willing to give up anything,—everything. He had been prepared to talk her over into a reconciliation with his mother, to admit that there had been faults on both sides, to come down from his high pedestal and discuss the matter as though Clara and his mother stood upon the same footing. Having recognised the spirit of his lady-love, he had told himself that so much indignity as that must be endured. But now, he had been carried so far beyond this, that he was willing, in the sudden vehemence of his love, to throw his mother over altogether, and to accede to any terms which Clara might propose to him. "Of course, I would wish you to be friends," he said, using now all the tones of a suppliant; "but if you found that it could not be so——"

"Do you think that I would divide you from your mother?"

"There need be no question as to that."

"Ah;—there you are wrong. There must be such questions. I should have thought of it sooner."

"Clara, you are more to me than my mother. Ten times more." As he said this he came up and knelt down beside her. "You are everything to me. You will not throw me over." He was a suppliant indeed, and such supplications are very potent with women. Men succeed often by the simple earnestness of their prayers. Women cannot refuse to give that which is asked for with so much of the vehemence of true desire. "Clara, you have promised to be my wife. You have twice promised; and can have no right to go back because you are displeased with what my mother may have said. I am not responsible for my mother. Clara, say that you will be my wife." As he spoke he strove to take her hand, and his voice sounded as though there were in truth something of passion in his heart.

CHAPTER XXIX.

THERE IS NOTHING TO TELL.

CAPTAIN AYLMER had never before this knelt to Clara Amedroz. Such kneeling on the part of lovers used to be the fashion, because lovers in those days held in higher value than they do now that which they asked their ladies to give,—or because they pretended to do so. The forms at least of supplication were used ; whereas in these wiser days Augustus simply suggests to Caroline that they two might as well make fools of themselves together,—and so the thing is settled without the need of much prayer. Captain Aylmer's engagement had been originally made somewhat after this fashion. He had not, indeed, spoken of the thing contemplated as a folly, not being a man given to little waggeries of that nature ; but he had been calm, unenthusiastic, and reasonable. He had not attempted to evince any passion, and would have been quite content that Clara should believe that he married as much from obedience to his aunt as from love for herself, had he not found that Clara would not take him at all under such a conviction. But though she had declined to come to him after that fashion,—though something more than that had been needed,—still she had been won easily, and, therefore, lightly prized. I fear that it is so with everything that we value,—with our horses, our houses, our wines, and, above all, with our women. Where is the man who has heart and soul big enough to love a woman with increased force of passion because she has at once recognised in him all that she has herself desired ? Captain Aylmer having won his spurs easily, had taken no care in buckling them, and now found to his surprise, that he was like to lose them. He had told himself that he would only be too glad to shuffle his feet free of their bondage ; but now that they were going from him, he began to find that they were very necessary for the road that he was to travel. " Clara," he said, kneeling by her

side, "you are more to me than my mother; ten times
more!"

This was all new to her. Hitherto, though she had
never desired that he should assume such attitude as this,
she had constantly been unconsciously wounded by his
coldness,—by his cold propriety and unbending self-possession. His cold propriety and unbending self-possession
were gone now, and he was there at her feet. Such an
argument, used at Aylmer Park, would have conquered
her,—would have won her at once, in spite of herself; but
now she was minded to be resolute. She had sworn to
herself that she would not peril herself, or him, by joining
herself to a man with whom she had so little sympathy,
and who apparently had none with her. But in what way
was she to answer such a prayer as that which was now
made to her? The man who addressed her was entitled to
use all the warmth of an accepted lover. He only asked
for that which had already been given to him.

"Captain Aylmer——," she began.

"Why is it to be Captain Aylmer? What have I done
that you should use me in this way? It was not I who,—
who,—made you unhappy at Aylmer Park."

"I will not go back to that. It is of no use. Pray get
up. It shocks me to see you in this way."

"Tell me, then, that it is once more all right between
us. Say that, and I shall be happier than I ever was
before;—yes, than I ever was before. I know how much
I love you now, how sore it would be to lose you. I have
been wrong. I had not thought enough of that, but I will
think of it now."

She found that the task before her was very difficult,—
so difficult that she almost broke down in performing it.
It would have been so easy and, for the moment, so
pleasant to have yielded. He had his hand upon her arm,
having attempted to take her hand. In preventing that
she had succeeded, but she could not altogether make herself free from him without rising. For a moment she had
paused,—paused as though she were about to yield. For a
moment, as he looked into her eyes, he had thought
that he would again be victorious. Perhaps there was
something in his glance, some too visible return of
triumph to his eyes, which warned her of her danger.

"No!" she said, getting up and walking away from him; "no!"

"And what does 'no' mean, Clara?" Then he also rose, and stood leaning on the table. "Does it mean that you will be forsworn?"

"It means this,—that I will not come between you and your mother; that I will not be taken into a family in which I am scorned; that I will not go to Aylmer Park myself, or be the means of preventing you from going there."

"There need be no question of Aylmer Park."

"There shall be none!"

"But, so much being allowed, you will be my wife?"

"No, Captain Aylmer;—no. I cannot be your wife. Do not press it further; you must know that on such a subject I would think much before I answered you. I have thought much, and I know that I am right."

"And your promised word is to go for nothing?"

"If it will comfort you to say so, you may say it. If you do not perceive that the mistake made between us has been as much your mistake as mine, and has injured me more than it has injured you, I will not remind you of it, —will never remind you of it after this."

"But there has been no mistake, and there shall be no injury."

"Ah, Captain Aylmer! you do not understand; you cannot understand. I would not for worlds reproach you : but do you think I suffered nothing from your mother?"

"And must I pay for her sins?"

"There shall be no paying, no punishment, and no reproaches. There shall be none at least from me. But, —do not think that I speak in anger or in pride,—I will not marry into Lady Aylmer's family."

"This is too bad,—too bad! After all that is past, it is too bad!"

"What can I say? Would you advise me to do that which would make us both wretched?"

"It would not make me wretched. It would make me happy. It would satisfy me altogether."

"It cannot be, Captain Aylmer. It cannot be. When I speak to you in that way, will you not let it be final?"

He paused a moment before he spoke again, and then he

turned sharp upon her. "Tell me this, Clara; do you
love me? Have you ever loved me?" She did not answer
him, but stood there, listening quietly to his accusations.
"You have never loved me, and yet you have allowed
yourself to say that you did. Is not that true?" Still she
did not answer. "I ask you whether that is not true?"
But though he asked her, and paused for an answer,
looking the while full into her face, yet she did not speak.
"And now I suppose you will become your cousin's wife?"
he said. "It will suit you to change, and to say that you
love him."

Then at last she spoke. "I did not think that you
would have treated me in this way, Captain Aylmer! I
did not expect that you would insult me!"

"I have not insulted you."

"But your manner to me makes my task easier than I
could have hoped it to be. You asked me whether I ever
loved you? I once thought that I did so; and so thinking, told you, without reserve, all my feeling. When I
came to find that I had been mistaken, I conceived myself
bound by my engagement to rectify my own error as best
I could; and I resolved, wrongly,—as I now think, very
wrongly,—that I could learn as your wife to love you.
Then came circumstances which showed me that a release
would be good for both of us, and which justified me in
accepting it. No girl could be bound by any engagement
to a man who looked on and saw her treated in his own
home, by his own mother, as you saw me treated at
Aylmer Park. I claim to be released myself, and I know
that this release is as good for you as it is for me."

"I am the best judge of that."

"For myself at any rate I will judge. For myself I
have decided. Now I have answered the questions which
you asked me as to my love for yourself. To that other
question which you have thought fit to put to me about my
cousin, I refuse to give any answer whatsoever." Then,
having said so much, she walked out of the room, closing
the door behind her, and left him standing there alone.

We need not follow her as she went up, almost mechani-
cally, into her own room,—the room that used to be her
own,—and then shut herself in, waiting till she should be
assured, first by sounds in the house, and then by silence,

that he was gone. That she fell away greatly from the
majesty of her demeanour when she was thus alone, and
descended to the ordinary ways of troubled females, we
may be quite sure. But to her there was no further
difficulty. Her work for the day was done. In due time
she would take herself to the cottage, and all would be
well, or, at any rate, comfortable with her. But what was
he to do? How was he to get himself out of the house,
and take himself back to London? While he had been in
pursuit of her, and when he was leaving his vehicle at the
public-house in the village of Belton, he,—like some other
invading generals,—had failed to provide adequately for his
retreat. When he was alone he took a turn or two about
the room, half thinking that Clara would return to him.
She could hardly leave him alone in a strange house,—him,
who, as he had twice told her, had come all the way from
Yorkshire to see her. But she did not return, and gradually he came to understand that he must provide for his
own retreat without assistance. He was hardly aware,
even now, how greatly he had transcended his usual modes
of speech and action, both in the energy of his supplication
and in the violence of his rebuke. He had been lifted for
awhile out of himself by the excitement of his position, and
now that he was subsiding into quiescence, he was unconscious that he had almost mounted into passion,—that he
had spoken of love very nearly with eloquence. But he
did recognise this as a fact,—that Clara was not to be his
wife, and that he had better get back from Belton to
London as quickly as possible. It would be well for him
to teach himself to look back on the result of his aunt's
dying request as an episode in his life satisfactorily concluded. His mother had undoubtedly been right. Clara,
he could now see, would have led him a devil of a life;
and even had she come to him possessed of a moiety of the
property,—a supposition as to which he had very strong
doubts,—still she might have been dear at the money.
"No real feeling," he said to himself, as he walked about
the room,—"none whatever; and then so deficient in
delicacy!" But still he was discontented,—because he
had been rejected, and therefore tried to make himself
believe that he could still have her if he chose to persevere. "But no," he said, as he continued to pace the

room, "I have done everything,—more than everything that honour demands. I shall not ask her again. It is her own fault. She is an imperious woman, and my mother read her character aright." It did not occur to him, as he thus consoled himself for what he had lost, that his mother's accusation against Clara had been altogether of a different nature. When we console ourselves by our own arguments, we are not apt to examine their accuracy with much strictness.

But whether he were consoled or not, it was necessary that he should go, and in his going he felt himself to be ill-treated. He left the room, and as he went down stairs was disturbed and tormented by the creaking of his own boots. He tried to be dignified as he walked through the hall, and was troubled at his failure, though he was not conscious of any one looking at him. Then it was grievous that he should have to let himself out of the front door without attendance. At ordinary times he thought as little of such things as most men, and would not be aware whether he opened a door for himself or had it opened for him by another;—but now there was a distressing awkwardness in the necessity for self-exertion. He did not know the turn of the handle, and was unfamiliar with the manner of exit. He was being treated with indignity, and before he had escaped from the house had come to think that the Amedroz and Belton people were somewhat below him. He endeavoured to go out without a noise, but there was a slam of the door, without which he could not get the lock to work; and Clara, up in her own room, knew all about it.

"Carriage;—yes; of course I want the carriage," he said to the unfortunate boy at the public-house. "Didn't you hear me say that I wanted it?" He had come down with a pair of horses, and as he saw them being put to the vehicle he wished he had been contented with one. As he was standing there, waiting, a gentleman rode by, and the boy, in answer to his question, told him that the horseman was Colonel Askerton. Before the day was over Colonel Askerton would probable know all that had happened to him. "Do move a little quicker; will you?" he said to the boy and the old man who was to drive him. Then he got into the carriage, and was driven out of Belton, devoutly purposing that he never would return; and as he made his way back to Perivale he thought of a certain Lady Emily, who would, as he assured himself, have behaved much better than Clara Amedroz had done in any such scene as that which had just taken place.

When Clara was quite sure that Captain Aylmer was off the premises, she, too, descended, but she did not immediately leave the house. She walked through the room, and rang for the old woman, and gave certain directions,—as to the performance of which she certainly was not very anxious, and was careful to make Mrs. Bunce understand that nothing had occurred between her and the gentleman that was either exalting or depressing in its nature. "I suppose Captain Aylmer went out, Mrs. Bunce?" "Oh yes, Miss, a went out. I stood and see'd un from the top of the kitchen stairs." "You might have opened the door for him, Mrs. Bunce." "Indeed then I never thought of it, Miss, seeing the house so empty and the like." Clara said that it did not signify; and then, after an hour of composure, she walked back across the park to the cottage.

"Well?" said Mrs. Askerton as soon as Clara was inside the drawing-room.

"Well," replied Clara.

"What have you got to tell? Do tell me what you have to tell."

"I have nothing to tell."

"Clara, that is impossible. Have you seen him? I know you have seen him, because he went by from the house about an hour since."

"Oh yes; I have seen him."

"And what have you said to him?"

"Pray do not ask me these questions just now. I have got to think of it all ;—to think what he did say and what I said."

"But you will tell me."

"Yes; I suppose so." Then Mrs. Askerton was silent on the subject for the remainder of the day, allowing Clara even to go to bed without another question. And nothing was asked on the following morning,—nothing till the usual time for the writing of letters.

"Shall you have anything for the post?" said Mrs. Askerton.

" There is plenty of time yet."

" Not too much if you mean to go out at all. Come, Clara, you had better write to him at once."

" Write to whom? I don't know that I have any letter to write at all." Then there was a pause. " As far as I can see," she said, " I may give up writing altogether for the future, unless some day you may care to hear from me."

" But you are not going away."

" Not just yet—if you will keep me. To tell you the truth, Mrs. Askerton, I do not yet know where on earth to take myself."

" Wait here till we turn you out."

" I've got to put my house in order. You know what I mean. The job ought not to be a troublesome one, for it is a very small house."

" I suppose I know what you mean."

" It will not be a very smart establishment. But I must look it all in the face; must I not? Though it were to be no house at all, I cannot stay here all my life."

" Yes, you may. You have lost Aylmer Park because you were too noble not to come to us."

" No," said Clara, speaking aloud, with bright eyes,— almost with her hands clenched. " No;—I deny that."

" I shall choose to think so for my own purposes. Clara, you are savage to me;—almost always savage; but next to him I love you better than all the world beside. And so does he. 'It's her courage,' he said to me the other day. ' That she should dare to do as she pleases here, is nothing; but to have dared to persevere in the fangs of that old dragon,'—it was just what he said,—' that was wonderful!' "

" There is an end of the old dragon now, as far as I am concerned."

" Of course there is;—and of the young dragon too. You wouldn't have had the heart to keep me in suspense if you had accepted him again. You couldn't have been so pleasant last night if that had been so."

" I did not know I was very pleasant."

" Yes, you were. You were soft and gracious,—gracious for you, at least. And now, dear, do tell me about it. Of course I am dying to know."

" There is nothing to tell."

" That is nonsense. There must be a thousand things to tell. At any rate, it is quite decided ?"

" Yes ; it is quite decided."

" All the dragons, old and young, are banished into outer darkness."

" Either that, or else they are to have all the light to themselves."

" Such light as glimmers through the gloom of Aylmer Park. And was he contented ? I hope not. I hope you had him on his knees before he left you."

" Why should you hope that ? How can you talk such nonsense ?"

" Because I wish that he should recognise what he has lost;—that he should know that he has been a fool;—a mean fool."

" Mrs. Askerton, I will not have him spoken of like that. He is a man very estimable,—of excellent qualities."

" Fiddle-de-dee. He is an ape,—a monkey to be carried on his mother's organ. His only good quality was that you could have carried him on yours. I can tell you one thing ;—there is not a woman breathing that will ever carry William Belton on hers. Whoever his wife may be, she will have to dance to his piping."

" With all my heart;—and I hope the tunes will be good."

" But I wish I could have been present to have heard what passed ;—hidden, you know, behind a curtain. You won't tell me ?"

" I will tell you not a word more."

" Then I will get it out from Mrs. Bunce. I'll be bound she was listening."

" Mrs. Bunce will have nothing to tell you ; and I do not know why you should be so curious."

" Answer me one question at least ;—when it came to the last, did he want to go on with it ? Was the final triumph with him or with you ?"

" There was no final triumph. Such things, when they have to end, do not end triumphantly."

" And is that to be all ?"

" Yes ;—that is to be all."

" And you say that you have no letter to write."

" None;—no letter; none at present; none about this
affair. Captain Aylmer, no doubt, will write to his mother,
and then all those who are concerned will have been
told."

Clara Amedroz held her purpose and wrote no letter,
but Mrs. Askerton was not so discreet, or so indiscreet, as
the case might be. She did write,—not on that day or on
the next, but before a week had passed by. She wrote to
Norfolk, telling Clara not a word of her letter, and by
return of post the answer came. But the answer was for
Clara, not for Mrs. Askerton, and was as follows:—

" Plaistow Hall, April, 186—.

" MY DEAR CLARA,

" I don't know whether I ought to tell you, but I
suppose I may as well tell you, that Mary has had a letter
from Mrs. Askerton. It was a kind, obliging letter, and I
am very grateful to her. She has told us that you have
separated yourself altogether from the Aylmer Park people.
I don't suppose you'll think I ought to pretend to be very
sorry. I can't be sorry, even though I know how much
you have lost in a worldly point of view. I could not
bring myself to like Captain Aylmer, though I tried hard."
Oh, Mr. Belton, Mr. Belton! " He and I never could have
been friends, and it is no use my pretending regret that
you have quarrelled with them. But that, I suppose,
is all over, and I will not say a word more about the
Aylmers.

" I am writing now chiefly at Mary's advice, and
because she says that something should be settled about
the estate. Of course it is necessary that you should feel
yourself to be the mistress of your own income, and understand exactly your own position. Mary says that this
should be arranged at once, so that you may be able to
decide how and where you will live. I therefore write
to say that I will have nothing to do with your father's
estate at Belton;—nothing, that is, for myself. I have
written to Mr. Green to tell him that you are to be considered as the heir. If you will allow me to undertake
the management of the property as your agent, I shall be
delighted. I think I could do it as well as any one else;

and, as we agreed that we would always be dear and close
friends, I think that you will not refuse me the pleasure of
serving you in this way.

"And now Mary has a proposition to make, as to which
she will write herself to-morrow, but she has permitted
me to speak of it first. If you will accept her as a visitor,
she will go to you at Belton. She thinks, and I think too,
that you ought to know each other. I suppose nothing
would make you come here, at present, and therefore
she must go to you. She thinks that all about the estate
would be settled more comfortably if you two were together. At any rate, it would be very nice for her,—and
I think you would like my sister Mary. She proposes
to start about the 10th of May. I should take her as
far as London and see her off, and she would bring her
own maid with her. In this way she thinks that she
would get as far as Taunton very well. She had, perhaps,
better stay there for one night, but that can all be settled
if you will say that you will receive her at the house.

"I cannot finish my letter without saying one word
for myself. You know what my feelings have been, and
I think you know that they still are, and always must be,
the same. From almost the first moment that I saw you
I have loved you. When you refused me I was very
unhappy; but I thought I might still have a chance, and
therefore I resolved to try again. Then, when I heard
that you were engaged to Captain Aylmer, I was indeed
broken-hearted. Of course I could not be angry with
you. I was not angry, but I was simply broken-hearted.
I found that I loved you so much that I could not make
myself happy without you. It was all of no use, for I
knew that you were to be married to Captain Aylmer.
I knew it, or thought that I knew it. There was nothing
to be done,—only I knew that I was wretched. I suppose
it is selfishness, but I felt, and still feel, that unless I can
have you for my wife, I cannot be happy or care for anything. Now you are free again,—free, I mean, from
Captain Aylmer;—and how is it possible that I should
not again have a hope? Nothing but your marriage
or death could keep me from hoping.

"I don't know much about the Aylmers. I know
nothing of what has made you quarrel with the people

at Aylmer Park ;—nor do I want to know. To me you
are once more that Clara Amedroz with whom I used to
walk in Belton Park, with your hand free to be given
wherever your heart can go with it. While it is free I
shall always ask for it. I know that it is in many ways
above my reach. I quite understand that in education
and habits of thinking you are my superior. But nobody
can love you better than I do. I sometimes fancy that
nobody could ever love you so well. Mary thinks that
I ought to allow a time to go by before I say all this
again ;—but what is the use of keeping it back ? It seems
to me to be more honest to tell you at once that the only
thing in the world for which I care one straw is that you
should be my wife.

" Your most affectionate Cousin,

" WILLIAM BELTON."

"Miss Belton is coming here, to the castle, in about a
fortnight," said Clara that morning at breakfast. Both
Colonel Askerton and his wife were in the room, and she
was addressing herself chiefly to the former.

"Indeed. Miss Belton ! And is he coming ?" said
Colonel Askerton.

"So you have heard from Plaistow ?" said Mrs. Askerton.

"Yes ;—in answer to your letter. No, Colonel Askerton, my cousin William is not coming. But his
sister purposes to be here, and I must go up to the house
and get it ready."

"That will do when the time comes," said Mrs. Asker
ton.

"I did not mean quite immediately."

"And are you to be her guest, or is she to be yours ?"
said Colonel Askerton.

"It is her brother's home, and therefore I suppose I
must be hers. Indeed it must be so, as I have no means
of entertaining any one."

"Something, no doubt, will be settled," said the Colonel.

"Oh, what a weary word that is," said Clara ; "weary,
at least, for a woman's ears ! It sounds of poverty and
dependence, and endless trouble given to others, and all
the miseries of female dependence. If I were a young
man I should be allowed to settle for myself."

"There would be no question about the property in that case," said the Colonel.

"And there need be no question now," said Mrs. Askerton.

When the two women were alone together, Clara, of course, scolded her friend for having written to Norfolk without letting it be known that she was doing so;— scolded her and declared how vain it was for her to make useless efforts for an unattainable end; but Mrs. Askerton always managed to slip out of these reproaches, neither asserting herself to be right, nor owning herself to be wrong. "But you must answer his letter," she said.

"Of course I shall do that."

"I wish I knew what he said."

"I shan't show it you, if you mean that.

"All the same I wish I knew what he said."

Clara, of course, did answer the letter; but she wrote her answer to Mary, sending, however, one little scrap to Mary's brother. She wrote to Mary at great length, striving to explain, with long and laborious arguments, that it was quite impossible that she should accept the Belton estate from her cousin. That subject, however, and the manner of her future life, she would discuss with her dear cousin Mary, when Mary should have arrived. And then Clara said how she would go to Taunton to meet her cousin, and how she would prepare William's house for the reception of William's sister; and how she would love her cousin when she should come to know her. All of which was exceedingly proper and pretty. Then there was a little postscript, "Give the enclosed to William." And this was the note to William :—

"DEAR WILLIAM,

"Did you not say that you would be my brother? Be my brother always. I will accept from your hands all that a brother could do; and when that arrangement is quite fixed I will love you as much as Mary loves you, and trust you as completely; and I will be obedient, as a younger sister should be.

"Your loving Sister,

"C. A."

" It's all no good," said William Belton, as he crunched the note in his hand. "I might as well shoot myself. Get out of the way there, will you?" And the injured groom scudded across the farmyard, knowing that there was something wrong with his master.

CHAPTER XXX.

MARY BELTON.

IT was about the middle of the pleasant month of May when Clara Amedroz again made that often-repeated journey to Taunton, with the object of meeting Mary Belton. She had transferred herself and her own peculiar belongings back from the cottage to the house, and had again established herself there so that she might welcome her new friend. But she was not satisfied with simply receiving her guest at Belton, and therefore she made the journey to Taunton, and settled herself for the night at the inn. She was careful to get a bed-room for an " invalid lady," close to the sitting-room, and before she went down to the station she saw that the cloth was laid for tea, and that the tea-parlour had been made to look as pleasant as was possible with an inn parlour.

She was very nervous as she stood upon the platform waiting for the new comer to show herself. She knew that Mary was a cripple, but did not know how far her cousin was disfigured by her infirmity; and when she saw a pale-faced little woman, somewhat melancholy, but yet pretty withal, with soft, clear eyes, and only so much appearance of a stoop as to soften the hearts of those who saw her, Clara was agreeably surprised, and felt herself to be suddenly relieved of an unpleasant weight. She could talk to the woman she saw there, as to any other woman, without the painful necessity of treating her always as an invalid. " I think you are Miss Belton ?" she said, holding out her hand. The likeness between Mary and her brother was too great to allow of Clara being mistaken.

" And you are Clara Amedroz ? It is so good of you to come to meet me !"

"I thought you would be dull in a strange town by
yourself."

" It will be much nicer to have you with me."

Then they went together up to the inn; and when they
had taken their bonnets off, Mary Belton kissed her cousin.
" You are very nearly what I fancied you," said Mary.

" Am I ? I hope you fancied me to be something that
you could like."

" Something that I could love very dearly. You are a
little taller than what Will said; but then a gentleman is
never a judge of a lady's height. And he said you were
thin."

" I am not very fat."

" No ; not very fat; but neither are you thin. Of course
you know, I have thought a great deal about you. It
seems as though you had come to be so very near to us ;
and blood is thicker than water, is it not ? If cousins are
not friends, who can be ?"

In the course of that evening they became very confidential together, and Clara thought that she could love Mary
Belton better than any woman that she had ever known.
Of course they were talking about William, and Clara was
at first in constant fear lest some word should be said on
her lover's behalf,—some word which would drive her to
declare that she would not admit him. as a lover; but
Mary abstained from the subject with marvellous care and
tact. Though she was talking through the whole evening
of her brother, she so spoke of him as almost to make Clara
believe that she could not have heard of that episode in his
life. Mrs. Askerton would have dashed at the subject at
once ; but then, as Clara told herself, Mary Belton was
better than Mrs. Askerton.

A few words were said about the estate, and they originated in Clara's declaration that Mary would have to be
regarded as the mistress of the house to which they were
going. " I cannot agree to that," said Mary.

" But the house is William's, you know," said Clara.

" He says not."

" But of course that must be nonsense, Mary."

" It is very evident that you know nothing of Plaistow
ways, or you would not say that anything coming from
William was nonsense. We are accustomed to regard all

his words as law, and when he says that a thing is to be so,
it always is so."

" Then he is a tyrant at home."

" A beneficent despot. Some despots, you know, always
were beneficent."

" He won't have his way in this thing."

" I'll leave you and him to fight about that, my dear. I
am so completely under his thumb that I always obey him
in everything. You must not, therefore, expect to range
me on your side."

The next day they were at Belton Castle, and in a very
few hours Clara felt that she was quite at home with her
cousin. On the second day Mrs. Askerton came up and
called,—according to an arrangement to that effect made
between her and Clara. " I'll stay away if you like it,"
Mrs. Askerton had said. But Clara had urged her to come,
arguing with her that she was foolish to be thinking always
of her own misfortune. " Of course I am always thinking
of it," she had replied, "and always thinking that other
people are thinking of it. Your cousin, Miss Belton,
knows all my history, of course. But what matters ? I
believe it would be better that everybody should know it.
I suppose she's very strait-laced and prim." " She is not
prim at all," said Clara. " Well, I'll come," said Mrs.
Askerton, " but I shall not be a bit surprised if I hear that
she goes back to Norfolk the next day."

So Mrs. Askerton came, and Miss Belton did not go back
to Norfolk. Indeed, at the end of the visit, Mrs. Askerton
had almost taught herself to believe that William Belton
had kept his secret, even from his sister. " She's a dear
little woman," Mrs. Askerton afterwards said to Clara.

" Is she not ?"

" And so thoroughly like a lady."

" Yes ; I think she is a lady."

" A princess among ladies ! What a pretty little conscious way she has of asserting herself when she has an
opinion and means to stick to it ! I never saw a woman
who got more strength out of her weakness. Who would
dare to contradict her ?"

" But then she knows everything so well," said Clara.

" And how like her brother she is !"

" Yes ;—there is a great family likeness."

" And in character too. I'm sure you'd find, if you were to try her, that she has all his personal firmness, though she can't show it as he does by kicking out his feet and clenching his fist."

" I'm glad you like her," said Clara.

" I do like her very much."

" It is so odd,—the way you have changed. You used to speak of him as though he was merely a clod of a farmer, and of her as a stupid old maid. Now, nothing is too good to say of them."

" Exactly, my dear ;—and if you do not understand why, you are not so clever as I take you to be."

Life went on very pleasantly with them at Belton for two or three weeks ;—but with this drawback as regarded Clara, that she had no means of knowing what was to be the course of her future life. During these weeks she twice received letters from her cousin Will, and answered both of them. But these letters referred to matters of business which entailed no contradiction,—to certain details of money due to the estate before the old squire's death, and to that vexed question of Aunt Winterfield's legacy, which had by this time drifted into Belton's hands, and as to which he was inclined to act in accordance with his cousin's wishes, though he was assured by Mr. Green that the legacy was as good a legacy as had ever been left by an old woman. " I think," he said in his last letter, " that we shall be able to throw him over in spite of Mr. Green." Clara, as she read this, could not but remember that the man to be thrown over was the man to whom she had been engaged, and she could not but remember also all the circumstances of the intended legacy,—of her aunt's death, and of the scenes which had immediately followed her death. It was so odd that William Belton should now be discussing with her the means of evading all her aunt's intentions,—and that he should be doing so, not as her accepted lover. He had, indeed, called himself her brother, but he was in truth her rejected lover.

From time to time during these weeks Mrs. Askerton would ask her whether Mr. Belton was coming to Belton, and Clara would answer her with perfect truth that she did not believe that he had any such intention. " But he must come soon," Mrs. Askerton would say. And when

Clara would answer that she knew nothing about it, Mrs. Askerton would ask further questions about Mary Belton. "Your cousin must know whether her brother is coming to look after the property." But Miss Belton, though she heard constantly from her brother, gave no such intimation. If he had any intention of coming, she did not speak of it. During all these days she had not as yet said a word of her brother's love. Though his name was daily in her mouth, —and latterly, was frequently mentioned by Clara,—there had been no allusion to that still enduring hope of which Will Belton himself could not but speak,—when he had any opportunity of speaking at all. And this continued till at last Clara was driven to suppose that Mary Belton knew nothing of her brother's hopes.

But at last there came a change,—a change which to Clara was as great as that which had affected her when she first found that her delightful cousin was not safe against love-making. She had made up her mind that the sister did not intend to plead for her brother,—that the sister probably knew nothing of the brother's necessity for pleading,—that the brother probably had no further need for pleading! When she remembered his last passionate words, she could not but accuse herself of hypocrisy when she allowed place in her thoughts to this latter supposition. He had been so intently earnest! The nature of the man was so eager and true! But yet, in spite of all that had been said, of all the fire in his eyes, and life in his words, and energy in his actions, he had at last seen that his aspirations were foolish, and his desires vain. It could not otherwise be that she and Mary should pass these hours in such calm repose without an allusion to the disturbing subject! After this fashion, and with such meditations as these, had passed by the last weeks;—and then at last there came the change.

"I have had a letter from William this morning," said Mary.

"And so have not I," said Clara, "and yet I expected to hear from him."

"He means to be here soon," said Mary.

"Oh, indeed!"

"He speaks of being here next week."

For a moment or two Clara had yielded to the agitation

caused by her cousin's tidings; but with a little gush she recovered her presence of mind, and was able to speak with all the hypothetical propriety of a female. " I am glad to hear it," she said. " It is only right that he should come."

" He has asked me to say a word to you,—as to the purport of his journey."

Then again Clara's courage and hypocrisy were so far subdued that they were not able to maintain her in a position adequate to the occasion. " Well," she said laughing, " what is the word?" I hope it is not that I am to pack up, bag and baggage, and take myself elsewhere. Cousin William is one of those persons who are willing to do everything except what they are wanted to do. He will go on talking about the Belton estate, when I want to know whether I may really look for as much as twelve shillings a week to live upon."

" He wants me to speak to you about—about the earnest love he bears for you."

" Oh dear! Mary;—could you not suppose it all to be said? It is an old trouble and need not be repeated."

" No," said Mary, " I cannot suppose it to be all said." Clara looking up as she heard the voice, was astonished both by the fire in the woman's eye and by the force of her tone. " I will not think so meanly of you as to believe that such words from such a man can be passed by as meaning nothing. I will not say that you ought to be able to love him; in that you cannot control your heart; but if you cannot love him, the want of such love ought to make you suffer,—to suffer much and be very sad."

" I cannot agree to that, Mary."

" Is all his life nothing, then? Do you know what love means with him;—this love which he bears to you? Do you understand that it is everything to him?—that from the first moment in which he acknowledged to himself that his heart was set upon you, he could not bring himself to set it upon any other thing for a moment? Perhaps you have never understood this; have never perceived that he is so much in earnest, that to him it is more than money, or land, or health,—more than life itself;—that he so loves that he would willingly give everything that he has for his love? Have you known this?"

" Clara would not answer these questions for a while.

What if she had known it all; was she therefore bound to sacrifice herself? Could it be the duty of any woman to give herself to a man simply because a man wanted her? That was the argument as it was put forward now by Mary Belton.

"Dear, dearest Clara," said Mary Belton, stretching herself forward from her chair, and putting out her thin, almost transparent, hand, "I do not think that you have thought enough of this; or, perhaps, you have not known it. But his love for you is as I say. To him it is everything. It pervades every hour of every day, every corner in his life! He knows nothing of anything else while he is in his present state."

"He is very good;—more than good."

"He is very good."

"But I do not see that;—that——Of course I know how disinterested he is."

"Disinterested is a poor word. It insinuates that in such a matter there could be a question of what people call interest."

"And I know, too, how much he honours me."

"Honour is a cold word. It is not honour, but love,—downright true, honest love. I hope he does honour you. I believe you to be an honest, true woman; and, as he knows you well, he probably does honour you;—but I am speaking of love." Again Clara was silent. She knew what should be her argument if she were determined to oppose her cousin's pleadings: and she knew also,—she thought she knew,—that she did intend to oppose them: but there was a coldness in the argument to which she was averse. "You cannot be insensible to such love as that!" said Mary, going on with the cause which she had in hand.

"You say that he is fond of me."

"Fond of you! I have not used such trifling expressions as that."

"That he loves me."

"You know he loves you. Have you ever doubted a word that he has spoken to you on any subject?"

"I believe he speaks truly."

"You know he speaks truly. He is the very soul of truth."

"But, Mary——"

"Well, Clara! But remember; do not answer me

lightly. Do not play with a man's heart because you have it in your power."

"You wrong me. I could never do like that. You tell me that he loves me;—but what if I do not love him? Love will not be constrained. Am I to say that I love him because I believe that he loves me?"

This was the argument, and Clara found herself driven to use it,—not so much from its special applicability to herself, as on account of its general fitness. Whether it did or did not apply to herself she had not time to ask herself at that moment; but she felt that no man could have a right to claim a woman's hand on the strength of his own love,—unless he had been able to win her love. She was arguing on behalf of women in general rather than on her own behalf.

"If you mean to tell me that you cannot love him, of course I must give over," said Mary, not caring at all for men and women in general, but full of anxiety for her brother. "Do you mean to say that,—that you can never love him?" It almost seemed, from her face, that she was determined utterly to quarrel with her new-found cousin, —to quarrel and to go at once away if she got an answer that would not please her.

"Dear Mary, do not press me so hard."

"But I want to press you hard. It is not right that he should lose his life in longing and hoping."

"He will not lose his life, Mary."

"I hope not;—not if I can help it. I trust that he will be strong enough to get rid of his trouble,—to put it down and trample it under his feet." Clara, as she heard this, began to ask herself what it was that was to be trampled under Will's feet. "I think he will be man enough to overcome his passion; and then, perhaps,—you may regret what you have lost."

"Now you are unkind to me."

"Well; what would you have me say? Do I not know that he is offering you the best gift that he can give? Did I not begin by swearing to you that he loved you with a passion of love that cannot but be flattering to you? If it is to be love in vain, this to him is a great misfortune. And, yet, when I say that I hope that he will recover, you tell me that I am unkind."

" No ;—not for that."

" May I tell him to come and plead for himself ?"

Again Clara was silent, not knowing how to answer that last question. And when she did answer it, she answered it thoughtlessly. " Of course he knows that he can do that."

" He says that he has been forbidden."

" Oh, Mary, what am I to say to you ? You know it all, and I wonder that you can continue to question me in this way."

" Know all what ?"

" That I have been engaged to Captain Aylmer."

" But you are not engaged to him now."

" No—I am not."

" And there can be no renewal there, I suppose ?"

" Oh, no !"

" Not even for my brother would I say a word if I thought——"

" No ;—there is nothing of that ; but——. If you cannot understand, I do not think that I can explain it." It seemed to Clara that her cousin, in her anxiety for her brother, did not conceive that a woman, even if she could suddenly transfer her affection from one man to another, could not bring herself to say that she had done so.

" I must write to him to-day," said Mary, " and I must give him some answer. Shall I tell him that he had better not come here till you are gone ?"

" That will perhaps be best," said Clara.

" Then he will never come at all."

" I can go ;—can go at once. I will go at once. You shall never have to say that my presence prevented his coming to his own house. I ought not to be here. I know it now. I will go away, and you may tell him that I am gone."

" No, dear ; you will not go."

" Yes ;—I must go. I fancied things might be otherwise, because he once told me that—he—would—be—a brother to me. And I said I would hold him to that ;— not only because I want a brother so badly, but because I love him so dearly. But it cannot be like that."

" You do not think that he will ever desert you ?"

" But I will go away, so that he may come to his own house. I ought not to be here. Of course I ought not to be at Belton,—either in this house or in any other. Tell

him that I will be gone before he can come, and tell him
also that I will not be too proud to accept from him what
it may be fit that he should give me. I have no one but
him;—no one but him;—no one but him." Then she
burst into tears, and throwing back her head, covered her
face with her hands.

Miss Belton, upon this, rose slowly from the chair on
which she was sitting, and making her way painfully
across to Clara, stood leaning on the weeping girl's chair.
" You shall not go while I am here," she said.

" Yes; I must go. He cannot come till I am gone."

" Think of it all once again, Clara. May I not tell him
to come, and that while he is coming you will see if you
cannot soften your heart towards him?"

"Soften my heart! Oh, if I could only harden it!"

" He would wait. If you would only bid him wait, he
would be so happy in waiting."

" Yes;—till to-morrow morning. I know him. Hold
out your little finger to him, and he has your whole hand
and arm in a moment."

" I want you to say that you will try to love him."

But Clara was in truth trying not to love him. She was
ashamed of herself because she did love the one man,
when, but a few weeks since, she had confessed that she
loved another. She had mistaken herself and her own
feelings, not in reference to her cousin, but in supposing
that she could really have sympathized with such a man as
Captain Aylmer. It was necessary to her self-respect that
she should be punished because of that mistake. She
could not save herself from this condemnation,—she would
not grant herself a respite,—because, by doing so, she
would make another person happy. Had Captain Aylmer
never crossed her path, she would have given her whole
heart to her cousin. Nay; she had so given it,—had done
so, although Captain Aylmer had crossed her path and
come in her way. But it was matter of shame to her to
find that this had been possible, and she could not bring
herself to confess her shame.

The conversation at last ended, as such conversations
always do end, without any positive decision. Mary wrote
of course to her brother, but Clara was not told of the
contents of the letter. We, however, may know them,

and may understand their nature, without learning above
two lines of the letter. "If you can be content to wait
awhile, you will succeed," said Mary; "but when were
you ever content to wait for anything?" "If there is any
thing I hate, it is waiting," said Will, when he received
the letter; nevertheless the letter made him happy, and
he went about his farm with a sanguine heart, as he
arranged matters for another absence. "Away long?" he
said, in answer to a question asked him by his head man;
"how on earth can I say how long I shall be away? You
can go on well enough without me by this time, I should
think. You will have to learn, for there is no knowing
how often I may be away, or for how long."

When Mary said that the letter had been written,
Clara again spoke about going. "And where will you
go?" said Mary.

"I will take a lodging in Taunton."

"He would only follow you there, and there would be
more trouble. That would be all. He must act as your
guardian, and in that capacity, at any rate, you must
submit to him." Clara, therefore, consented to remain at
Belton; but, before Will arrived, she returned from the
house to the cottage.

"Of course I understand all about it," said Mrs.
Askerton; "and let me tell you this,—that if it is not all
settled within a week from his coming here, I shall think
that you are without a heart. He is to be knocked
about, and cuffed, and kept from his work, and made to
run up and down between here and Norfolk, because
you cannot bring yourself to confess that you have been
a fool."

"I have never said that I have not been a fool," said
Clara.

"You have made a mistake,—as young women will do
sometimes, even when they are as prudent and circumspect
as you are,—and now you don't quite like the task of
putting it right."

It was all true, and Clara knew that it was true. The
putting right of mistakes is never pleasant; and in this
case it was so unpleasant that she could not bring herself
to acknowledge that it must be done. And yet, I think,
that by this time. she was aware of the necessity.

CHAPTER XXXI.

TAKING POSSESSION.

"I want her to have it all," said William Belton, to Mr. Green, the lawyer, when they came to discuss the necessary arrangements for the property.

"But that would be absurd."

"Never mind. It is what I wish. I suppose a man may do what he likes with his own."

"She won't take it," said the lawyer.

"She must take it if you manage the matter properly," said Will.

"I don't suppose it will make much difference," said the lawyer,—"now that Captain Aylmer is out of the running."

"I know nothing about that. Of course I am very glad that he should be out of the running, as you call it. He is a bad sort of fellow, and I didn't want him to have the property. But all that has had nothing to do with it. I'm not doing it because I think she is ever to be my wife."

From this the reader will understand that Belton was still fidgeting himself and the lawyer about the estate when he passed through London. The matter in dispute, however, was so important that he was induced to seek the advice of others besides Mr. Green, and at last was brought to the conclusion that it was his paramount duty to become Belton of Belton. There seemed in the minds of all these councillors to be some imperative and almost imperious requirement that the acres should go back to a man of his name. Now, as there was no one else of the family who could stand in his way, he had no alternative but to become Belton of Belton. He would, however, sell his estate in Norfolk, and raise money for endowing Clara with commensurate riches. Such was his own plan;—but having fallen among councillors, he would not exactly follow his own plan, and at last submitted to an arrangement in accordance with which an annuity of eight hundred pounds a year was to be settled upon Clara, and this was to lie as a charge upon the estate in Norfolk.

"It seems to me to be very shabby," said William Belton.

"It seems to me to be very extravagant," said the leader among the councillors. She is not entitled to sixpence."

But at last the arrangement as above described was the one to which they all assented.

When Belton reached the house which was now his own he found no one there but his sister. Clara was at the cottage. As he had been told that she was to return there, he had no reason to be annoyed. But nevertheless he was annoyed, or rather discontented, and had not been a quarter of an hour about the place before he declared his intention to go and seek her.

"Do no such thing, Will; pray do not," said his sister.

"And why not?"

"Because it will be better that you should wait. You will only injure yourself and her by being impetuous."

"But it is absolutely necessary that she should know her own position. It would be cruelty to keep her in ignorance:—though for the matter of that I shall be ashamed to tell her. Yes;—I shall be ashamed to look her in the face. What will she think of it after I had assured her that she should have the whole?"

"But she would not have taken it, Will. And had she done so, she would have been very wrong. Now she will be comfortable."

"I wish I could be comfortable," said he.

"If you will only wait——"

"I hate waiting. I do not see what good it will do. Besides, I don't mean to say anything about that,—not to-day, at least. I don't indeed. As for being here and not seeing her, that is out of the question. Of course she would think that I had quarrelled with her, and that I meant to take everything to myself, now that I have the power."

"She won't suspect you of wishing to quarrel with her, Will."

"I should in her place. It is out of the question that I should be here, and not go to her. It would be monstrous. I will wait till they have done lunch, and then I will go up."

It was at last decided that he should walk up to the

cottage, call upon Colonel Askerton, and ask to see Clara in the Colonel's presence. It was thought that he could make his statement about the money better before a third person who could be regarded as Clara's friend, than could possibly be done between themselves. He did, therefore, walk across to the cottage, and was shown into Colonel Askerton's study.

"There he is," Mrs. Askerton said, as soon as she heard the sound of the bell. "I knew that he would come at once."

During the whole morning Mrs. Askerton had been insisting that Belton would make his appearance on that very day,—the day of his arrival at Belton, and Clara had been asserting that he would not do so.

"Why should he come?" Clara had said.

"Simply to take you to his own house, like any other of nis goods and chattels."

"I am not his goods or his chattels."

"But you soon will be; and why shouldn't you accept your lot quietly? He is Belton of Belton, and everything here belongs to him."

"I do not belong to him."

"What nonsense! When a man has the command of the situation, as he has, he can do just what he pleases. If he were to come and carry you off by violence, I have no doubt the Beltonians would assist him, and say that he was right. And you of course would forgive him. Belton of Belton may do anything."

"That is nonsense, if you please."

"Indeed if you had any of that decent feeling of feminine inferiority which ought to belong to all women, he would have found you sitting on the door-step of his house waiting for him."

That had been said early in the morning, when they first knew that he had arrived; but they had been talking about him ever since,—talking about him under pressure from Mrs. Askerton, till Clara had been driven to long that she might be spared. "If he chooses to come, he will come," she said. "Of course he will come," Mrs. Askerton had answered, and then they heard the ring of the bell. "There he is. I could swear to the sound of his foot. Doesn't he step as though he were Belton of Belton, and conscious that

everything belonged to him?" Then there was a pause.
" He has been shown in to Colonel Askerton. What on
)arth could he want with him?"

" He has called to tell him something about the cottage,"
said Clara, endeavouring to speak as though she were calm
through it all.

"Cottage! Fiddlestick! The idea of a man coming to
look after his trumpery cottage on the first day of his
showing himself as lord of his own property! Perhaps he
is demanding that you shall be delivered up to him. If he
does, I shall vote for obeying."

"And I for disobeying,—and shall vote very strongly, too."

Their suspense was yet prolonged for another ten
minutes, and at the end of that time the servant came in
and asked if Miss Amedroz would be good enough to go
into the master's room. "Mr. Belton is there, Fanny?"
asked Mrs. Askerton. The girl confessed that Mr. Belton
was there, and then Clara, without another word, got up
and left the room. She had much to do in assuming a look
of composure before she opened the door; but she made the
effort, and was not unsuccessful. In another second she
found her hand in her cousin's, and his bright eye was
fixed upon her with that eager, friendly glance which
made his face so pleasant to those whom he loved.

" Your cousin has been telling me of the arrangements
he has been making for you with the lawyers," said Colonel
Askerton. "I can only say that I wish all ladies had
cousins so liberal, and so able to be liberal."

"I thought I would see Colonel Askerton first, as you
are staying at his house. And as for liberality,—there is
nothing of the kind. You must understand, Clara, that a
fellow can't do what he likes with his own in this country.
I have found myself so bullied by lawyers and that sort of
people, that I have been obliged to yield to them. I
wanted that you should have the old place, to do just what
you pleased with it."

" That was out of the question, Will."

" Of course it was," said Colonel Askerton. Then, as
Belton himself did not proceed to the telling of his own
story, the Colonel told it for him, and explained what was
the income which Clara was to receive.

" But that is as much out of the question," said she, " as

the other. I cannot rob you in that way. I cannot and I shall not. And why should I? What do I want with such an income? Something I ought to have, if only for the credit of the family, and that I am willing to take from your kindness; but——"

"It's all settled now, Clara."

"I don't think that you can lessen the weight of your obligation, Miss Amedroz, after what has been done up in London," said the Colonel.

"If you had said a hundred a year——"

"I have been allowed to say nothing," said Belton; "those people have said eight,—and so it is settled. When are you coming over to see Mary?"

To this question he got no definite answer, and as he went away immediately afterwards he hardly seemed to expect one. He did not even ask for Mrs. Askerton, and, as that lady remarked, behaved altogether like a bear. "But what a munificent bear!" she said. "Fancy;—eight hundred a year of your own. One begins to doubt whether it is worth one's while to marry at all with such an income as that to do what one likes with! However, it all means nothing. It will all be his own again before you have even touched it."

"You must not say anything more about that," said Clara gravely.

"And why must I not?"

"Because I shall hear nothing more of it. There is an end of all that,—as there ought to be."

"Why an end? I don't see an end. There will be no end till Belton of Belton has got you and your eight hundred a year as well as everything else."

"You will find that—he—does not mean—anything— more," said Clara.

"You think not?"

"I am—sure of it." Then there was a little sound in her throat as though she were in some danger of being choked; but she soon recovered herself, and was able to express herself clearly. "I have only one favour to ask you now, Mrs. Askerton, and that is that you will never say anything more about him. He has changed his mind. Of course he has, or he would not come here like that and have gone away without saying a word."

" Not a word ! A man gives you eight hundred a year, and that is not saying a word !"

" Not a word except about money ! But of course he is right. I know that he is right. After what has passed he would be very wrong to—to—think about it any more. You joke about his being Belton of Belton. But it does make a difference."

" It does ;—does it ?"

" It has made a difference. I see and feel it now. I shall never—hear him—ask me—that question—any more."

" And if you did hear him, what answer would you make him ?"

" I don't know."

" That is just it. Women are so cross-grained that it is a wonder to me that men should ever have anything to do with them. They have about them some madness of a phantasy which they dignify with the name of feminine pride, and under the cloak of this they believe themselves to be justified in tormenting their lovers' lives out. The only consolation is that they torment themselves as much. Can anything be more cross-grained than you are at this moment? You were resolved just now that it would be the most unbecoming thing in the world if he spoke a word more about his love for the next twelvemonths——"

"Mrs. Askerton, I said nothing about twelvemonths."

" And now you are broken-hearted because he did not blurt it all out before Colonel Askerton in a business interview, which was very properly had at once, and in which he has had the exceeding good taste to confine himself altogether to the one subject."

" I am not complaining."

" It was good taste ; though if he had not been a bear he might have asked after me, who are fighting his battles for him night and day."

" But what will he do next ?"

" Eat his dinner, I should think, as it is now nearly five o'clock. Your father used always to dine at five."

"I can't go to see Mary," she said, "till he comes here again."

" He will be here fast enough, I shouldn't wonder if he was to come again to-night." And he did come again that night.

When Belton's interview was over in the Colonel's study he left the house,—without even asking after the mistress, as that mistress had taken care to find out,—and went off, rambling about the estate which was now his own. It was a beautiful place, and he was not insensible to the gratification of being its owner. There is much in the glory of ownership,—of the ownership of land and houses, of beeves and woolly flocks, of wide fields and thick-growing woods, even when that ownership is of late date, when it conveys to the owner nothing but the realisation of a property on the soil; but there is much more in it when it contains the memories of old years; when the glory is the glory of race as well as the glory of power and property. There had been Beltons of Belton living there for many centuries, and now he was the Belton of the day standing on his own ground,—the descendant and representative of the Beltons of old,—Belton of Belton without a flaw in his pedigree! He felt himself to be proud of his position,—prouder than he could have been of any other that might have been vouchsafed to him. And yet amidst it all he was somewhat ashamed of his pride. "The man who can do it for himself is the real man after all," he said.

"But I have got it by a fluke,—and by such a sad chance too!" Then he wandered on, thinking of the circumstances under which the property had fallen into his hands, and remembering how and when and where the first idea had occurred to him of making Clara Amedroz his wife. He had then felt that if he could only do that he could reconcile himself to the heirship. And the idea had grown upon him instantly, and had become a passion by the eagerness with which he had welcomed it. From that day to this he had continued to tell himself that he could not enjoy his good fortune unless he could enjoy it with her. There had come to be a horrid impediment in his way,—a barrier which had seemed to have been placed there by his evil fortune, to compensate the gifts given to him by his good fortune, and that barrier had been Captain Aylmer. He had not, in fact, seen much of his rival, but he had seen enough to make it matter of wonder to him that Clara could be attached to such a man. He had thoroughly despised Captain Aylmer, and had longed to show his contempt of the man by kicking him out of the hotel at the London railway station. At that moment all the world had seemed to him to be wrong and wretched.

But now it seemed that all the world might so easily be made right again! The impediment had got itself removed. Belton did not even yet altogether comprehend by what means Clara had escaped from the meshes of the Aylmer Park people, but he did know that she had escaped. Her eyes had been opened before it was too late, and she was a free woman,—to be compassed if only a man might compass her. While she had been engaged to Captain **Aylmer** Will had felt that she was not assailable. Though he had not been quite able to restrain himself,— as on that fatal occasion when he had taken her in his arms and kissed her,—still he had known that as she was an engaged woman, he could not, without insulting her, press his own suit upon her. But now all that was over. Let him say what he liked on that head, she would have no proper plea for anger. She was assailable;—and, as this was so why the mischief should he not set about the work at once? His sister bade him to wait. Why should he wait when one fortunate word might do it? Wait! He could not wait. How are you to bid a starving man to wait when you put him down at a well-covered board? Here was he, walking about Belton Park,—just where she used to walk with him;—and there was she at Belton Cottage, within half an hour of him at this moment, if he were to go quickly; and yet Mary was telling him to wait! No; he would not wait. There could be no reason for waiting. Wait, indeed, till some other Captain Aylmer should come in the way and give him more trouble!

So he wandered on, resolving that he would see his cousin again that very day. Such an interview as that which had just taken place between two such dear friends was not natural,—was not to be endured. What might not Clara think of it! To meet her for the first time after her escape from Aylmer Park, and to speak to her only on matters concerning money! He would certainly go to her again on that afternoon. In his walking he came to the bottom of the rising ground on the top of which stood the rock on which he and Clara had twice sat. But he turned away, and would not go up to it. He hoped that he might go up to it very soon,—but, except under certain circumstances, he would never go up to it again.

"I am going across to the cottage immediately after dinner," he said to his sister.

"Have you an appointment?"

"No; I have no appointment. I suppose a man doesn't want an appointment to go and see his own cousin down in the country."

"I don't know what their habits are."

"I shan't ask to go in; but I want to see her."

Mary looked at him with loving, sorrowing eyes, but she said no more. She loved him so well that she would have given her right hand to get for him what he wanted;—but she sorrowed to think that he should want such a thing so sorely. Immediately after his dinner, he took his hat and went out without saying a word further, and made his way once more across to the gate of the cottage. It was a lovely summer evening, at that period of the year in which our summer evenings just begin, when the air is sweeter and the flowers more fragrant, and the forms of the foliage more lovely than at any other time. It was now eight o'clock, but it was hardly as yet evening; none at least of the gloom of evening had come, though the sun was low in the heavens. At the cottage they were all sitting out on the lawn; and as Belton came near he was seen by them, and he saw them.

"I told you so," said Mrs. Askerton, to Clara, in a whisper.

"He is not coming in," Clara answered. "He is going on."

But when he had come nearer, Colonel Askerton called to him over the garden paling, and asked him to join them. He was now standing within ten or fifteen yards of them, though the fence divided them. "I have come to ask my cousin Clara to take a walk with me," he said. "She can be back by your tea time." He made his request very placidly, and did not in any way look like a lover.

"I am sure she will be glad to go," said Mrs. Askerton. But Clara said nothing.

"Do take a turn with me, if you are not tired," said he.

"She has not been out all day, and cannot be tired," said Mrs. Askerton, who had now walked up to the paling

" Clara, get your hat. But, Mr. Belton, what have I done
that I am to be treated in this way ? Perhaps you don't
remember that you have not spoken to me since your
arrival."

" Upon my word, I beg your pardon," said he, endeavouring to stretch his hand across the bushes. " 1
forgot I didn't see you this morning."

" I suppose I mustn't be angry, as this is your day of
taking possession; but it is exactly on such days as this
that one likes to be remembered."

" I didn't mean to forget you, Mrs. Askerton : I didn't,
indeed. And as for the special day, that's all bosh, you
know. I haven't taken particular possession of anything
that I know of."

" I hope you will, Mr. Belton, before the day is over,"
said she. Clara had at length arisen, and had gone into
the house to fetch her hat. She had not spoken a word,
and even yet her cousin did not know whether she was
coming. " I hope you will take possession of a great deal
that is very valuable. Clara has gone to get her hat."

" Do you think she means to walk ?"

" I think she does, Mr. Belton. And there she is at the
door. Mind you bring her back to tea."

Clara, as she came forth, felt herself quite unable to
speak, or walk, or look, after her usual manner. She knew
herself to be a victim,—to be so far a victim that she could
no longer control her own fate. To Captain Aylmer, at
any rate, she had never succumbed. In all her dealings
with him she had fought upon an equal footing. She had
never been compelled to own herself mastered. But now
she was being led out that she might confess her own
submission, and acknowledge that hitherto she had not
known what was good for her. She knew that she would
have to yield. She must have known how happy she was
to have an opportunity of yielding; but yet,—yet, had
there been any room for choice, she thought she would
have refrained from walking with her cousin that evening.
She had wept that afternoon because she had thought that
he would not come again ; and now that he had come at
the first moment that was possible for him, she was almost
tempted to wish him once more away.

" I suppose you understand that when I came up this

morning I came merely to talk about business," said Belton, as soon as they were off together.

"It was very good of you to come at all so soon after your arrival."

"I told those people in London that I would have it all settled at once, and so I wanted to have it off my mind."

"I don't know what I ought to say to you. Of course I shall not want so much money as that."

"We won't talk about the money any more to-day. I hate talking about money."

"It is not the pleasantest subject in the world."

"No," said he; "no indeed. I hate it,—particularly between friends. So you have come to grief with your friends, the Aylmers?"

"I hope I haven't come to grief,—and the Aylmers, as a family, never were my friends. I'm obliged to contradict you, point by point,—you see."

"I don't like Captain Aylmer at all," said Will, after a pause.

"So I saw, Will; and I dare say he was not very fond of you."

"Fond of me! I didn't want him to be fond of me. I don't suppose he ever thought much about me. I could not help thinking of him."—She had nothing to say to this, and therefore walked on silently by his side. "I suppose he has not any idea of coming back here again?"

"What; to Belton? No, I do not think he will come to Belton any more."

"Nor will you go to Aylmer Park?"

"No; certainly not. Of all the places on earth, Will, to which you would send me, Aylmer Park is the one to which I should go most unwillingly."

"I don't want to send you there."

"You never could be made to understand what a woman she is; how disagreeable, how cruel, how imperious, how insolent."

"Was she so bad as all that?"

"Indeed she was, Will. I can't but tell the truth to you."

"And he was nearly as bad as she."

"No, Will; no; do not say that of him."

"He was such a quarrelsome fellow. He flew at me just because I said we had good hunting down in Norfolk."

"We need not talk about all that, Will."

"No;—of course not. It's all passed and gone, I suppose."

"Yes;—it is all passed and gone. You did not know my Aunt Winterfield, or you would understand my first reason for liking him."

"No," said Will; "I never saw her."

Then they walked on together for a while without speaking, and Clara was beginning to feel some relief,—some relief at first; but as the relief came, there came back to her the dead, dull, feeling of heaviness at her heart which had oppressed her after his visit in the morning. She had been right, and Mrs. Askerton had been wrong. He had returned to her simply as her cousin, and now he was walking with her and talking to her in this strain, to teach her that it was so. But of a sudden they came to a place where two paths diverged, and he turned upon her and asked her quickly which path they should take. "Look, Clara," he said, "will you go up there with me?" It did not need that she should look, as she knew that the way indicated by him led up among the rocks.

"I don't much care which way," she said, faintly.

"Do you not? But I do. I care very much. Don't you remember where that path goes?" She had no answer to give to this. She remembered well, and remembered how he had protested that he would never go to the place again unless he could go there as her accepted lover. And she nad asked herself sundry questions as to that protestation. Could it be that for her sake he would abstain from visiting the prettiest spot on his estate,—that he would continue to regard the ground as hallowed because of his memories of her? "Which way shall we go?" he asked.

"I suppose it does not much signify," said she, trembling.

"But it does signify. It signifies very much to me. Will you go up to the rocks?"

"I am afraid we shall be late, if we stay out long."

"What matters how late? Will you come?"

"I suppose so,—if you wish it, Will."

She had anticipated that the high rock was to be the at which the victim was to be sacrificed; but now he would not wait till he had taken her to the sacred spot. He had of course intended that he would there renew his offer; but he had perceived that his offer had been renewed, and had, in fact, been accepted, during this little parley as to the pathway. There was hardly any necessity for further words. So he must have thought; for, as quick as lightning, he flung his arms around her, and kissed her again, as he had kissed her on that other terrible occasion, —that occasion on which he had felt that he might hardly hope for pardon.

"William, William," she said; "how can you serve me like that?" But he had a full understanding as to his own privileges, and was well aware that he was in his right now, as he had been before that he was trespassing egregiously. "Why are you so rough with me?" she said.

"Clara, say that you love me."

"I will say nothing to you because you are so rough."

They were now walking up slowly towards the rocks. And as he had his arm round her waist, he was contented for awhile to allow her to walk without speaking. But when they were on the summit it was necessary for him that he should have a word from her of positive assurance. "Clara, say that you love me."

"Have I not always loved you, Will, since almost the first moment that I saw you?"

"But that won't do. You know that is not fair. Come, Clara; I've had a deal of trouble,—and grief too; haven't I? You should say a word to make up for it;—that is, if you can say it."

"What can a word like that signify to you to-day? You have got everything."

"Have I got you?" Still she paused. "I will have an answer. Have I got you? Are you now my own?"

"I suppose so, Will. Don't now. I will not have it again. Does not that satisfy you?"

"Tell me that you love me."

"You know that I love you."

"Better than anybody in the world?"

"Yes;—better than anybody in the world."

"And after all you will be—my wife?"

"Oh, Will,—how you question one!"

"You shall say it, and then it will all be fair and honest.'

" Say what? I'm sure I thought I had said everything."

" Say that you mean to be my wife."

" I suppose so,—if you wish it."

" Wish it!" said he, getting up from his seat, and throwing his hat into the bushes on one side; "wish it! I don't think you have ever understood how I have wished it. Look here, Clara; I found when I got down to Norfolk that I couldn't live without you. Upon my word it is true. I don't suppose you'll believe me."

" I didn't think it could be so bad with you as that."

" No;—I don't suppose women ever do believe. And I wouldn't have believed it of myself. I hated myself for it. By George, I did. That is when I began to think it was all up with me."

" All up with you! Oh, Will!"

" I had quite made up my mind to go to New Zealand. I had, indeed. I couldn't have kept my hands off that man if we had been living in the same country. I should have wrung his neck."

" Will, how can you talk so wickedly?"

" There's no understanding it till you have felt it. But never mind. It's all right now; isn't it, Clara?"

" If you think so."

" Think so! Oh, Clara. I am such a happy fellow. Do give me a kiss. You have never given me one kiss yet."

" What nonsense! I didn't think you were such a baby."

" By George, but you shall;—or you shall never get home to tea to-night. My own, own, own darling! Upon my word, Clara, when I begin to think about it I shall be half mad."

" I think you are quite that already."

" No, I'm not;—but I shall be when I'm alone. What can I say to you, Clara, to make you understand how much I love you? You remember the song, 'For Bonnie Annie Laurie, I'd lay me down and dee.' Of course it is all nonsense talking of dying for a woman. What a man has to do is to live for her. But that is my feeling. I'm ready to give you my life. If there was anything to do for you, I'd do it if I could, whatever it was. Do you understand me?"

" Dear Will! Dearest Will!"

"Am I dearest?"

"Are you not sure of it?"

"But I like you to tell me so. I like to feel that you are not ashamed to own it. You ought to say it a few times to me, as I have said it so very often to you."

"You'll hear enough of it before you've done with me."

"I shall never have heard enough of it. Oh, heavens, only think, when I was coming down in the train last night I was in such a bad way."

"And are you in a good way now?"

"Yes; in a very good way. I shall crow over Mary so when I get home."

"And what has poor Mary done?"

"Never mind."

"I dare say she knows what is good for you better than you know yourself. I suppose she has told you that you might do a great deal better than trouble yourself with a wife."

"Never mind what she has told me. It is settled now; —is it not?"

"I hope so, Will."

But not quite settled as yet. When shall it be? That is the next question."

But to that question Clara positively refused to make any reply that her lover would consider to be satisfactory. He continued to press her till she was at last driven to remind him how very short a time it was since her father had been among them; and then he was very angry with himself, and declared himself to be a brute. "Anything but that," she said. "You are the kindest and the best of men;—but at the same time the most impatient."

"That's what Mary says; but what's the good of waiting? She wanted me to wait to-day."

"And as you would not, you have fallen into a trap out of which you can never escape. But pray let us go. What will they think of us?"

"I shouldn't wonder if they didn't think something near the truth."

"Whatever they think, we will go back. It is ever so much past nine."

"Before you stir, Clara, tell me one thing. Are you really happy?"

" Very happy."

" And are you glad that this has been done ?".

·" Very glad. Will that satisfy you ?"

" And you do love me ?"

" I do—I do—I do. Can I say more than that ?"

" More than anybody else in the world ?"

" Better than all the world put together."

" Then," said he, holding her tight in his arms, " show me that you love me." And as he made his request he was quick to explain to her what, according to his ideas, was the becoming mode by which lovers might show their love. I wonder whether it ever occurred to Clara, as she thought of it all before she went to bed that night, that Captain Aylmer and William Belton were very different in their manners. And if so, I must wonder further whether she most approved the manners of the patient man or the man who was impatient.

CHAPTER XXXII.

CONCLUSION.

ABOUT two months after the scene described in the last chapter, when the full summer had arrived, Clara received two letters from the two lovers, the history of whose loves have just been told, and these shall be submitted to the reader, as they will serve to explain the manner in which the two men proposed to arrange their affairs. We will first have Captain Aylmer's letter, which was the first read ; Clara kept the latter for the last, as children always keep their sweetest morsels.

" Aylmer Park, August, 186—.

" MY DEAR MISS AMEDROZ,

" I heard before leaving London that you are engaged to marry your cousin Mr. William Belton, and I think that perhaps you may be satisfied to have a line from me to let you know that I quite approve of the marriage." I do not care very much for his approval or disapproval, said Clara as she read this. " No doubt it will be the best thing you can do, especially as it will heal all the sores arising from the entail." " There never was any sore," said Clara. " Pray give my compliments to Mr. Belton, and offer him my congratulations, and tell him that I wish him all happiness in the married state." " Married fiddlestick!" said Clara. In this she was un·reasonable; but the euphonious platitudes of Captain Aylmer were so unlike the vehement protestations of Mr. Belton that she must be excused if by this time she had come to entertain something of an unreasonable aversion for the former.

" I hope you will not receive my news with perfect indifference when I tell you that I also am going to be married. The lady is one whom I have known for a long time, and have always esteemed very highly. She is Lady Emily Tagmaggert, the youngest daughter of the Earl of Mull." Why Clara should immediately have conceived a feeling of supreme contempt for Lady Emily Tagmaggert, and assured herself that her ladyship was a thin, dry, cross old maid with a red nose, I cannot explain; but I do know that such were her thoughts, almost instantaneously, in reference to Captain Aylmer's future bride. " Lady Emily is a very intimate friend of my sister's; and you, who know how our family cling together, will feel how thankful I must be when I tell you that my mother quite approves of the engagement. I suppose we shall be married early in the spring. We shall probably spend some months every year at Perivale, and I hope that we may look forward to the pleasure of seeing you sometimes as a guest beneath our roof." On reading this Clara shuddered, and made some inward protestation which seemed to imply that she had no wish whatever to revisit the dull streets of the little town with which she had been so well acquainted. " I hope she'll be good to poor Mr. Possitt," said Clara, " and give him port wine on Sundays."

" I have one more thing that I ought to say. You will remember that I intended to pay my aunt's legacy immediately after her death, but that I was prevented by circumstances which I could not control. I have paid it now into Mr. Green's hands on your account, together with the sum of £59 18s. 3d., which is due upon it as interest at the rate of five per cent. I hope that this may be satisfactory." "It is not satisfactory at all," said Clara, putting down the letter, and resolving that Will Belton should be instructed to repay the money instantly. It may, however, be explained here that in this matter Clara was doomed to be disappointed; and that she was forced, by Mr. Green's arguments, to receive the money. "Then it shall go to the hospital at Perivale," she declared when those arguments were used. As to that, Mr. Green was quite indifferent, but I do not think that the legacy which troubled poor Aunt Winterfield so much on her dying bed was ultimately applied to so worthy a purpose.

"And now, my dear Miss Amedroz," continued the letter, "I will say farewell, with many assurances of my unaltered esteem, and with heartfelt wishes for your future happiness. Believe me to be always,

"Most faithfully and sincerely yours,

"FREDERIC F. AYLMER."

"Esteem!" said Clara, as she finished the letter. "I wonder which he esteems the most, me or Lady Emily Tagmaggert. He will never get beyond esteem with any one."

The letter which was last read was as follows:—

"Plaistow, August, 186—.

"DEAREST CLARA,

"I don't think I shall ever get done, and I am coming to hate farming. It is awful lonely here, too; and I pass all my evenings by myself, wondering why I should be doomed to this kind of thing, while you and Mary are comfortable together at Belton. We have begun with the wheat, and as soon as that is safe I shall cut and run. I shall leave the barley to Bunce. Bunce knows as much about it as I do,—and as for remaining here all the summer, it's out of the question.

"My own dear, darling love, of course I don't intend to urge you to do anything that you don't like; but upon my honour I don't see the force of what you say. You know I have as much respect for your father's memory as anybody, but what harm can it do to him that we should be married at once? Don't you think he would have wished **it** himself? It can be ever so quiet. So long as it's done, I don't care a straw how it's done. Indeed for the matter of that I always think it would be best just to walk to church and to walk home again without saying anything to anybody. I hate fuss and nonsense, and really I don't think anybody would have a right to say anything if we were to do it at once in that sort of way. I have had a bad time of it for the last twelvemonths. You must allow that, and I think that I ought to be rewarded.

"As for living, you shall have your choice. Indeed you shall live anywhere you please;—at Timbuctoo if you like it. I don't want to give up Plaistow, because my father and grandfather farmed the land themselves; but I am quite prepared not to live here. I don't think it would suit you, because it has so much of the farm-house about it. Only I should like you sometimes to come and look at the old place. What I should like would be to pull down the house at Belton and build another. But you mustn't propose to put it off till that's done, as I should never have the heart to do it. If you think that would suit you, I'll make up my mind to live at Belton for a constancy; and then I'd go in for a lot of cattle, and don't doubt I'd make a fortune. I'm almost sick of looking at the straight ridges in the big square fields every day of my life.

"Give my love to Mary. I hope she fights my battle for me. Pray think of all this, and relent if you can. I do so long to have an end of this purgatory. If there was any use, I wouldn't say a word; but there's no good in being tortured, when there is no use. God bless you, dearest love. I do love you so well!

"Yours most affectionately,
"W. Belton."

She kissed the letter twice, pressed it to her bosom, and then sat silent for half an hour thinking of it;—of it, and the man who wrote it, and of the man who had written the other letter. She could not but remember how that other man had thought to treat her, when it was his intention and her intention that they two should join their lots together;—how cold he had been; how full of caution and counsel; how he had preached to her himself and threatened her with the preaching of his mother; how manifestly he had purposed to make her life a sacrifice to his life; how he had premeditated her incarceration at Perivale, while he should be living a bachelor's life in London! Will Belton's ideas of married life were very different. Only come to me at once,—now, immediately, and everything else shall be disposed just as you please. This was his offer. What he proposed to give,—or rather his willingness to be thus generous, was very sweet to her; but it was not half so sweet as his impatience in demanding his reward. How she doted on him because he considered his present state to be a purgatory! How could she refuse anything she could give to one who desired her gifts so strongly?

As for her future residence, it would be a matter of indifference to her where she should live, so long as she might live with him; but for him,—she felt that but one spot in the world was fit for him. He was Belton of Belton, and it would not be becoming that he should live elsewhere, Of course she would go with him to Plaistow Hall as often as he might wish it; but Belton Castle should be his permanent resting-place. It would be her duty to be proud for him, and therefore, for his sake, she would beg that their home might be in Somersetshire.

"Mary," she said to her cousin soon afterwards, "Will sends his love to you."

"And what else does he say?"

"I couldn't tell you everything. You shouldn't expect it."

"I don't expect it; but perhaps there may be something to be told."

"Nothing that I need tell,—specially. You, who know him so well, can imagine what he would say."

"Dear Will! I am sure he would mean to write what was pleasant."

Then the matter would have dropped had Clara been so minded,—but she, in truth, was anxious to be forced to talk about the letter. She wished to be urged by Mary to do that which Will urged her to do;—or, at least, to learn whether Mary thought that her brother's wish might be gratified without impropriety. "Don't you think we ought to live here?" she said.

"By all means,—if you both like it."

"He is so good,—so unselfish, that he will only ask me to do what I like best."

"And which would you like best?"

"I think he ought to live here because it is the old family property. I confess that the name goes for something with me. He says that he would build a new house."

"Does he think he could have it ready by the time you are married?"

"Ah;—that is just the difficulty. Perhaps, after all, you had better read his letter. I don't know why I should not show it to you. It will only tell you what you know already,—that he is the most generous fellow in all the world." Then Mary read the letter. "What am I to say to him?" Clara asked. "It seems so hard to refuse anything to one who is so true, and good, and generous."

"It is hard."

"But you see my poor dear father's death has been so recent."

"I hardly know," said Mary, "how the world feels about such things."

"I think we ought to wait at least twelve months," said Clara, very sadly.

"Poor Will! He will be broken-hearted a dozen times before that. But then, when his happiness does come, he will be all the happier." Clara, when she heard this, almost hated her cousin Mary,—not for her own sake, but on Will's account. Will trusted so implicitly to his sister, and yet she could not make a better fight for him than this! It almost seemed that Mary was indifferent to her brother's happiness. Had Will been her brother, Clara thought, and had any girl asked her advice under similar circumstances, she was sure that she would have answered in a different way. She would have told such girl that her first duty was owing to the man who was to be her husband, and would not have said a word to her about the feeling of the world. After all, what did the feeling of the world signify to them, who were going to be all the world to each other?

On that afternoon she went up to Mrs. Askerton's; and succeeded in getting advice from her also, though she did not show Will's letter to that lady. "Of course, I know what he says," said Mrs. Askerton. "Unless I have mistaken the man, he wants to be married to-morrow."

" He is not so bad as that," said Clara.

" Then the next day, or the day after. Of course he is impatient, and does not see any earthly reason why his impatience should not be gratified."

" He is impatient."

" And I suppose you hesitate because of your father's death."

" It seems but the other day ;—does it not ?" said Clara.

" Everything seems but the other day to me. It was but the other day that I myself was married."

" And, of course, though I would do anything I could that he would ask me to do——"

" But would you do anything ?"

" Anything that was not wrong I would. Why should I not, when he is so good to me ?"

" Then write to him, my dear, and tell him that it shall be as he wishes it. Believe me, the days of Jacob are over. Men don't understand waiting now, and it's always as well to catch your fish when you can."

" You don't suppose I have any thought of that kind ?"

" I am sure you have not ;—and I'm sure that he deserves no such thought ;—but the higher that are his deserts, the greater should be his reward. If I were you, I should think of nothing but him, and I should do exactly as he would have me." Clara kissed her friend as she parted from her, and again resolved that all that woman's sins should be forgiven her. A woman who could give such excellent advice deserved that every sin should be forgiven her. " They'll be married yet before the summer is over," Mrs. Askerton said to her husband that afternoon. " I believe a man may have anything he chooses to ask for, if he'll only ask hard enough."

And they were married in the autumn, if not actually in the summer. With what precise words Clara answered her lover's letter I will not say ; but her answer was of such a nature that he found himself compelled to leave Plaistow, even before the wheat was garnered. Great confidence was placed in Bunce on that occasion, and I have reason to believe that it was not misplaced. They were married in September ;—yes, in September, although that letter of Will's was written in August, and by the beginning of October they had returned from their wedding trip to Plaistow. Clara insisted that she should be taken to Plaistow, and was very anxious when there to learn all the particulars of the farm. She put down in a little book how many acres there were in each field, and what was the average produce of the land. She made inquiry about four-crop rotation, and endeavoured, with Bunce, to go into the great subject of stall-feeding. But Belton did not give her as much encouragement as he might have done. "We'll come here for the shooting next year," he said; "that is, if there is nothing to prevent us."

"I hope there'll be nothing to prevent us."

"There might be, perhaps; but we'll always come if there is not. For the rest of it, I'll leave it to Bunce, and just run over once or twice in the year. It would not be a nice place for you to live at long."

"I like it of all things. I am quite interested about the farm."

"You'd get very sick of it if you were here in the winter. The truth is that if you farm well, you must farm ugly. The picturesque nooks and corners have all to be turned inside out, and the hedgerows must be abolished, because we want the sunshine. Now, down at Belton, just about the house, we won't mind farming well, but will stick to the picturesque."

The new house was immediately commenced at Belton, and was made to proceed with all imaginable alacrity. It was supposed at one time,—at least Belton himself said that he so supposed,—that the building would be ready for occupation at the end of the first summer; but this was not found to be possible. "We must put it off till May, after all," said Belton, as he was walking round the unfinished building with Colonel Askerton. "It's an awful bore, but there's no getting people really to pull out in this country."

"I think they've pulled out pretty well. Of course you couldn't have gone into a damp house for the winter."

"Other people can get a house built within twelve months. Look what they do in London."

"And other people with their wives and children die in consequence of colds and sore throats and other evils of that nature. I wouldn't go into a new house, I know, till I was quite sure it was dry."

As Will at this time was hardly ten months married, he was not as yet justified in thinking about his own wife and children; but he had already found it expedient to make arrangements for the autumn, which would prevent that annual visit to Plaistow which Clara had contemplated, and which he had regarded with his characteristic prudence as being subject to possible impediments. He was to be absent himself for the first week in September, but was to return immediately after that. This he did; and before the end of that month he was justified in talking of his wife and family. " I suppose it wouldn't have done to have been moving now,—under all the circumstances," he said to his friend, Mrs. Askerton, as he still grumbled about the unfinished house.

" I don't think it would have done at all, under all the circumstances," said Mrs. Askerton.

But in the following spring or early summer they did get into the new house; and a very nice house it was, as will, I think, be believed by those who have known Mr. William Belton. And when they were well settled, at which time little Will Belton was some seven or eight months old,—little Will, for whom great bonfires had been lit, as though his birth in those parts was a matter not to be regarded lightly; for was he not the first Belton of Belton who had been born there for more than a century? —when that time came visitors appeared at the new Belton Castle, visitors of importance, who were entitled to, and who received, great consideration. These were no less than Captain Aylmer, member for Perivale, and his newly-married bride, Lady Emily Aylmer, *née* Tagmaggert. They were then just married, and had come down to Belton Castle immediately after their honeymoon trip. How it had come to pass that such friendship had sprung up,—or rather how it had been revived,—it would be bootless here to say. But old alliances, such as that which had existed between the Aylmer and the Amedroz family, do not allow themselves to die out easily, and it is well for us all that they should be long-lived. So Captain Aylmer brought his bride to Belton Park, and a small fatted calf was killed, and the Askertons came to dinner,—on which occasion Captain Aylmer behaved very well, though we may imagine that he must have had some misgivings on the score of his young wife. The Askertons came to dinner, and the old rector, and the squire from a neighbouring parish; and everything was very handsome and very dull. Captain Aylmer was much pleased with his visit, and declared to Lady Emily that marriage had greatly improved Mr. William Belton. Now Will had been very dull the whole evening, and very unlike the fiery, violent, unreasonable man whom Captain Aylmer remembered to have met at the station hotel of the Great Northern Railway.

"I was as sure of it as possible," Clara said to her husband that night.

"Sure of what, my dear?"

"That she would have a red nose."

"Who has got a red nose?"

"Don't be stupid, Will. Who should have it but Lady Emily?"

"Upon my word I didn't observe it."

"You never observe anything, Will; do you? But don't you think she is very plain?"

"Upon my word I don't know. She isn't as handsome as some people."

"Don't be a fool, Will. How old do you suppose her to be?"

"How old? Let me see. Thirty, perhaps."

"If she's not over forty, I'll consent to change noses with her."

"No;—we won't do that; not if I know it."

"I cannot conceive why any man should marry such a woman as that. Not but what she's a very good woman, I dare say; only what can a man get by it? To be sure there's the title, if that's worth anything."

But Will Belton was never good for much conversation at this hour, and was too fast asleep to make any rejoinder to the last remark.

THE END.

A CATALOGUE OF
SELECTED DOVER BOOKS
IN ALL FIELDS OF INTEREST

A CATALOGUE OF SELECTED DOVER
BOOKS IN ALL FIELDS OF INTEREST

RACKHAM'S COLOR ILLUSTRATIONS FOR WAGNER'S RING. Rackham's finest mature work—all 64 full-color watercolors in a faithful and lush interpretation of the *Ring*. Full-sized plates on coated stock of the paintings used by opera companies for authentic staging of Wagner. Captions aid in following complete Ring cycle. Introduction. 64 illustrations plus vignettes. 72pp. 8⅝ x 11¼. 23779-6 Pa. $6.00

CONTEMPORARY POLISH POSTERS IN FULL COLOR, edited by Joseph Czestochowski. 46 full-color examples of brilliant school of Polish graphic design, selected from world's first museum (near Warsaw) dedicated to poster art. Posters on circuses, films, plays, concerts all show cosmopolitan influences, free imagination. Introduction. 48pp. 9⅜ x 12¼. 23780-X Pa. $6.00

GRAPHIC WORKS OF EDVARD MUNCH, Edvard Munch. 90 haunting, evocative prints by first major Expressionist artist and one of the greatest graphic artists of his time: *The Scream, Anxiety, Death Chamber, The Kiss, Madonna*, etc. Introduction by Alfred Werner. 90pp. 9 x 12. 23765-6 Pa. $5.00

THE GOLDEN AGE OF THE POSTER, Hayward and Blanche Cirker. 70 extraordinary posters in full colors, from Maitres de l'Affiche, Mucha, Lautrec, Bradley, Cheret, Beardsley, many others. Total of 78pp. 9⅜ x 12¼. 22753-7 Pa. $5.95

THE NOTEBOOKS OF LEONARDO DA VINCI, edited by J. P. Richter. Extracts from manuscripts reveal great genius; on painting, sculpture, anatomy, sciences, geography, etc. Both Italian and English. 186 ms. pages reproduced, plus 500 additional drawings, including studies for *Last Supper*, Sforza monument, etc. 860pp. 7⅞ x 10¾. (Available in U.S. only) 22572-0, 22573-9 Pa., Two-vol. set $15.90

THE CODEX NUTTALL, as first edited by Zelia Nuttall. Only inexpensive edition, in full color, of a pre-Columbian Mexican (Mixtec) book. 88 color plates show kings, gods, heroes, temples, sacrifices. New explanatory, historical introduction by Arthur G. Miller. 96pp. 11⅜ x 8½. (Available in U.S. only) 23168-2 Pa. $7.95

UNE SEMAINE DE BONTÉ, A SURREALISTIC NOVEL IN COLLAGE, Max Ernst. Masterpiece created out of 19th-century periodical illustrations, explores worlds of terror and surprise. Some consider this Ernst's greatest work. 208pp. 8⅛ x 11. 23252-2 Pa. $6.00

UNCLE SILAS, J. Sheridan LeFanu. Victorian Gothic mystery novel, considered by many best of period, even better than Collins or Dickens. Wonderful psychological terror. Introduction by Frederick Shroyer. 436pp. 5⅜ x 8½. 21715-9 Pa. $6.00

JURGEN, James Branch Cabell. The great erotic fantasy of the 1920's that delighted thousands, shocked thousands more. Full final text, Lane edition with 13 plates by Frank Pape. 346pp. 5⅜ x 8½. 23507-6 Pa. $4.50

THE CLAVERINGS, Anthony Trollope. Major novel, chronicling aspects of British Victorian society, personalities. Reprint of Cornhill serialization, 16 plates by M. Edwards; first reprint of full text. Introduction by Norman Donaldson. 412pp. 5⅜ x 8½. 23464-9 Pa. $5.00

KEPT IN THE DARK, Anthony Trollope. Unusual short novel about Victorian morality and abnormal psychology by the great English author. Probably the first American publication. Frontispiece by Sir John Millais. 92pp. 6½ x 9¼. 23609-9 Pa. $2.50

RALPH THE HEIR, Anthony Trollope. Forgotten tale of illegitimacy, inheritance. Master novel of Trollope's later years. Victorian country estates, clubs, Parliament, fox hunting, world of fully realized characters. Reprint of 1871 edition. 12 illustrations by F. A. Faser. 434pp. of text. 5⅜ x 8½. 23642-0 Pa. $5.00

YEKL and THE IMPORTED BRIDEGROOM AND OTHER STORIES OF THE NEW YORK GHETTO, Abraham Cahan. Film *Hester Street* based on *Yekl* (1896). Novel, other stories among first about Jewish immigrants of N.Y.'s East Side. Highly praised by W. D. Howells—Cahan "a new star of realism." New introduction by Bernard G. Richards. 240pp. 5⅜ x 8½. 22427-9 Pa. $3.50

THE HIGH PLACE, James Branch Cabell. Great fantasy writer's enchanting comedy of disenchantment set in 18th-century France. Considered by some critics to be even better than his famous *Jurgen*. 10 illustrations and numerous vignettes by noted fantasy artist Frank C. Pape. 320pp. 5⅜ x 8½. 23670-6 Pa. $4.00

ALICE'S ADVENTURES UNDER GROUND, Lewis Carroll. Facsimile of ms. Carroll gave Alice Liddell in 1864. Different in many ways from final Alice. Handlettered, illustrated by Carroll. Introduction by Martin Gardner. 128pp. 5⅜ x 8½. 21482-6 Pa. $2.50

FAVORITE ANDREW LANG FAIRY TALE BOOKS IN MANY COLORS, Andrew Lang. The four Lang favorites in a boxed set—the complete *Red, Green, Yellow* and *Blue* Fairy Books. 164 stories; 439 illustrations by Lancelot Speed, Henry Ford and G. P. Jacomb Hood. Total of about 1500pp. 5⅜ x 8½. 23407-X Boxed set, Pa. $15.95

A MAYA GRAMMAR, Alfred M. Tozzer. Practical, useful English-language grammar by the Harvard anthropologist who was one of the three greatest American scholars in the area of Maya culture. Phonetics, grammatical processes, syntax, more. 301pp. 5⅜ x 8½. 23465-7 Pa. $4.00

THE JOURNAL OF HENRY D. THOREAU, edited by Bradford Torrey, F. H. Allen. Complete reprinting of 14 volumes, 1837-61, over two million words; the sourcebooks for *Walden*, etc. Definitive. All original sketches, plus 75 photographs. Introduction by Walter Harding. Total of 1804pp. 8½ x 12¼. 20312-3, 20313-1 Clothbd., Two-vol. set $70.00

CLASSIC GHOST STORIES, Charles Dickens and others. 18 wonderful stories you've wanted to reread: "The Monkey's Paw," "The House and the Brain," "The Upper Berth," "The Signalman," "Dracula's Guest," "The Tapestried Chamber," etc. Dickens, Scott, Mary Shelley, Stoker, etc. 330pp. 5⅜ x 8½. 20735-8 Pa. $4.50

SEVEN SCIENCE FICTION NOVELS, H. G. Wells. Full novels. *First Men in the Moon, Island of Dr. Moreau, War of the Worlds, Food of the Gods, Invisible Man, Time Machine, In the Days of the Comet*. A basic science-fiction library. 1015pp. 5⅜ x 8½. (Available in U.S. only) 20264-X Clothbd. $8.95

ARMADALE, Wilkie Collins. Third great mystery novel by the author of *The Woman in White* and *The Moonstone*. Ingeniously plotted narrative shows an exceptional command of character, incident and mood. Original magazine version with 40 illustrations. 597pp. 5⅜ x 8½. 23429-0 Pa. $6.00

MASTERS OF MYSTERY, H. Douglas Thomson. The first book in English (1931) devoted to history and aesthetics of detective story. Poe, Doyle, LeFanu, Dickens, many others, up to 1930. New introduction and notes by E. F. Bleiler. 288pp. 5⅜ x 8½. (Available in U.S. only) 23606-4 Pa. $4.00

FLATLAND, E. A. Abbott. Science-fiction classic explores life of 2-D being in 3-D world. Read also as introduction to thought about hyperspace. Introduction by Banesh Hoffmann. 16 illustrations. 103pp. 5⅜ x 8½. 20001-9 Pa. $2.00

THREE SUPERNATURAL NOVELS OF THE VICTORIAN PERIOD, edited, with an introduction, by E. F. Bleiler. Reprinted complete and unabridged, three great classics of the supernatural: *The Haunted Hotel* by Wilkie Collins, *The Haunted House at Latchford* by Mrs. J. H. Riddell, and *The Lost Stradivarious* by J. Meade Falkner. 325pp. 5⅜ x 8½. 22571-2 Pa. $4.00

AYESHA: THE RETURN OF "SHE," H. Rider Haggard. Virtuoso sequel featuring the great mythic creation, Ayesha, in an adventure that is fully as good as the first book, *She*. Original magazine version, with 47 original illustrations by Maurice Greiffenhagen. 189pp. 6½ x 9¼. 23649-8 Pa. $3.50

TONE POEMS, SERIES II: TILL EULENSPIEGELS LUSTIGE STREICHE, ALSO SPRACH ZARATHUSTRA, AND EIN HELDEN-LEBEN, Richard Strauss. Three important orchestral works, including very popular *Till Eulenspiegel's Marry Pranks,* reproduced in full score from original editions. Study score. 315pp. 9⅜ x 12¼. (Available in U.S. only)
23755-9 Pa. $8.95

TONE POEMS, SERIES I: DON JUAN, TOD UND VERKLARUNG AND DON QUIXOTE, Richard Strauss. Three of the most often per-formed and recorded works in entire orchestral repertoire, reproduced in full score from original editions. Study score. 286pp. 9⅜ x 12¼. (Avail-able in U.S. only)
23754-0 Pa. $7.50

11 LATE STRING QUARTETS, Franz Joseph Haydn. The form which Haydn defined and "brought to perfection." (*Grove's*). 11 string quartets in complete score, his last and his best. The first in a projected series of the complete Haydn string quartets. Reliable modern Eulenberg edition, otherwise difficult to obtain. 320pp. 8⅜ x 11¼. (Available in U.S. only)
23753-2 Pa. $7.50

FOURTH, FIFTH AND SIXTH SYMPHONIES IN FULL SCORE, Peter Ilyitch Tchaikovsky. Complete orchestral scores of Symphony No. 4 in F Minor, Op. 36; Symphony No. 5 in E Minor, Op. 64; Symphony No. 6 in B Minor, "Pathetique," Op. 74. Bretikopf & Hartel eds. Study score. 480pp. 9⅜ x 12¼.
23861-X Pa. $10.95

THE MARRIAGE OF FIGARO: COMPLETE SCORE, Wolfgang A. Mozart. Finest comic opera ever written. Full score, not to be confused with piano renderings. Peters edition. Study score. 448pp. 9⅜ x 12¼. (Available in U.S. only)
23751-6 Pa. $11.95

"IMAGE" ON THE ART AND EVOLUTION OF THE FILM, edited by Marshall Deutelbaum. Pioneering book brings together for first time 38 groundbreaking articles on early silent films from *Image* and 263 illustra-tions newly shot from rare prints in the collection of the International Museum of Photography. A landmark work. Index. 256pp. 8¼ x 11.
23777-X Pa. $8.95

AROUND-THE-WORLD COOKY BOOK, Lois Lintner Sumption and Marguerite Lintner Ashbrook. 373 cooky and frosting recipes from 28 countries (America, Austria, China, Russia, Italy, etc.) include Viennese kisses, rice wafers, London strips, lady fingers, hony, sugar spice, maple cookies, etc. Clear instructions. All tested. 38 drawings. 182pp. 5⅜ x 8.
23802-4 Pa. $2.50

THE ART NOUVEAU STYLE, edited by Roberta Waddell. 579 rare photographs, not available elsewhere, of works in jewelry, metalwork, glass, ceramics, textiles, architecture and furniture by 175 artists—Mucha, Seguy, Lalique, Tiffany, Gaudin, Hohlwein, Saarinen, and many others. 288pp. 8⅜ x 11¼.
23515-7 Pa. $6.95

THE ANATOMY OF THE HORSE, George Stubbs. Often considered the great masterpiece of animal anatomy. Full reproduction of 1766 edition, plus prospectus; original text and modernized text. 36 plates. Introduction by Eleanor Garvey. 121pp. 11 x 14¾. 23402-9 Pa. $6.00

BRIDGMAN'S LIFE DRAWING, George B. Bridgman. More than 500 illustrative drawings and text teach you to abstract the body into its major masses, use light and shade, proportion; as well as specific areas of anatomy, of which Bridgman is master. 192pp. 6½ x 9¼. (Available in U.S. only) 22710-3 Pa. $3.50

ART NOUVEAU DESIGNS IN COLOR, Alphonse Mucha, Maurice Verneuil, Georges Auriol. Full-color reproduction of *Combinaisons ornementales* (c. 1900) by Art Nouveau masters. Floral, animal, geometric, interlacings, swashes—borders, frames, spots—all incredibly beautiful. 60 plates, hundreds of designs. 9⅜ x 8-1/16. 22885-1 Pa. $4.00

FULL-COLOR FLORAL DESIGNS IN THE ART NOUVEAU STYLE, E. A. Seguy. 166 motifs, on 40 plates, from *Les fleurs et leurs applications decoratives* (1902): borders, circular designs, repeats, allovers, "spots." All in authentic Art Nouveau colors. 48pp. 9⅜ x 12¼. 23439-8 Pa. $5.00

A DIDEROT PICTORIAL ENCYCLOPEDIA OF TRADES AND INDUSTRY, edited by Charles C. Gillispie. 485 most interesting plates from the great French Encyclopedia of the 18th century show hundreds of working figures, artifacts, process, land and cityscapes; glassmaking, papermaking, metal extraction, construction, weaving, making furniture, clothing, wigs, dozens of other activities. Plates fully explained. 920pp. 9 x 12. 22284-5, 22285-3 Clothbd., Two-vol. set $40.00

HANDBOOK OF EARLY ADVERTISING ART, Clarence P. Hornung. Largest collection of copyright-free early and antique advertising art ever compiled. Over 6,000 illustrations, from Franklin's time to the 1890's for special effects, novelty. Valuable source, almost inexhaustible.
Pictorial Volume. Agriculture, the zodiac, animals, autos, birds, Christmas, fire engines, flowers, trees, musical instruments, ships, games and sports, much more. Arranged by subject matter and use. 237 plates. 288pp. 9 x 12. 20122-8 Clothbd. $14..50

Typographical Volume. Roman and Gothic faces ranging from 10 point to 300 point, "Barnum," German and Old English faces, script, logotypes, scrolls and flourishes, 1115 ornamental initials, 67 complete alphabets, more. 310 plates. 320pp. 9 x 12. 20123-6 Clothbd. $15.00

CALLIGRAPHY (CALLIGRAPHIA LATINA), J. G. Schwandner. High point of 18th-century ornamental calligraphy. Very ornate initials, scrolls, borders, cherubs, birds, lettered examples. 172pp. 9 x 13. 20475-8 Pa. $7.00

AN AUTOBIOGRAPHY, Margaret Sanger. Exciting personal account of hard-fought battle for woman's right to birth control, against prejudice, church, law. Foremost feminist document. 504pp. 5⅜ x 8½.
20470-7 Pa. $5.50

MY BONDAGE AND MY FREEDOM, Frederick Douglass. Born as a slave, Douglass became outspoken force in antislavery movement. The best of Douglass's autobiographies. Graphic description of slave life. Introduction by P. Foner. 464pp. 5⅜ x 8½. 22457-0 Pa. $5.50

LIVING MY LIFE, Emma Goldman. Candid, no holds barred account by foremost American anarchist: her own life, anarchist movement, famous contemporaries, ideas and their impact. Struggles and confrontations in America, plus deportation to U.S.S.R. Shocking inside account of persecution of anarchists under Lenin. 13 plates. Total of 944pp. 5⅜ x 8½.
22543-7, 22544-5 Pa., Two-vol. set $12.00

LETTERS AND NOTES ON THE MANNERS, CUSTOMS AND CONDITIONS OF THE NORTH AMERICAN INDIANS, George Catlin. Classic account of life among Plains Indians: ceremonies, hunt, warfare, etc. Dover edition reproduces for first time all original paintings. 312 plates. 572pp. of text. 6⅛ x 9¼. 22118-0, 22119-9 Pa.. Two-vol. set $12.00

THE MAYA AND THEIR NEIGHBORS, edited by Clarence L. Hay, others. Synoptic view of Maya civilization in broadest sense, together with Northern, Southern neighbors. Integrates much background, valuable detail not elsewhere. Prepared by greatest scholars: Kroeber, Morley, Thompson, Spinden, Vaillant, many others. Sometimes called Tozzer Memorial Volume. 60 illustrations, linguistic map. 634pp. 5⅜ x 8½.
23510-6 Pa. $10.00

HANDBOOK OF THE INDIANS OF CALIFORNIA, A. L. Kroeber. Foremost American anthropologist offers complete ethnographic study of each group. Monumental classic. 459 illustrations, maps. 995pp. 5⅜ x 8½.
23368-5 Pa. $13.00

SHAKTI AND SHAKTA, Arthur Avalon. First book to give clear, cohesive analysis of Shakta doctrine, Shakta ritual and Kundalini Shakti (yoga). Important work by one of world's foremost students of Shaktic and Tantric thought. 732pp. 5⅜ x 8½. (Available in U.S. only)
23645-5 Pa. $7.95

AN INTRODUCTION TO THE STUDY OF THE MAYA HIEROGLYPHS, Syvanus Griswold Morley. Classic study by one of the truly great figures in hieroglyph research. Still the best introduction for the student for reading Maya hieroglyphs. New introduction by J. Eric S. Thompson. 117 illustrations. 284pp. 5⅜ x 8½. 23108-9 Pa. $4.00

A STUDY OF MAYA ART, Herbert J. Spinden. Landmark classic interprets Maya symbolism, estimates styles, covers ceramics, architecture, murals, stone carvings as artforms. Still a basic book in area. New introduction by J. Eric Thompson. Over 750 illustrations. 341pp. 8⅜ x 11¼.
21235-1 Pa. $6.95

THE DEPRESSION YEARS AS PHOTOGRAPHED BY ARTHUR ROTH-STEIN, Arthur Rothstein. First collection devoted entirely to the work of outstanding 1930s photographer: famous dust storm photo, ragged children, unemployed, etc. 120 photographs. Captions. 119pp. 9¼ x 10¾.
23590-4 Pa. $5.00

CAMERA WORK: A PICTORIAL GUIDE, Alfred Stieglitz. All 559 illustrations and plates from the most important periodical in the history of art photography, Camera Work (1903-17). Presented four to a page, reduced in size but still clear, in strict chronological order, with complete captions. Three indexes. Glossary. Bibliography. 176pp. 8⅜ x 11¼.
23591-2 Pa. $6.95

ALVIN LANGDON COBURN, PHOTOGRAPHER, Alvin L. Coburn. Revealing autobiography by one of greatest photographers of 20th century gives insider's version of Photo-Secession, plus comments on his own work. 77 photographs by Coburn. Edited by Helmut and Alison Gernsheim. 160pp. 8⅛ x 11.
23685-4 Pa. $6.00

NEW YORK IN THE FORTIES, Andreas Feininger. 162 brilliant photographs by the well-known photographer, formerly with Life magazine, show commuters, shoppers, Times Square at night, Harlem nightclub, Lower East Side, etc. Introduction and full captions by John von Hartz. 181pp. 9¼ x 10¾.
23585-8 Pa. $6.95

GREAT NEWS PHOTOS AND THE STORIES BEHIND THEM, John Faber. Dramatic volume of 140 great news photos, 1855 through 1976, and revealing stories behind them, with both historical and technical information. Hindenburg disaster, shooting of Oswald, nomination of Jimmy Carter, etc. 160pp. 8¼ x 11.
23667-6 Pa. $5.00

THE ART OF THE CINEMATOGRAPHER, Leonard Maltin. Survey of American cinematography history and anecdotal interviews with 5 masters—Arthur Miller, Hal Mohr, Hal Rosson, Lucien Ballard, and Conrad Hall. Very large selection of behind-the-scenes production photos. 105 photographs. Filmographies. Index. Originally Behind the Camera. 144pp. 8¼ x 11.
23686-2 Pa. $5.00

DESIGNS FOR THE THREE-CORNERED HAT (LE TRICORNE), Pablo Picasso. 32 fabulously rare drawings—including 31 color illustrations of costumes and accessories—for 1919 production of famous ballet. Edited by Parmenia Migel, who has written new introduction. 48pp. 9⅜ x 12¼. (Available in U.S. only)
23709-5 Pa. $5.00

NOTES OF A FILM DIRECTOR, Sergei Eisenstein. Greatest Russian filmmaker explains montage, making of Alexander Nevsky, aesthetics; comments on self, associates, great rivals (Chaplin), similar material. 78 illustrations. 240pp. 5⅜ x 8½.
22392-2 Pa. $4.50

DRAWINGS OF WILLIAM BLAKE, William Blake. 92 plates from Book of Job, *Divine Comedy, Paradise Lost,* visionary heads, mythological figures, Laocoon, etc. Selection, introduction, commentary by Sir Geoffrey Keynes. 178pp. 8⅛ x 11. 22303-5 Pa. $4.00

ENGRAVINGS OF HOGARTH, William Hogarth. 101 of Hogarth's greatest works: *Rake's Progress, Harlot's Progress, Illustrations for Hudibras, Before and After, Beer Street and Gin Lane,* many more. Full commentary. 256pp. 11 x 13¾. 22479-1 Pa. $12.95

DAUMIER: 120 GREAT LITHOGRAPHS, Honore Daumier. Wide-ranging collection of lithographs by the greatest caricaturist of the 19th century. Concentrates on eternally popular series on lawyers, on married life, on liberated women, etc. Selection, introduction, and notes on plates by Charles F. Ramus. Total of 158pp. 9⅜ x 12¼. 23512-2 Pa. $6.00

DRAWINGS OF MUCHA, Alphonse Maria Mucha. Work reveals draftsman of highest caliber: studies for famous posters and paintings, renderings for book illustrations and ads, etc. 70 works, 9 in color; including 6 items not drawings. Introduction. List of illustrations. 72pp. 9⅜ x 12¼. (Available in U.S. only) 23672-2 Pa. $4.00

GIOVANNI BATTISTA PIRANESI: DRAWINGS IN THE PIERPONT MORGAN LIBRARY, Giovanni Battista Piranesi. For first time ever all of Morgan Library's collection, world's largest. 167 illustrations of rare Piranesi drawings—archeological, architectural, decorative and visionary. Essay, detailed list of drawings, chronology, captions. Edited by Felice Stampfle. 144pp. 9⅜ x 12¼. 23714-1 Pa. $7.50

NEW YORK ETCHINGS (1905-1949), John Sloan. All of important American artist's N.Y. life etchings. 67 works include some of his best art; also lively historical record—Greenwich Village, tenement scenes. Edited by Sloan's widow. Introduction and captions. 79pp. 8⅜ x 11¼. 23651-X Pa. $4.00

CHINESE PAINTING AND CALLIGRAPHY: A PICTORIAL SURVEY, Wan-go Weng. 69 fine examples from John M. Crawford's matchless private collection: landscapes, birds, flowers, human figures, etc., plus calligraphy. Every basic form included: hanging scrolls, handscrolls, album leaves, fans, etc. 109 illustrations. Introduction. Captions. 192pp. 8⅞ x 11¾. 23707-9 Pa. $7.95

DRAWINGS OF REMBRANDT, edited by Seymour Slive. Updated Lippmann, Hofstede de Groot edition, with definitive scholarly apparatus. All portraits, biblical sketches, landscapes, nudes, Oriental figures, classical studies, together with selection of work by followers. 550 illustrations. Total of 630pp. 9⅛ x 12¼. 21485-0, 21486-9 Pa., Two-vol. set $15.00

THE DISASTERS OF WAR, Francisco Goya. 83 etchings record horrors of Napoleonic wars in Spain and war in general. Reprint of 1st edition, plus 3 additional plates. Introduction by Philip Hofer. 97pp. 9⅜ x 8¼. 21872-4 Pa. $4.00

THE EARLY WORK OF AUBREY BEARDSLEY, Aubrey Beardsley. 157 plates, 2 in color: *Manon Lescaut, Madame Bovary, Morte Darthur, Salome,* other. Introduction by H. Marillier. 182pp. 8⅛ x 11. 21816-3 Pa. $4.50

THE LATER WORK OF AUBREY BEARDSLEY, Aubrey Beardsley. Exotic masterpieces of full maturity: *Venus and Tannhauser, Lysistrata, Rape of the Lock, Volpone,* Savoy material, etc. 174 plates, 2 in color. 186pp. 8⅛ x 11. 21817-1 Pa. $5.95

THOMAS NAST'S CHRISTMAS DRAWINGS, Thomas Nast. Almost all Christmas drawings by creator of image of Santa Claus as we know it, and one of America's foremost illustrators and political cartoonists. 66 illustrations. 3 illustrations in color on covers. 96pp. 8⅜ x 11¼. 23660-9 Pa. $3.50

THE DORÉ ILLUSTRATIONS FOR DANTE'S DIVINE COMEDY, Gustave Doré. All 135 plates from Inferno, Purgatory, Paradise; fantastic tortures, infernal landscapes, celestial wonders. Each plate with appropriate (translated) verses. 141pp. 9 x 12. 23231-X Pa. $4.50

DORÉ'S ILLUSTRATIONS FOR RABELAIS, Gustave Doré. 252 striking illustrations of *Gargantua and Pantagruel* books by foremost 19th-century illustrator. Including 60 plates, 192 delightful smaller illustrations. 153pp. 9 x 12. 23656-0 Pa. $5.00

LONDON: A PILGRIMAGE, Gustave Doré, Blanchard Jerrold. Squalor, riches, misery, beauty of mid-Victorian metropolis; 55 wonderful plates, 125 other illustrations, full social, cultural text by Jerrold. 191pp. of text. 9⅜ x 12¼. 22306-X Pa. $7.00

THE RIME OF THE ANCIENT MARINER, Gustave Doré, S. T. Coleridge. Dore's finest work, 34 plates capture moods, subtleties of poem. Full text. Introduction by Millicent Rose. 77pp. 9¼ x 12. 22305-1 Pa. $3.50

THE DORE BIBLE ILLUSTRATIONS, Gustave Doré. All wonderful, detailed plates: Adam and Eve, Flood, Babylon, Life of Jesus, etc. Brief King James text with each plate. Introduction by Millicent Rose. 241 plates. 241pp. 9 x 12. 23004-X Pa. $6.00

THE COMPLETE ENGRAVINGS, ETCHINGS AND DRYPOINTS OF ALBRECHT DURER. "Knight, Death and Devil"; "Melencolia," and more—all Dürer's known works in all three media, including 6 works formerly attributed to him. 120 plates. 235pp. 8⅜ x 11¼. 22851-7 Pa. $6.50

MECHANICK EXERCISES ON THE WHOLE ART OF PRINTING, Joseph Moxon. First complete book (1683-4) ever written about typography, a compendium of everything known about printing at the latter part of 17th century. Reprint of 2nd (1962) Oxford Univ. Press edition. 74 illustrations. Total of 550pp. 6⅛ x 9¼. 23617-X Pa. $7.95

GEOMETRY, RELATIVITY AND THE FOURTH DIMENSION, Rudolf Rucker. Exposition of fourth dimension, means of visualization, concepts of relativity as Flatland characters continue adventures. Popular, easily followed yet accurate, profound. 141 illustrations. 133pp. 5⅜ x 8½.

23400-2 Pa. $2.75

THE ORIGIN OF LIFE, A. I. Oparin. Modern classic in biochemistry, the first rigorous examination of possible evolution of life from nitrocarbon compounds. Non-technical, easily followed. Total of 295pp. 5⅜ x 8½.

60213-3 Pa. $4.00

PLANETS, STARS AND GALAXIES, A. E. Fanning. Comprehensive introductory survey: the sun, solar system, stars, galaxies, universe, cosmology; quasars, radio stars, etc. 24pp. of photographs. 189pp. 5⅜ x 8½. (Available in U.S. only)

21680-2 Pa. $3.75

THE THIRTEEN BOOKS OF EUCLID'S ELEMENTS, translated with introduction and commentary by Sir Thomas L. Heath. Definitive edition. Textual and linguistic notes, mathematical analysis, 2500 years of critical commentary. Do not confuse with abridged school editions. Total of 1414pp. 5⅜ x 8½.   60088-2, 60089-0, 60090-4 Pa., Three-vol. set $18.50